PRAISE FOR CAR

Hummingbird Lane

"Brown's (*The Daydream Cabin*) gentle story of a woman finding strength within a tight-knit community has just a touch of romance at the end. Recommended for readers who enjoy heartwarming stories about women overcoming obstacles."

—*Library Journal*

Miss Janie's Girls

"[A] heartfelt tale of familial love and self-acceptance."

—*Publishers Weekly*

"Heartfelt moments and family drama collide in this saga about sisters."

—*Woman's World*

The Banty House

"Brown throws together a colorful cast of characters to excellent effect and maximum charm in this small-town contemporary romance . . . This first-rate romance will delight readers young and old."

—*Publishers Weekly*

The Family Journal

HOLT MEDALLION FINALIST

"Reading a Carolyn Brown book is like coming home again."

—*Harlequin Junkie* (top pick)

The Empty Nesters

"A delightful journey of hope and healing."
—*Woman's World*

"The story is full of emotion . . . and the joy of friendship and family. Carolyn Brown is known for her strong, loving characters, and this book is full of them."
—*Harlequin Junkie*

"Carolyn Brown takes us back to small-town Texas with a story about women, friendships, love, loss, and hope for the future."
—*Storeybook Reviews*

"Ms. Brown has fast become one of my favorite authors!"
—*Romance Junkies*

The Perfect Dress

"Fans of Brown will swoon for this sweet contemporary, which skillfully pairs a shy small-town bridal shop owner and a softhearted car dealership owner . . . The expected but welcomed happily ever after for all involved will make readers of all ages sigh with satisfaction."
—*Publishers Weekly*

"Carolyn Brown writes the best comfort-for-the-soul, heartwarming stories, and she never disappoints . . . You won't go wrong with *The Perfect Dress!*"
—*Harlequin Junkie*

The Magnolia Inn

"The author does a first-rate job of depicting the devastating stages of grief, provides a simple but appealing plot with a sympathetic hero and heroine and a cast of lovable supporting characters, and wraps it all up with a happily ever after to cheer for."

—Publishers Weekly

"*The Magnolia Inn* by Carolyn Brown is a feel-good story about friendship, fighting your demons, and finding love, and maybe just a little bit of magic."

—Harlequin Junkie

"Chock-full of Carolyn Brown's signature country charm, *The Magnolia Inn* is a sweet and heartwarming story of two people trying to make the most of their lives, even when they have no idea what exactly is at stake."

—Fresh Fiction

Small Town Rumors

"Carolyn Brown is a master at writing warm, complex characters who find their way into your heart."

—Harlequin Junkie

The Sometimes Sisters

"Carolyn Brown continues her streak of winning, heartfelt novels with *The Sometimes Sisters*, a story of estranged sisters and frustrated romance."

—All About Romance

"This is an amazing feel-good story that will make you wish you were a part of this amazing family."

—Harlequin Junkie (top pick)

the Lucky Shamrock

ALSO BY CAROLYN BROWN

CONTEMPORARY ROMANCES

The Devine Doughnut Shop
The Sandcastle Hurricane
Riverbend Reunion
The Bluebonnet Battle
The Sunshine Club
The Hope Chest
Hummingbird Lane
The Daydream Cabin
Miss Janie's Girls
The Banty House
The Family Journal
The Empty Nesters
The Perfect Dress
The Magnolia Inn
Small Town Rumors
The Sometimes Sisters
The Strawberry Hearts Diner
The Lilac Bouquet
The Barefoot Summer
The Lullaby Sky
The Wedding Pearls
The Yellow Rose Beauty Shop
The Ladies' Room
Hidden Secrets
Long, Hot Texas Summer
Daisies in the Canyon
Trouble in Paradise

CONTEMPORARY SERIES

The Broken Roads Series

To Trust
To Commit
To Believe
To Dream
To Hope

Three Magic Words Trilogy

A Forever Thing
In Shining Whatever
Life After Wife

HISTORICAL ROMANCE

The Black Swan Trilogy

Pushin' Up Daisies
From Thin Air
Come High Water

The Drifters & Dreamers Trilogy

Morning Glory
Sweet Tilly
Evening Star

The Love's Valley Series

Choices
Absolution
Chances
Redemption
Promises

the Lucky Shamrock

CAROLYN BROWN

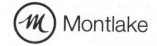 Montlake

Text copyright © 2023 by Carolyn Brown

Published by Montlake, Seattle

www.apub.com

Amazon, the Amazon logo, and Montlake are trademarks of Amazon.com, Inc., or its affiliates.

ISBN-13: 9781542038607 (paperback)
ISBN-13: 9781542038614 (digital)

Cover design by Leah Jacobs-Gordon
Cover image: © Evrymmnt / Getty © Creative Stock Studio/Shutterstock;
© Artman96/Shutterstock; © lkpro/Shutterstock;
© NicholasGeraldinePhotos/Shutterstock

Printed in the United States of America

This book is for my cousins,
Keith and Cindy Harvill
and
Tommy and Becky Edwards

Chapter One

No, no, no!" Taryn slapped the steering wheel with each word. Nana Irene hadn't said anything about bringing her two cousins, Jorja and Anna Rose, back to Shamrock for the summer. But right there, parked in front of the flower shop, were Jorja's car, with its "Honk If You Love Jesus" bumper sticker, and Anna Rose's truck, with its own statement to the world stuck to the back window: "Forget the Blarney Stone. Kiss a Cowboy." Taryn jerked her phone off the dash holder in her SUV and called her grandmother.

"Are you there yet?" Irene asked.

"I'm here, but I'm not sure I'm even going in," Taryn answered.

Irene laughed. "Suck it up, buttercup. You'll be so busy that you'll be glad for their help. I've put Clinton McEntire on the payroll as a full-time employee, too. It'll take all four of you to keep up with the weddings and funerals this summer, on top of the small jobs."

"Can I live in the upstairs apartment?" Taryn asked.

"Nope, I gave that space to Clinton last fall, when he came home from the service," Irene said. "You'll be living in the trailer out back with your two cousins. Believe me, they aren't happy with the arrangement, either, but you're three grown women. You don't have to like each other, but you do have to work together till I get back. I've taken the guns out of the shop, so the only things there for the next few weeks are floral knives and a hammer in the storage room. We'll see y'all on Saturday for a late lunch. One o'clock. Other than that, don't be calling me every day. Learn to get along and work together. Bye, now."

Taryn laid her head on the steering wheel for several minutes, then raised up and sighed. She'd promised Nana Irene that she would help run the flower shop—the Lucky Shamrock—after Nana's best friend, Ruby, had fallen and broken her hip, and Taryn wasn't one to go back on her word. Truth was, she was afraid of the lecture she'd get from her grandmother if she did, so she had no choice but to suck it up. She'd worked in the flower shop, right along with Anna Rose and Jorja, every summer since before she was old enough to go on the payroll. Nana Irene had given the three of them a generous allowance to help her in the summer months. She was of the firm belief that working together helped build friendships; Taryn thought that might have been the only time her grandmother had been dead wrong about an issue.

"She also said it was to teach us responsibility and to keep us out of trouble. The first part worked. The second, not so much—at least in mine and Anna Rose's stories. Jorja didn't do so bad, but then, she loves Jesus more than we do," Taryn muttered as she got out of her vehicle.

A soft breeze ruffled the petunia blossoms in the hanging baskets on either side of the door into the shop. Nana Irene had taught her that some plants could withstand the hot western sun of the Texas Panhandle in early summer, but nothing would survive the scorch of July and August. Taryn made a mental note to take the baskets inside before that time came. She opened the door, heard the familiar jingle of the bells, and did her best to put a smile on her face.

Anna Rose looked up from behind the counter and frowned. "It's about time you got here. We've got a funeral on Wednesday, and we're swamped. I've been running back and forth between making a wreath in the back room and coming up here to take orders."

"I'm ready to go to work." Taryn wedged her purse beside two others on the shelf under the counter. One was pink with a Bible verse embroidered on the front. The leather one beside it was embellished with sparkly gemstones. "Where is Jorja?"

"She's in the back. We're taking turns waiting on customers." Anna Rose tucked a strand of her curly chestnut-brown hair up into the messy bun on top of her head. She wore skinny jeans with a top that hugged her curvy body and showed just a little bit of cleavage. Her green eyes—the only thing all three cousins had inherited from their Irish roots—twinkled with mischief, just like always.

"Isn't this awesome?" Jorja came out from the back room with a big smile on her face and wrapped Taryn up in a hug. "God is really good to give us this time together."

Except for the eyes, no one would have ever guessed that Jorja was related to the other two women. She was tall and slender, and she wore her blonde hair in two thick braids that wrapped around her head like a crown. Somewhere, there was a nice figure, but Jorja hid it under what folks called *mom jeans* and a baggy chambray shirt that buttoned up the front. Taryn knew because she'd seen Jorja in a swimsuit before they all grew up and split seven ways to Sunday, as her grandmother had often complained.

Jorja took a step back. "We're making the flowers for poor Miz Leona Gatlin. She only needed a few days to reach her hundredth birthday, but the Lord decided it was time to take her home." Her tone reminded Taryn of the day they had found a dead bird on the porch of the trailer and Jorja insisted that they bury the poor thing and have a funeral. Anna Rose had dug a shallow grave with a spoon she borrowed from the kitchen. Jorja had wrapped the bird in a paper towel and said a few words over him—and her voice sounded the same this morning, even though more than twenty years had passed.

Anna Rose rolled her eyes toward the ceiling and pursed her full lips. Evidently, she was already tired of listening to religion, but Jorja was probably tired of listening to bar stories and jokes. Taryn just nodded and hoped they each took that to mean she understood.

"Well, I suppose . . . ," Taryn started, but stopped when a tall man with black hair darkened the doorway.

"Hello," he drawled as he stuck out his hand. "I'm Clinton McEntire. You must be Taryn."

She shook hands with him. "Yes, I am, and I understand that you'll be here, too, until Nana Irene can come back to work?"

"That's right. Miz Irene gave me a job delivering flowers for her after I left the military last fall. When we didn't have deliveries, she and Ruby taught me the business," he answered. "I'm just part-time here, but Irene wants me to work full-time at least until the end of summer."

"She usually knows what's best," Taryn said. "I understand that we've got a funeral this week, so I guess we'd better get busy." She headed toward the back room, where all the work went on.

Clinton moved to the side to let her pass and then followed her. Nana Irene hadn't told her that he had a limp—or that he was one of those tall, dark, and handsome guys Taryn was attracted to. Thank goodness he wasn't wearing tight-fitting jeans and boots, or Anna Rose would have already staked a claim. Not that Taryn was thinking about flirting with him—oh, no. Never. She had a steadfast rule about dating men whom she worked with. Even though the last fiasco had been several years before, she remembered what could and did happen when things went south in a relationship and she still had to work with the fellow. Nana Irene's favorite saying, *Don't shit where you eat*, came to mind. That applied to life in general, for sure.

Clinton sat down on a tall stool behind the worktable. "Y'all know the system. Orders are in that basket. Miz Irene says that you take the top one, and you don't get to pick and choose."

Jorja pointed to a half-done wreath. "That's what I'm working on. The order of things around here hasn't changed in the past ten years."

Anna Rose put a pink-and-white-striped bow on the bottom front of a wreath and set it to the side, then grabbed the ticket at the top of the basket. "This one is for a peace lily. All I have to do is make a bow and fill out a card."

Taryn took the next order. "A bouquet of pink and white carnations," she said as she opened the glass-front cooler and took out a half a dozen of each, along with some feathery greenery. She remembered Leona Gatlin very well and had helped make her a birthday bouquet a couple of times back when she worked in the shop with her grandmother.

Taryn was thinking about Leona's deep southern accent and all the stories she'd told about living down on the bayou as she laid her flowers on the table, picked out a pretty white vase, and sat down on the only vacant stool—the one beside Clinton. Anna Rose twisted wire around a pale pink ribbon across the table from her. Jorja was cutting the stems from pink roses and placing them on a heart-shaped wreath. Clinton had finished the greenery for the base of the casket piece and had begun to add an array of different flowers—from roses to carnations and even hydrangeas and orchids.

"Miz Leona did love pink," Jorja said.

"The funeral is going to look like a gender-reveal party." Anna Rose glanced around at a dozen arrangements and threw up both palms in a jazz-hands gesture. "The baby is a girl!"

Jorja shot a dirty look her way. "That's disrespectful."

"I was making a joke," Anna Rose defended herself.

Jorja stuck her nose in the air. "Well, it's not funny."

Here we go, Taryn thought as she looked up at the clock. *Less than ten minutes into the morning, and they're already arguing.*

The bell above the door rang, and Jorja slid off her stool and headed toward the front room of the shop with Anna Rose right behind her.

"I can take care of the customer," Jorja snapped.

"There are two customers. I heard two car doors slam." Anna Rose's tone was even colder than Jorja's. "Maybe one of them will order something other than pink. And besides, not everyone that comes in here needs you to preach at them."

"Well, you shouldn't tell them that you'll meet them at the bar on Saturday night, either," Jorja hissed under her breath.

"Aren't you the peacemaker?" Clinton whispered.

"Not anymore," Taryn told him. "I'm tired of it. I'm only supposed to call Nana Irene if there's blood or broken bones—her words, not mine. They're grown women. They can hate each other or make up and act like cousins. I'm tired of being the go-between for them."

He kept working on the casket piece. "Miz Irene told me that the three of you didn't get along, but that Anna Rose and Jorja particularly don't like each other."

"What else did she tell you?" Taryn asked.

"You are the oldest. Anna Rose is next, and Jorja is the baby of the group. Anna Rose likes to party. Jorja likes to pray. And you are the peacemaker. What did she tell you about me?"

"That she had hired someone to deliver flowers on a part-time basis and that you were a veteran. I learned today that you are living in the apartment above the shop, and that I have to live with *those two* in the trailer out back, with Anna Rose trying to loosen up Jorja and Jorja trying to save, sanctify, and dehorn Anna Rose," Taryn said as she finished her arrangement and set it to the side. "That's all I know. How long were you in the service, and what branch?"

"Air force—ten years," Clinton answered. "I finished up two years of college before I enlisted and almost finished the second enlistment before I got a medical discharge."

"I only did one tour of duty, also air force," Taryn said. "Coming back takes some adjustment. I hated all the rules and regulations. How about you?"

"I didn't mind the regs, but coming back to civilian life was a big adjustment," Clinton said.

"More pink," Anna Rose said with a groan when she sat back down on her stool. "And not even for the funeral. I've got to make a vase with sixteen pink roses for a birthday and deliver it before noon to McDonald's, where the girl works."

"Do we have that many roses left?" Clinton asked.

Jorja took four white roses from the cooler. "Looks like there's about two dozen."

"We should be good until tomorrow, then. I'll deliver what we have made up and the casket piece as soon as I get it finished, and then I'll order another two dozen to be brought in on Wednesday morning," Clinton said. "We'll have a few last-minute orders for the funeral. Y'all want me to pick up lunch from McDonald's while I'm out making the deliveries?"

"Double cheeseburger, fries, and a chocolate shake," Anna Rose said as she counted roses in the cooler and whipped around to glare at Jorja. "You said there was two dozen. There's only sixteen. We'll be out after I make this bouquet."

"Count your blessings," Jorja hissed. "You're lucky we've got that many, after all the orders we've had for Leona. She was so well liked in town that everyone wants to send something."

"Enough!" Taryn said, raising her voice. "We're all either thirty or looking it right in the eye!" She shot a look toward Jorja. "Act like adults, not bickering teenagers."

Jorja stuck her nose in the air and looked down at Taryn. "Why are you looking at me? Anna Rose started it—and I can see you haven't changed much. I'll have to say an extra prayer for you that you get your temper under control."

"I'll need some help loading and delivering this," Clinton said. "I'm not so good at arranging the flowers and plants in the funeral home, so maybe you could go along with me and help, Taryn."

"Why does she get to go?" Jorja asked. "I'm good at arranging things. I've taken care of the flowers for holidays at my church for the past five years."

"Hey, wait a minute," Anna Rose piped up. "I've put together more arrangements than you have this morning, so if anyone should get out of this place for an hour, it should be me."

Clinton picked up the huge casket piece and headed toward the back door. "Because you two are still working on things that aren't part of Leona's funeral."

Taryn could have given Clinton a hug right there in front of her cousins, God, and whoever else might be watching. She had always been the one who had to keep peace, so she surely did appreciate the help.

"I changed my mind about my order. I want a double-meat burger, no cheese, fries, and the biggest cup of sweet tea they make," Anna Rose said and gave Taryn a dirty look. "Looks like Clinton is the boss now, not you, Taryn."

Taryn picked up a peace lily in one hand and a wreath in the other. "I gave the job to him willingly. I'm tired of it. If he doesn't want it, y'all can duel it out behind the shop. I'll call Nana Irene if there's blood or broken bones. She said that she took her pistol home, but there's always florist knives and a hammer or two in the storage room."

Jorja raised her chin a notch. "That's an ugly attitude. I really will pray for your spirit."

"I need all the prayers I can get," Taryn said with a shrug. She wasn't just being glib with her cousin, even though Jorja was acting a little self-righteous. She did need prayers, if she was going to survive the next few weeks in the shop with Anna Rose and Jorja constantly bickering.

When Clinton brought out the last two bud vases and put them in the special holders on the walls of the van, Taryn was already in the passenger's seat. Her younger cousins had been fussing about her being the favorite and always getting special privileges as she'd carried out the last wreath. Putting the two of them together had always been like adding gasoline to a bonfire, so it surprised her to see them join forces against her.

"Oh, well," she muttered. "I'll take the heat if they'll get along. It's only for a few weeks, and then I'm leaving. I probably won't see them again until Christmas, if I even come back here then. Siberia is beginning to look better by the minute."

"Ruby and Irene were sure right about all y'all." Clinton chuckled as he got into the van and started the engine. "So, you joined the air force right out of high school?"

"Yep," Taryn said.

He drove out to the street and turned left. "How did Irene take that?"

"Just fine," Taryn answered, "but my mother was so angry that she didn't speak to me for three months. Daddy was proud because he was still serving out the last of his twenty-year career and thought that all of us should do at least one stint. He said that it would have done Jorja and Anna Rose both good to do four years, but they had college on their minds. I only stayed for one enlistment, then got out and went to a two-year business school."

"How did all three of you manage to take six weeks' vacation time to come to Shamrock?" he asked as he braked for a stop sign.

"I work from home and have built up enough vacation time to do this. Jorja is a teacher at a religious private school, so she has the summer free. Anna Rose is a freelance photographer with a couple of books already doing very well on the market, so she's flexible," Taryn answered. "I just don't understand why Nana Irene had to bring all three of us here. She and Ruby have run the place all alone for years until she hired you to help with deliveries. You and I could have taken care of things without having to listen to all the bickering."

"Neither Irene nor Ruby are in good health." Clinton waited until a couple of cars went by and then drove ahead. "You already know that Ruby slipped at work and broke her hip. Irene has two bad knees and won't get them fixed because"—he shrugged—"who would run the shop? I do what I can, but they're independent old gals. These next few weeks will be good for both of them. Ruby just needs someone to cook or get her meals and take her to therapy. Irene needs to get off her legs for a while. They hired me because they couldn't lift the big pots or get all the flowers set up for weddings, and they each did the work of three people—so believe me when I say it will take all of you to keep up."

"Speaking of that, I understand that we've got six weddings on the calendar in June and three for July," Taryn said. "That's more than one a week this next month."

"Yep. First one is the first day of June, so we'll start making pew bows this week. Thank goodness the bride wants all silk flowers instead of fresh ones. We can make them ahead of time instead of waiting for the last couple of days," Clinton said with a nod as he parked the van in front of the funeral home door. "And who knows how many funerals will pop up in the next six weeks? Folks can't plan a death like they can a wedding, so they just come out of nowhere. No more thousand-piece puzzles for us to work on."

"Puzzles?" Taryn asked.

"When we aren't busy, we clean off the worktable and put puzzles together. Irene and Ruby love doing them, and I get to hear all the town gossip while we work on them," he said with a wide grin.

By the time he'd reached the van door and slid it open, Taryn was right beside him. "Guys like you listen to gossip?"

"What do you mean, like me?" Clinton asked. "Because I'm a vet or because I'm tall and brawny?" He winked.

Taryn stared at his sand-colored military boots and let her eyes travel all the way up to his brown eyes. "The vets I've worked with are all macho alpha males. What makes you think you're brawny?"

"Well, I'm dang sure not scrawny," Clinton protested, the humor fading from his face.

"You didn't answer my question about gossip," Taryn countered as she picked up two wreaths and started for the door.

"I call it 'getting to know my neighbors,' not gossip," he said. "If I listened to rumors, you'd be in trouble."

Taryn blushed. "I guess I would. So even after more than a decade, folks are still talking about me?"

"Yep, they are, and Anna Rose and Jorja—all three of you. When there's nothing else to feed the rumor mill, someone remembers the time when Jorja held a prayer vigil for the football team in the pouring-down rain," he answered with a chuckle.

"And no one showed up but her, and we lost the ball game. I told her that God had better things to do than referee a state playoff game." Taryn laughed.

"Then there was the time that you stole a trunkload of watermelons from some farmer's field," he went on.

"Would you believe me if I told you that there were two other girls—not related to me—who were in on that thievery?" she asked. "I didn't rat them out, so I had to do community work for a month to pay for the watermelons, and they got off free."

"Why would you do that?" Clinton asked.

"Two reasons." She held up one finger. "Because I'm not a tattle-tale." She pointed another one up. "Because I thought at the time that they were my friends and wouldn't let me take all the blame when it came down to the wire. I was wrong about that."

"Irene said that was the way things often went," Clinton replied. "It looks like neither of your cousins have changed much. Have you?"

"That's classified/redacted stuff," she threw over her shoulder. "And your security level isn't high enough to get the original rumor file on my past. I'm just glad that I moved away from here right after high school. I hoped that the rumors would die down when I left. What did you hear?"

"Nothing much, just a few rumors about teenage pranks," Clinton said with a chuckle.

Taryn smiled and held the door open for him to bring in the casket piece. "That's in the past. You want to talk about all the stupid stunts you pulled when you were young?"

"I'm Scottish to the bone, and we are known for our wild and wicked ways," he said, "and I've never been a rat, either. Thanks for holding the door. We'll put these at the front of the viewing room and then get the funeral home cart to bring in the rest."

"For Leona?" the funeral director asked as he came down the hallway.

"Yes, sir," Clinton answered.

"First room on the right. The family will be arriving in an hour for a private viewing, so it will be nice to have the flowers a little early," he said.

Taryn took one look at Leona lying in the casket, gasped, and slumped down in one of the chairs in front of the casket.

Clinton was a blur as he rushed over to her side. "Are you all right?"

"No, I'm not," she answered. "I'd forgotten how much Leona looks like Ruby. They were distant cousins."

He sat down beside her. "Do you need a drink of water? Maybe you should put your head between your knees."

"I'll be fine in a minute," she said. "I've always thought Nana Irene and Ruby would live forever, and the sudden shock of realizing that it could have been one of them here"—she paused—"in this place . . . Well, it flat-out took me by surprise."

Clinton draped an arm around her shoulders and gave her a gentle squeeze. "We aren't ever prepared to lose a loved one. Not even if they've been sick for a long time."

Taryn attributed the jolt that ran through her body at his touch to her relief that it was Leona and not Ruby in the casket. "You are so right, but I'm over my shock now. Let's get the rest of those flowers out of the heat before they wilt. If Nana Irene heard that we delivered ugly arrangements to her friend's funeral, she might bring her guns back to the shop."

"She just might," Clinton said with a chuckle. "She runs a tight ship."

You have no idea just how tight that ship really is, Taryn thought.

Chapter Two

"Why do we have to live in this cramped space?" Anna Rose complained that evening when she dragged two big suitcases into the trailer. "The closet in my room is so small that I can barely get my clothes in it. I'll be living out of a suitcase for six weeks!"

Jorja brought in her baggage—one small suitcase and a tote bag—and headed down the hallway. "It could be longer than six weeks. Nana Irene told me that she was staying with Ruby until she could come back to work—and at her age, that could be even longer. Maybe until August. I'm not worried, though. I don't have to be back at school until the first week of September, and I've already told my church family that I'll be gone most of the summer."

"I'm taking the bedroom at the end of the hall," Anna Rose said and rushed past Jorja to claim it. "The closet is bigger in that one."

Taryn rolled her eyes but didn't say anything. The end of summer sounded like an eternity and three days away to her. She agreed with Anna Rose's complaint about living in the cramped space of a single-wide trailer that had to be at least thirty years old. The thing would definitely be overcrowded with three grown women living in it, and it looked pitiful. Back when Nana Irene had lived there, when Taryn was a little girl, it had seemed plenty big enough. But now the blue on the lower half of the outside had faded, the white on the upper part had a few rust spots, and the inside wasn't big enough to cuss a cat without getting a hair in Taryn's mouth—another of Nana Irene's sayings.

After all three of the cousins had graduated from Shamrock High School—*go, Shamrock Irish!*—Nana Irene bought the house next door to Ruby's. Then she had offered the single-wide to folks who needed a temporary roof over their heads until they could get back on their feet. Taryn couldn't complain too much. The place had a good roof and air-conditioning, and was just a temporary thing. Being cramped wouldn't kill any of them—at least, Taryn hoped that it wouldn't.

Taryn took her single suitcase to the first bedroom down the hall on the right, by far the smallest of the three. But hey, she didn't need a big closet. She was used to working at home in pajama pants and an oversize T-shirt, and she had no problem living out of a suitcase. She liked to move every few months, so she usually rented an Extended Stay room and paid rent by the month. That way she didn't have to worry about moving towels, bedding, or even kitchen items, and she didn't make fickle friends who would betray her.

"I've got dibs on the bathroom since you got first choice of bedrooms," Anna Rose shouted.

"Don't you dare use all the hot water," Jorja yelled.

Taryn heard the bathroom door close and the old pipes under the trailer clank when Anna Rose turned the water on. *Lord, I'm not as good at praying as Jorja, but please keep the plumbing going while we're living here,* she thought.

That's when it hit her: they had to share the one tiny bathroom, and the hot-water tank wasn't big enough to support three hot showers. That meant that by the time it was her turn, she would have to wait until the water got hot again. Her stomach let her know that her lunch had long since gone, and it was time to eat. She opened the pantry and found that Nana Irene had stocked it well. A peek inside the refrigerator showed that there was food in there as well. She poured herself a bowl of junk cereal, covered it with milk, and carried it outside.

She had only taken the first bite when a little red sports car pulled up and parked right beside what had to be Clinton's black pickup truck. A tall, thin blonde got out and carried a covered dish up the stairs to the landing. She knocked on the door with the toe of one of her high-heeled shoes, with soles that matched her car, and did a little hip wiggle while she waited for Clinton.

Taryn set her bowl of cereal to the side, slipped her phone from her hip pocket, and called her grandmother.

"Which one of you has blood or broken bones? Do I need to come to the hospital?" Irene answered.

"None of the above. It hasn't come to that . . . yet," Taryn said. "Who's the blonde that Clinton is seeing?"

Irene giggled out loud. "Red sports car?"

"That's right, and she carried a casserole up the stairs to his apartment," Taryn answered.

"That one is Elaine Ferguson. Most likely she bought the casserole from the frozen-food section at the grocery store and put it in something fancy so she'll have a reason to come back and get her dish," Irene told her. "Plus, everyone in town knows that woman can't boil water without creating a disaster."

"'That one'? How many are there?" Taryn's opinion of Clinton was falling by the second.

"Just about every unmarried, divorced, or separated woman in Shamrock," Irene answered. "They're constantly pestering him in the evenings with food or some other excuse to come around. Didn't I tell you that he's the town hero and the most eligible bachelor in Wheeler County?"

"'Town hero'?" Taryn's voice went all high and squeaky on the last word.

"That would be his story to tell, not mine," Irene said. "This is your one freebie call for this week. I'll see you on Saturday, and you can learn all the gossip then."

"But Nana Irene," Taryn begged, "who am I supposed to talk to? You know I can't visit with Jorja or Anna Rose."

"You figure that out. All three of you need to be a family," Irene said. "Do you still know how to make a chocolate cake? I hear that's

Clinton's favorite, and he's a good listener if you need someone to talk to."

"Sounds to me like he's already occupied with keeping the female population of Shamrock busy, so he doesn't need anyone to visit with him," Taryn said with a sigh.

"Bye, now," Irene said, and the screen went dark.

Taryn picked up her bowl and ate a couple more bites of her cereal. After a few minutes, Elaine came out of Clinton's apartment. From the look on her face, she hadn't gotten the kind of reception she'd thought she might. She shot Taryn a dirty look across the parking lot between the trailer and shop, got into her car, and slung gravel all over the place when she peeled out. She'd only driven a few yards when she braked, and more gravel flew across the parking lot. She backed the vehicle up, climbed out, and stomped toward the trailer. The expression on her face said that she meant to mop up the streets of Shamrock with Taryn. But poor Elaine didn't realize that Taryn wasn't a teenager protecting her so-called friends anymore, and if push came to shove, she didn't mind getting dirty.

A rousing, good fight might be just what Taryn needed. However, she did feel sorry for Elaine's expensive shoes. That pretty red on the underside of the high heels had suffered horribly when she stormed across the gravel parking area.

When Elaine reached the trailer's ratty porch steps, she shook her finger at Taryn. "Stay away from him. That goes for all three of you. I'm going to win this contest no matter what it takes. Elaine Ferguson does not lose."

"What contest, and why are you angry with *me*?" Taryn asked. "I'm just sitting here, eating my cereal and minding my own business."

"You were a couple of years ahead of me in school, and I remember *you* very well." She accentuated her words with a jab of her finger. "I'm telling you to leave Clinton McEntire alone. He's mine! The contest is none of your business, either." She whipped around and stormed back to her car.

"Well, that was childish," Taryn muttered. "I might be the one with the reputation in this town for being a pushover, but I grew up. Evidently, she didn't."

Jorja came through the door and sat down beside Taryn. "Is that Elaine Ferguson? What's she doing here? I hope you told her that the shop is closed."

"Did you know her when we lived here?" Taryn asked.

"She was in my class at school and always claimed she was royalty, even kin to the duchess of York, that Fergie from England," Jorja said. "You didn't answer my question. What is she doing here?"

"Evidently telling us to stay out of some contest that's going on in town," Taryn said. "It must have something to do with Clinton because she told me to stay away from him and informed me that he was hers. And she was pretty definite about it."

Jorja stood up and started back into the trailer but stopped at the door. "Could be that there's another contest going on, but I bet it's the wreath contest for all the businesses in town—the one that the Chamber of Commerce sponsors for the Fourth of July." She frowned and shook her head. "But Elaine doesn't own a store, so why would she be all up in our face about that? And why would Clinton have anything to do with that contest?" Another frown. "She must be talking about something else." Jorja waved the gravel dust from around her face. "But I don't care if Elaine thinks she's royalty. She's not telling me what to do. I'll make the biggest, best wreath in the whole dang town, and we'll win first prize."

"I got the impression that the contest she's talking about has to do with just Clinton, because she warned all three of us to stay away from him—but now that you mention the wreath contest, I vote that we make one with a veteran theme to honor our fallen heroes," she suggested.

"Sounds like a good idea. You won't talk Anna Rose into that, you know. She'll want to have a cowboy or Western theme," Jorja said.

So much for slipping in and out of town without anyone remembering me, Taryn thought, and then muttered, "The past is always lurking in the shadows."

"What's going on out here?" Anna Rose asked as she stood to the side and let Jorja enter the trailer.

"I'm going to make myself some supper," Jorja said. "After that lunch we had, I'm just having a salad."

Good old Jorja. Always doing the right thing, Taryn thought, but she didn't say anything out loud.

"Don't give me that look," Jorja protested. "I know I need to lose about five pounds—but then, so do both of y'all."

"What'd I say or do?" Taryn asked. "I didn't say a word, so don't jump on my case."

Jorja threw up her palms, rolled her eyes, and slammed the door.

Anna Rose sat down beside Taryn. "You can share my pizza with me when it gets here. If you work with flowers all day, then whatever you eat before midnight has no calories or fat grams."

"I thought that only worked if you drank a diet soda with it," Taryn said.

"That sounds like something you'd say when you were bossing us around when we were all kids," Anna Rose said. "You told us that Clinton is the boss now."

"And he's all wrapped up in some kind of contest now, so I might have to take the title back," Taryn told her.

"What contest?" Anna Rose asked.

Taryn told her about Elaine Ferguson's visit to Clinton's apartment. "According to the little I could get out of Nana Irene, something is going on among a bunch of local women who are chasing after him. Would you throw your hat into the race for who wins this battle? You always did enjoy a good contest."

Anna Rose shook her head. "Not me. If there's that many women after him, then I'd feel like just another notch on his bedpost. When I get ready to walk down the aisle with someone—if I ever do—I want to feel like I'm special. How about you?"

"Elaine looked like she could whip off one of those knockoff red-soled shoes and beat me to death with it if I gave her any competition, so I don't think I'm interested," Taryn replied.

Anna Rose nudged her on the shoulder. "I always figured you were bulletproof—or in this case, high-heel-shoe proof. I've never known you to back down from a fight—at least not after we got to be adults."

Taryn set her cereal bowl and spoon to the side, took a rubber band from her pocket, and used it to pull her red hair up into a ponytail. "I'll fight a forest fire with a cup of water if I want something bad enough to drag it out of the blazes, but I don't know Clinton well enough to get near that fire called Elaine. Besides, he's been to war and brought home a limp to prove it, so he knows how to take care of himself."

"Did you ever think that Nana Irene might have brought us all home to protect him?" Anna Rose asked.

"I'm only protecting you and Jorja from each other," Taryn protested.

"Well, good luck with that," Anna Rose snapped. "She drives me crazy. I can't remember a time when she didn't look down her nose at me, especially after she got out of high school and got even more wrapped up in Jesus than she'd been her whole life. I'm surprised she's not doing missionary work with her mama and daddy in whatever country they're in now."

Taryn tilted her head to the side. "I'm thinking that something might have happened to her about the time that she graduated. When I was in the service, I saw soldiers get religious after a traumatic event. I wonder if she almost wrecked that car her dad bought her for her sixteenth birthday or if she got drunk and felt guilty about it. Aunt Yvonne was always big in the church, and Jorja hung on to her mother's skirt."

"I'm glad that my mama has always been full of life and fun," Anna Rose said.

"Yep, I love Aunt Molly's smile," Taryn agreed. She thought about Anna Rose's mother and how much fun she had when she went there for a visit; then she remembered Jorja's folks. They had always been so staid and proper that she felt awkward and afraid she would do something wrong when she spent time there. No wonder Jorja had problems. She was probably fighting against normal desires and the fear of not being perfect enough for her folks.

A car turned into the parking lot. Anna Rose stood up and pulled a bill from her pocket to pay the delivery person. "Just in time to keep me from starving to death."

A tall, curvy brunette got out of the car, smoothed her hands down over the butt of her jeans, and picked up what looked to be a pie from the passenger's seat. She glanced over at Anna Rose and Taryn but didn't even wave at them.

"Maybe you can tackle her for whatever is in that pie shell," Taryn whispered.

Jorja brought out a huge bowl filled with salad and a sleeve of saltine crackers and sat down on the steps beside them. "Who's that?"

"Evidently it's another contestant vying to win Clinton's hand in marriage," Anna Rose answered. "He's already got the main-course casserole up there, and now dessert. If you'd take that salad up to him, y'all could have a whole meal."

"What are y'all talking about?" Jorja asked.

"We think this contest is a fight to the finish. The winner gets to rope Clinton into walking down the aisle with her. You want to give her some competition?" Taryn asked.

"Not interested," Jorja said. "I don't know why Nana is keeping him through the summer, since we're here. There's three of us. We can run the shop by ourselves."

"Nana always has a motive for what she does," Anna Rose said. "We might never know what she's got up her sleeve, but believe me, she's got something in mind."

"I don't believe you," Jorja said. "Nana Irene is a fine Christian woman, and she knows that God doesn't like people who manipulate others."

The crunch of gravel announced another car minutes before it parked behind the bright blue car that was already there. A kid who couldn't be older than seventeen got out and carried a pizza up to the porch. "Got a delivery for Anna Duquette."

Anna Rose stood up, took the box, and handed the kid a twenty-dollar bill. "Keep the change and thank you."

"Thank *you*," he said and hurried back to his vehicle.

She sat back down. "I love pizza from our little local place. It's the best I've ever had. Not even the famous New York slices compare to this, in my book, and I miss it when I'm not in Shamrock. I always have it at least once when I come to visit."

"Yep, me too, and I've tested it all over the United States," Taryn agreed. "Are you going to open that lid, or are we just going to sit here and smell it all evening?"

Anna Rose eased the lid open and took out a large slice. "I'm going to eat three slices. That leaves five for y'all to fight over."

Taryn picked up one and took a bite from the pointed end. "Jorja is trying to lose weight, so that leaves five for me."

The driver of the blue car left Clinton's apartment, got into her vehicle, and drove away without even so much as a nod toward the three cousins, but at least she didn't leave a cloud of gray dust to settle over their pizza.

"Holy smoke!" Jorja gasped and dropped what salad she had on her fork back into the bowl. "That was Mallory Jones. She graduated with me, too. She always had her nose stuck in the air so high that if it came a good old West Texas rain, she would have drowned. She and Elaine were best friends. I wonder, if this is really a fight for Clinton like y'all think it is, whether it will ruin their friendship." She set her salad on the porch, reached across Taryn, and picked up a slice of pizza. "Why would they want him anyway?" She pointed toward his truck with her free hand. "He drives that, not a Cadillac, and he has a limp."

"He got that limp serving his country, so don't make fun of him for it," Taryn scolded.

Jorja shot an evil eye toward her. "I don't make fun of people. That would make Jesus ashamed of me. I'm just stating facts."

Anna Rose pointed at the slice of pizza in her cousin's hand. "I thought you were watching your weight."

"I am helping y'all out with your extra weight. If I have two slices, then you and Taryn won't eat all of it and gain five pounds." Jorja's tone had turned sharp.

"*Well, bless your heart* for protecting your fat cousins," Taryn said as she finished off the last bite of her slice and reached for another one. "And thank you, Anna Rose, for supper."

"You don't have to be sarcastic," Jorja snapped.

"I wonder what Clinton's got up there in his apartment," Anna Rose said. "We should have gone up there and crashed his party with Mallory. He can't eat a whole casserole and a pie by himself."

Taryn shook her head. "Y'all can go if you want . . ." She stopped midsentence when a big yellow cat came out from under the porch. "Nana didn't mention that she had a cat. Did y'all see any cat food in the pantry?"

"Nope. Nana doesn't even like cats." Anna Rose tossed her crust toward the animal. "Guess it's just a hungry stray who likes pizza. I've been working on pictures for a cat book. If it's still here tomorrow, I may take some photos of it."

"What kind of cat pictures?" Jorja asked.

"Ones for the millions of people in this world who dote on their animals," Anna Rose answered. "Think of all the pet memes you can find on the internet and all the coffee mugs with cats and dogs on them, or toys for fur babies you can buy in just about every store you go into. My agent says a cat picture book will go over well."

Jorja picked up her salad and started to head back into the house. "I've seen dozens of devotionals with cat pictures in them. I thought maybe you were beginning to change your way of life. See y'all in the morning."

"Why is she like that?" Anna Rose whispered when their cousin had closed the door.

"Who knows?" Taryn said with a shrug. "We all had different attitudes and burdens to carry out of Shamrock when we left. I'm not sure what hers was or if she's managed to even get rid of any of it."

Anna Rose pointed at Taryn. "You were mine when I left."

"Hey, now!" Taryn protested. "You were as ornery as I was. The only difference was that you didn't get caught as often as I did, and folks didn't lay the blame on you for every wild and wicked thing that happened in Shamrock."

Anna Rose drew herself up straight and looked down her nose at Taryn. "Anna Rose Duquette. I understand that you are related to Taryn O'Reilly. Is that right?"

Taryn finished off her pizza and reached for the last slice. "If you're trying to imitate Mr. Barron, you're doing a good job."

"Yes, sir. Taryn is my cousin," Anna Rose said in her own voice. "That's when Mr. Barron went to the board, wrote my name, and put two demerits after it and said, 'Three demerits from any of you, and you will spend a day over at the in-school suspension room.'"

Taryn almost choked on a bite of pizza. "I never knew about that."

"I asked him why I got two when I didn't do anything," Anna Rose said. "And he told me that I was guilty by association. What did you do, anyway?"

"I took the blame for a couple of things in his class to keep others from getting a third demerit," Taryn said, "and I spent several days in the suspension room for doing it. I wasn't an angel, but I wasn't a snitch, either."

"Why would you do that?" Anna Rose asked.

"I wanted to fit in and for those girls to like me, but they were just using me to dodge blame for what they did. They'd better take a step back if they think I'm the same person I was then," Taryn answered and realized how cold and bitter her tone was.

"I didn't give a damn if anyone liked me or not, and still don't," Anna Rose said. "Think Mallory will come back and tell us to stay away from Clinton like Elaine did?"

"At least she's not wearing high heels, and she doesn't have enough room in those skintight jeans to hide a pistol, so we might come out with just a black eye if push comes to shove," Taryn answered.

"Honey, if she lights into one of us, you can bet your butt that she'll come out with worse than a little bruising around her eyes." Anna Rose stood, picked up the empty pizza box, and put it in the trash bin at the end of the porch. "I'm going inside. You and Goldie can deal with Mallory if she wants to stake her claim."

"Goldie?" Taryn asked.

Anna Rose crossed the porch. "That's what I'm naming the cat. I'm going to take pictures of her with the sunrise behind her and maybe some against the old, faded trailer house. I can already see that last shot in my mind."

Chapter Three

*C*linton couldn't remember the name of the artist or even the title of the song he was humming when he made it to the shop the next morning, but he remembered one line: something about news traveling fast in a small town. The song seemed to be written just for the three cousins. Folks were standing outside on the sidewalk, talking and waiting for someone to open the front door. Was all that chatter about the cousins' return, he wondered, or about this stupid contest to win his affection? Or were they all here to make last-minute floral orders for Leona's funeral? He hoped the latter was the issue, because he didn't like being the center of all the gossip.

"Good morning!" Clinton pushed through the back door with a box in his hands. "I brought a Mexican chicken casserole and a cherry pie for lunch today. We've got some of those little containers of vanilla ice cream in the freezer to go on the pie, and we can heat up the casserole in the oven."

"You cook?" Taryn asked.

"Yes, I do, but I didn't make this stuff." Clinton busied himself by putting the casserole in the refrigerator and then making a pot of coffee. Women bringing so much food to his house was embarrassing, but at least it cut down on the grocery bill. The cousins didn't need to know the real reason behind all the silliness going on in Shamrock. "Some of the ladies in town have started feeling sorry for me the past few months, and so they bring me food. I've been sharing with Irene and Ruby, but I won't be offended if y'all would rather grab some fast food."

Taryn shook her head. "Not me. I'll be glad to share anytime you bring it to us—but I heard that the women weren't just 'feeling sorry' for you."

Anna Rose covered a yawn with the back of her hand. "I heard the same thing. Have you decided which one is going to win? What's the criteria? Does she have to wear tight jeans or make a mean pie?"

The last cousin, Jorja, rushed into the shop, hurried to the front, and put her purse under the counter, then returned, breathless, to the back room. "Sorry I'm late. It took longer to do my prayers this morning than usual. I had to pray for extra strength, patience, and love to fill my heart." She cut her eyes around at Anna Rose. "Your eyes are bloodshot. Did you sneak out to the bars last night?"

"I don't sneak around. If I do it, I own it," she snapped.

"Clinton brought food for lunch. And, Jorja, Anna Rose is a big girl. She can go wherever she wants without either of us getting into her business if she shows up for work on time," Taryn answered.

Anna Rose pointed at the clock. "At least I'm on time, and I don't blame God and Jesus for being late. I smell coffee."

Jorja muttered all the way through the shop as she went to open the front door. In seconds, the place was full of folks milling around, looking at plants, crosses to hang on their walls or set on a shelf, and other gift items suitable for funerals or birthdays.

Clinton glanced over at Taryn, who shrugged, poured herself a cup of coffee, took a sip, and set it to the side. "Nana Irene thinks we'll all learn to be friends. I'm not sure that even her prayers and Jorja's combined can make that happen."

"You never know. Irene and Ruby both might have a hotline to heaven," Clinton said with a chuckle.

"Maybe so, but I won't hold my breath," she said and went to the front to help wait on customers.

The conversations in the front of the shop all mingled together, but Clinton could easily make out Taryn's husky voice. It reminded him of good whiskey, with a bit of honey thrown in to sweeten the fire.

"Good morning, everyone. Who can I help?" she asked.

"That would be me," a feminine-sounding voice answered.

"Well, hello there, Mrs. Sullivan. How is Kaitlin doing these days?"

Clinton slid off his barstool and took a few steps toward the archway leading from one room to the other so he could hear better. Linda Sullivan had a reputation for being a gossip, and he didn't want to miss a word that she had to say to Taryn.

"I didn't come in here to buy a flower or a present," Linda said, so low that Clinton had to strain to hear her words. "I came to tell you to stay away from Kaitlin and her family. She's married to Ford Chambers and has two little children. She and Ford help out with the youth at our church, and I don't want you comin' around them."

Clinton peeked around the corner in time to see Linda whip around to face Jorja, now with a sunny smile on her face. "Kaitlin and Ford are bringing the kids and coming to my house for dinner after church on Sunday. We'd be glad to have you join us at our place of worship, and maybe while you are here, you could help her teach the kindergarten class."

"Thanks for asking, but I've already got plans for after church on Sunday," Jorja said.

Well, now! That's the coldest tone I've heard Jorja use, Clinton thought. *Why was her face set like flint?* Her eyes even had that deer-in-the-headlights look to them. Clinton could almost smell the fear. He'd seen that in soldiers too many times not to recognize PTSD, but Jorja had never served in the military and had lived a very sheltered life.

"Then maybe another day this summer," Linda suggested and left the shop without looking back.

Clinton went back to the prep space and finished what he'd been working on. Half an hour later, the chatter had died down, and the cousins all returned to their places at the worktable. "Did you tell a big fat lie, Jorja Butler?" Taryn asked.

"It's a sin to lie, and I do my best not to sin," Jorja answered.

"What have you got to do that you can't go to Sunday dinner with Linda and Kaitlin? And why did you do that?" Taryn asked.

"I plan to write get-well cards to send to the sick or shut-ins in my church at home on Sunday afternoon." Jorja dropped a fistful of orders in the basket. "As for why—Kaitlin told everyone we could meet up at Amos's barn for our graduation party and urged me to go. I knew it was wrong to drink, but I wanted to be included with the rest of the class."

"And?" Taryn asked.

"And nothing," she whispered and shivered at the same time. "I believe that she set me up . . ." She stopped midsentence.

"Set you up for what?" Anna Rose asked.

"To go against my beliefs and to probably make a laughingstock of me," Jorja answered.

The pinched expression on her face, the haunted look in her eyes, and the cold tone in her voice told Clinton that she was hiding something painful. She shook her head as if trying to erase a bad memory.

"I will forgive her because God says I have to, but He doesn't say I have to like her. I don't intend to spend time with her and her family or step foot in their church. I can go to another one. It's not like that is the only place to worship in Shamrock—and besides, Nana Irene doesn't attend services there, anyway."

"And I thought you refused the invitation because we're family and you love your cousins so much," Taryn teased.

Clinton knew that they shouldn't joke about the demons in Jorja's heart and soul, but he understood. It wasn't his place to say a word.

Jorja moved a small picture frame from the bottom shelf to the top one. "We are family, but that wasn't the whole reason. I just don't like hypocrites. At least you and Anna Rose are up-front about who you are. Now, let's take care of these orders and forget about Linda Sullivan."

"I dunno, you told a white lie up there, and that's not easy to forget," Anna Rose said with a grin.

"Did not." Jorja reached over and grabbed the next order. "Three red roses in a vase with a get-well card to be taken to Ruby's house. And just to be clear, it was not a lie. I do have plans for Sunday afternoon, even if I had to create them on the spot." She slid off the stool and went to the cooler for the flowers she needed. "I may not even go to any of the local churches while I'm here. My church at home televises their services each week, so I can sit in the living room at the trailer and watch it in my pajamas."

"You're not even going to help with Vacation Bible School at Nana Irene's church?" Anna Rose asked.

"Maybe I'll do that, but I can get my dose of spirituality from the television," she answered.

Anna Rose finished up a small wreath and set it aside for delivery. "If you do, you're going to wear earphones. If you wake me up before noon to preachin' on the television, I *will* throw things at you."

Jorja laid her flowers out on the worktable, chose a vase, and went to work. "A bit of spirituality wouldn't hurt either of you, but so you won't go tattling to Nana Irene, I'll watch my church service on my laptop in my bedroom—with my earphones. Far be it from me to force religion on either of you."

Taryn threw up her palms. "Don't go clumping me into y'all's argument. I'm just minding my own business here, putting together a bow to go on the last peace lily we've got in the building for Leona's funeral."

"I promise not to force you to go to a bar with me if you'll use your earphones, but I seem to remember that you liked to dance when you were younger," Anna Rose said. "And, Taryn, darlin', you started this whole thing when you said that Jorja told a big fat lie. Looking back, I wonder how many arguments you instigated in the past just so you could step in and save the day."

Clinton swallowed a chuckle. Things were back to normal, but he still wondered if Jorja hadn't experienced something more than just setting aside her faith out at Amos's old barn on graduation night.

"Don't ever look back." Jorja paled. "Just ask for forgiveness for the dark things that live in your past and keep your eyes forward."

"No comeback on that?" Clinton whispered for Taryn's ears only.

"Not today," Taryn answered.

The bell above the door announced a customer, and Anna Rose pointed at Clinton. "It's your turn. We took care of all the folks earlier."

"I don't wait on people. Ruby and Irene did that—and now it's y'all's jobs, not mine. I arrange. I deliver. I bring lunch when it shows up on my doorstep. I'll even pick up burgers and fries for all of you, but I don't go to the front," he said.

"Yoo-hoo!" A high, squeaky voice floated from the front to the back room.

Clinton rolled his eyes. "And that is why I stay in the back, especially since this damned contest started."

"Clinton, darlin', are you here?" the voice went on, getting louder with each word.

Taryn slid off her stool. "I recognize that voice. I'll go this time." Some folks never change, but she couldn't say the same for Diana Marlow. Her hair had been brown back in high school, but now it was platinum blonde. And she had to be wearing colored contacts, because her brown eyes were now light blue. "Hello, Diana. I don't think I've seen you since I left Shamrock more than ten years ago, but I'd recognize your voice anywhere."

"Not seeing you is a good thing. I haven't forgotten how much trouble followed you around. Some of us are good members of society now. Where's Clinton?" She tipped up her chin and looked down her nose at Taryn.

"He's not here, but I'll be glad to give him a message." Taryn was amazed at her calmness—but then, maybe she was getting to be more like Nana Irene. None of the girls were worried if their grandmother raised her voice at them . . . but if she whispered, that was a different matter.

"I wanted to give this to him myself, but . . ." Diana sighed and set a bright red platter wrapped in cellophane on the counter. "It's a loaf of pumpkin bread from my family's secret recipe and a dozen chocolate chip cookies. You be sure he gets it, and tell him I'll be by his apartment in a couple of days with a nice pot roast."

"I will do that." Taryn felt the chill in her own voice and hoped that when Diana shivered, it was caused by more than the air-conditioning. "Anything else I can help you with this morning?"

"Not a thing. I'll be glad when Ruby and Irene are back. This shop is going to suffer without them," Diana threw over her shoulder as she went out the front door.

Taryn carried the platter to the back and set it on the table beside the coffee maker. "How many women are trying to swindle an engagement ring out of you by bringing you food?"

"Tell us more about this contest," Anna Rose said. "Do you own half the state of Texas or something?"

Clinton finished the vase of flowers he had been working on and set it aside. "This all started when my grandfather, Harry McEntire, was featured on the front of a magazine. Until then, I was a nobody, but folks put my name and his together. Evidently, you can find out anything about anyone on the internet."

"You are from *that* McEntire family?" Jorja gasped. "He's the biggest oil baron in the state. I read that article—he talked about someday leaving it all to his grandson, Clinton."

Clinton tore the plastic wrap off the bread and cookies. "That would be me. My grandfather will be running the corporation until he's a hundred years old, so I don't have to worry about my inheritance. Right now, I'm not interested in oil or any of those other new investments he made. Material things aren't at the top of my priority list. Neither are women that are after me because they think I'm rich."

"Why don't you just tell them that?" Anna Rose asked.

"I have," Clinton said with a shrug. "It didn't change anything. It's like they have selective hearing. And Google searches and what's on the internet are both as eternal as God and heaven."

"Please lead them on a little bit until Nana Irene and Ruby get back," Taryn said with a chuckle as she picked up a cookie. "I like the idea of good food being brought in, and these cookies are still warm."

"That's not very nice," Jorja scolded.

Clinton took the whole platter to the worktable and then poured four cups of coffee. "Let's have a midmorning snack, and then I'll make the deliveries. Looks like we've got a full van. We might have to go out a couple of times by the end of the day."

Taryn helped him carry the cups to the worktable.

Anna Rose cleaned a floral knife and cut several slices of bread. "This is almost as good as Nana Irene's, and that's giving her a lot of praise. I'm throwing my vote in with Taryn's about not running your admirers off until Nana Irene and Ruby are back in the shop. Then, if you can't make them understand, turn it over to Nana Irene. She'll put the fear of God into them."

"Don't I get a vote?" Jorja took a bite of her bread.

"Sure, you do, but it won't matter," Taryn answered. "You're already outvoted two to one."

"My vote is that you don't tell the women to get lost until we're gone," Jorja said between bites. "They deserve whatever happens for making you the prize in a contest."

Taryn dipped the edge of a cookie into her coffee. "Clinton, you should call Nana Irene and tell her that—for what may well be the first time ever—we have agreed on something."

"You call her," Clinton said.

Anna Rose shook her head. "We can't. There's no blood or broken bones."

"Oh, hush about that," Jorja said. "And for y'all's information, none of those three women that we've seen would listen anyway. You know what they say about changing a leopard's spots. They'll all be gold diggers forever, but I do wish Kerry Smith would join the contest. Her momma makes the best gingerbread and lemon sauce I've ever tasted."

"She brought me some of that, and Irene and Ruby said the same thing—but here lately, it's just been Elaine, Mallory, and Diana coming around," Clinton said with a grin.

He ate a second cookie and a slice of pumpkin bread and finished off his coffee. "While we're discussing me, I'll tell you this: I'm not a hero. I didn't run into a burning building to save my air force buddies, and I didn't get this limp from an explosion over in Kuwait or Afghanistan. I moved to Shamrock because my grandfather grew up here, and I started a small nonprofit business out of my apartment where I advocate for wounded vets. The minute folks realized who I was, they assumed I had been wounded in battle, and when they found out I was running a military-related nonprofit organization, and didn't need a wagonload of money, that just made them more sure of the fact. I tried to tell them I wasn't a hero or interested in my grandfather's money, but I might as well have been whistling in the wind."

"How *did* you get hurt?" Jorja asked.

"We had a five-mile run over rough terrain for our PT test. I stepped in a hole and broke my hip, fractured my tibia, broke my fibula in three places, and tore up my knee all at the same time. They did what they could, including a lot of therapy after the surgeries, but I got a limp out of the deal, which got me a medical discharge," he answered. "Enough about me. Now, I'm going to make these deliveries, and then after lunch today and until noon tomorrow, y'all are on your own. I have back-to-back appointments with vets." He stretched the cellophane over the platter and set it back on the table with the coffeepot.

"I'd say you are between the old proverbial rock and a hard place," Taryn said. She had never heard of a fall causing so much damage to a leg and hip. Maybe what had really happened to him was classified.

"You are so right," Clinton agreed with a nod and a wink. "After a dozen people told me they understood that I couldn't talk about my limp because it was classified—including several vets here in town—I didn't even try to explain."

Taryn took the next ticket from the stack in the basket. "Smart man. Protesting too loudly would just cause the nosy people to believe you even less. Besides, it has to be a bit of an ego boost for folks to think you're a hero, right?"

"Not really," Clinton answered and grabbed a couple of plants to take out to the van. "Knowing about my family's money and thinking that I'm some kind of hero is what started this contest between the single women."

"You might want to wait to deliver until I get this last one done," Taryn said.

"As fast as you are, you'll have it done by the time I get all these loaded," Clinton said.

"She *is* fast," Jorja said.

"What's that supposed to mean?" Taryn bristled, though the barb from her cousin shouldn't have surprised her one bit.

Jorja picked up a dust rag and headed to the front office. "Take it any way you want to."

The last order was for an ivy plant to be delivered to Ruby. Taryn was more than a little bit jealous that Clinton got to go see her grandmother and Ruby, but if she insisted on going with him, the other two would pitch a hissy fit.

She remembered visiting her grandmother on Mother's Day, but that seemed like months—maybe years—ago. Jorja had been doing something with her church, and Anna Rose was somewhere on the East Coast, taking pictures of lighthouses for a calendar. She'd had a lovely day with Irene and Ruby. In true southern tradition, she had bought a red-rose corsage for herself—signifying that her mother was still living—and white ones for Ruby and Irene because their mothers had passed. She had taken them to church that morning and then out to dinner afterward. Ruby had needed a nap, but Taryn and her grand-mother spent the afternoon sitting on the porch swing and looking at old photo albums.

When Clinton left, Anna Rose hopped down from her barstool and poured herself another cup of coffee. "Do you believe that story about falling in a hole?"

Taryn was jerked out of her memory in time to hear the last few words. "Who fell?"

"Where's your mind today?" Anna Rose asked, then repeated the question.

"Why would he lie to us, and what difference does it make?" Jorja asked. "I don't really care how he got that limp. What I want to know is why Taryn is flirting with him after just one day. I mean, I could understand it if, after we've been here a month, you figure out that you kind of liked him. But only one day? Are you that desperate?"

"I *was not* flirting with him," Taryn protested.

"Yeah, you were," Anna Rose said.

"If it gives you two something to agree on, then yes, I was flirting with him," Taryn told them. "And if it will stop you from bickering, I'll flirt with him every day we are here—and FYI, I am not desperate."

Anna Rose held up a palm. "I was not agreeing with Jorja. If we had the same opinion twice in one day, the world might come to an end, and there's cowboys out there that I have not flirted with or kissed. For the record, I was just stating a fact."

"You *cannot* start a relationship with Clinton." Jorja's tone was so sharp that it reminded Taryn of one of her military-training instructors.

"Why not?" Taryn had no intentions of doing more than just being work friends with Clinton, but Jorja dang sure wasn't going to tell her what she could or could not do. "Maybe I believe in love at first sight."

"I'm not sure if I believe in that," Anna Rose said with a giggle, "but I really, really believe in lust at first sight, and I intend to see if I can find a healthy dose of that real soon."

"You should go to church, not to bars," Jorja scolded.

Anna Rose flipped her brown hair back over her shoulders in a dramatic gesture and did a little hip wiggle. "Maybe my church is a bar, and my hymns are good country music on a jukebox, and my salvation is a good-lookin' cowboy willin' to come home with me."

Jorja shivered even worse than she had earlier when she had mentioned her dark past or when Linda had invited her to Sunday dinner. "That's sacrilege. You go stand on the other side of the room. When lightning shoots down from the cloudless sky and zaps you into dust, I don't want to be close to you."

"Don't worry, Anna Rose," Taryn said. "If that happens, I'll scoop up every bit of your ashes and throw them out in the parking lot of that bar over the Oklahoma-Texas line that you've always liked."

"Promise?" Anna Rose asked with a gleam in her green eyes. "Will you do that for me and then have a wake in the bar? I want the last handful of my ashes put into that vase right there"—she pointed at a shiny black one on the shelf—"and set on the jukebox so I can be there for all the fun."

Jorja got the window cleaner out from under the counter and started to work on the glass door. "Y'all are both awful."

"Don't worry, darlin'," Taryn teased. "If you get struck by lightning, I'll make sure your ashes are placed on the altar of the church of your choice and that we'll all sing 'I'll Fly Away' at your services. I'll even do the eulogy and tell the mourners that you were trying to save a sinner when the bolt came down through the rafters toward Anna Rose." She stopped and sighed. "And that it got you by mistake."

"And I'll pass out really nice tissues at the door," Anna Rose chimed in. "The kind that comes in pretty little individual packages."

"I'm not talking to either of you," Jorja declared, "and I'm telling Nana Irene that you've both been ugly."

"We can't tattle until we close up on Saturday and go to Ruby's to eat lunch with the two of them," Anna Rose reminded her.

"But if you want to get hurt bad enough to go to the emergency room, I expect Nana Irene will come see you, and you can tattle then," Taryn said.

Jorja whipped around and gave them a look that was probably meant to fry them on the spot. "You've both tested the Jesus in me really hard today. Right now, I could probably put both of you in the ER and get away with it on Judgment Day after the way y'all have been talking."

"Then Nana Irene would just make you take care of us and run the shop without us," Anna Rose teased.

"We'll be good if you'll tell us what made you shiver when you were talking about something that happened in your past," Taryn said. "I thought you were born with wings and a halo, so what has happened to you that wasn't so holy and sanctified in your past? Did you get really drunk on your graduation night, or did something else happen?"

"That would be need-to-know, and neither of you do." Jorja shivered again. "You both ran off to do your own thing when you graduated and left me here in Shamrock alone, so you don't get to pry into the ugly moments of my past. And because Jesus says that I have to love you, I will pray for your souls tonight."

"Thank you for that," Taryn said. "I know that, for myself, I can use all the prayers I can get. Especially in this town, where it seemed to me like I got blamed for everything that happened, even when I could prove I didn't do it."

"You did plenty, and so did I," Anna Rose said.

"And I paid for it," Jorja grumbled.

"I'm sorry about that . . . whatever it was," Taryn told her with a grimace. "But if you ever want to talk about it, I'll listen."

"But then you'd tell Anna Rose, and she would tease me," Jorja said, almost whining.

"You can talk to both or either of us," Anna Rose declared. "We might not like each other, but we are cousins."

"Amen!" Taryn said, and she meant it.

Chapter Four

Jorja had flipped the sign around to let people know they were open, but the bell above the door hadn't rung all morning. The shelves were dusted and straightened, all the glass had been polished, and now there was nothing to do. She was bored to tears. Maybe if she got out the Christian romance book she'd been reading, they would get a dozen customers. It usually worked that way when she tried to read at home. No more than one page into the story, and the phone would ring.

"Get out a puzzle," Taryn said to Anna Rose.

"You're having Clinton withdrawal," Anna Rose told her.

"I am not," Taryn protested.

"Yes, you are," Jorja agreed with Anna Rose. "And for the record, I don't do puzzles. That seems like a waste of time to me. I'd rather read a book."

"I'm going out back to set my camera up," Anna Rose said, and turned to head out of the shop. "Maybe Goldie will be willing to do a photo shoot. Call me if y'all get busy."

"I didn't take time for breakfast, so I *will* have some pumpkin bread and a cup of coffee while we're waiting on an order or two." Jorja uncovered the platter holding what was left of the bread. Only a few crumbs of the cookies remained.

"I thought you were trying to lose five pounds," Taryn said. "I don't know why, since you are the tallest and thinnest one of us." She brought out a knife and cut two thick slices of the bread and then slathered hers with cream cheese.

"When Daddy was a little kid, they called him hyperactive—but now, that is diagnosed as ADHD," Jorja explained. "I inherited being hyper from him and some of Mama's OCD, so when I'm not busy, I want to cook or eat or both. And being the tall one in this family is nothing to brag about in the overall picture. Last time I was measured, I was just five feet six inches. That's not really tall."

"If you were barely topping out at five three like me and Anna Rose, it would be a lot to boast about," Taryn said between bites. "We'd love to have your blonde hair and cheekbones. And your skin is flawless—not a single freckle."

Jorja touched her face with her free hand. "I'd trade complexion and height for a little of your confidence."

"Honey, confidence is ninety percent bluff," Taryn said as she cut another piece of the bread.

"What's the other ten percent?" Jorja asked.

Anna Rose came through the back door. "I heard most of what y'all just said—and, Jorja, that last ten percent is either ego or fear, or a mixture of both."

The bell rang, and the aroma of warm chocolate floated through to the back room. Jorja took a sip of coffee and led the way to the front part of the shop, with Taryn right behind her. When she was a little girl, she'd called it the "pretty part" of the shop. The back had always been strewn with bits of ribbon and flower stems, and that drove Jorja crazy with her desire to keep things neat and in place. But the display room had always looked like it came out of a fancy magazine.

Diana, Elaine, and Mallory all stood in front of the counter with food in their hands and anger written all over their faces. Three foolish women, who had once been such close friends that they all wore matching *BFF* necklaces, had let a man turn them into enemies. And they were standing right there, in front of Taryn and Jorja. They all looked different—a brunette, a blonde, and a platinum blonde—but had the same fury in their expressions.

"Good morning," Jorja said cheerfully. "No one told me there was a bake sale here today. Where is it, and do they have any more of those chocolate pies?"

"There's not a bake sale anywhere!" Diana barked. "I brought this chocolate sheet cake for Clinton. Where is he?"

"He's not here," Anna Rose said as she rounded the end of the counter and stood beside Jorja. "What can I help you ladies with today? We don't have a lot of fresh flowers until our delivery arrives around noon, but I could rustle up some daisies or mums if you want a bouquet."

Elaine eyed both Jorja and Anna Rose like horns had suddenly sprouted from the tops of their heads. "I'm not interested in flowers of any kind. I brought this chocolate pie to Clinton. He loves his chocolate and his Mexican food. You can tell him that my pie is homemade, and these other two brought things they either bought or had someone make for them."

Diana turned on the woman standing beside her and hissed, "You bitch!"

Are you still bored? Jorja's inner voice asked.

No, she answered. *Things are getting kind of interesting, and I hope they don't have a food fight with all that good stuff they've brought in.*

Taryn stepped between the two of them. "We have a policy that says if you break it, you buy it, so you might take your fighting out on the sidewalk. Or if you don't want anyone to see you trying to snatch each other bald, you can leave by the back door and have it out in the parking lot. I can't guarantee that Anna Rose won't take pictures and post them on Instagram, but it's your choice to make. And one more thing before push comes to shove—Elaine, you can bring that Mexican casserole once a week. We had it for lunch just yesterday. And, Mallory, your cherry pie was really good, too."

Elaine whipped around and looked down her nose at Taryn. "That casserole wasn't for you. That was for Clinton."

Jorja wondered which one would win if they did decide to duke it out, and she secretly wished she could figure out a way to get them all mad at Kaitlin—or even better, sic them on Ford.

"When you gave it to him, did you tell him not to share?" Anna Rose asked.

Elaine set her pie down on the counter and popped her hands on her hips. "I didn't have to tell him that before you three moved in on my territory. He knows that whatever I bring him is made with love just for him."

"Then I guess he had better fall in love with the Mexican restaurant down the street, because I found their sticker on the bottom of the fancy dish you brought the other day." Jorja was amazed at the words that came out of her mouth.

Mallory pointed a finger at Elaine. "I knew you couldn't boil water without burning down the house." Then she turned back to the three cousins, who were now lined up behind the counter. "He told me that he likes brownies better than pie or cake, so I just took these out of the oven five minutes ago so they would be warm for him—and you can tell him that I made them myself."

"Why are the three of you bringing him more food than one man can eat?" Taryn asked.

Elaine glared at all three cousins with such heat that Jorja wondered how they weren't melting into a pile of bones and fat right there behind the counter. "I'm doing it because I intend to win this contest and make him love me," she said, with enough venom in her voice to kill a person graveyard dead.

Jorja glanced out the window to see if lightning bolts could be coming from a clear blue sky. But then, who needed a flash of fire when Elaine could zap a person even quicker with words? Jorja shifted her gaze back to the three women and decided that they were all the devil's minions. No self-respecting Christian woman would be so rude and unkind.

"I can learn to cook, if that's what it takes. Besides, I've already picked out my wedding dress, and Mama is looking at venues." Elaine gave her a fake smile.

"Hmmph!" Mallory snorted. "You just want him for his money. I want to marry him because I love him. He's a hero, don't you know? And, *honey*"—she shook her finger at Elaine—"don't buy that dress yet. Not until he makes up his mind which one of us he wants."

Diana set her cake on the counter. "Neither of you have a chance when I'm in the running."

"All of you have rocks for brains," Jorja said in a voice so icy that she didn't even recognize it, but she was determined to be more like her cousins and tell people exactly what she thought. "A man does not like to be chased down like a feral hog. The way you are acting, you might as well load up a shotgun and force him to pick among the three of you. You should be ashamed of yourselves."

Diana sucked in a lungful of air and let it out slowly. "Everyone knows that the way to a man's heart is through his stomach, and I intend to show him that I can cook."

"A man's heart is his to give to a woman he loves." Jorja liked the feeling of being bluntly honest with people other than her two cousins. "Whether she can cook or not doesn't really matter. There are restaurants everywhere—and Clinton can cook for himself, so he won't be getting married just to have a chef in the kitchen."

Anna Rose finally spoke up. "And, ladies, this is a place of business, not a delivery drop-off for baked goods. I agree with Jorja. If you want to fight over him like he's a plate of nachos and you are starving, then get on out of our shop."

Elaine picked up her pie and gave the cousins one last dirty look. "I'll take my pie to him tonight in his apartment. Believe me when I tell you that I will find a way to win this contest."

"He'll share it with us tomorrow," Anna Rose called out. "I've always loved the pies from the bakery in town, and chocolate is my favorite."

Mallory grabbed her brownies. "I'll feed these to the birds before I let you eat a one of them."

"Anna Rose knows a cat that might like them better than a bunch of birds, so if you've got a mind to throw them out, please put them on the trailer porch," Jorja said. She heard her cousins' smarty-pants words coming from her mouth and wasn't sure she liked the sound, but she couldn't stop the tone or what she was saying.

Diana was the only one left in the shop, and she smirked at the cousins, "I don't like any of you, but I do owe you a thank-you for getting rid of those two. I'll leave the cake right here. That gives me more points for today. See to it that he gets this cake when he comes back."

"Did you not hear a thing Jorja said?" Taryn asked. "You are all three making fools of yourselves."

Diana's smile got even bigger. "Maybe so, but I'm going to have a wedding, and Elaine and Mallory are going to be standing on the sidelines."

"Didn't you all used to be good friends?" Taryn asked.

"We were—and we might be again, someday." Diana flipped her hair back over her shoulder. "But right now, all is fair in love and war. We started out with a dozen women in the contest, and we all put five hundred dollars in the pot. Whoever gets an engagement ring wins all six thousand dollars. I'll use the money to help buy my wedding dress."

Jorja slapped the glass-topped counter, rattling the cute little container with pens in it. "I hope that he refuses all of you, but you can bring all the food you want. We were just having a slice of your pumpkin bread when you got here."

Diana stared at the cake, then finally turned around and opened the door. "After that smart-aleck remark, you won't be invited to the wedding."

"Honey, none of us want to come to your wedding, anyway. We might go to Clinton's if he ever gets married, but I'd bet dollars to cow chips that it won't be to any one of you three," Anna Rose shot back, raising her voice so Diana could hear every word before the door closed.

For several seconds, the silence was deafening; then Jorja glanced over at Taryn and giggled. "You are right. Confidence is mostly bluff with a little ego and fear thrown into the mix."

"Yep," Anna Rose agreed with a nod. "I'm proud of you for the way you stood up to them today. They've been full of themselves since they were just little girls, and what they've got is mostly ego. Living in a small town where they are all big shots makes them that way. Drop them in a place like Dallas or Houston, and they would die."

"You're right, but I was talking about myself. I felt like I had some confidence right then," Jorja said.

Taryn patted her on the back. "You did, and I'm proud of you, too."

"'You done good,' as Nana Irene says when we do something right." Anna Rose picked up the cake and started for the back room. "This is still warm, and I do love chocolate cake."

"Maybe we should call Clinton since it was meant for him." Jorja whipped out her phone and went to the refrigerator-door notepad, where phone numbers had been scribbled in her grandmother's handwriting. She found Clinton's number after hers, Anna Rose's, and Taryn's; she added it to her contact list. Then she called him.

"Hello, is everything all right down there?" Clinton asked.

"Just peachy," Jorja answered. "No, that's not right. Everything is chocolaty, not peachy. We've got a chocolate cake from Diana. Do you want us to wait to cut it or just dive in, or would you like for me to bring it up to your apartment?"

"Dive right in," Clinton chuckled. "I've got dozens and dozens of cookies up here that I've been sending home with the vets who come in for help. My last appointment is at three, and it might last an hour. I'll be down there after that, but I left the company credit card in the cash register so you can pay the fresh-flower deliveryman when he gets there. See you later."

She didn't even have time to tell him thank you before the call ended.

"Well?" Anna Rose asked. "Do we cut the cake, or do we wait?"

"He says that we can cut it," Jorja said. "Evidently, those women really have been bombarding him with food. He said that he's got dozens of cookies up in his apartment. Milk or coffee?"

"Both," Anna Rose answered. "And while we eat, I'll show you the pictures of Goldie that I took this morning. I wonder who she belongs to."

Jorja brought a stack of disposable plates and napkins to the worktable. "We'll have to ask Nana Irene on Saturday, or maybe Clinton knows. If we don't start eating better, we'll all be diabetics by the time we leave here."

She set the milk on the table, poured a cup of coffee for Anna Rose, and looked over at Taryn with a raised eyebrow.

"Milk, please. But what a way to go! I'm glad there's a contest going on, if it means that we get food every day," Taryn declared.

A miracle had just happened—at least, in Jorja's way of thinking. They had stood together on something more important than a vote about food, and they weren't arguing now.

"Hey, y'all hungry for something besides that chocolate cake Anna Rose is carrying?" Clinton asked.

"What have you got there?" Taryn sniffed the air. "Do I smell lasagna?"

"You sure do," Clinton answered.

Taryn motioned him toward the trailer. "Bring it on in. I'll make a salad and some garlic bread to go with it. How much food have you got up there, anyway?"

"Enough to feed a whole family reunion," he answered with a smile. "My little freezer is full. The refrigerator is full, and several bins are full of cookies. Unless y'all want something special, I can probably provide supper for the next six weeks."

"Sounds good to me," Anna Rose said, holding the door open. "How many women are there that bring food?"

"At first, there were at least a dozen women coming around all the time." Clinton frowned. "Then it narrowed down to about six, and it seems like lately there's only the three. Honestly, ladies, I've tried to tell them that if I want to date, I will ask them. It's like they don't even hear me. I tell them that I don't want any more food, and yet they come back several times a week with cakes, pies, and casseroles."

"Their ears can only hear money jingling around for their wedding day," Jorja said.

Clinton set the lasagna on the cabinet and suddenly looked like he'd been poleaxed—as Nana Irene said when reality hit a person right in the core of their brain. "Wedding day? I thought the contest was to see who could get me to go out with them. Do you mean they're wanting marriage *for real*? Y'all aren't just teasing me?"

Taryn pulled the lettuce and tomatoes from the refrigerator and set about making a salad. "They are picking out wedding dresses and venues. You might want to run for the hills."

Anna Rose took a loaf of Italian bread from the pantry and started slicing it. "We'll protect you as best we can until we leave—but when we're gone, you'll be on your own, feller. I'm not sure Nana Irene and Ruby together can keep those rabid skunks at bay by the end of summer."

Clinton swiped his hand across his brow. "Why didn't someone tell me this was about more than a date or two before now? Irene and Ruby had to have known."

"They probably liked the food, just like we do," Jorja said. "But I'm wondering what those women will do next when they figure out that the way to the altar isn't through your stomach."

"I shudder to even think about it," Clinton whispered. "Marriage? Are you sure?"

Jorja nodded. "Elaine wouldn't be buying a wedding dress if she wasn't pretty sure that she was going to win the diamond, the man, and a walk down the aisle on her father's arm. I imagine she already has visions of being invited to parties in the governor's mansion in Austin."

Clinton sighed. "I thought they were bringing food to the poor, crippled man because he is a *war hero*"—he threw up air quotes—"and they just wanted to date me because of that."

Taryn set the bowl of salad on the bar beside the pan of lasagna. "I don't know about that. I think they see dollar signs more than a slight limp."

What do you *see?* her inner voice asked.

I see a good man, she answered honestly.

Jorja set the table and poured four glasses of sweet tea. "Looks like we're ready to eat."

Clinton stood up and glanced at the round table. "Where do I sit?"

"Anywhere you want," Taryn answered. "Nana Irene said that she bought a round table so that we wouldn't fuss about who got to be the queen and sit at the head. I imagine that any one of the three women who are vying for a diamond ring the size of an ice rink will be sure to have a table where they can reign as queen in whatever big mansion that you build for them. For tonight, we're all just work friends, so pick up a plate and help yourself."

"But first, we pray," Jorja said and held out her hand to Taryn. "And we have to hold hands because that's what Nana Irene made us do when she said grace. She said it was the one time in the day when we had to be nice to each other for a minute or two."

Clinton took Taryn's hand in his right one and Anna Rose's in his left. Taryn simply had to get out more, because plenty of chemistry flowed through her hand—just like it had when he had put his arm around her in the funeral home. She didn't even hear Jorja's prayer, but when her cousin said, "Amen," and Clinton dropped her hand, Taryn glanced over at him, and their eyes locked for a brief moment.

Taryn blinked and looked away before either of her cousins could accuse her of flirting.

"I didn't have time to eat anything but a few cookies today, so I'm starving," he said.

She reached over to the table and handed him a plate. "Guests first, especially when you've been working all day and we've only had a total of three customers. Mostly what we did was finish off the pumpkin bread and eat cake."

"I'm not a guest," Clinton protested. "I'm a partner—at least until Irene and Ruby get back, and then I'm back to a hired hand. But I won't argue about going first."

He loaded up his plate, sat down at the table, and waited on the others to join him before he took the first bite. "So, it was a slow day? Did y'all get the puzzles out?"

"Nope, but . . ." Taryn told him about the three women coming in to bring chocolate cake, pie, and brownies.

"But Elaine and Mallory took theirs back," Jorja said. "I really like those pies that the bakery here in town makes, so I wish Elaine would have left it."

"Thank God!" Clinton said. "I've already taken a lot of stuff to the homeless shelter."

Anna Rose patted him on the shoulder. "I can eat lasagna for breakfast, so if there's more up in your apartment, save it for us rather than taking it to the shelter."

"I would gladly cook every evening if they would leave me alone," Clinton said.

"Doesn't look like that's going to happen anytime soon," Taryn said. "I kind of wished that they had gotten into a catfight today. That way they would have had to pay for all the things they broke, and we would have made some money."

Anna Rose reached behind her for the bowl of bread and set it on the table. "I was just waiting for them to throw punches or scratch each other with those fake nails. If they had, I would have stepped in and helped break a few things. I never have liked those orange vases."

"Anna Rose!" Jorja scolded. "That would be deceitful."

"Maybe so, but those hideous vases would be gone," Anna Rose said.

"I'm afraid to think about what they would do next if they didn't bring food," Clinton said.

"Probably declare that they are pregnant, and the baby is yours," Taryn said. "This is Texas, and daddies don't take well to guys who sleep with their daughters and then refuse to marry them when there's a bun in the oven."

"Lock your doors after work, and don't answer when anyone knocks," Jorja said. "One of us will be with you during the day."

"But . . ." Taryn raised an eyebrow. "Elaine was there Monday night, so in six weeks, she just might . . ."

Clinton shook his head. "Nothing has happened with any of them."

Anna Rose laid a hand on his arm. "Don't worry, darlin'. If they make accusations like that, I will say that we've taken turns spending the night with you and there's no way you have energy enough for two women a night."

"Good Lord!" Clinton gasped. "That would be even worse than the contest they've got going."

"Like I said, we'll protect you as long as you share your bounty of casseroles and food with us," Anna Rose said with a smile.

"I won't go that far," Jorja said from across the table. "These other two can spread that kind of gossip, but I'm not losing my reputation."

"Y'all better not be telling that kind of thing." Clinton took a piece of bread from the bowl. "Irene would shoot me, and Ruby would bury me in her rose garden."

Taryn's knee brushed against Clinton's under the table, and the same tingly feeling she got when he'd held her hand swept over her. She really needed to get out and date, but how was she supposed to meet anyone working from home?

Her nana's voice popped into her head: *You could go out to eat rather than calling that place that delivers. Or maybe go to church—or heck, even a bar once in a while. Just don't get involved with any of those dating sites on the computer. You could wind up getting hurt, and I would have to take care of things. It's not that I mind spending my last days in prison, but Ruby would be lost without me.*

Taryn giggled.

"What Clinton said wasn't *that* funny," Jorja said.

"Didn't you see that glazed-over look in her eyes?" Anna Rose asked. "She wasn't listening to Clinton. She was off in la-la land. Were you thinking of wedding cake and venues, Taryn?"

"I was not," Taryn declared. "I know it sounds silly, but sometimes Nana Irene's voice pops into my head. She was telling me that I don't get out enough."

"She does that all the time to me," Jorja said.

"Me too," Anna Rose said with a nod.

Clinton pushed back his chair, stood up, and got the pitcher of tea from the bar. "Got to admit that she does the same with me." He refilled his glass and then topped off the other three. "I kind of appreciate it. Her advice is always good."

"Right now, all we can get is what little she hands out to us when she pops into our heads," Taryn grumbled, "since we can't go see her or call her through the week. Why did she make such a stupid rule, anyway?"

"She has her reasons for what she does," he said.

Taryn had figured Clinton would defend Irene.

"Well, I for one would like to ask her about the big yellow cat that seems to have taken up homesteading under our porch," Anna Rose said.

"I can help with that," Clinton said, picking up the bread bowl and passing it over to Taryn. "That would be the cat with no name. She started showing up at the back door of the shop about a month ago. Irene and Ruby told me not to feed her or she would never leave, and I was sure not supposed to name her. I couldn't stand to see her begging for food, but I also didn't want her on my landing every morning, so when I had scraps, I fed her on the trailer porch."

"I've named her Goldie, and when I leave, I may take her with me since she poses for me," Anna Rose said.

"If you don't, I could adopt her, and I wouldn't even make her change her name," Taryn offered. "I kind of like Cat with No Name, but she'll have to learn to travel. I'm never in one place for more than six months."

"Why?" Clinton asked. "I thought that you worked from home?"

"I do, but why work from one place when I can travel and see other places?" Taryn said. "I guess the go bug hit me when I was in the service. My job was constantly taking me to different bases for computer work, and I like to travel, so when I finished my enlistment, I went to work for an insurance company. I work from home so I can do what I do from anywhere. I don't know that I'll ever be ready to settle down to one place. You were in the military longer than I was, Clinton. Don't you ever get the urge to pack up and go somewhere else?"

"Nope," Clinton answered. "I like the roots I'm putting down in this area. Helping vets gives me a sense of accomplishment, and working in the flower shop brings me peace."

Taryn glanced around the table at her two cousins and Clinton. "That's great, but this would never be a peaceful place for me to put down roots if I ever decided to do something like that." She thought about the turmoil she had suffered in the past, and always trying to make peace between her cousins surely was not something she would want to do on a permanent basis.

"Why?" Jorja asked. "It's where we were born and grew up. The houses that we all lived in are still standing."

"All three sets of your parents moved away. Was there any kind of reason behind it?" Clinton asked.

"My folks left because Mama had nurse training and Daddy was a pharmacist. Their dream had always been to go to Africa and help bring Jesus to the underprivileged, so that's what they're doing. They change countries there now and again," Jorja answered.

"Daddy was still in the military, and without a kid at home, Mama could go wherever he was, but they decided I needed a permanent home, so she stayed here in Shamrock most of the time. Sometimes in the summer, we would go to wherever he was for several weeks. They were in England while Daddy finished up his career, and they loved it there, so they just stayed," Taryn said.

"My dad was a long-distance truck driver, and Mama did the same as Taryn's. She stayed around here so I would have roots. They're in Canada now, living in a travel trailer." Anna Rose shrugged. "I guess Daddy's wandering ways got into my blood. My folks say they're settling in Canada, but I figure they'll get bitten by the go bug before they get around to building the cabin they're talking about. And Goldie belongs to me, Taryn. There could be enough blood and broken bones to call Nana Irene about if you try to take her away from me."

"Girl, if I ever get into a real fight with you, it will be over something more important than a cat," Taryn said. "You can have her with my blessing, but you better ask Jorja about it first. You know how she pouts if we make decisions without her."

"I do not pout," Jorja protested. "And I am sitting right here!"

Clinton finished off his supper and helped himself to a piece of cake. "Looks to me like you were all born with one foot planted solid on the ground and one that longs to run away."

"Which one wins the race?" Taryn muttered.

Clinton smiled over at her. "Whichever one you feed."

"What's that supposed to mean?" Taryn asked.

"My grandfather tells the old story about the two wolves in each of us. One is evil, and one is good. In your case, one wolf would be the one who roams the hills; the other is the one that builds a home and stays in one place. Whichever one you feed is the one that wins the race," Clinton answered.

"There would have to be something spectacular to keep me in Shamrock," Jorja said.

"Hey, we are working at the Lucky Shamrock," Anna Rose declared. "Could be that this is our lucky summer, and we will find something that makes us want to stay."

Yeah, right, Taryn thought. *It would take more than a sign and a green shamrock on the door of the flower shop to make this a lucky place for me.*

Chapter Five

*G*ood grief!" Taryn groaned at all the orders that had been placed in the basket by noon on Thursday morning. "I'd forgotten that this was Memorial Day weekend, but it seems like everyone in the county remembered today."

"I didn't even think to question the delivery guy when he brought in so many red and white carnations. Thank goodness he did," Jorja said as she took the ticket off the top and began making a small round wreath.

"Good morning, or maybe I should say afternoon," Clinton said, backing into the shop with a baby carrier in his hand and a diaper bag thrown over his shoulder. "I'd like you all to meet Zoe. She will be joining us for the next six weeks."

Taryn hadn't been knocked speechless very many times in her life, but she was right then. A thousand questions ran through her mind, yet when she opened her mouth, words would not come out.

Clinton set the carrier in the middle of the worktable and slid the diaper bag off his shoulder with such ease that Taryn wondered if Zoe was his daughter. Was that why none of the women who had put up their money in the contest had a chance with him? Was he involved with Zoe's mother?

"A baby?" Jorja frowned. "Where did that come from?"

"I could answer that question, but your face would go up in flames," Anna Rose teased.

"And why do you have it?" Taryn asked. "Are those witches sending you babies instead of cakes now?" She peered into the carrier to see a fat-cheeked infant dressed in a pink onesie. She had dark hair, thick lashes, and looked like a little angel.

Clinton shook his head with a smile. "Zoe's mother is one of the vets I've been counseling and helping use her VA benefits. She's got PTSD, and the doctors think it's best if she goes into a rehab facility for six weeks."

"But—" Jorja started.

"How?" Anna Rose butted in.

"She gave me temporary custody of Zoe to keep her from going into the foster system," Clinton said and picked up a ticket. "I've kept her for a couple of days at a time before when her mama was having problems, so she knows me. Irene and Ruby loved having her in the shop."

Taryn sat down on the stool beside Clinton, but she couldn't keep from staring at the baby. Even though the baby's eyes were closed, Taryn thought for a moment that they would be brown. She had fallen in love with a friend's baby when she was in the air force—a little girl with dark hair and brown eyes. She had often babysat her, and Taryn had cried until her eyes were swollen when Alicia's family was sent to Germany.

"Her father's name was Larry," Clinton went on to say. "I knew him very well."

"Was?" Taryn asked.

"He was killed when an IED went off under the Humvee he was driving. Rebecca had finished her second enlistment and had been sent back to the States a few months earlier. She was six months pregnant when Larry was killed. His time was up in another month, and as soon as he got home and discharged, they were going to get married. His death put her in a tailspin that she can't seem to crawl up out of."

Taryn looked down at the sleeping baby and sighed. "Poor little darlin'. How old is she?"

"Four months today," Clinton answered. "Irene and Ruby have helped me with her when I had to go out for deliveries."

"Don't expect me to do that," Jorja said.

Taryn whipped around and glared at her cousin. "You teach kindergarten. You have to like kids."

"I like them just fine." Jorja met her gaze with one just as cold. "After they are potty-trained and won't throw up on me. I'll wait on the front, do floral arrangements, or even clean the bathroom, but don't ask me to change diapers or babysit that child. That's why I teach the five- to eight-year-old Sunday school class. I love kids, not babies."

"If she's asleep, I'll help with her," Anna Rose said, "but I'm with Jorja on the diaper duty. No, thank you. I would like to take some pictures of her with Goldie, though. People drool over baby and kitty-cat pictures."

"I'll help with whatever she needs, and if you've got evening appointments, I'll babysit her," Taryn said. "Is Rebecca from here in Shamrock?"

"No, she lives across the Oklahoma border in Erick," Clinton answered. "I appreciate the help. Irene told me, if I got in a bind, to bring her over to Ruby's place, but she's got enough on her plate."

"No problem." Taryn couldn't take her eyes off the baby. "I'm glad to help. That's a lot for Rebecca to have to live with. I feel so sorry for her."

"I'll pray for her," Jorja said as she gathered flowers for a bouquet.

"When she gets well, I'll take her dancing if Taryn will babysit," Anna Rose said.

"Thank all y'all," Clinton said.

Taryn was staring at Zoe when the baby opened her eyes and smiled at her. "Did you see that, Clinton? She smiled at me. Is it okay if I take her out of the carrier?"

"Of course," Clinton answered with a nod. Of the three, he would have guessed that Jorja would be the one who loved babies the most.

The baby snuggled right down into Taryn's chest when she picked her up. "Hello, sweet darlin'," Taryn whispered. "I wonder what color your eyes will be when you get a little older. You and I are going to be good friends, and I can already tell that I'm going to hate to see you leave in a few weeks."

The bell above the door let them know a customer had arrived, so Taryn carried Zoe to the front. "What can I help you with?" Clinton heard her ask.

"Whose baby is that?" came Elaine's muffled demand.

"Good Lord, why don't they leave me alone?" Clinton whispered.

"All three want to win your love and affection," Anna Rose answered.

"And your money," Jorja added.

Anna Rose put her finger on her lips. "Shhh. I want to hear how Taryn handles this."

All the talk in the back room stopped so they could listen to the conversation.

"If you lose the attitude and apologize for being so hateful to me and my cousins, I might tell you," Taryn answered.

"I won't apologize to you for anything," Elaine practically growled.

Taryn turned, and it looked like Elaine could then see Zoe better. "Then you'll have to guess who her mama is. Do you think her eyes will be green when she's a little older?"

"She's your child, isn't she? Who's the father?" Elaine asked and took a step back.

"I don't kiss and tell—but look at her dark hair and think about it."

Clinton could hear the conversation in the front, and he couldn't have held back the smile if he'd tried. Taryn probably shouldn't be leading Elaine on, but the woman deserved it—and more. Trying to coerce him into marriage . . . What self-respecting woman did that?

"Does Irene know about this?" Elaine snapped.

"She does," Taryn answered. "And she thinks Zoe is adorable."

"I would have expected something like this from you," Elaine said in a huff. "Do you even know who the father is?"

"Like I said, I do not kiss and tell." Taryn shot her a smirk.

"Is that . . . Did you . . . Is Clinton . . . ," Elaine stammered.

"Are you ready to leave Clinton alone and quit trying to lead him down the aisle like a lamb to slaughter?" Taryn asked.

"I'll be a wonderful wife to him," Elaine said.

"And mother to his children?" Taryn asked.

"I don't like kids and never intend to spoil my body by having them," Elaine hissed.

If Clinton had had doubts about being nice to Elaine, they were squelched like a bug right that second. He wanted children of his own someday. He eased off the barstool so he could peek around the corner and see what was happening.

Taryn covered one of Zoe's ears with her hand. "It's all right, baby girl. Don't pay any attention to her. Lots of people don't like babies, but I love them. You're going to grow up to be smart and even more beautiful than you are now." Then she leaned forward. "Clinton loves children, so if you don't like babies, you might consider cutting your losses and dropping out of the contest."

"Never!" Elaine stormed out of the shop.

"Well, crap!" Clinton groaned. "I thought maybe I'd be done with that one."

"I guess she didn't want to buy anything or bring us something special for our midmorning snack," Taryn said with a laugh and started back to the workroom.

On his way to the cooler to get flowers, Clinton could see the baby give Taryn a toothless smile and a giggle when the bell rang for the second time that morning. He quickly ducked to the side of the archway when he saw Diana breeze into the shop. Her makeup was all done just perfect, and her cute little flowing sundress revealed her shoulders. But she still didn't appeal to Clinton. Being chased like a rabbit by a bunch of coyotes would make any man gun-shy. He loved his work helping vets, and his best air force buddy, Quincy, had said that he was interested in coming to Shamrock to help with the workload, which kept getting bigger every week. They were about to be a real firm. But that day, Clinton was fighting the urge to pick up and run from all the drama going on with these pushy women.

"Do you get your hair done every week to keep the roots from showing?" Taryn asked. "And how often do you spend time in a tanning bed?"

"That's none of your business." Diana glared at her. "Whose kid is that?"

"Elaine was just here," Taryn replied. "I figured she would have told you since you've always been best friends. Y'all had to have passed each other on the street."

"We aren't talking until this contest is over," Diana said. "That kid has your face shape and . . ." She clamped a hand over her mouth.

"Does this baby change anything about the contest?" Taryn asked.

"She does not," Diana said. "I'm here to ask Clinton to go to a picnic with me on Sunday afternoon. Our family reunion is always held on the Sunday before Memorial Day, and I want to introduce him to all my relatives. *You* can babysit that day."

He could hear Taryn biting back a grin. "This is Clinton's weekend to have Zoe, so if he goes to the picnic, the baby goes with him. You can show him what a good little stepmother you would make."

Clinton stepped out of the doorway and took Zoe out of Taryn's arms. "Thank you for the invitation, but Zoe and I have plans for the whole weekend."

"Doing what?" Diana asked.

"That's his business," Taryn answered before he could.

"You should have stayed away from Shamrock." Diana left the shop in a huff.

"Two down and one to go," Clinton chuckled. "Why did you do that?"

Taryn shrugged. "Do what? I did not tell one lie or say that Zoe belonged to me *or* you. Both of those women drew their own conclusions—but now you know what kind of mothers they will make if you decide that you want a family sometime in the future. One wants a sitter for a family reunion, which would cause the children to think they weren't wanted. The other one would hire a nanny and send the kid off to boarding school as soon as he or she was potty-trained."

"If I was interested—which I'm not—I'd be more curious to see what kind of wife each of them would make at first," Clinton said. "Would one of them be willing to live in a little one-bedroom apartment above a flower shop? Would they be content to let me spend hours working with vets? And maybe even helping out with someone else's child once in a while?"

"No, no, and no," Taryn answered, "and that's judging from what I've seen this week."

Anna Rose burst out laughing. "It's not blood or broken bones, but it sure was hilarious. I was tempted to call Nana Irene. I'm proud of you, girl."

"So am I," Clinton said.

"We had a terrible time keeping quiet back there," Jorja chimed in with a giggle. "That was ingenious—but what happens when Zoe disappears after six weeks?"

"We won't be here in six weeks, so it won't matter," Anna Rose said.

"We could always say that we gave her up for adoption," Taryn said. "Until then, Diana and Elaine can heat up the Shamrock gossip vine."

"Set it on fire, is more like it," Anna Rose said. "But we've got more than a dozen tickets in the basket, so the fun stops now and the work begins."

"We'll probably get swamped today and tomorrow, and then it will be time to start getting ready for the first wedding of the summer," Jorja added as she followed her cousin. She picked up a ticket and went to work on a red, white, and blue wreath.

Clinton laid Zoe in her carrier and disappeared into one of the storage rooms. After a minute, he came out with a folded playpen in his hands. He popped it open, adjusted the mobile with bright-colored butterflies that hung above, and pressed a button to make it go around. Then he moved Zoe over into it. She cooed and kicked her chubby little legs.

"The mobile will play for thirty minutes," he said as he started placing flowers in a half-finished saddle piece for a tombstone. "Then she'll be ready for her midmorning bottle. She's a good baby."

"You said you had plans for Saturday, right?" Taryn said as she started on a centerpiece done all in red.

"Zoe and I are going to Irene's on Saturday for dinner after we close the shop. Then, on Sunday, I'm planning to take her to the park; maybe there will be a squirrel that will entertain us for a while. Monday is free, but if one of the contest women comes in with an invitation, we may go back to the park," he said.

"Does Rebecca get to see the baby while she's in rehab?" Taryn couldn't fathom spending that much time away from her baby, if she ever had one.

Clinton's shoulder raised in a half shrug. "I'm not sure she wants to see Zoe—maybe not ever again. Every time she looks at the baby, she remembers losing Larry. I'm hoping that the trauma-treatment center helps with that."

"Doesn't she have family that would help with the baby and be a support for her?" Anna Rose asked.

"Both she and Larry were foster kids," Clinton answered.

"Do they have specialists that are trained to work with PTSD?" Jorja asked.

"Yes, they do, and I'm hoping that in six weeks, she's got a grip on life and is ready to move on with her daughter past Larry's death," Clinton answered.

Taryn glanced over at Zoe and fought back tears. She and her parents didn't see each other often, but at Christmas, Nana Irene's three children and granddaughters all tried their best to come home for the holidays. Sometimes it was just for a day, but when they could, they would stick around until New Year's Day. But even at that, she couldn't imagine a time when they wouldn't come from the far ends of the earth to help her if she needed them. To not have the support of a family was sad, and she felt so sorry for Rebecca. At the same time, she admired Clinton for taking on such a responsibility and for trying to help their fellow vets.

"What happens if she doesn't think she can raise Zoe?" Taryn's voice sounded hollow in her own ears.

"We'll cross that bridge when it comes time. Until then, I'm her legal guardian," Clinton answered.

"Won't you get attached to her?" Taryn asked.

"I already am," Clinton whispered. "I just hope she sleeps better than she did last night. Rebecca dropped her off with the legal papers she'd signed and left as fast as she came. We just couldn't let her go into the system."

"Maybe a few weeks away from her will help," Taryn said.

"I'm worried she'll need more than six weeks to get her legs under her. The VA rehab center she's checking into will be a good starting point, but it may not be a cure. She's got to want to get better for it to happen. I just hope that she figures that out," Clinton said.

The day went by without any more excitement, and when evening came, Clinton had vanished up the stairs with the baby carrier when Taryn called out to him, "Hey, why don't you let me take the baby and that diaper bag? You're supposed to bring one of those casseroles you've got stashed away down for our supper, remember?"

He didn't argue with her when she climbed up the stairs and took the diaper bag from his shoulder and slung it over hers.

"What are you bringing tonight?" she asked.

"There's a chicken-and-rice dish in the fridge that we could just heat up," he said.

"Sounds great." Taryn's hand brushed his when she grabbed the handle of the carrier. "I'll boss Anna Rose and Jorja into making some sides while I rock the baby. They can turn on the oven, too."

Clinton nodded, opening the door into his apartment. "Come on in. I'll need to add some diapers and another bottle or two to her diaper bag."

He had only taken a step into the room when his phone rang. He fished it out of his hip pocket.

"Hello?" He put it on speaker and set about shoving things into the diaper bag.

"This is Rebecca." Taryn didn't know her, but anyone could tell by the sound of her voice that she was at the end of her rope. "I'm all checked in. This looks like a nice place. I can't call much, what with all the scheduled stuff, but I wanted you to have this number in case of an emergency."

"I'm glad to hear from you," Clinton said. "Remember, you have to open up and work at the program for it to help."

"Right now, I don't know if anything will help me, but I'll give it a try. Bye, now," she said and ended the call.

"Zoe has been spoiled . . . ," he started to say, before he must have realized that Rebecca had ended the call. He shoved the phone back in his pocket.

Taryn didn't hand out sympathy like candy at Halloween, but right then she felt sorry for Clinton. "She didn't even ask about Zoe—but then, she's only been gone a day. It's good that she called to give you an emergency number, though."

"You noticed that, too," Clinton said with a sigh. "I'm not sure what is going to happen at the end of this time that she's away. I've got a playpen for the baby to sleep in, but she'll outgrow it soon and need a real crib. But where would I put it if Rebecca just disappears and doesn't come back for her?"

Taryn looked around his apartment. There was absolutely no place to put another piece of furniture or anything else for Zoe. There certainly wasn't room in the trailer for a baby bed, either, or she'd offer to put one over there.

"That's not today's worry," Taryn said. "We'll have to trust that Rebecca is going to get better—and if she doesn't, we'll cross that bridge when we have to." She felt just like Clinton, and she'd only known Zoe for less than twenty-four hours. This precious child needed someone to love and support her forever.

He finished repacking the diaper bag and took the casserole from the fridge. "You could carry this, and I'll take Zoe."

"Okay," she agreed and slung the diaper bag over her shoulder before taking the dish from him. "One day at a time, like the song says. We'll ask Jorja to pray that Rebecca gets her feet on solid ground in the next few weeks. My prayers don't get past the ceiling, but hers go all the way to heaven."

"I hope you are right," he said and led the way down the stairs.

"When we get to the trailer, you can drag the wooden rocking chair out to the front porch. This baby needs some fresh air. I'm going to rock her and relax. You can sit with me while Jorja and Anna Rose get everything set for dinner," Taryn told him.

"Maybe they'd rather rock the baby," Clinton said.

"Fat chance." Taryn giggled. "I'll give them a choice of watching the baby or making the sides to go with the casserole. You can see what they choose. They don't love babies like I do. I think I got that from Nana Irene. A good friend of mine in the service had a baby I adored. Alicia was about this age when her mama and her dad got orders for Germany. Since then, they've moved to London, and when they finished their enlistment, they settled in New Zealand. I see pictures of Alicia, and

I talk to her and her parents every few months, but . . ." She paused. "It was surprisingly hard to have her leave. Besides, Zoe is bored from being inside the shop all day."

"I feel the same way." Clinton took the food inside, and after a minute, he dragged the rocking chair out to the porch. Taryn sat down in the chair and turned Zoe around so she could see everything. Then she began to tell her a story about a princess—one of Alicia's favorites. The high-pitched voice she used elicited a giggle from the baby.

"You are really good with her. Why aren't you already married and have a couple or three kids of your own?" Clinton asked.

"I haven't found the right person yet. I had a serious relationship when I was in the service, so I can relate to Rebecca's situation a little. It was with another serviceman, who turned out to be a lucky guy when I found out he had a wife and kids back home."

"How would that make him lucky?" Clinton asked as he sat down in the chair.

"My dad was on his last deployment overseas." Taryn shifted the baby to a different position so she could see more. "If he'd been stateside, my dad might have had to spend the rest of his life in prison for assault."

Goldie hopped onto the porch step and crawled up in Clinton's lap. "Is that why you travel a lot and work from home?"

"Probably." She kissed Zoe on the top of her head and hugged her closer. "But there's benefits to it, because I now get to visit with this precious baby. What about you? How did you get into helping vets?"

"I had a friend who needed some help navigating the system, and then he had a cousin who couldn't figure out the paperwork or where to go," Clinton answered. "It snowballed, and the VA people kind of got to know me, so they work with me and help with whatever resources they have. The VA offered to hire me, but I'd rather do what I do pro bono. I don't need the money, and I want to help my fellow soldiers."

"I admire you for doing that—and for helping out Nana Irene and Ruby." Taryn stood up with the baby, carried her over to the steps, and sat down beside Clinton.

"No thanks necessary. I enjoy both of my jobs," Clinton said.

"Look, Zoe, this is a kitty cat," Taryn said and held the baby's little hand over to touch Goldie's long yellow fur. "I read that it's good to let them feel different textures and to read to them even when they're this young. I think she likes Goldie's soft fur."

"It probably reminds her of her favorite blanket," Clinton chuckled.

Holding a baby made Taryn realize how much she wanted a family. She still had plenty of time to consider that idea. After all, she was only thirty, and lots of women didn't get married and start a family until they were almost forty.

Taryn nudged Clinton on the shoulder. "Have you about got that basket of wool finished yet?"

"What?" Clinton frowned.

"Your expression told me that you were woolgathering," she answered.

"I was thinking about my mother. She was like Jorja and didn't like kids. After I was born, she gave me to my father—no, that's not right." He shook his head. "She made an agreement with him. For a big cash settlement, she handed me off to my father and left town. She never looked back, and I've only seen her a couple of times: once when she came to her mother's funeral and then when she returned to Shamrock for her grandmother's services. I was about six or seven."

"That's rough," Taryn said. "I bet that's why you didn't want Zoe being put into the system. You're going to make a wonderful father when you get around to having a family."

"Thanks. I had a good father. He passed when I was in the service. I still have the best grandfather—but sometimes I worry about whether I have enough sense to choose a woman who would be a wonderful mother. Neither my grandfather nor my father have ever done a good job when it came to choosing wives, and maybe poor judgment in that area is hereditary."

Taryn turned and looked right into his eyes. "I disagree with you. Choices can't be blamed on heredity. I think that you'll make a wonderful husband and father, Clinton. Proof is in the way this baby has bonded with you and the kindness you show everyone."

Chapter Six

Taryn couldn't count the number of times she had stretched out on the sofa in the trailer and rested her head on the arm. As far back as she could remember, she had spent a lot of time either in the flower shop, playing out in the gravel parking lot, or taking naps on that very sofa. Anna Rose had invited her to go to the bar and have a few drinks with her that evening. Jorja had asked if she wanted to go to church and find a place to help with Vacation Bible School.

Taryn had declined both just so she could have some peace and quiet. Five days of working with her cousins all day, then coming home to spend the evenings with them would have tarnished an angel's halo.

Someone knocked. "Anybody home?" Clinton stuck his head in the door.

"Come on in. I'm the only one here," Taryn answered, but her limbs felt so heavy that she didn't move from her position.

He had a diaper bag thrown over his shoulder and was carrying Zoe in his arms rather than in her carrier. "She's fussy tonight and nothing seems to help."

Taryn reached out her arms, and Clinton gave her the baby. She loved the way that Zoe cuddled against her shoulder and the trust Clinton had in her to just hand over the baby anytime she asked for her.

"She usually has her bath right after supper, takes a bottle, and sleeps until five or six the next morning. But tonight, she's fighting it."

With her back to the sofa, Taryn cuddled Zoe up next to her chest and started to hum a lullaby that Nana Irene had sung to all three cousins. In seconds, the baby's eyes fluttered shut, and she wiggled down into a comfortable position and went to sleep.

Clinton settled into a well-worn recliner and popped up the footrest. "Will you come live with me and do that every night?"

"Why, Clinton McEntire, we've known each other less than a week, and we haven't even been out on a date," Taryn teased.

Clinton wiped his brow in a mock gesture of shock. "I've got women coming out my ears who have visions of wedding cakes. What I need is a nanny, not a girlfriend."

"Well, that's about the sexiest thing a guy has ever said to me," Taryn said with a giggle. "We don't need a nanny, darlin'. Between the two of us, we've got this. Why don't you stretch out on that recliner and take a nap while she's sleeping? You've been running hard all day."

Clinton covered a yawn with his hand. "You don't have to ask me twice. You are a good friend, Taryn."

"So are you," she told him.

Friends aren't a bad thing, she thought. *I like Clinton, and I'm not a gold digger like these women circling him with lassos.*

Jorja left her air-conditioned car and stepped out into the hot breeze flowing across the church parking lot. "Vacation Bible School, Friday through Sunday, 6–8 p.m."—that's what the sign outside the church said. She figured she would show up as a volunteer and they'd put her to work somewhere that evening. She was not expecting folks to gather round her the moment she walked into the sanctuary.

"Is Irene really not going to help with VBS this year?" Ora Mae Stephens asked. "We've worked together every year for more than thirty years."

"No, she's not," Jorja answered. "She's taking care of Ruby."

Ora Mae was a tiny little woman, but what she had in spunk made up for her size. The doggie broach she wore on the lapel of her bright blue jacket seemed to go with her short gray hair, which reminded Jorja of a poodle that needed grooming.

Ora Mae patted her on the shoulder. "Well, I'm glad you're here. I remember when you were just a little girl and came to Bible school with Irene. You were such a good little girl."

Good girls make bad mistakes, Jorja thought, but she said, "We made jewelry boxes out of macaroni and cigar boxes, and we sprayed them with gold paint."

"Yes, we did, but kids today have to have more than that," Ora Mae said with a long sigh. "All those ridiculous videos we play now."

"I think getting out of the house and giving Ruby some breathing room would be good for her," Nettie Jones said.

All the women around them nodded.

"But I'm here." Jorja managed a smile. "Put me to work. I'm willing for anything, except the nursery."

"We don't have a nursery," Nettie explained. "Bible school starts with four-year-olds."

"I can use some help," Ora Mae piped up. "I've got a six- and seven-year-old class, and this year's theme is the Castle of Courage. Don't you teach kindergarten kids?"

Jorja stepped over closer to Ora Mae. "Yes, ma'am, I teach kindergarten in a small town north of Houston. We did that theme in my church last year."

"Then you should be able to help me corral these young'uns. Things aren't like they were when you was a little girl. Kids today don't mind like they did then," Ora Mae said.

Going to church. Worshipping. Helping with the smaller kids. This was definitely Jorja's place in the world, and she loved it so much more than she did teaching—even in the Christian school where she taught nine months out of the year. The other ladies all disappeared, leaving only Jorja and Ora Mae.

"Follow me." Ora Mae motioned with a flick of her blue-veined hand. "We've got a few last-minute preparations to get done before the kids all get here."

Jorja fell in behind the older woman and inhaled deeply, taking in the lemony smell of the stuff the ladies used to clean the church. She liked the aroma of fresh flowers because it reminded her of her childhood, but she just loved the scent of a sanctuary when she first walked in.

"It reminds me of Jesus," she whispered.

"What does?" Ora Mae asked.

She certainly does not need hearing aids, Jorja thought.

"The sanctuary, when it's all fresh and a bunch of bodies with shaving lotion and cologne hasn't messed it all up," Jorja answered.

Ora Mae opened the door to the classroom at the end of the hallway. "You got that right. This is our room right here. I'd complain about having to walk so far on these old knees, but it is right across from the ladies' room, so that's a good thing."

Positive attitude, Jorja thought. *This is what I need after a day of arguing with Anna Rose.*

"Oh. My. Goodness. This is awesome," Jorja gasped when she entered the classroom behind Ora Mae. "You've done a much better job than the class I helped with last year. The kids are going to love this."

The first banner hanging on the wall had a knight standing tall on one end and "Stand in Your Love" on the other.

"The lesson we'll teach is standing up for Jesus when someone asks if you go to church. We have to keep it simple so this age understands." Ora Mae pointed to another banner that had a castle printed on it, along with the words "Be Ye Kind" across it. The third had knights on horses on either side, with "Name the First Five Books of the Bible" written above them.

"We've got a coloring sheet to match each of the banners. One for each day. I've found that teaching a lesson while they color gets the message across to them better than anything. Then, for our craft project that they get to take home on the last day, I bought little castles for them to paint." Ora Mae beamed, but then her expression changed.

"Are you okay?" Jorja asked.

"I'm fine, just a little sad. This will be my last year to teach Bible school," Ora Mae answered. "I wanted it to be real special, and you helping me out is just the icing on the cake—but I'm an old dinosaur, and kids today need someone who's up on all the technology and has a lot more energy than I do. Why don't you move back to Shamrock and take my job? Most of the projects now come in digital form, but I'm too outdated to know all that PowerPoint stuff."

Jorja stashed her purse under a desk that had been turned into a piece of the castle and sidestepped the question. "Why are you quitting?"

"I've been planning on moving to an assisted-living center in Amarillo with my older sister. 'Course, I have to wait for a spot, but I want to be ready to move when I can," Ora Mae answered. "I'm so glad you like the room. I've been working on it since last Monday. We just need to get the craft table set up so they can paint their castles after they've had their snacks in the fellowship hall. That way the lesson is first, and we break it up with snacks; then they come back and work on their little projects . . ." She continued to talk as she set a dozen small plaster castles around a worktable. "You can put a watercolor set beside each one."

"And a little cup of water to clean their brushes, right?" Jorja began to hum as she picked up the box with the paint supplies.

"Even though I miss Irene, I'm glad you came to help out," Ora Mae said. "I should have asked before now, but how are Irene and Ruby doing? We all thought it would be Irene who'd be down with knee surgery. Didn't dawn on us that Ruby might break a hip and need help before Irene would."

"They seem to be coping pretty well," Jorja answered. "We would gladly go over every evening after we close the shop to help them, but Nana Irene has a bur in her saddle. She says we can only call and go see her on Saturday afternoon."

Ora Mae glanced up at the clock hanging on the far wall. "That could be because she wants the bunch of you to learn to get along and lean on each other. She's told me several times about how she prays that someday y'all will be a proper family instead of a bickering one. Now, it's time for us to go gather up our students."

"I'm not sure I'll ever be able to lean on Anna Rose." Jorja crossed the room and stood to the side to let Ora Mae go first. "Maybe I could learn to get along with Taryn, but even that's doubtful."

Ora Mae made a clucking sound like an old hen gathering in her chickens. "Well, darlin', if they haven't changed their ways, then that's understandable, but don't go judging them too harshly. A lot of things that got blamed on Taryn weren't her fault, and Anna Rose just liked to have a good time. If any of you ever need to talk through the week, though, I'm glad to listen."

"Yes, ma'am, and thank you," Jorja said with a long sigh. "I'm trying to be tolerant, but it's tough some days." She tried to think of something positive to say, and it finally came to her. "At least I've got VBS in the evenings for the next few days, and my church at home is televising their services on Sunday, so I'll feel at home then—but I'm never moving back to Shamrock. There's too many dark memories here."

Ora Mae patted her on the shoulder. "I know, honey." She stopped at the door leading into the sanctuary and lowered her voice. "Not all of us are blind and deaf to what happens or happened, but please know you are always welcome to come join me on Sunday mornings for services. I'll be glad to save you a seat beside me and Amos on the front pew, or you can slip in and sit beside Forrest at the back."

Jorja opened it for Ora Mae. "Thank you for the invitation. I'll think about it. What does Forrest do these days? I haven't seen him since we graduated."

Ora Mae stopped walking and turned to face Jorja. "Amos hired him to help with the watermelons and cotton out on his farm in the summertime when Forrest was just a kid and then put him on full-time when he finished school. The foster system tossed him out when he was eighteen, just before y'all finished school, so Amos took him in."

"I didn't even know he was a foster kid," Jorja said. "But I'm glad he's doing well."

"He's shy and backward, socially, but that feller knows watermelons and cotton as well as Amos these days," Ora Mae said and then leaned toward Jorja and whispered, "I heard that Taryn has a baby, and it could belong to Clinton."

"Clinton is babysitting for one of his vet friends, and Taryn loves babies. None of us have children of our own," Jorja said. "But keep that under your hat. Clinton is tired of all this contest thing going on with women trying to drag him to the altar."

Ora Mae drew her brows down and pursed her mouth. "Those women are silly for chasing after a man like they're doing. Clinton is a good man for doing what he can for his friend. Do you think Taryn might be interested in helping with the nursery on Sunday morning?"

Jorja tried to hold back a giggle, but she failed. "How many young mothers here in Shamrock would leave their children in a room with her?"

Ora Mae nodded. "You've got a point there. She left behind a bad reputation."

"Yes, she did," Jorja agreed. "But, like you said, at least half of what she got blamed for shouldn't be laid to her credit. She sure wasn't as bad as people thought."

Ora Mae patted her on the shoulder. "You are so right. I see the preacher headed up to the pulpit to welcome everyone. We'd better get on in there."

Jorja had expected to float on what she called her *Jesus high* all evening, and maybe even until the next day, when she returned to help Ora Mae again, but it didn't happen. The kids weren't interested in the Bible lesson about how Joseph went through hard times but finally lived in a castle. One of them even asked if there was a video game about it. After sugary snacks of cookies and juice packs, they were all hyper, and then there was an argument over one of them saying that another girl had stolen her idea of how to paint her castle, which had almost ended in fisticuffs. Their bickering reminded Jorja of her cousins—and herself—when they worked together in the shop.

At the end of the event, Jorja couldn't wait to leave the church and sit in her car for a few minutes. If her students ever acted like those little hooligans, she would quit teaching tomorrow and join her folks in their missionary work. She turned on the engine so she could have air-conditioning and laid her head back. She tried to find the joy and peace that she'd had when she first got a whiff of the clean sanctuary—but it wasn't there.

She started back to the trailer, but when she reached the final turn, she felt herself ease off the gas pedal and slow to a stop. She didn't want to talk to either of her cousins, and she would have to speak to them on her way back to her bedroom. She took her foot off the brake and drove to the park where she'd played as a child.

Jorja parked and got out of the car, went straight to the swings, and sat down in one of them. A warm breeze blew her blonde hair back from her face as she set the swing in motion with her foot and pretended that she was a little girl again. No worries except to figure out which bow she would wear in her hair the next day or whether she wanted a rainbow snow cone or a grape one when her mama took her home from the park that evening.

Then the memories that haunted her dreams on a regular basis and made her doubt that Jesus loved her washed over her. "Get thee behind me, Satan," she whispered. "I repented and I've been celibate since that night. Jesus promised to love those who are sorry."

She hopped up off the swing and headed toward her car, trying to leave the past behind. All she had ever wanted was to have a good Christian marriage and a place to raise a family—maybe with a white picket fence and rosebushes. But in trying to find the excitement that her cousins knew, she'd turned down a path that would forever keep her from realizing—or even deserving—any of her dreams.

The sun had fully dropped behind the horizon by the time she made it back to the trailer. The lights were still on, which meant she had to walk past her cousins. She assured herself that she could do it and sent up a silent prayer that she wouldn't have the nightmares and wake up in a cold sweat again. Evidently, coming to Shamrock had triggered the dreams again—just when she'd thought she had finally put the horror of that time behind her.

She stopped on the porch and petted Goldie while she listened intently to see if Anna Rose and Taryn were talking, but she heard nothing. She left the cat behind and eased the door open to find Clinton sound asleep in the recliner. Taryn was sitting on the sofa with Zoe in her arms. She put a finger over her lips. Jorja nodded and tiptoed to her bedroom. Some prayers got answered after all.

Anna Rose sang along with the radio that Friday evening as she drove across the Texas border into Oklahoma and stopped at the first bar she came to. She flipped the visor down and, using the tiny mirror, checked her makeup and fluffed up her dark brown hair. Then she opened the truck door, set her cowboy boots on the ground, and headed across the parking lot. The jukebox was turned up loud enough that she could hear Luke Bryan singing "One Margarita," and she sang along with him when the lyrics said that everyone there wasn't from there, but they were there doing their thing.

"That's me," she said as she twirled around with a fake partner. "I'm not from here anymore, but I'm here at this bar, doing my thing."

She wasn't aware of anyone around her until someone slipped his hand into hers and proceeded to do some fancy footwork in a swing dance. When the song ended, he brought her hand to his lips and kissed her knuckles.

"Thank you for the dance, gorgeous," he said. "My name is Hank. Is yours Angel? Where are you hiding your wings and halo?"

"I'm Anna Rose," she said with a giggle. "And, honey, that's the lamest pickup line I've ever heard."

"I've danced the first one with you," Hank said. "Will you save me the last one?"

Anna Rose took a step back. Her eyes traveled from his scuffed-up cowboy boots all the way up to his creased jeans, his silver belt buckle with a bull rider on it, and his Western-cut shirt. She reached his chin with its cute little dimple and went on up to lock with his bright blue eyes. "Depends on who else dances with me," she flirted. "The night is still young, Mr. Hank—if that's even your real name."

"Just Hank, darlin'." He tipped his hat and grinned. "Mr. Hank is my grandpa. I'll see you inside. If you get bored, come find me."

"I just might do that." Anna Rose could feel his eyes on her as she walked past him and up to the bar.

She claimed the last barstool, ordered a beer, and listened to a couple of songs while she drank. When the music stopped and everyone seemed to be ordering drinks, she gave up her seat and went over to the vintage jukebox. She was amazed to see that it still only took quarters, but not so much when she realized that she only got two plays for her money. She dug four coins from her pocket and plugged them into the machine.

"Eight," she muttered. "Do I want to do some line dancing or two-steppin'?"

She chose four for two-stepping and two for line dancing, starting with Chris Stapleton's "Tennessee Whiskey" and ending with Tim McGraw's "I Like It, I Love It."

"May I have this dance?" A good-looking guy held out his hand to her.

The bright lights around the jukebox lit up his gold wedding band like a neon sign that told her to step away. "Darlin', I don't dance with married men. Go find your wife."

"It's just a dance," he protested.

Hank stepped up from behind the guy. "There you are, my sweet Anna Rose. I believe this is our song."

He wrapped his arms around her and began a slow country waltz around the dance floor. "You don't want to dance with that guy. His wife will come in here in about thirty minutes. There will be an argument, and whoever he is dancing with will wind up with a bloody nose. When they have a big fight, which is about once a week, he comes in here. She comes in after him and blames whoever he's flirting with for whatever they were arguing about."

"Oh, really? And where is your wife?" Anna Rose asked.

"Don't have one. Don't want one." Hank held up his hand to show there wasn't even a white mark where a ring had been. "I'm too big of a flirt to settle down."

Just my kind of guy, Anna Rose thought. "Thanks for rescuing me. I wouldn't want to explain a broken nose to my roommates."

"Anytime, darlin'." He tipped his hat when the song ended. "I've got your back, sweet Anna Rose. You really should let me buy you a drink since I saved your life."

Anna Rose held up a forefinger. "One drink—but you saved my nose, not my life."

She drank only half the beer that Hank bought for her, then left when he went to the men's room. The clock above the bar read nine o'clock when she slid off the stool. "Boredom this early means no hangover in the morning," she whispered as she made her way across the parking lot and unlocked her truck.

Darkness had settled in when she got back to Shamrock, but she didn't want to go home—not just yet. She headed straight to the Dairy Queen and was the last customer of the evening. She ordered a chocolate milkshake and was home before ten. She found Goldie sitting on the rocking chair, so she picked her up and held her in her lap while she drank her shake.

The lights were on, but she didn't hear anything until the door opened and Clinton came out, carrying the baby. He nodded toward her and almost tiptoed across the parking area and up the steps.

Taryn brought out a tall glass of sweet tea and sat down on the top porch step. "You're home earlier than I figured you would be—and you're alone."

"Yep, I am," Anna Rose said with a sigh. "I met a cowboy named Hank, and he was sexy. But . . ."

"You mean there's a *but* when it comes to you and a sexy cowboy?" Taryn asked.

Anna Rose raised her shoulders in a shrug. "Maybe there's something in the water around here that makes us want to have something permanent in our lives."

"Or maybe Jorja is rubbing off on you," Taryn teased.

"God, I hope not!" Anna Rose declared.

"Did I hear my name?" Jorja asked as she came out onto the porch. She wore pajama pants with crosses printed on them and a T-shirt with "Love Thy Neighbor" on the front.

"How did Bible school go?" Taryn asked.

Jorja sat down on the step beside her. "I could say just wonderful, but that would be a lie. I was glad when it was over—and truthfully, I dread having to go back."

"Then don't go," Anna Rose said. "You could be too tired for tomorrow night since we'll be swamped with last-minute Memorial Day orders. If that's not enough, we might have to run errands for Nana Irene and Ruby after we have lunch tomorrow."

"I couldn't do that to Ora Mae. She's depending on me," Jorja said. "And besides, why are you trying to help me out? I figured you'd be glad to get rid of me on Saturday night so you could bring home a one-night stand."

"If you don't want to do Bible school, then you shouldn't do it," Anna Rose told her. "That's hours of your time that you can never get back. Go do something fun or read a good, juicy novel during that time. And for your information, I could have brought a guy home with me tonight."

"Why didn't you?"

Anna Rose shrugged.

Taryn giggled. "She got bored with the whole bar scene for the first time in her life, and she thinks there's something in the water here in Shamrock that's affecting her."

Jorja nodded in agreement. "It could very well be just that. I've never wanted to leave church before. Those kids are the same age as the ones in my class back home, but they were little demons tonight. My kids don't act like that, and if they did, I wouldn't teach another day. They actually reminded me of the bickering between Diana, Elaine, and Mallory when they came into the shop today, with a touch of when the three of us argue about every little thing."

"Childish, huh?" Anna Rose asked.

"Yep," Jorja said. "You aren't happy in a bar. I'm not happy at church. How's it affecting you, Taryn?"

"My biological clock is groaning," she answered. "I wonder if we're getting a double dose of whatever is in that water when we make tea with it and take showers."

"You could scrape up five hundred dollars and enter the contest," Anna Rose said. "You're already a family of sorts since you help out with Zoe so much."

Taryn shook her head. "No, thank you. Clinton and I are becoming friends, and I don't date friends or people that I work with. I tried that, had a broken heart to prove it, and vowed it wouldn't happen again. How about you two? Y'all ever really get into a serious relationship?"

"Nope, and don't intend to," Anna Rose declared. "Why rope myself down to one guy when there's so many out there?"

Jorja's face turned so red that Anna Rose could see the glow by the light of the moon. "Fess up, Jorja," she said. "What was his name, and how did he hurt you?"

"I don't want to talk about it," Jorja whispered. "I've never told another soul about what happened. It's too humiliating—and for y'all's information, part of it is your fault."

"Have you told Jesus?" Taryn pressured. "If Jesus knows and it's our fault, then we have to repent."

"I have. I repented, and then later, I begged forgiveness again because I felt guilty for being relieved," Jorja answered. "And that's all you are getting out of me."

"Well, that's sure enough a vague answer," Anna Rose snapped. "I thought we were making progress tonight and talking without arguing."

Tears began to stream down Jorja's face. Taryn threw an arm around her shoulders and hugged her, and Anna Rose left the rocking chair and sat down on the other side of her. "It's okay, Jorja. You don't have to tell us what happened, but we're here if you want to talk."

"I just wanted to do something exciting like y'all, and I disappointed Jesus. Mama and Daddy don't even know, and . . ." She began to sob. "I've never talked about it to anyone other than Jesus, not once."

"Good Lord!" Anna Rose gasped. "Did you kill someone? If you did, we'll protect you."

"I kind of did, because I prayed and prayed for a death, and God answered my prayer." Jorja cried even harder.

"Where's the body buried?" Taryn whispered.

Jorja finally raised her head. "There wasn't a body."

"Get it off your chest," Taryn said. "Whatever it is, you'll feel better if you tell someone. If you don't want to talk to us, then talk to a therapist or your preacher."

Jorja dried her wet cheeks on the hem of her T-shirt. "Y'all were both gone, but you were like legends here in Shamrock, and I was the wallflower. So, on the night we graduated, Kaitlin invited me to a party, and I decided to go out to the red barn and just see what it was like to be around a fun crowd—and I kind of pretended that I was like y'all. I put on tight jeans and a shirt that was pretty snug. Somebody brought me a beer, and I opened it. It tasted horrible, but I must've drank about half of it, and then Ford Chambers handed me a drink that he called a bathtub daiquiri. I liked it better than the beer, and so I downed the whole thing. Then he was holding me and dancing with me all nice-like, and I felt like I belonged. I never thought that someone who was so popular would tell me that I looked nice and had beautiful eyes."

Anna Rose's quick intake of breath caused Jorja to stare at her. She'd had an ugly couple of years in her life, too, but now wasn't the time to tell her story. Tonight was all about Jorja.

"What?" Jorja asked.

"He was playing you, and you were so innocent that you didn't know it," Taryn answered.

"I figured that out, but not until it was too late," Jorja said.

"You got drugged, didn't you?" Taryn asked.

Jorja nodded. "I was aware of something happening, but I felt like I was floating and looking down at what was going on. I should have fought with him, but my arms and legs wouldn't move; then everything went dark. When I woke up, I was in the back seat of my car with my skirt up over my body, and my underpants were gone. I knew what had happened because I was so sore. I was afraid to go to the doctor, afraid to tell Mama, and afraid of what Daddy would do if he found out. I didn't know that I was pregnant until I missed my second period and took a test, and I was already getting my things ready for college." Jorja's voice quivered.

Anna Rose reached out and took her hand. Bless her cousin's heart. Anna Rose had been around the block herself and should have recognized the signs long before she did when her bad experience happened. Jorja had been naive and sheltered. She wouldn't have seen it coming.

"That's when I prayed and asked God to take the baby to heaven before it was born, and I miscarried at eleven weeks. It was my first week at college, so no one had to know, and I was eighteen, so they couldn't call Mama or Daddy unless I gave them permission. So I kind of killed someone, and I've lived with the guilt for a decade. Sometimes when I pray, it's like Jesus doesn't even want to look at me," Jorja said.

Taryn patted her on the shoulder. "You poor girl, having to live with all that bottled up inside of you."

"None of that was your fault," Anna Rose assured her.

"Yes, it was," Jorja argued. "I went to that party, and I took that drink from Ford, so part of it is my fault. I didn't pray about going, so now I have to face the consequences for the rest of my life. Ford is married to Kaitlin, and that's really the reason I turned down Linda's invitation to go to dinner with them after church. I'm pretty sure it was his baby, since he gave me the drink, and I found his wallet in the back seat of my car. But something worse could have happened if he'd invited others to . . ."

"You don't have to go on," Taryn said. "We get the picture."

"What did you do with the wallet?" Anna Rose asked.

"I threw it in a mud puddle on the way home," Jorja said. "And I can't get past the hate in my heart for that man even yet. Jesus says I have to forgive him, and I've tried, but I can't."

"Want us to take care of him for you?" Anna Rose asked. "I would enjoy a bit of revenge."

Jorja shook her head. "It's not your place. Vengeance belongs to God."

"Maybe He's busy and needs a little help," Taryn suggested.

Jorja almost smiled. "Y'all are right. It does feel good to get it off my chest. Maybe someday I will forgive him. God says I need to do that, but He doesn't say I have to like the sorry bastard."

"No, He does not." Anna Rose slapped Jorja's arm. "I'm not hitting you. I'm killing a mosquito the size of a buzzard."

"Thanks for that, then," Jorja said, "and thanks for listening to me tonight. I'm going to turn in now and hope that I don't have nightmares again."

"Anytime," Anna Rose said, still wishing that she would have taken out more revenge on the man who had abused her.

"We're here for you," Taryn assured her.

Anna Rose stood up at the same time Jorja did, but she went back to the rocking chair instead of going inside. Poor little Jorja, with her religious upbringing and ideas, shouldn't have had something like that happen to her. God help Ford if Anna Rose ever found him out alone on a dark road. She was not nearly as nice as her cousins, and she vowed that he would pay for what he had done in some way before the end of summer.

Chapter Seven

Taryn glanced at the seven people around the dinner table that afternoon. Ruby had never married and had become a second grandmother—or maybe she was a great-aunt—to the three cousins. Her dark hair had turned gray years ago, but the sparkle in her crystal-blue eyes was still there, even after surgery. Nana Irene sat next to her, and she seemed more rested than she had in years, but her gray roots were showing. With Clinton and the cousins, the little dining area was crowded.

"Nana, I would be glad to come visit with Ruby a couple of hours next week if you want to schedule a trip to the hairdresser," Taryn said as she passed the platter of roast beef over to her grandmother.

"Thanks for the offer, darlin'"—Irene took the platter and put a slice on her plate—"but I'm going to let it grow out. I'm tired of dyeing it. I figure by the end of summer, it will be grown out, and I can get all the red cut off and won't look so much like a skunk."

"I've been trying to get her to do that for years. All that stuff on your scalp can't be good for you," Ruby said. "Did she tell you that the last time Lacy Jones down at the beauty shop was covering the roots, she dropped a blob of that dye on the countertop?"

"What happened?" Jorja asked.

"It ate right through the white paint and down to the wood," Ruby answered. "It's a wonder that crap hasn't eaten through Irene's flesh and bone and into her brain."

Irene turned and winked at Taryn. "I bet that's what's wrong with my knees. The danged stuff bypassed my brain, got into my bloodstream, and ate the cartilage right out of my poor little kneecaps."

Ruby shook her fork at Irene. "This is not a joking matter, and I refuse to let you go back on your word. We should be growing old with dignity, and that means gray hair."

"Ruby, darlin'"—Irene raised her eyebrows—"I do not intend to grow old with dignity. I will have a good time right up until the day I die. I want to roll into heaven on roller skates with every ounce of what is Irene O'Reilly all used up and not a single regret."

"Some people never grow up," Ruby grumbled. "You girls take a lesson from your grandmother in what *not* to be."

"All due respect," Taryn said, "but I want to grow up to be just like her—except after that story you just told, I may never let my hairdresser mess with hair dye."

"That's my girl," Ruby said with a nod.

Taryn tuned out the conversation and let her eyes settle on Zoe, who was strapped into a high chair at the end of the table. She vaguely remembered Jorja using the same chair when she was just a baby. That would have been when Taryn and Anna Rose were probably sitting on thick books or maybe even a big pot from the kitchen.

"Taryn, are you listening to a word I'm saying?" Irene asked.

"I'm sorry, I was thinking about that high chair. Didn't Jorja sit in it when she was a baby? What did I miss?"

"All of my three kids and then all of you girls used that same high chair, but I was asking if y'all remembered to make small wreaths for the family members in the cemetery," Irene answered.

Taryn shook her head. "I'm sorry, but we totally forgot—but we'll get it done this evening and take them out to the cemetery tomorrow."

"It's kind of like the story of the cobbler's kids' shoes that you used to tell us about," Jorja said. "He made shoes for everyone else and forgot his own children."

Ruby nodded. "That's right, but no worries. We've got a list made. Just a small wreath on the graves without vases on the tombstones will be fine."

"And don't forget to take a pail, a scrub brush, and some cleaner to shine up the tombstones," Irene told them. "And I expect all three of you to work together on this. Anna Rose, don't you run off to party. Jorja, don't you try to get out of it by saying you have to go to Vacation Bible School."

"Yes, ma'am," Anna Rose and Jorja said at the same time.

"Zoe and I'll be glad to help out," Clinton offered.

Irene picked up the basket of hot rolls and passed them to him. "Thank you. They might need a referee."

"I thought they all were doing better," Ruby said. "I haven't heard an argument since they arrived. That could be a record."

"Either that or they're trying to snow me." Irene grabbed a hot roll when they came back to her. "If they aren't bickering, then they might be thinking they could come over here every night."

"We're not trying to snow you," Anna Rose protested.

"We'll give it another week or two to be sure," Irene said with a chuckle.

"Have y'all heard about the contest to get Clinton to the altar?" Jorja asked.

Bless your heart for changing the subject, Taryn thought and then wondered what Nana Irene would say if she found out about what Ford had done to Jorja.

"Oh, yes, we've heard," Ruby answered. "And, Clinton, honey, I don't meddle in other people's lives, but my advice is to steer clear of all those money-hungry coyotes."

"Hmmph," Irene snorted. "You'll still be meddling when you get to the Pearly Gates."

Ruby pointed her fork at Irene for the second time. "That's the pot calling the kettle black, for sure."

Anna Rose giggled. "Just where do y'all think we learned to bicker?"

Irene narrowed her eyes. "At your age, you should have learned from old women's mistakes."

"I'm not old," Ruby snapped.

Taryn giggled, and soon everyone was laughing. When she got control and had wiped her eyes with her napkin, she looked around at everyone. "I missed this so much. I'm glad we all came home to help out this summer."

"Me too." Anna Rose nodded.

They both stared at Jorja, who finally said, "Okay, okay! I'm glad to be here, too. But don't expect me to agree with everything y'all say. Just because I'm the youngest doesn't mean you can order me around."

"Wouldn't dream of it," Anna Rose whispered and then straightened up. "I want to talk about the cat with no name, Nana Irene. Do you care if I take her home with me when y'all are able to come back to the shop?"

"What home?" Ruby asked. "I thought you moved around a lot. That's no way for a cat to live. They need a place that they can call their own."

"I always rent an apartment for six months or a cabin in the woods or . . ."

Irene threw up a palm. "You can't have the cat with no name if you don't have a permanent dwelling place. She might get eaten by coyotes or bears if you're living out in the forest."

"She has a name," Jorja said. "Anna Rose named her Goldie."

"That doesn't sound like a cat's name," Irene argued. "She should be Queen or maybe Princess. She carries herself high and mighty. Goldie sounds like . . ."

Ruby laughed. "You didn't even want that stupid cat to be around the shop. It would have starved if Clinton hadn't fed the poor thing. I agree that Goldie is a poor name, but if that's what Anna Rose wants to call her, then it is what it is."

Taryn put a forkful of mashed potatoes in her mouth, and she felt Clinton's knee nudge hers. His touch set off another volley of sparks even warmer than the ones she had experienced before, but she wasn't willing to admit that she was attracted to him. They were friends, and if she spoiled that, then it'd ruin both things at the flower shop and with their new baby visitor. She glanced over at him, and he gave her a sly wink.

The sparks can fly around like Fourth of July fireworks, and I'm going to ignore them, she thought, but when he reached for the salt and his shoulder touched hers, she had trouble sticking to her vow.

"This is so much fun. I'm having a great time," he said out of the corner of his mouth. "I love a family like this. Mine has always been so stuffy."

"You're welcome to all you want of it." She smiled and went back to eating.

"I'll take all I can have," he said.

Before them sat life in all its stages: Zoe as the baby, Taryn and her cousins and Clinton in the middle, and Ruby and Nana Irene in their golden years. Start to nearly finish around one table, making up a family—whether they were related by blood or not.

Yet the end of their time with Zoe would come when Rebecca had recovered and returned to Shamrock to take her away. Having seen Miz Leona in the casket brought home the fact that her grandmother—as active and sassy as she was—was not a spring chicken anymore. And those were Irene's words, not Taryn's.

Life is an emotional roller coaster, she thought.

"I didn't really want to do all this now. It's kind of depressing," Taryn said as she unlocked the back door to the shop and flipped on the lights.

"Me too," Anna Rose agreed. "Have y'all even looked at the long list of folks' graves that they want us to put flowers on? It's kind of depressing to think of so many of their family and friends already being gone."

Jorja laid the list on the table and headed to the shelves where the artificial flowers were kept. "Looks like we've got half a dozen vase arrangements and a few more wreaths. Nana only wanted one tombstone saddle for Grandpa."

"That means about four or five each, right?" Anna Rose gathered up a fistful of pink and yellow flowers. "I'll do the two baby girls first."

Clinton brought Zoe in and laid her in the playpen. "Poor little darlin' is worn out from all the excitement at Irene's place. She fell asleep on the way home and will probably take a long nap. I'll get to work on the saddle for your grandfather's grave. Irene told me as we were leaving that she wants it in red, white, and blue because he was a veteran. She just said to make the rest of them look pretty!"

"Daddy followed in his father's footsteps," Taryn said as she ran her finger down the list and decided to make a wreath for Ruby's father. "Nana Irene said that she lived in fear every day that two uniformed military guys would come to her doorstep and tell her that he was missing in action or dead like they did when Grandpa died."

"She never got over that happening with Grandpa," Jorja said with a sigh.

Anna Rose wrapped a Styrofoam wreath in a wide pink ribbon and glued a bouquet of baby's breath and tiny yellow rosebuds to it. "Can you imagine it? There she was, with three little kids to raise, and her husband wasn't coming home."

"When did they confirm that he was gone and not just MIA?" Clinton asked.

"About five years later," Taryn answered. "They sent his body home from Vietnam, and she finally had a funeral and got a little bit of closure. She doesn't talk about it much, but when I was a little girl, I'd see her holding his picture up to her heart."

"How could *you* go into the military knowing that?" Jorja asked.

Taryn talked as she worked. "I wanted out of Shamrock. I didn't like the idea of college, and it seemed like a better thing than flipping burgers."

Taryn hadn't thought about the fear that her grandmother must have faced over the years that her son and granddaughter had been in the military. Had Taryn's mother worried about hearing that knock on the door? She tried to imagine how she would feel if Zoe came in during the last weeks of her senior year and told her that she would be joining the air force the day after graduation.

That's crazy, the pesky voice in her head shouted. *Zoe is not your child. You've only known her a few days, and she will be going back to her mother about the same time you leave Shamrock.*

Taryn shook off the voice and kept working on the wreath. She had gone with her grandmother to the cemetery to put flowers on the graves just before she left for basic training, but she hadn't been back since. She remembered the general area they were located in; the O'Reilly family was under a big shade tree, and the O'Malleys—Nana Irene's mama and daddy and siblings—weren't far away.

"Did y'all ever go help Nana Irene put flowers out?" she asked.

"Not me," Anna Rose answered.

"I wasn't here last year," Clinton said.

Jorja shook her head. "Or me, either. Did you?"

"Yes, I did, and she told me the stories of each person as we scrubbed the tombstones and freshened up the grave sites," Taryn said. "She and Grandpa got married a few weeks before he went off to the military. She got pregnant when he came home from basic and had my dad while Grandpa was in his training. She stayed right here and worked at the flower shop. That was back before she and Ruby pooled their money and bought the place. She wound up having three kids in less than five years and raised them right here in this shop—kind of like we're doing with Zoe."

Anna Rose finished the first small wreath and set it to the side. "Guess it was named right and was lucky in some ways. She had a job that let her bring her children to work, and later, she and Ruby could buy it."

"What about all these other arrangements and wreaths?" Jorja asked.

"Their names are on the lists. You should remember most of them from what Ruby and Nana Irene told us about their families when we were kids."

Jorja marked through each one as they finished making the arrangements. "Looks like she wants this next wreath done in yellow roses for Grandpa's mama. As fast as we're working, I believe we'll be done in plenty of time for me to get to VBS."

"And for me to get changed to go see if I can find a good-lookin' cowboy to kiss on," Anna Rose said with half a giggle. "You sure you don't want to blow off VBS and join me? I bet if you put on some tight jeans and borrowed a pair of my boots, you'd be swamped with guys begging to dance with you or buy you a drink."

"And I might wind up in the . . ." Jorja paused, blushed, and then went on, "I've got a better idea: Why don't you come to VBS with me?"

Clinton finished up the saddle wreath by putting a small flag on either end. "Which way are you going, Taryn? Are you going to chase cowboys or Jesus this evening?"

"Depends on what you've got in the freezer," she answered. "I'm tired. I'd rather have a long bath and then have supper and play with Zoe when she wakes up. I can chase a good time or religion any day. I don't get to rock a baby very often. You want to go with either of my cousins, you are welcome to do so. I'll babysit for you."

Clinton shook his head. "No thanks. I'd fall asleep in church, and my limp makes it kind of tough to do any boot scootin'. I've got a cheesy thing with chicken and tater tots in it up there, and a ripe cantaloupe. Does that sound good for supper?"

"Yes, sir," Jorja answered. "If we hurry up with these last arrangements, I'll have time to eat before I go—and Anna Rose never leaves until after seven."

"Doors don't open until eight," Anna Rose said. "There! I'm done with mine."

Just as Taryn finished her job, Zoe awoke and reached out her little arms. Taryn rushed over and picked her up. "Did you have a good nap? Are you ready to sit on the porch and look at the birds and the cat?"

"Lord help us all!" Jorja declared.

"What?" Clinton asked.

"When Rebecca gets done with rehab and takes Zoe with her, Taryn is going to go right into a deep, dark funk," Anna Rose answered. "I'm glad that we'll be about done here by that time. I don't like Taryn when she's all moody."

"Or sometimes when she's not moody and just plain old bossy," Jorja added.

"Well, I like her when she's being a pseudo mama," Clinton said. "I didn't realize how tough it was to have a baby around for more than a couple of nights."

Taryn picked up the diaper bag. "I'll see y'all at the trailer. Zoe and I are going to see if Goldie is out and about and maybe even spot a bird or two while y'all get supper ready. I didn't think I'd be hungry again until morning after that late dinner, but I am."

"You do the baby thing, and we'll gladly take care of heating up a casserole and cutting up a cantaloupe," Jorja told her as she walked out the door with Clinton right behind her.

His limp looked worse when he climbed the stairs to his apartment—but then, he'd worked all morning, taking care of last-minute orders and deliveries. Taryn wondered if maybe keeping Zoe twenty-four seven would change his mind about having a family—if he ever had that idea to begin with.

"It sure hasn't changed mine," she whispered as she sat down in the rocking chair. "I can't wait to have a baby just like you, Miz Zoe, or maybe a whole yard full of them, but that doesn't look like it's going to happen anytime soon."

Jorja sat down on the top porch step, but Anna Rose went on inside the trailer. "You really are good with her. I wonder what kind of mother I would have made if . . ."

"You would have been amazing," Taryn said. "Do you think you would have kept the baby if you hadn't lost it?"

"I doubt it. I wouldn't have even been through my first year of college, and . . ." She paused. "And a baby needs parents that love and want it. I didn't want to be pregnant, and I couldn't love a child that was conceived because of nothing short of rape."

"Why didn't you just terminate it?" Taryn asked.

Tears ran down Jorja's cheeks. "Jesus would have really forsaken me if I did that."

"You *have* to talk to someone," Taryn said.

Jorja wiped her face with the back of her hand. "I'm talking to you. Telling anyone else would be too embarrassing."

"How did that news not get out all over town?" Taryn wondered out loud.

"I guess Ford was afraid that if he bragged, everyone would tease him about sleeping with a nerd," Jorja answered. "But I lived in fear that he would tell someone. I was glad to leave at the end of summer, and even more so when my folks left town to do missionary work."

"Ever wonder how much Nana Irene must miss her three kids being split seven ways to Sunday? One is up in Canada, one is in a third world country, and the other one is living in England," Taryn said with a sigh. "And none of us three come back very often. It's like she raised all of us and we just left without looking back."

"Never thought of it that way," Jorja answered.

Taryn kissed Zoe on the top of her head. "Neither have I, until this moment. Maybe I'll stick around after she and Ruby come back to work. I can live here in the trailer and do my computer work in the evenings."

Jorja stood up when she saw Clinton coming down the steps. "Not me. I can't wait to go back to my job this fall. I love Nana Irene, and I'm sorry she's here without family, but this place isn't for me."

"Afraid you'll run into Ford?" Taryn asked.

"Afraid of doing something that Jesus couldn't forgive me for if I did," Jorja answered and went into the trailer.

"Only if you get to him first," Taryn whispered.

Chapter Eight

*D*ark clouds covered the sky when the three cousins piled into the company van to drive to the cemetery that Sunday morning. Jorja was glad that Clinton had not mentioned going with them. Since she had opened up to her cousins about what had happened to her, she wanted to talk about it more, but not with Clinton around. That would be too embarrassing.

"You do know where all the graves are located, right, Taryn?" Jorja asked.

Taryn started the engine and drove out of the parking lot. "Not right offhand. It's been years since I've been here on Memorial Day, but I can remember the general area."

"If we get in a bind, we can always call Nana Irene," Anna Rose said. "Either she or Ruby will be able to guide us right to them."

"Has anyone checked the weather?" Just the thought of storms made Jorja nervous. She remembered hoping that God was sending lightning down from heaven to strike Ford dead that horrible night. Later, she figured He was sending it to remind her that she shouldn't have let her herself be put in that position and that what had happened was her fault.

"I did," Taryn answered. "I'm not sure you can depend on the weatherman, since Texas has a mind of its own. But we've got a fifty percent chance of scattered storms and rain all day."

"Tomorrow is supposed to be hot and sunny," Anna Rose added. "That means it'll be muggy if it rains today."

"These arrangements are artificial, so they will withstand a little rain," Taryn said. "And they won't mind the high humidity."

Jorja shivered. "I hate storms. That night that"—she paused and swallowed several times, trying to get the lump in her throat to go away—"it happened, it was storming. I guess I associate hard rain and the noise of a storm with the pain and humiliation, and the lack of ability to do anything about what was happening."

"You really need to see a therapist and work through this," Anna Rose told her.

"All I would do is sit on a therapist's couch or chair and talk," Jorja snapped. "She or he wouldn't tell me what to do. They would just ask me how it makes me feel. I've watched enough shows on television to know how it works."

"Okay, then," Taryn said as she drove through the arch and into the Shamrock Cemetery, pulling off near the big O'Reilly tombstone. "How do the dark clouds up there in the sky make you feel? Tell us about your emotions. We've got all day, unless you want to get back in time for church services."

Jorja sucked in a lungful of air and let it out slowly. "Are you serious, or are you being sarcastic?"

"I don't know about Taryn, but I'm as serious as this danged hangover I have," Anna Rose answered.

Jorja gasped. "You drove home drunk last night?"

Anna Rose slipped her sunglasses out from her purse and put them on. "I wasn't drunk enough to let Hank talk me into spending the night at his place. That's my gauge about whether I should drive or not—but mixing beer with Jack Daniel's is not a good idea."

"You should have a designated driver," Jorja scolded.

Anna Rose slid open the panel door on the side of the van. "Then *you* can start going with me. You know Nana Irene would be furious if I wrecked my truck on the way home."

"I'm not going to a bar," Jorja declared.

"Then it's on you if I crash into a tree or a telephone pole or even an Angus bull on the way home." Anna Rose got out of the van and headed toward the back.

By the time Jorja joined her, Anna Rose had already opened the double doors and picked up the saddle for their grandfather's tombstone. Jorja wanted to ignore what her cousin had just said, but she couldn't. "I've only ever drank a beer and one fruity drink in my life, and look what that got me."

"Designated drivers do not drink. That's the point," Anna Rose threw over her shoulder as she carried the arrangement across the grass to the tombstone. "You can just sit in the corner at a table and glare at people who do. Maybe you could even run off any cowboys that have wedding bands or a white stripe where a ring used to be."

Jorja gave her a double dose of stink eye. "Taryn can do all that for you."

Anna Rose raised her voice. "Taryn has baby fever, and we can't take Zoe into the bar. So it's up to you. If you're worried about me, then you can be my driver next weekend. If you don't care if I live or die, then that's on you."

A streak of lightning zigzagged through the dark sky, and then thunder rolled. Jorja dropped the wreath she was carrying and covered her head with her hands. "I know it's childish," she said, "but I can't seem to shake this feeling."

Taryn picked up the wreath and then wrapped an arm around her shoulders. "We're here for you, darlin'. Let's get this job done, and then we'll go home. We can make popcorn and hot chocolate and close all the blinds so the lightning can't come through."

Jorja nodded, took the flowers from Taryn, read the small tag on the tripod, and headed toward the grave where it belonged. When she got there, she placed it in front of the gravestone and whispered the name: "Esther Elizabeth O'Malley. The poor little baby was born and died the same day. I didn't even think about a name for my baby." She slid down on the ground, braced her back against the heart-shaped tombstone, and laid her hand on her stomach. "I'm so sorry for not wanting you and for praying that God would just take you."

Anna Rose dropped down beside her. "Are you okay? I'm not interrupting your prayers, am I?"

Before she could answer, Taryn was on the other side of her. "Why are you crying? It looks like the storm is going south of us."

"My poor baby," Jorja sobbed. "Nobody wanted her."

"It was a girl?" Anna Rose asked.

"I have no idea—but when I dream about her, she has blonde pigtails and big green eyes, and she loves kittens." Just admitting that she saw her baby in her dreams made her sob even harder. "I don't ever deserve to have a child after what I did."

"You didn't do anything wrong," Anna Rose said. "Miscarriages happen to women all the time. You can talk about your feelings to us anytime you want, but you are a strong woman, and you can get through this."

"How do I ever get over it?" Jorja asked.

"I said get *through* it, not get *over* it," Anna Rose told her.

"You don't ever really get over the loss of a child," Taryn said. "You were a mother for almost three months, whether you wanted to be or not. If you really believe in God and Jesus, then you know that they won't put more on you than they'll give you the strength to get through."

Jorja had buried the pain so deeply that when it surfaced, she could hardly breathe for the ache. She had been the good cousin, the one who never got into trouble and always went to church.

"It's not fair," she groaned.

"What?" Taryn asked. "That you had to endure a horrible experience? Do you think you're the only one who had something terrible in her background? Do you really believe that you were singled out to have to live through something terrible? That you are this generation's equivalent of Job in the Bible?" Taryn's voice had an edge to it.

"Don't talk to me like that," Jorja snapped. "I trusted you and Anna Rose to help me, not to be hateful."

"Sometimes you don't need to be mollycoddled, but you need someone to jerk you up by the bootstraps and tell you how it is," Anna Rose told her. "Bad things happen to good people, and we have to deal with it. Sometimes bad things happen to bad people. Either way, you don't have to let it control the rest of your life. If you want a family, you need to work through what happened and move on."

"What happened to the two of you that makes you understand?" Jorja asked.

"That's a conversation for another day," Taryn answered. "Today, we're helping you move on. Tomorrow, we may need help ourselves, but not now. You're not even thirty yet, so your biological clock isn't ticking."

"I don't know what I want," Jorja whispered, "but I know I don't like feeling like this."

Two huge drops of rain fell on her face, and she wondered if the angels were weeping with her or if maybe her baby daughter had sent them to tell her that she was fine in heaven with little Esther Elizabeth O'Malley. Either one, or both, brought a little measure of peace to her heart—something that she hadn't known or felt in years.

Taryn jumped up and headed toward the van. "Guess we'd better take this party home or else to the McDonald's for some breakfast."

"I could eat a couple of sausage biscuits." Anna Rose held out a hand to Jorja. "Come on, girl. You can't sit here in the rain—and besides, we're under a big old oak tree. Lightning could get us both, and you'd never get to be my designated driver."

Jorja put her hand into her cousin's and let her pull her up. "I'm never going to a bar, and the lightning has . . ."

A flash crackled through the air so close that Jorja could have sworn it parted her hair.

"You were saying?" Anna Rose took off jogging toward the van.

"I was about to say that the lightning had stopped," Jorja yelled above the thunder and beat Anna Rose to the van. "In this weather, we'll wait until another day to clean the tombstones. We'll be lucky if we can get the flowers put out before the storm."

"How can you eat sausage with a hangover?" Jorja asked with a shiver.

"I've got my own hangover cure," Taryn piped up. "That's a banana, soft scrambled eggs, and a cup of black coffee, in that order. Daddy told me about it before he retired from the military, and it works—almost all the time."

"My daddy told me that any kind of breakfast food helped cure it but to always have a couple of aspirin and a cup of coffee first," Anna Rose replied.

Jorja unwrapped the paper from her bacon, egg, and cheese biscuit. "I don't think either of my folks ever needed a hangover cure."

"I don't imagine they did," Taryn said with a smile. "Aunt Yvonne was always the perfect person, like you were. I never heard her raise her voice—but my mama was a different matter. She used to fuss at me for taking the blame for things I didn't do and for not ratting out the folks who were with me when I did do something bad. In the same breath, she would tell me to pray for those kids."

"Why didn't you stand up for yourself?" Anna Rose asked.

"I really thought those folks I wouldn't tattle on were my friends, but I was just the scapegoat," Taryn answered.

"When you figured that out, why didn't you start right then and . . ." Jorja paused. She sure hadn't done much to own up to her problems; she had buried them deep inside and never told anyone until recently.

Taryn held up a palm. "Ever heard that old saying about not being able to fight city hall? That applies to a bad reputation once you have it. By senior year, I was pretty much a loner. I couldn't trust any of my past so-called friends because they had all betrayed me. I wasn't about to fight them after they blamed me for things I didn't do, because that would have gone on my permanent record."

"It's hard to believe that Nana Irene raised her kids in the same home and they all turned out so different. Her only son went to the service and married Aunt Lisa. She had a good set of lungs when me and you got into trouble, Taryn," Anna Rose said with a giggle. "Nana Irene used to say that she had to be that way to live with Uncle Patrick."

Taryn's smile turned into a soft giggle of her own. "He does have the Irish temper and gift of gab. But he's a good father, and he would go to battle for any one of us three girls—then or now. I'd hate to see what he would do if Jorja told him what happened."

Jorja didn't even have to close her eyes to see her Uncle Patrick, with his crop of red hair and his brilliant green eyes that always seemed to be happy—except for when he was mad, and then they could bore holes into a person.

"I always loved his stories," Jorja said. "Coming to your house was so different from mine, where everything was so quiet you could have heard dust dropping from the ceiling fan to the floor."

"That's what I'm talking about when I say kids raised in the same house can turn out so different. Your mama never met a bit of dust she couldn't conquer," Anna Rose said. "My mama used to say you didn't even need plates at her sister's house—that you could eat right off the floors."

Jorja nodded in agreement. That her mother didn't have blisters on her hands from all the cleaning bordered on a miracle. She often repeated that saying about cleanliness being next to godliness. All through her life, Jorja figured that her mother probably had wings folded up her undershirt and a halo sitting at a perfect angle above her head.

Anna Rose snapped her fingers in front of Jorja's face. "Are you off in la-la land?"

Both Jorja and Taryn jumped.

"Yes, I was," Jorja admitted. "I was thinking about how perfect my mother has always been, both physically and spiritually. I couldn't tell her what happened, for fear that she would think I was dirty and not worthy to be her daughter."

"Bless your heart, Jorja," Taryn said, "and I mean that in a good way. I'm so sorry you have had to live with all those emotions without anyone to even talk to. Did Aunt Yvonne ever tell you about sex?"

"Good Lord, no!" Jorja declared as she laid her hand over her heart. "I'm not sure that I wasn't conceived by immaculate conception. Mama and Daddy never even kissed each other in front of me."

"You poor baby," Anna Rose said. "Daddy kissed Mama every time he left on a long haul in his truck, and she jumped into his arms and wrapped her legs around his waist every time he came home. I can't imagine living in such a sterile house."

Jorja finally smiled for the first time that day. "It was home—but I have to say that I loved Aunt Molly's sense of humor, and it was always a treat for me to get to spend a day or two with her. Nana Irene told me that Molly was one of those 'surprise babies.'" She made air quotes with her fingers. "God must've known, though, that Nana Irene needed some humor in her life and sent Molly to be part of the family. Don't you miss her horribly?"

"Yep, I do, but we FaceTime a couple of times a week and that helps," Anna Rose answered.

"Do you tell her about the times when you have a hangover?" Jorja asked.

"I tell my mama everything," Anna Rose answered. "Don't you?"

Jorja shook her head slowly. "No, I don't. I know she prays for me and that she loves me, but she would be so disappointed in me if she knew . . ."

"You might be surprised," Taryn said.

"No, I wouldn't." Jorja shook her head. "Mama's heart and soul are as clean as her house. I'd talk to either of your mothers before I would her."

Anna Rose patted her on the arm. "My mama would be glad to talk to you. She's pretty good at listening and not passing judgment."

Jorja suddenly understood why Nana Irene wanted the three of them to be closer, like a real family instead of bickering all the time. They were all only children, and their parents had moved away from them. They were all she had left of family, and when it was time for Nana Irene to leave this earth—in the far distant future, in Jorja's mind—she wanted to go with the assurance that her granddaughters all had one another's backs.

She heard a quick intake of breath and looked up to see all the color drain from Ford Chambers's face as he and his family came into the McDonald's out of the rain. Kaitlin Sullivan—now Chambers— hadn't changed all that much in the past ten years. She still wore her shoulder-length blonde hair in the same style and applied entirely too much eye makeup.

Taryn wadded up her trash and tossed it onto the bright red tray in the middle of the table. "We should probably go. We can use the back exit door and not go past them. I'm sure Kaitlin's mother has warned her to stay away from me."

"No!" Jorja slapped the table with enough force to rattle the tray. "I'm through hiding. If I'm ever going to get past this, I have to face it." She stood up and headed toward the door like a woman on a mission to save the world.

Anna Rose slid out of the booth. "I'll go with you. You look like you're about to explode. If we end up in jail, maybe Nana Irene would come bail us out?"

"I doubt it," Taryn said and followed them both across the dining area. "I've got enough money in my purse to get us out of jail. But I want y'all to let me get one good punch in. I want to do my best to break Ford Chambers's nose."

"Kaitlin." Jorja stopped right in front of her and ignored Ford altogether. "I haven't seen you since I got back in town. Are y'all out having breakfast before church services this morning?"

Kaitlin looked like a scared bunny trying to outrun a coyote. "Yes, we are. I heard that y'all were back in town. Mother said she'd been in the shop and . . ."

"Yes, she was," Jorja said with a curt nod. "She even invited me to lunch, but if Taryn and Anna Rose aren't welcome in y'all's homes, then I'm not."

"We don't want any trouble from any of you," Kaitlin whispered.

Jorja took two steps forward and laid a hand on Ford's chest. "*You* deserve trouble for reasons you know all too well, but I expect that you've had an up-front and long talk with Jesus and repented of your sins, right?"

"Take your hand off me," he practically growled.

"If I don't, will you bring me a spiked drink and possibly call in your friends for a good time?" Jorja hissed.

His gaze dropped to the floor. "I don't know what you're talking about."

Jorja removed her hand and took a step back when she got a whiff of his cologne—the same kind that he had worn that night. She fought back a gag, straightened her shoulders, and looked at the top button on his shirt. She couldn't bring herself to lock eyes with him again for fear that she would throw up on his shoes. His two sons didn't need to see something like that. "God might forgive you for what you did, but I still don't have it in my heart to do so," she said. "And if today He asked my opinion on whether you get to pass through those Pearly Gates, I'm afraid you'd be told to go straight to hell." She turned around and forced a fake smile at Kaitlin. "Nice seeing you, Kaitlin. Y'all enjoy the services this morning," she said in a saccharine voice as she walked right past them and made her weak knees take a step toward the door.

"What were y'all talking about?" Kaitlin asked her husband.

As Jorja left the store, she heard Ford assuring Kaitlin that she had always been a little weird and he had no idea why she was being so hateful to them.

Taryn draped an arm around her cousin's shoulders. "That man is digging his way to hell with a teaspoon." She popped open her umbrella and shared it with Jorja. "Sin is sin, and a lie is just as deadly as raping an innocent girl."

"What was that?" Anna Rose asked as she got into the vehicle.

"Ford Chambers is going to have to face what he's done someday, and I hope I'm around to see the fallout," Taryn answered and turned around to check on Jorja, who was settling into the back seat. "Are you okay?"

"Of all the scenarios that I've played through in my head, this wasn't one. Thank you both for being there. It gave me confidence," she answered.

"Why didn't you really lay it out for him?" Taryn asked.

"Those two little kids didn't need to know that about their father. He doesn't deserve protecting—and after what Kaitlin did to you, she doesn't either, but those children . . ." Jorja sighed and then went on, "Maybe my dad wasn't the saint I thought he was, but I don't want anyone bursting my bubble about him. And I'm twenty-eight years old, not . . ." Another sigh. "A six- or seven-year-old who just wants to eat a kids' meal and go to Sunday school."

"You are a better person than I am, for sure," Taryn said with a grin. "He called you *weird*."

"I *was* weird in *everyone's* eyes back then, not just his," Jorja said with a big smile. "That means he knew he shouldn't have treated me like he did. God will exact vengeance on him when the time is right. I just hope his sons don't have to pay for his sins."

Clinton parked out in front of the hotel and called his grandfather. "We're here. Want to meet in the lobby, or should I come up to your room?" Even though, at this point in his life, he had no desire to run the corporation, he did love his grandfather and was always excited to get to spend time with him.

"I've got a small conference room booked for us, and I'm in the elevator coming down to the lobby right now," Harry told him. "See you in a minute."

Clinton slipped the phone into his pocket, got out of his truck, and opened the back door to get Zoe. "Are you tired of riding? Ready to go in and meet my grandfather? He already loves babies, but you're going to win his heart even more than most."

Zoe flashed a bright, toothless grin.

He toted the carrier in one hand and slung the diaper bag over his shoulder as he made his way up the sidewalk and into the hotel lobby. His grandfather met them halfway across the room and gave him a brief hug. "It's good to see you. Been a while."

"About three months." Clinton smiled. "You should come up this way more often."

"I'm not real fond of the panhandle," Harry said as he led the way down a long hallway. "It's too flat for me. I like a few trees and maybe a rolling hill or two—but I've got to admit, this area is good for the oil business. I've got a meeting at the Mesquite Oil Company this afternoon. You can join me and bring the baby. She's a cutie." He opened the door to a small room with a long table to one side that had all kinds of finger foods laid out, along with coffee and a pitcher of sweet tea. "Help yourself. We might as well eat while we talk business. Let me take the baby while you load up a plate."

Clinton handed the carrier over to Harry and dropped the diaper bag on a chair. "Thanks, Grandpa. This all looks good."

"I understand that you love what you're doing, and I've got a good crew to run things after I'm gone," Harry said as he unstrapped Zoe and took her out of the carrier. "But I do wish you would be at the company in Houston on a daily basis—you'd be the CEO at that point."

"Grandpa, I love you, but my heart is in the nonprofit business I'm building," Clinton said.

"If that's what you want to do, then you can't continue to run it out of your hip pocket. I've had the lawyers set up a corporation, and the papers are ready to sign. The way it's growing even now, you will need help. A man can't run a business like that on his own and take in babies at the same time, and you can't run it out of an upstairs apartment much longer," Harry told him. "We set up a budget, and you'll have whatever funds you need for payroll or expenses." Zoe reached up and patted his cheek with her chubby little hand. "Maybe the first thing you better do is hire a nanny."

Clinton carried his plate to the table and sat down. "Maybe later on down the road, I will—or set up a day care center for the vets who need to work and have no place to leave their children. But you'll remember Quincy, my military buddy that came home with me for Christmas a few years back. He's thinking about joining me. We're supposed to talk in a little bit."

"I liked that guy when I met him," Harry said. "Offer him a salary worth his while, and give yourself one also—and for God's sake, buy a building for your office. Now, tell me about this baby. When is her mother coming back?"

"I honestly don't know, Grandpa," Clinton answered. "She's got a really bad case of PTSD." He went on to tell him the whole story of Larry and Rebecca. "I'm hoping that the therapy she gets over the next few weeks helps her get to the point that she can handle the responsibilities of being a mother. She's served her country, but so many of the vets I work with have come home broken."

"Reminds me of your dad," Harry said. "He wasn't in the service, but he had the same symptoms when your mother left. I made him go to therapy, and it helped him; hopefully, Rebecca will get the coping skills she needs for all the issues she's having. Your dad finally accepted that he had married a woman who wanted his money, not his child. It took me a while to come to that conclusion with your grandmother way back when, and I raised your dad by myself. When you find a woman, make sure you can trust her, and break this terrible chain."

"Yes, sir," Clinton said, and a vision of Taryn holding Zoe flashed through his mind. She knew about his money and didn't seem to be interested in it—not like those three women who were constantly badgering him.

He took a sip of his sweet tea, and then his cell phone pinged. He pulled his phone out of his shirt pocket and saw that the call was from Quincy. "Hello?" he answered.

"Did I get you at a good time? We have to hammer this out," Quincy said.

"I'm putting you on speaker," Clinton said. "My grandpa and I are setting things in motion now. It's Quincy, Grandpa."

"Hello, Mr. McEntire," Quincy said.

"Nice to talk to you again, Quincy, even this long since Clinton got out of the air force," Harry told him. "So, I hear you are interested in helping out with this venture my grandson has been trying to run out of a tiny apartment."

"Yes, sir, I am. My enlistment is up, and I see a need," Quincy answered.

"Well, how about . . ." Harry quoted him a salary figure. "I think that's probably at least twice as much as you made in the service, right?"

"Yes, sir, it is, and it's very generous," Quincy replied. "But I can work for less, and we can put the rest of the money back into helping other vets."

"You'll be working long hours most likely, so I insist that you're paid right," Harry informed him in a no-nonsense tone. "Your first job is to find a building—preferably with some good handicap parking—where you and my grandson can set up a proper office."

Even though his grandfather had been disappointed in his choices, he had always supported him. But this kind of backing totally surprised Clinton.

"Yes, sir," Quincy said. "I can be in Shamrock in a few days and get right on that."

"That's good. Now, you and Clinton can visit more while Zoe and I have a visit," Harry told him,

Clinton took the phone off speaker and said, "So, you're really going to do this?"

"I'd do it for room and board," Quincy said. "You and I both know what these vets need, and I want to help them."

"Me too," Clinton told him. "Let me know when you are getting into town, and I'll book you a hotel room until we can find something better for you to live in."

"Will do," Quincy said.

The sun had set and taken some of the heat of the day with it, leaving behind a muggy night. Taryn had tossed and turned for more than an hour that evening, but she couldn't shut her thoughts down. She should be worried about Jorja's problem, not thinking about Clinton and Zoe, but that's where her mind got stuck. Finally, she gave up on sleep, tip-toed down the hallway, and went out onto the porch.

Nana Irene's voice was clear in her head: *Clinton is a grown man. He doesn't have to call you and tell you where he's going or give you a time frame about when he's coming home. Did you girls call him and give him a play-by-play of what you were doing today?*

"No," she whispered, and then heard a vehicle turn into the parking lot.

Clinton's truck came to a stop not far from the steps up to his apartment. He got out and slung the diaper bag over his shoulder. He opened the door to the back seat, hefted the baby carrier out, and limped up the stairs.

The light from the waning moon let Taryn see that Zoe was in the carrier and sleeping soundly. He had just gotten into his apartment when the trailer door eased open, and Anna Rose tiptoed out and sat down on the top porch step. Her nightshirt that had Betty Boop riding a horse on the front of it barely covered her underpants.

"Have trouble sleeping?" Taryn asked.

Anna Rose jumped and gasped at the same time. "You scared the bejesus out of me."

"Sorry about that," Taryn apologized. "What's got you coming out here on this muggy night?"

"I kept worrying about Jorja," Anna Rose admitted. "She's a pain in my ass, but she's blood kin, and she was an innocent. I lost my virginity at sixteen. I thought I was in love with Jeremy Baker, and he told me that he loved me. We'd been dating for two years, and it seemed the right thing to do at the time. Jorja was different than me and you, Taryn. She had all that religion drilled into her from birth, and Aunt Yvonne was so prim and proper."

"Do you think that Nana Irene found out about what happened, and she expects us to fix Jorja?" Taryn asked.

"Maybe, but maybe we just need her to kiss the Blarney Stone and learn to live outside of a church family." Anna Rose looked up at the sky. "I'm not saying that you aren't good, God. I'm saying that—"

"Are you praying?" Jorja asked as she opened the door.

"I'm just telling God what I think." Anna Rose's voice held a sharp edge.

"That's praying." Jorja sat down on the other side of the top step and stretched her long legs out past the bottom one. She wore a pair of boxer shorts and a tank top that showed off her lean figure. If she ever wore a pair of tight jeans and a fitted shirt to a bar, Taryn thought, she dang sure wouldn't be sitting alone at a table for more than ten minutes.

"Not in my book," Anna Rose said. "What are you doing out here?"

"I can't sleep. I keep thinking about that baby, Esther Elizabeth O'Malley. I wonder if she died because something was wrong with her, and if my baby had the same thing. If I did decide to move on and trust someone with my heart, would I ever carry a child to full term?" She paused and took a deep breath. "I bet little Esther's mama wanted her to live and was devastated when she didn't."

Taryn set the rocking chair in motion with her foot. "Probably so—but then, she was having that child with a man she loved. Your circumstances were a whole lot different than whatever happened to that child."

For several minutes, there was no sound except for a cricket and a tree frog's duet over near the big pecan tree at the end of the porch. Taryn was not a therapist, and she didn't know what else to say, but a nagging feeling in her heart told her that she needed to say some more comforting words—yet nothing would come.

"Y'all are right," Jorja said. "It's time for me to find myself—not who Mama wants me to be or who y'all think I should be. But to figure out what I want out of life."

"That requires putting the past in a box, taping it shut, and either burying it or setting it on fire," Taryn told her, but she wasn't sure if she was advising her cousin or herself.

Jorja jumped up and headed inside. "Don't go away. I'll be right back."

Anna Rose shifted her position and leaned her back against the porch post. "If she brings her Bible and a match out here, I'm heading for the shop. There are stars in the sky, but I bet lightning could come down and zap this whole trailer if she does that."

"I'll be right behind you," Taryn said.

"I'm a little superstitious," Jorja said as she came back out with a shoebox, a roll of tape, and the metal trash can from the bathroom in her hands.

"You don't expect us to dance around a fire and chant, do you?" Anna Rose asked.

"Only if you take off all your clothes and do it naked," Jorja snapped. "I'm going to figuratively put all those memories of that summer in this box, tape it shut, and burn it. Hopefully, that will help me move on."

"Can I put some of mine in there with yours?" Taryn remembered the heartache she had felt when her military boyfriend told her he had a wife and a couple of kids, and that what they'd had was just a good time between two consenting adults.

Jorja opened the box and set it on the railing. "If you've got crap you don't want in your life anymore, close your eyes and put it in the box."

"I've got a few things I want to add," Anna Rose said and stood up.

The three cousins gathered around the box, but before they could close their eyes, Taryn reached out and took Jorja's hand in her left one and Anna Rose's in her right. "All right, we'll close our eyes now and mentally pack away all the bad stuff from our past."

"Do we forgive the ones who hurt us?" Jorja whispered.

"I'm not in a forgiving mood tonight," Anna Rose said.

Taryn nodded in agreement. "Tonight, we just burn the past. Maybe later, we'll have a forgiving ceremony."

"With wine," Anna Rose declared.

"I don't drink," Jorja said.

"Even Jesus drank wine, girlfriend," Taryn reminded her. "Heck, he *made* wine."

"Moving on. New life. Maybe one small glass of wine when I'm ready to forgive—but by then I'll be so old, I won't remember what I'm forgiving." Jorja squeezed Taryn's hand. "I'm closing my eyes and packing all those ugly moments into the box right now."

The moment Taryn closed her own eyes, she got a visual of Mitchell in his uniform. He had claimed a barstool beside her and laid on a heavy dose of flirting. For the next two months, the relationship had been hot and heavy, and Taryn was ready to say yes if he proposed before they finished their enlistment. Without even folding the memory like a favorite shirt, she crammed it into the box and mentally stomped it with her boots. Then she added several more memories from her youth.

When she opened her eyes, both of her cousins were staring at her. "What?" she asked.

"I reckon the box is full. Think we can get it taped shut?" Anna Rose asked.

Jorja let go of Taryn's hand, slammed the lid onto the box as if it were overflowing with heavy stuff, and quickly taped it shut. Then she put it in the trash can and carried it off the porch. "We are burning the past and moving forward. All of us. Not just me. So we're all three going to strike a match and set it on fire."

Taryn had never been superstitious—except for black cats crossing her path. But when Jorja handed her the first match and she struck it, she felt a bit of the heaviness in her heart disappear and began to think maybe there was something to the ritual. Anna Rose and Jorja each lit up another corner, and soon, a blaze lit up the area and smoke floated upward. The wind carried tiny pieces of paper out onto the gravel, but they soon burned out and died right there.

Jorja covered a yawn with her hand. "Now maybe we can all sleep. The past is gone; the future is ahead of us."

"Are you sure you don't want to undress and do a victory dance around the trash can?" Anna Rose teased.

"I guess some things, like *your* smart-ass attitude, can't be burned up," Jorja said.

Anna Rose gave her two thumbs up. "Jorja just said a bad word. I think the ritual has already begun to work. Good night to you both." She headed toward the porch but turned at the bottom step and said, "I'm taking another shower to get the smell of smoke and sweat off me. Don't worry, I won't use all the hot water."

"I'm having cookies and milk while I wait on Anna Rose." Jorja left the trash can, and in a few long strides, she was inside the trailer.

Taryn stared at the red embers in the bottom of the can. Leaving them outside could cause a disaster. One big puff of wind could pick them up, send them to the wooden porch, and then the fire trucks would be waking up the whole city. She could see the headline in the local newspaper: Trash Can Fire Causes Major Catastrophe. Just that much could reinstate her as the biggest troublemaker Shamrock, Texas, had ever produced. She scooped up gravel in her hands and put it into the trash can until all the fire was smothered completely.

By the time she got into the house, Anna Rose was out of the shower and Jorja was having her turn. Taryn poured herself a glass of milk and put a fistful of lemon cookies on a paper towel, then carried her snack over to the recliner. She'd only been teasing when she told Jorja to bury or burn all the past, but doing it had sure brought Taryn peace.

Could it really be that she, herself, had just left all the hurt and pain behind and was ready to move forward?

Chapter Nine

*W*hat are y'all doin' in here? This is a holiday," Clinton asked as he came into the shop through the back door. "I thought you'd be enjoying a day away from flowers and ribbons. Why didn't y'all call me when the trash can caught on fire? Did you get burned taking it out of the house?"

"We are all fine," Jorja answered. "We had a cleansing ceremony. We took the trash can out into the yard and set the fire ourselves. Not to worry—we knew where the water hose was if the blaze had gotten out of hand."

Clinton raised a dark eyebrow and set the baby carrier on the worktable. He took Zoe out of the carrier and started toward the playpen with her. "What is a cleansing ceremony—or do I even want to know?"

"It's where we all burn what is holding us back from moving forward with our lives. We put all the bad memories in a shoebox and burned it in the trash can," Anna Rose explained. "And the reason we're in the shop today is that we're bored with nothing to do, so we are making pew bows for the first wedding on the list. These things look like they belong at a baby shower instead of a wedding, don't they?"

"Maybe so," Clinton answered with a grin.

Taryn laid down the bow she had been working on and held out her arms to take Zoe from Clinton. When his arms brushed hers, sparks flew again—but then, that was no big surprise. However, she did wonder if he felt the same thing. Did he cover it up as well as she did? Or maybe he didn't feel a thing? She avoided eye contact with him and talked to the baby: "Good mornin', sweet girl. Did you want to come to the shop, where there's pretty colors and excitement? Do you like these pink ribbons, or are you a red or purple girl?"

"Maybe she likes orange best," Anna Rose said. "She always reaches for the orange tiger on her mobile."

Taryn figured that she would miss Zoe when Rebecca came back for her, but the way Anna Rose's and Jorja's eyes lit up when the baby was close by left her with no doubt that they would be sad to see her leave, too.

"I missed the baby, but I missed that food from your apartment even more," Anna Rose continued. "We had to cook for ourselves, and you and Zoe weren't there to buffer our arguments."

Clinton sat down on his usual stool and picked up a roll of ribbon. "There's still lots of casseroles up there, but I'm tired of those things. If the stores weren't all closed for Memorial Day, I'd buy a grill so we could have real meat—like maybe steak—tonight. Yesterday, we stopped at the Dairy Queen in Pampa, and I had a big juicy burger. It tasted so good. Zoe had a bottle, but I promised her when she got a little older she could have an ice cream cone."

"When is she even old enough to have big-people food?" Taryn held Zoe out from her body and studied her face. "Did you sleep all right, baby girl, after a big trip like that?"

"And, Mommy Taryn, she slept just fine," Clinton answered.

Taryn laid Zoe in the playpen and started the mobile. "I would love to be her mommy, so thank you for that." *Did I really say that out loud?* She wondered. And if she did, would her cousins take it the wrong way—or, worse yet, would Clinton?

"For real?" Jorja's eyes widened.

"Of course." Taryn flinched just a little as she hopped back up on her barstool. "I want a family, and I'd gladly start with Zoe." *Good Lord!* She had to bite her tongue to keep from saying anything else.

"So, you drove all the way to Pampa with a baby for a hamburger?" Jorja asked.

Taryn could have hugged her youngest cousin for changing the subject.

"Nope, not just for a burger."

Taryn was mesmerized at how fast his big hands whipped the ribbon around and tied it off with floral wire. A visual of his hands cupping her face as he leaned in to kiss her popped into her head. She moistened her lips in anticipation of the kiss. Then she realized what she had done and blushed.

He finished that bow and started another one. "My grandfather flew into the area for a business meeting, and he had papers for me to sign since I'm on the board of directors, whether I want to be or not. Plus, we had to set up all the legal corporation stuff for my veteran's business, and Zoe charmed everyone there."

"They were open on Sunday *and* on a holiday weekend?" Taryn was relieved that he hadn't gone to a picnic with one of the women chasing after him. But then, was he telling the truth? Could she trust him?

"When Harry McEntire comes to town, everyone comes to the hotel to meet with him, no matter what day it is, and not one single person complains," Clinton answered without even looking up.

Taryn took her place beside him. "They must love him a lot to give up a Monday holiday like that."

"I'm not so sure it's love for him or if it's love for a nice bump in their paychecks," Clinton said. "They get double pay if they work a day on the weekend—plus, since it was a holiday weekend, that turns into triple pay."

"Do *we* get double pay for working on a holiday?" Anna Rose asked.

"Of course you do," Clinton replied, but Taryn could feel his eyes on her when he talked. "Since you are working on a holiday, your extra pay is that you get to choose what you want from McDonald's for lunch since that's one of the few places open today—and you can even have dessert. Or I can get into the petty cash fund, and we can buy some hot dogs and grill them and maybe get a watermelon from the roadside stand and celebrate Memorial Day with a party in the parking area out back for supper."

"Just how are you going to grill?" Taryn asked. "You should have thought about picking one up at Walmart while you were in Pampa."

"Mommy Taryn is beginning to nag like Wifey Taryn," Anna Rose teased.

Taryn shot a dirty look across the table. "That's not funny."

"It is a little bit," Jorja said with a giggle. "You said you were ready to be a mommy. Are you ready to be a wifey?"

"That's a loaded question, and I'm not going to answer it," Taryn told her. No way was she going to say a single word with Clinton in the room.

"Okay, changing the subject to keep y'all from bickering," Clinton said. "I've got an idea. That little trash can out back is already ruined. We could start another fire in it and roast hot dogs over it. If I straighten out a few wire coat hangers, they'll make great skewers."

"I'm in," Taryn said before her cousins could continue the teasing. "Let's have McDonald's for lunch and do that for supper. I agree with Clinton: a juicy burger for lunch and then hot dogs with mustard and relish for supper sounds pretty dang good. And we can invite Nana Irene and Ruby. They might like to get out for an evening. I'll go get them in my SUV—it will be easier for them to get in and out of than a car or pickup."

Taryn realized she was talking too much and way too fast—but then, that was what she did when she was nervous. Just the idea of being a wife gave her heart palpitations. What if she committed to that kind of relationship, then found out that her husband wasn't the man she'd thought he was when they married? What if he was kind and sweet until she said "I do," and then he turned into someone she hardly knew? Just like Mitchell. No, Taryn O'Reilly was not ready to be a "wifey"—not now and maybe not ever.

Anna Rose was talking when Taryn tuned back in to the conversation.

"Sounds like fun to me, and I bet Nana Irene and Ruby will jump at the chance to get out this evening," Anna Rose agreed. "But we don't have to buy anything. We have hot dogs in the freezer and buns and condiments in the pantry. I'll spring for a watermelon and pick it up at the fruit stand, and I'll buy some cold beer and chips at the convenience store."

"I'll make a pitcher of sweet tea," Jorja offered. "I'll also grate some cheese and heat up a can of chili for anyone who wants to put that on their hot dogs."

"*You*"—Taryn pointed at her—"will have a cold beer. You can make a pitcher of tea for Ruby since she can't drink with her meds . . . But remember, *you* are moving on."

"Moving on from what?" Clinton asked.

"A personal problem that she probably doesn't want to talk about," Anna Rose answered.

Jorja glared at Taryn. "I couldn't . . . What if . . . it would . . . ," she stammered.

"Yes, you can, and *what ifs*—right along with *would* or *might*—got burned up last night with all those bad things we put in the shoebox," Taryn told her. "You can taste it, and if you really don't like it, I'll finish it for you. We never waste beer or liquor."

"Or better yet, I'll get a six-pack of bitch beer," Anna Rose said with a giggle.

"What is that, and are you calling me a bi . . . bi . . . ?" Poor Jorja had trouble even saying the word.

"Nope, I am not," Anna Rose answered. "It's flavored beer. I'm partial to watermelon or peach."

"Why do they call it that?" Jorja's face was scarlet, most likely from thinking about letting what she considered a bad word fall from her lips, combined with the idea of actually drinking something with alcohol in it.

"It's because men make fun of us for drinking fruity beers," Anna Rose answered.

"Then buy a six-pack for us," Jorja declared. "We'll prove to the lot of them that we can drink our fruity beer with pride."

"That's really moving on with determination and purpose, and I'm proud of you." Anna Rose shot a smile across the table toward her.

"Wow!" Taryn laid a hand on her chest in a dramatic gesture, but in all seriousness, she was also both surprised and happy that Jorja was making progress. "This is a celebration day. You two were kind to each other."

"I kind of like a bottle of that stuff every now and then," Clinton chimed in. "Especially the watermelon flavor on a hot day. I keep a couple of six-packs up in my apartment all the time. That's all my best friend, Quincy, drinks. He's going to join me in my vet business in a few days. I can't wait for all y'all to meet him."

"That would be great," Taryn said. "But why does he only drink that?"

"He hates the taste of the real stuff and of any kind of hard liquor," Clinton explained. "He says life is too good to lose part of it by passing out drunk."

"Amen," Jorja said and cut her eyes around at Anna Rose.

"Don't give me your old stink eye," Anna Rose snapped. "I've never passed out, and when I have more than I should, I can say that I had a good time doing it."

"Hey, we've all got a past," Clinton said. "But we have a million futures in front of us, and it's up to us to choose which path is right."

"Where'd you get those words of wisdom?" Taryn asked and wondered if she would take the path to have a relationship with Clinton if it ever opened up.

"I heard the part about a million futures on a television show," Clinton answered. "The rest I kind of figured out for myself. The past is gone and should be put away. But we have dozens upon dozens of futures ahead of us, and it's our decision about which one to choose each day."

"That's right," Taryn said and then reached across the table to lay a hand on Jorja's arm. "I don't want you to go against your morals, but I want *you* to decide what's right for *you*. Same goes for you, Anna Rose." The voice inside her head said that she was preaching to the choir, and she agreed with it wholeheartedly.

"And for you," Clinton asked.

"Especially for me," Taryn said with a nod toward Clinton.

"Thank you for offering to come get us," Irene said as she helped Ruby into Taryn's SUV. "There's no way I could get this old woman in my small car."

"You just wait until you get those new bionic knees and see how quick you can get in and out of a car," Ruby teased.

"No problem," Taryn said. "We're just glad y'all are going to join us. They should be getting the hot dogs roasted by the time we get there."

Ruby settled into the passenger seat and fastened her seat belt. "You kids are so inventive. I would never have thought to build a fire in an old metal trash can—and for your information, Irene O'Reilly, I'm not as old as you are and never will be."

"Oh, right!" Irene declared. "I'm ten days older, and that makes me ten days smarter."

Taryn folded Ruby's walker. "Clinton gets the credit for the trash can plan. We just went along with it, and we're glad y'all decided to join us. It's just hot dogs and then watermelon for dessert, but it will be fun."

"When we get there, I get to hold that baby first," Ruby said.

"Why do you get to hold her first?" Irene asked.

"Because I had surgery, and I get to be pampered, and because you held her first on Saturday," Ruby answered.

"All right, but she's going to fuss and want me in less than a minute. Babies always love me more than you," Irene said.

"Y'all argue more than us three cousins," Taryn muttered as she took the walker to the back and loaded it in.

They were still arguing when she got behind the wheel and started the engine, and they hadn't stopped by the time they reached the trailer. To Taryn's way of thinking, the two old gals had been together too much and needed some time apart, even if it was just for an hour or two.

But that doesn't make sense, the voice in her head argued, *because Anna Rose and Jorja can be apart a whole year and start bickering the moment they see each other.*

"Okay, ladies, your limousine has arrived." Taryn parked the car. "From that smoking trash can, I'd say that the hot dogs are ready, and the party has moved inside. As hot as it is this evening, no one is getting an argument from me about not eating on the porch."

"Well, rats," Irene complained. "I wanted to roast a hot dog on the fire myself. I haven't done that in years."

Ruby winked at Taryn. "Don't pout, Irene. We can always do s'mores sometimes this week in our backyard. Maybe we'll be lucky enough to set the grass on fire."

"Why would you do that?" Taryn asked.

"So those good-lookin' firemen can come rescue two little old ladies," Ruby answered. "We haven't had much excitement these past few weeks. It's really time for us to come back to the shop. I miss hearing all the gossip and knowing when folks die, have babies, or get married before I have to read it in the newspaper."

"Amen!" Irene said with a giggle.

Then their laughter filled the vehicle.

A cold chill chased down Taryn's back at the very thought of leaving Shamrock.

And to think you didn't even want to spend a few weeks here, the voice in her head reminded her.

"We could come over and build a small firepit in the yard for y'all and celebrate getting it built by having a s'mores evening. We could ask Clinton to bring a couple of his casseroles for supper and . . ."

"Nope." Irene shook her head. "We're not having a firepit, and you are not talking us into coming over more than one day a week. You'd all three corner me and tattle on each other. You need to learn to get along without me settling arguments. Now, get Ruby's walker out before she decides she needs to do something worse than build a fire in the yard."

"Yes, ma'am!" Taryn followed her grandmother's orders and then helped Ruby out of the SUV. Together they guided her up the steps to the porch and into the house, where she went straight to the recliner, sat down, and held out her arms.

"Clinton, you can take the baby out of that bucket and give her to me," she said. "And, Anna Rose, get me one of those flavored beers to sip on." She started rocking and humming the moment Zoe was in her lap.

The baby reached one little hand up and touched Ruby's cheek.

Ruby's smile lit up the whole room. "See? She likes me better than you, Irene."

Irene sat down on the sofa and propped her feet up on the coffee table. "She does not—and you're not distracting me into an argument, so I won't notice when Anna Rose brings you a beer. You can have a glass of sweet tea or a bottle of lemonade. The doctor said no liquor of any kind for six weeks."

"Party pooper," Ruby grumbled. "Bring me a lemonade, then, and don't be timing me with this baby. I get her as long as I want."

Jorja set a bowl of grated cheese on the bar next to her drink and then took a seat beside her grandmother. "I'm glad y'all felt like coming out this evening. Does being back in the trailer bring back memories?"

Irene leaned slightly and lowered her voice. "I can't believe my eyes. Are you really drinking a beer? What has happened in this place?"

"Yes, I am, and it's pretty good," Jorja said. "I've decided to go on a journey to find myself, and so tonight, I'm having one beer."

Anna Rose brought her grandmother a beer and Ruby a lemonade, then pulled out a chair and sat down at the kitchen table. "Jorja is turning over a new leaf and trying new things."

"But I'm not forsaking my beliefs or my church," Jorja declared.

"A beer is not going to keep anyone out of heaven," Irene said.

"If I die before this hip is healed, I hope they have beer in heaven," Ruby said with a sigh.

"What makes you think *you'll* ever get past the Pearly Gates?" Irene asked.

"Because I'm going to sneak in on your coattails," Ruby retorted. "Besides, if you got to go and I didn't, I'd throw a big old hissy fit, and the devil wouldn't want me in hell."

"Even if you get past the front gates, you'll be a spirit and won't be able to drink other spirits, if you see what I mean," Irene reminded her.

Ruby cocked her head to the side and narrowed her eyes. "Just for that smart-ass remark, you don't get to hold the baby"—she lowered her voice to a whisper—"and when I find out how they talked Jorja into drinking even one of those silly beers, I'm not telling you."

"The older you get, the harder you are to put up with," Irene told her.

"Are we going to have to separate you two?" Clinton asked.

"Ain't nobody been big enough or brave enough to do that in the past," Ruby answered. "Me and Irene have been best friends since we could walk. We might argue and fuss amongst the two of us, but nobody better even try to come between us. Here, Taryn, you take this baby. I can't even drink this lemonade with a baby in my lap. She keeps lookin' up at me with those pretty eyes, and I know she's too young to have it."

Taryn picked up Zoe and kissed her on the forehead. "Just wait until you are old enough, baby girl, and then you can have ice cream and Popsicles."

"*I* might need a Popsicle if there's a red one," Ruby said. "This heat takes it out of a person, and your granny ate the last of our ice cream last night."

Irene got up and headed for the kitchen. "Well, you scarfed down the last two pieces of pecan pie, and the doctor said you should be watching your sugar intake."

"Nana Irene, we've got everything under control, so you go on back in there and sit down," Anna Rose said. "Soon as I get this watermelon cut up, we'll be ready to eat, and you both can have ice cream if you want. You told me that anything you eat on a holiday doesn't have fat, sugar, or calories. Remember?"

"Speak for yourself," Ruby said. "You guys should know that this woman is a tyrant. Not only does she boss me around but she is also a demon about my at-home therapy. I keep telling her that payback is a b-i-t-c-h, and I will deliver it with a smile on my face when she gets her knees done."

"Why are you spelling that word?" Clinton asked.

"Zoe doesn't need to hear bad words," Ruby told him.

Taryn giggled. "I don't think she'll remember much of what we're saying here tonight."

"And one more thing: the girls are all home now, so when I get my knees done, they can take care of me and you won't have to even see me for six weeks." Irene groaned when she sat back down.

"There'll be a blizzard in hell before that happens," Ruby smarted off. "We ain't gone without seeing each other for one day in our whole lives, and it ain't damn likely to start now."

Taryn didn't ask, but she wondered just when her grandmother was planning on having knee surgery and if she really thought all three of them would be staying past the summer. She could do her work in Shamrock for a while if Nana Irene needed her—but if she was doing that, who would run the shop?

"Okay, everyone," Clinton said. "Looks like we're ready to eat. Ruby, what do you want on your hot dog? I'll make it for you and bring it right to the recliner."

"Everything and extra cheese," she said. "And thank you for being such a gentleman."

Jorja set her beer on the table and said, "But first we say grace. I still love Jesus, even if I do like this beer." She bowed her head, and everyone else did the same.

Taryn didn't listen to her cousin's prayer, but she sent up one of her own asking God not only to help Jorja find her way but also to show all three of them the path they should be taking.

"Amen," Jorja said. "I might need to say an extra prayer tonight for what I'm about to say, but my beer is sacri-licious."

"I'd say you've turned the first page of the new chapter in your life," Anna Rose told her. "I'm proud of you!"

Taryn giggled and looked over at Clinton, who had a big smile on his face. She had never wanted to kiss a man more than she did right then—but not with the whole family surrounding her.

The shop is called the Lucky Shamrock, but it can only do so much. It's up to you to do the rest, the pesky voice in her head said.

"Turn out the lights; the party's over," Irene singsonged at nine o'clock. "It's time for these old birds to go home to roost."

"See how bossy she is?" Ruby fussed. "I could stay until midnight. But if I did, I might feel the need to put on some music and dance, and maybe even teach y'all the dances of the sixties and seventies. We had some real moves back then."

Taryn unfolded Ruby's walker and set it before the recliner. "When your hip gets better, we'll let you have beer—and even a double shot of Jameson if you want it—and you and Nana Irene can teach us the dances."

"You'll have to find the right music," Irene said. "That music you kids listen to today doesn't have the kind of beat for the dances that we did."

"All except for country music." Ruby groaned when she got up out of the recliner. "Guess I sat a little too long. My old bones are jealous of the new hip, and sometimes they get testy just to show me that they're still around."

Clinton gathered up Zoe's toys and put them in the diaper bag. "It's past time for me and Zoe to go home, too. She's used to having her bath and being asleep by this time. She'll start to get cranky pretty soon if we don't get going, but it's sure been a great evening."

Taryn wondered if that idea about Ruby's old bones being jealous of a new hip worked for moods as well as joints. She and her cousins had been getting along the past few days, but would a time come when the old attitudes resurfaced just to test their new relationships? She was still thinking about that when she settled Zoe into her carrier and kissed her good night.

Anna Rose pouted. "It's not fair that you get to spend time with Nana Irene without us."

"How do you figure she's doing that?" Clinton asked as he picked up the diaper bag with one hand and the carrier with the other.

"She gets time with them in her SUV, both coming over here and going back," Jorja answered and then shot Taryn a dirty look. "If you are gone more than half an hour, then we get to go over to Nana Irene's separately later in the week."

Irene shook her finger in Jorja's direction. "Young lady, you don't call the shots on this issue. Taryn is my cab driver. If you are jealous because she gets to drive me back and forth, then trade that little car of yours in on something that Ruby and I can get in and out of."

Taryn gave her cousin a cocky smile, and Irene whipped around to point at her. "You don't get to lord it over the other two, young lady. Do y'all think I like being right across town and not seeing each of you every day? If you do, you've got rocks for brains. I'm making you lean on each other because the day will come when I won't be here, and family is important."

Her last words landed with a jolt. Taryn didn't want to think about a time when Nana Irene would be gone. Her grandmother was and had always been the stability for the whole family, and they needed her to boss them around, give advice, and keep them in line.

Irene dropped her finger. "Ruby and I will see y'all on Saturday, unless we decide we need to get out and go for a ride and then drop in here for a little visit. If that happens, you can draw straws to see who will bring Taryn's SUV and chauffeur us around."

"Yes, ma'am," Jorja said and came around the end of the bar separating the kitchen from the dining area to give her grandmother a hug. "But please don't talk about dying. It makes me sad."

Irene wrapped her arms around Jorja and then stepped back. "Darlin', we all have an expiration date, and the closer we get to it, the less it bothers us. Don't be sad when I'm gone. Be happy for all the good times we've had together—like tonight."

"That goes for me, too," Ruby said, "but I'm not planning a trip into eternity anytime soon, so you don't have to rush out and buy extra tissues."

Jorja swiped a tear from her cheek. "That's easier said than done, so I'm just not going to think about it. Good night, Nana. 'Night, Ruby."

Taryn knew that her cousins were close to Nana Irene and Ruby, but she wasn't so sure that anyone—not even her mother and her siblings—could love Nana Irene any more than Jorja did.

"'Night," Irene and Ruby said at the same time.

"Now, Taryn, you can help me get Ruby down those steps and into your vehicle," Irene said.

"I hate not being able to do for myself," Ruby said with a long sigh.

Irene helped Ruby get the walker out onto the porch. "I'm going to hate it, too, when I get new knees at the end of summer, and I intend to whine about it even worse than you do. But with the girls' and Clinton's help, we'll get through it."

"I don't whine," Ruby argued.

Taryn followed them and then held on to Ruby while she slowly made her way down the porch steps to the ground. Ruby was a little woman, not even as tall as Taryn, and frail looking. If she had gotten off-balance, Taryn was sure she was strong enough to scoop Ruby up and carry her to the bottom of the steps with no trouble.

Irene had opened the doors and was settled into the back seat by the time Taryn and Ruby reached the SUV. "What's this thing between you and Clinton?" she asked.

Taryn started to speak but didn't know how to tell the truth or even divine whatever it was between them. She also didn't know—after all these years—how to tell her grandmother about her fear of trusting anyone after the last fiasco with a married man.

"We're friends, and I help with Zoe," Taryn finally answered.

"Oh, honey!" Ruby got situated and fastened her seat belt. "The way you two were looking at each other, you are more than friends. If you aren't willing to admit it now, you better get ready because I could feel the heat between y'all, and I'm an old woman."

"Don't confuse what you feel for Zoe now with what you might feel with Clinton in time," Irene said. "You have absolutely fallen in love with that baby."

"You're going to be devastated when Zoe's mama takes her away," Ruby said.

"I've thought of that," Taryn said as she slid in behind the steering wheel and started the engine. "Did you ever hear that song by Garth Brooks called 'The Dance'?"

"Of course," Ruby answered.

"Well, that's kind of the way I feel about Zoe." She took a few minutes to tell them about the way she had bonded with Alicia. "I could refuse to let myself get close to Zoe and miss the pain when she leaves, but I would have to miss the joy of knowing her. I'm choosing joy," Taryn said as she drove out of the parking area.

Irene sighed loudly. "I was in pain when my three kids all moved away, but I wouldn't have them stick around here and be miserable. I had the joy of being close to them for more than forty years. And now, I have you girls to bring me happiness—even if it is in short spurts. But I agree with Ruby: there's what you kids call *vibes* between you and

Clinton. He's putting down roots, and you've had wings to flit around wherever your heart leads you for the past few years. I worry that you might start something that can't ever be finished. He's a good man, and you're a great woman, but be sure of your feelings for him before you start doing more than casual dating. I don't want to see either of you get hurt."

Ruby laid a hand on Taryn's shoulder. "Whatever you do, just do it without regrets."

Taryn parked in the driveway at her grandmother's house. She wouldn't argue with her grandmother or with Ruby, but she wasn't so sure they—either one—had a thing to worry about. Still, to appease them, she said, "I promise I will think long and hard about taking another step with Clinton, but y'all don't have a thing to worry about. We're just friends who share a love for a little baby."

Chapter Ten

"This whole church looks like it's been sprayed down with Pepto-Bismol," Taryn muttered as she followed along behind Clinton. He affixed silver hangers to the end of each pew, and she hung the pink bows with sprigs of baby's breath on each one.

Jorja had always liked pink and even thought that if she ever got married, she might want her bridesmaids to wear that color. But she changed her mind right then and there.

Anna Rose stood back to look at the floral arrangement on top of the piano, then moved it a couple of inches to the left. "There, that's better. Taryn, you stole that line from an old movie. We watched it with Nana Irene and Ruby when we were teenagers. It's still one of their favorites, and they both tear up every time they see it."

"*Steel Magnolias*," Jorja said as she set flameless candles in crystal wineglasses in each of the windows lining the sides of the sanctuary. "Nana Irene gave me that movie for my graduation present. I wish I was as strong as every one of the characters. I wonder if the bride got the idea for all this pink from that. I'm surprised that they didn't want us to drape the walls with pink satin."

"Shhh." Clinton waved his hand at her. "We've still got a couple of hours before the ceremony, and the bride could decide to bring in bolts of satin for the walls, and maybe even the ceilings, at the last minute." He picked up the baby carrier with Zoe sitting in it and carried it to the front.

"Not my zoo. Not my monkeys," Jorja said. "If they bring in satin, the bride can crawl up on a ladder in her wedding gown and cover the walls herself. We're here to set up the equipment and attach the pew bows."

"Amen," Taryn agreed. "But I can't believe you have gotten so sassy, Jorja Butler!"

Jorja shrugged. "I turned another page in my new-life book." Saying that felt good, but the relief in her heart was even better—bordering on great—than just uttering the words.

"And, Jorja, *Steel Magnolias* came out more than thirty years ago," Anna Rose said. "Unless the bride's mama or grandma saw the show, the idea for all this pink probably didn't come from there."

"Maybe Victoria's Secret," Jorja said, feeling her face heat up. "That company's signature color is pink, isn't it?"

"You *are* moving on," Taryn said. "I didn't think you would even look sideways at one of those stores as you passed by it in the mall."

"I only buy my nail polish from there," Jorja said, trying to nip this conversation in the bud. *What would Clinton think—and in church?* "Mama would have a cardiac arrest if she thought I was buying other things in that place."

"You are supposed to be finding yourself," Anna Rose reminded her. "We'll drive down to Amarillo and go to Westgate Mall. There's a Victoria's Secret there, and we'll do some shopping for the new and improved Jorja Butler."

"In your dreams," Jorja snapped. "*If* I find myself, it won't be in one of those places."

"Where will it be?" Clinton asked and set the carrier down on the altar facing the pulpit.

"I'm not sure because I just started on this journey," Jorja answered. "But I'm not going to change my values. Besides, this business of finding me should begin inside, not with a new, fancy look on the outside."

"You're probably right about that," Clinton agreed as he sat the arch upright and then placed a candelabra on each side of it. "These folks have rented just about everything we have in the storage room. This could be the biggest wedding we will do all summer. Taryn, if you'll watch Zoe, I'll bring in the kneeling bench."

"Will do," Taryn agreed with a nod and took the baby out of the carrier. Zoe laid her head on Taryn's shoulder and cuddled against her chest. "I know you are tired of that thing. Helping set up a wedding isn't fun for you, is it? We'll go sit on the third or fourth pew and tell these folks what looks best."

"That's my job!" Kaitlin Chambers waved from the back of the church and then slowly came down the center aisle, checking each bow along the way. "The bride is my cousin, and I'm her wedding planner, so I'll be deciding where to place everything. To start with, some of the candles in the windows look off-center to me, and I believe that we ordered half-inch ribbons on the stems of the wineglasses. Those look a little narrow to me, but"—she whipped out a metal tape measure from her pink tote bag—"I'll measure them to be sure, and if they aren't right, you can get busy redoing them. And a couple of these bows look a tad bit smaller than the others, so I hope you brought a few more for emergencies."

"Holy . . . ," Taryn whispered under her breath.

"Crap on a cracker," Anna Rose added, finishing the sentence for her cousin and flopping down next to her on the third pew. "This is going to be a long day."

"This is a nightmare," Jorja whispered. The room seemed to fade away for a split second; then she slumped down on a pew and got control of herself.

Taryn quickly made her way over to her cousin and sat down beside her. "We're here. Don't let that woman get under your skin."

Anna Rose joined them and draped an arm around Jorja's shoulders. "The dream might be horrible, but you *will* eventually wake up."

"We'll be done in a couple of hours, and we won't have to come back to tear it all down until tomorrow, after we close up the shop," Taryn assured her. "The preacher is going to be out of town until six o'clock after the wedding, but he said that he would open the church for us when he gets back so we can gather up our equipment."

Clinton brought in the white kneeling bench from the back door and raised a dark eyebrow. "Where do I put this? Is everything all right?"

"I guess things are done according—" Jorja started.

"The boss lady says that we aren't doing things right." Taryn nodded toward Kaitlin, who was busy wielding her tape measure.

"Looks like these ribbons are okay," Kaitlin said with a weighty sigh. "If I'd realized how they would look, I would have ordered wider ones, but they'll"—she gave another sigh—"*have* to do. Some of them aren't dead center, so you'll have to work on that. It's your job to make everything perfect."

Jorja could not believe her attitude.

"How many other weddings around these parts are you helping with this summer?" Clinton asked.

"Five," Kaitlin answered. "But this is the only one booked through the Lucky Shamrock. Jorja, I'll loan you my tape measure. Please see to it that these candles are centered properly. And, Anna Rose, I want you to work on the pew bows. Some of them seem to be leaning just a bit."

Taryn glared at the woman with such heat that Jorja felt a rush of it blow over her like what she got when she opened a hot oven's door.

"I'm quitting my job tomorrow morning," Anna Rose whispered as she stood up.

"Right behind you," Jorja said out of the corner of her mouth. "What about you, Taryn? That look you gave Kaitlin should have fried her right there on the spot."

"Not me," Taryn declared.

"Whoa, wait just a minute," Clinton said, raising his voice. "Kaitlin, you hired us to make the flowers and bring them to the church. You did not pay for extra help. I have the invoice right here with all your orders on ribbon width, colors, and everything else that the bride wanted—so please *back off*. We'll do our jobs and leave you to your tape measure when we get finished. You told me and Irene that *you* were the wedding planner, so anything above and beyond delivering the flowers and set-ting up the equipment is on you."

Kaitlin spun around like a prima donna and popped her hands on her hips. "I will report your attitude to Irene."

Taryn took a few steps forward as Jorja felt her hands ball into fists. Jorja started to step between them but decided that if Taryn slapped the woman, she might just get one good hit in, too.

With her free hand, Taryn pulled her phone from her hip pocket and held it out to Kaitlin. "Here's my phone. She's on the contact list. You are obviously aggravated over the incident in McDonald's and taking it out on us, but we are not your servants. Perhaps it's time you hired an assistant."

"Don't you have any community pride?" Kaitlin's tone had changed from belligerent to whiny in an instant. "I'm not even charging my cousin for my services. It looks like you could help make this day perfect for her without expecting extra pay."

"She's not *my* cousin," Anna Rose said and went to the front of the sanctuary to help Clinton get the bench set in the right place. "If you want to bring your tape measure to the pulpit, you can move these things around without much trouble. The bows all look fantastic to me, and the arrangements that were ordered have been placed in the correct places. The bride's and the twelve bridesmaids' bouquets are on the back pew. All the corsages and boutonnieres are marked and laying in a flat box next to them."

"Kaitlin, darling . . ." Ford came through the door and stopped in his tracks. "I . . . came . . . I thought . . . ," he stammered.

Jorja's hands went clammy. That Ford would show up for chap-el-decorating had never even crossed her mind. She had to conquer the feelings she had every time she was around him. If she didn't, she would never be able to live in Shamrock again.

So you're planning to move back here? the pesky voice in her head asked.

"I'll need your help to make this perfect for Paige," Kaitlin whined, bringing Jorja back to the moment. "They've made a mess of everything. The candles aren't centered, and the pew bows are horrible. I will never do business with the Lucky Shamrock again after this summer."

"It's all beautiful, darlin'," Ford said as he crossed the room and took her in his arms. "Paige is so nervous that she won't even see the imperfections. She sent me to find you because it's time for you to do her makeup. Why don't you just leave this to these folks and come take care of her?"

"I need to check the fellowship hall"—Kaitlin cut her eyes to Taryn—"to see if the centerpieces are right before I go take care of Paige's makeup."

"They will be fine." Her husband shot a dirty look toward Jorja. Then he gently turned Kaitlin around and headed out of the sanctuary.

Jorja's sweaty hands knotted into fists so tightly that her fingernails bit into her palms. She glanced around for something to throw at him—anything would do, but a Bible would be perfect.

Kaitlin stopped in her tracks after a couple of steps and threw the metal tape measure at Jorja. "Do the job right—and those centerpieces in the fellowship hall had better be perfect."

Jorja reached up and caught the thing in midair. "I'll put this on top of the bride's cake for you."

"You wouldn't dare!" Kaitlin yelled.

"Don't test me!" Jorja shouted after her.

"I thought we really might have to call Irene. I'm glad we don't have to work with her on any more weddings," Clinton said with a chuckle after Kaitlin and Ford had disappeared.

"Why's that?" Taryn asked.

"Looked to me like there would have been blood or broken bones if that thing had hit Jorja in the face," he answered. "I was just hoping that y'all wouldn't break any of those wineglass candles during the fight. Y'all saw the contract. It says that it's our responsibility to deliver everything in good shape."

"If this"—Jorja held up the tape measure—"had hit me in the face, I would have snatched that woman bald and gladly paid for whatever I broke out of my own savings. Wrath is a sin, but every time I see either one of them, I can't help but get angry."

"And rightly so," Anna Rose told her.

"You really won't put the tape measure on top of the wedding cake, will you?" Taryn asked.

"No, but she can wonder about it the whole time she's doing Paige's makeup." A wave of satisfaction swept over Jorja for even threatening Kaitlin with such a thing. She had always hated confrontation, but she was finding that in some instances, it felt dang good.

"Okay, then." Taryn held up the invoice with prices and the special notes written out in her grandmother's hand. "The prayer bench is to be set about a foot in front of the altar. I guess that the bride and groom will stand under the arch and then come forward to take their first Communion together and then kneel for their first prayer. Now that y'all have it in place, I believe we are done in here. Let's go check out the fellowship hall and escape before anyone else comes in and tells us that the ribbons and flowers on the arch aren't right."

Jorja laid the tape measure on top of the prayer bench. "Maybe if she sees it here, she will think it's a sign to pray about her ugly attitude."

"Good for you," Anna Rose said. "When you get married, are you going to have a pink wedding?"

"Good Lord, no!" Jorja gasped. "How about you?" Marriage was for other people—women who didn't flinch every time they thought of going to bed with a man.

"If I ever take that step—and that's a real big *if*—I will have a black-and-white wedding. That means my groom will wear black jeans, and I will wear a white dress, but nothing froufrou. We'll get married at the courthouse," Anna Rose answered. "What color will you have?"

"Navy blue and cream," Jorja replied even though she doubted that she would ever have to plan a wedding for herself. "I shouldn't wear white . . ." She paused. "But *if*—and that's a big, enormous *if*—I do want a nice wedding. I will have memories. It won't be anything huge like this, but something with pictures so if I get dementia like my grandma on my daddy's side of the family did, I'll have them."

"Today's etiquette gurus say that it's perfectly okay to wear white even at a fifth or sixth or tenth wedding," Anna Rose told her. "How about you, Taryn? What kind of wedding do you want?"

"I'm having a cruise wedding," Taryn said without hesitation. "Maybe one to Alaska—and you are both invited but only if you can get along for seven days."

"That leaves me out," Anna Rose said.

"Me too," Jorja added.

Clinton picked up the empty baby carrier. "Oh, come on, girls. By the time Taryn gets married, all of you will be best friends, and you'll have a great time on the cruise."

Anna Rose snapped her fingers close to Clinton's face. "Wake up, soldier! You are dreaming."

Jorja could see Taryn having a cruise wedding, but up until they'd all come home to Shamrock, she'd never thought about her cousin asking her or Anna Rose to be in the wedding party.

"You were thinking about that cruise wedding, weren't you, Taryn?" Anna Rose asked. "Did your groom have a face?"

"You'll never know, since you won't be there," Taryn answered. "And neither will Jorja."

Yep, I was right, Jorja thought.

"You can plan it during the school year, and then Jorja can't go anyway," Anna Rose suggested. "My job doesn't tie me down, and I could take all kinds of gorgeous pictures for an Alaska book while we were at sea. Who knows? The cruise line might even hire me as their professional photographer on the trip."

"Y'all left me behind once, and look what happened." Jorja stomped her foot. "I'm going on that cruise with you."

"It's not even real, so why are y'all arguing about it?" Clinton asked and then opened the door into the fellowship hall.

"Because it might be real someday," Jorja answered.

Dark clouds covered the sky, and the first big drops of rain hit the windshield of the van just as Clinton parked behind the shop that evening after they'd left the church. "I heard somewhere that rain on the day of the wedding brought good luck to the marriage," he said.

"If the cotton and watermelon farmers around these parts find out about that, they might be willing to finance a wedding once a week," Taryn said as she slid the side door of the van open. The idea of a cruise wedding had stuck in her head. She'd only been joking at the time, but after thinking about it, the idea didn't seem so far-fetched. A vision of Clinton waiting at the front of a ship's small chapel popped into her head. In her scenario, he wore a white shirt and khaki shorts, and she had chosen a simple white cotton dress. White baby rosebuds were tucked into her hair, and they were both barefoot.

The vision vanished when Zoe reached out her little arms for Taryn to take her out of the car seat.

Anna Rose looked up at the dark clouds. "Looks like we've got a toad strangler on the way."

Clinton got out of the van and reached to take the baby from Taryn. "Yep, and Zoe and I are going to run between the raindrops and go right upstairs. We'll see y'all in the morning."

Jorja and Anna Rose had already made a beeline for the trailer without even looking back, but Taryn sat down in the rocking chair on the porch and watched Clinton until he and the baby were safe in his apartment. His limp seemed a little worse that night—but then, there had been a lot of lifting and walking involved in setting up the church for the wedding. Her legs and feet felt like they could use a massage or, at the very least, a long soaking bath in a nice claw-foot tub. Neither of which was going to happen that evening. The tub in the trailer's bathroom was so shallow that when she sank down into it, her boobs still floated like two balloons, and the nearest place for a good massage was probably in Amarillo.

A streak of lightning lit up the sky in a long zigzag show, and thunder followed soon after. Then the rain got serious, falling in sheets so thick that she could barely even see a flicker of the light shining through Clinton's apartment window.

Anna Rose brought out a kitchen chair and sat down on it, and together, they watched the rain for a while. "I love the smell of rain after a hot day."

"Me too, and I don't even mind the storm. Like that song that Miranda Lambert sings," Taryn said.

"That would be 'Storms Never Last.' I like the line that talks about bad times passing with the wind. Too bad that can't be our story. This wind could carry away the bad times that we've all three had to experience, especially the ones that Jorja went through."

The porch light came on so suddenly that Taryn closed her eyes and shivered. A memory of that last evening when she switched off the porch light behind Mitchell as he left her apartment.

"I'm facing my fears," Jorja said as she dragged a chair out onto the porch, "and I was thinking of an old country song . . ."

"Was it 'Storms Never Last'?" Taryn asked. "Anna Rose and I were talking about that one as we watched this storm."

"No, it was 'Hard Rain Don't Last.' It talks about holding on until morning," Jorja answered. "It's an old song, too, but I've kind of leaned on the lyrics for the past ten years."

"Don't stand there as stiff as a board and ready to run when it thunders again," Taryn fussed at her cousin. "Face your fear of the storm. No one is going to hurt you when me and Anna Rose are close by. Have a seat and join us."

Jorja did what Taryn suggested without argument, but she sat on the edge of the chair with her back as straight as a rod. "Thank you for that."

Anna Rose reached over and patted Jorja on the shoulder. "We may fight and argue amongst ourselves, but Lord help anyone who tries to come between us."

"You don't know how tough this is for me, even with y'all here with me," Jorja whispered. "What I want to do is hide in my bedroom with the blinds pulled down and listen to music with my earbuds."

"Breathe in. Breathe out. Enjoy the sweet smell of rain and think about how it's making everything all clean and pretty. You can even try to imagine it washing all the past away and leaving nothing but pure joy in its wake," Anna Rose said.

"I'm trying, but . . . ," Jorja muttered.

"Getting past those feelings takes time," Taryn told her.

"Kind of like baby steps. You take a step and fall on your butt, but you get up and take another one anyway," Anna Rose assured her.

"How do you two know?" Jorja asked.

"Long story," Anna Rose answered. "But I went to a lot of meetings for abuse before I could move past it, and sometimes even yet, when those feelings of helplessness come back, I go to a meeting."

"Someone abused you?" Jorja gasped.

"Yep," Anna Rose answered. "I started dating a fellow photographer about five years ago, and at first, he was wonderful to me. It was an amazing time—he was the most romantic guy I'd ever met. I didn't even notice how we slowly stopped seeing my friends and then my parents and even Nana Irene over the next year. Then, one evening, he wanted to go out to dinner, and I wanted to stay home and work on my photographs. We argued, and he hit me more than once. I fought with him and finally got my hands on a butcher knife I'd been using to cut carrots and held him off."

"You didn't use the knife on him?" Taryn couldn't picture her sassy cousin letting any man control her.

"No, but I called the police," Anna Rose answered. "They stayed on the property while I got my things together and left. I didn't file charges, because I'd told myself—just like you did, Jorja—that I deserved what I got." She stopped for a breath and then went on. "I told myself that I had brought the whole thing on myself by letting him manipulate me. He texted me the next day with all kinds of apologies and begged me to come back to him."

"Did you even think about going back to him?" Jorja asked.

"Nope," Anna Rose answered. "But it took me a while to rebuild my self-confidence. Good God! I had let someone else determine what I would take pictures of and slowly tear me down until I thought I was worthless as a woman and as a photographer. That's where the meetings came into play. They helped me so much. I figured out that there were other people just like me and that, together, it was possible for me to regain what I'd had lost. People often consider abuse to be something like what you went through with Ford, but there's also mental abuse from manipulation, with or without being hit, or what Taryn went through when she found out she had fallen in love with a married man. It all falls under the same category of abuse."

"Did you tell Nana Irene?" Taryn asked.

"Did you tell her about your married man?" Anna Rose shot back at her.

"I did not," Taryn answered. "Other than y'all, I've never told anyone."

"Do you trust yourself to get into another relationship?" Anna Rose asked.

"Nope. Do you?" Taryn fired right back.

"Not yet," Anna Rose answered. "Maybe not ever."

"Looks like all of us have trust issues," Jorja said, "and justly so. But y'all handle yours so much better than I do."

"We talked about our issues to someone instead of burying them inside our hearts and letting them fester." Taryn hoped that what she and Anna Rose had told Jorja wasn't too much for her new fragile self to endure. "Anna Rose went to meetings. I just cried and cussed. We've all felt pretty stupid about the choices we made, but we don't have to let those mistakes define us, do we?"

"I'm not going to," Anna Rose declared.

"But you still flirt and date and have one-night stands." Jorja covered her ears when another clap of thunder rattled the windows. "I can't even think about holding hands with a guy."

"Again, I got help and you haven't until now," Anna Rose scolded. "I'm way on down the road after my heartbreak, and so is Taryn. We have trust issues, but we started working on our problems right after the troubles started. You turned to religion when a lot of girls who experienced what you did would have drunk more, partied more, and probably self-medicated—anything to take away the pain and guilt of what happened."

"I wanted Jesus to forgive me for the choice I made to go to that party," Jorja whispered. "I never even thought about drinking or doing drugs."

"It's a wonder you didn't end up in a toxic relationship or friendship," Taryn said.

"Did you?" Jorja asked.

"Almost, but then I woke up pretty quick and figured out that I didn't need toxic people in my life," Taryn answered.

"And you both travel a lot to keep from putting down roots where you might find someone and get hurt again, right?" Jorja asked.

"Now who's the therapist?" Anna Rose answered. "I never thought that my traveling to take pictures was a part of the healing process, but I guess it is."

"Too bad no one has made a one-time pill to cure trust issues," Taryn said and wished there were such a medication. She would pop it into her mouth without even reading the long list of side effects on the paper from the pharmacist.

Chapter Eleven

aryn had just said whatever had popped into her mind when she told Clinton and her cousins that she was having a wedding on a cruise ship, but when she walked into the sanctuary that Friday evening, she found new determination never to have a big church ceremony. Even the preacher, Brother James, sighed when he saw the mess that had been left behind.

"Kaitlin said that you folks are supposed to clean this up?" he asked.

"No, sir," Clinton answered. "We were hired to bring the flowers, set up the equipment, and then come back and take the rented items back to the shop. We have a copy of the invoice if you need to see it or make a copy to show her."

"The arch, the candelabras, and the prayer bench are the only things that we need to take back," Taryn told him. "What happened in here?"

Several of the wineglass candles had been broken, and the glass was scattered all over the floor and the windowsills. Silk rose petals hadn't just been left lying down the center aisle—it looked like they'd been shot out of a bazooka and landed all over the sanctuary. The bride's veil was draped over the top of the piano. Then there were the candy wrappers and punch cups tossed about on almost every pew.

"Everything was pretty normal until I introduced them as a married couple, and then some kind of wild music started. The bride threw off her veil and it landed on the piano. The new couple started dancing up the aisle"—Brother James took a deep breath and let it out in a loud whoosh—"like two chickens with their heads cut off, and rose petals began floating like they were raining from the rafters. I've never seen anything like it, and I've been performing weddings for forty years. The fellowship hall was full, so I suspect the reception spilled over back into the sanctuary after I left. You can see what happened. Had I known this kind of riot would break out in the church, I wouldn't have scheduled a meeting with the Ministerial Alliance on the same evening as the wedding."

"Since Kaitlin was the wedding coordinator, you'll need to call her about the mess," Jorja said.

"I will do that right now. Kaitlin has more weddings that she's planning to help with, but I can guarantee you that she and I are going to have a talk about this mess. Usually, the church is pristine the morning after a wedding, even if the friends and family have to stay until dawn to get it cleaned up," Brother James said. "Your things are sitting in the foyer. I was shocked when I unlocked the door. Do you have anything in the fellowship hall? I'm almost afraid to even go in there."

"We have a cake server and matching knife that was rented," Anna Rose answered, and headed that way. Her gasp when she opened the door could have been heard halfway back to the flower shop.

Taryn peeked over her shoulder and couldn't believe that Kaitlin expected them to clean up. At least a third of the bride's cake and a little less of the groom's cake had been left behind. Cake was smeared in several places on the floor, and a few flies floated in the leftover punch.

"The bride and groom were very young," the preacher said. "Young folks tend to be a little rowdier than the more mature couples. I guess we need to form a committee to make some rules about what should and should not be done at weddings. If I have to hire a professional crew to clean the punch stains off the pew cushions, Kaitlin will be paying the fees."

Taryn stepped around the nasty mess on the floor and retrieved the knife and server from the bride's table, then made her way back. "Maybe you should think about making them put up a healthy deposit that's returnable if the church and fellowship hall are left spotless. We ask for a deposit on each of our rental pieces—and after seeing this, we'll check them out carefully."

"That's probably a good idea." The preacher nodded as he rubbed a hand over his brow.

Clinton had already loaded the items that needed to go back to the shop into the van when Taryn and Anna Rose came out with the two things that they had recovered from the fellowship hall. "I've been working for the flower shop for the better part of a year, and I've never seen a mess like this or dealt with someone like Kaitlin. I took pictures of the sanctuary with my phone and sent them to Irene."

"I did the same in the fellowship hall," Anna Rose said as she and Jorja slid into the wide bench back seat of the van.

"I feel like they should hire someone to perform exorcism rites. A wedding is supposed to be a beautiful, serious exchanging of vows, not a melee that wrecks a church," Jorja said. "It's going to take hours to clean the cake icing from the arch, and the prayer bench will have to be reupholstered. No amount of scrubbing will clean the chocolate icing off the white velvet. If they wanted to have a wild and wicked wedding, they should have rented a bar, not had it in the church. Good Lord!" She threw up her hands in disgust. "I'm glad Zoe is too young to remember seeing such a thing, but I can't unsee it."

"And to think, Kaitlin assumed we would clean it up," Clinton said as he started the engine and drove away. "I'm sure glad we don't have to work with her anymore."

Taryn slipped her phone from her hip pocket when it pinged. "Hello, Nana Irene."

"I've seen the pictures, and Kaitlin will not get back a dime of her deposit. Replacing that prayer bench alone will cost more than she put up for damages." Irene's voice got louder with each word. "I've been in this business for decades, and I've never seen such a sight."

"Yes, ma'am," Taryn said. "We were thinking the exact same thing."

"Y'all get another bench ordered for the next wedding. From here on out, the security deposit will be the replacement price of whatever piece of equipment anyone is renting." Irene's voice had settled back to normal. "If she wants to book anything else with us, don't tell her no—tell her *hell* no."

"We can do that," Taryn said with a smile. "I'll even let the new and improved Jorja do it so that she can use a swear word."

"We've got to talk when y'all get here tomorrow," Irene told her. "There's something going on between you three, and I don't know whether to be worried or celebrate—but for now, I've got supper on the stove. Bye, now."

"Bye," Taryn said and ended the call.

"What am I using a swear word about?" Jorja asked.

Taryn explained what Irene had said. "So, no more working with Kaitlin on anything. Her deposit won't cover the damages."

"I'll gladly use a swear word to not have to deal with her again," Jorja declared as Clinton made the turn into the parking lot at the back of the shop.

Anna Rose pointed toward Kaitlin, who was standing beside her car and glaring at them. "Maybe you better whisper a few bad words for practice because it looks like you're going to have to find some of those words sooner than later."

"Maybe you better pray before we get out of the van," Taryn teased Jorja.

"It's better to ask for forgiveness than permission in a case like this," Clinton said.

Taryn nodded. "Forget what I told you. Do what Clinton said."

The expression on Kaitlin's face reminded Taryn of something her grandmother used to tell them when they were all little girls: "If you don't get that look off your face, it's going to freeze like that, and you'll be sorry every time you look in the mirror."

Clinton parked and got out of the van; then he slid the side panel door open. Jorja and Anna Rose climbed out at the same time Taryn slid out of the passenger seat. She unhooked all the straps and then picked the baby up, leaving the carrier in the van.

"The shop is closed right now, so whatever you've got to say will have to wait until business hours," Taryn said.

"I'm here for Paige's deposit," Kaitlin said. "Our preacher called me a few minutes ago and said that you all refused to clean up. I paid enough for the rentals and the flowers that I figured that job was included when you picked up the arch and those things."

"You figured wrong," Jorja told her. "Did you even read the invoice that you signed?"

Anna Rose took a couple of steps forward. "I would be ashamed to leave a church in the mess that you did. That poor preacher was trying to pick up trash and clean up, and that's not his job. That will not look good on you since you're the wedding coordinator."

"I'll hire someone to clean it up first thing tomorrow morning," Kaitlin hissed.

"Girl, have you no business sense at all?" Jorja asked. "Whoever you hire is going to gossip about what an unholy mess you left behind, and no one is going to want you to do their events. If you go in there right now and work until daylight, you might be able to salvage your reputation as a planner. Just a word of advice: you better rent a steam cleaner because all those red punch stains on the pew cushions are going to be tough to get out."

Kaitlin opened her mouth, but Anna Rose threw up a palm. "Plus, I can't even imagine how many pictures are already on Instagram and videos that are probably all over social media by now that show what a mess was made. You are skating on thin ice."

"Just give me the deposit, and the rest is none of your business," Kaitlin practically growled.

"You don't get that deposit back," Taryn said. "The prayer bench alone is ruined."

Clinton opened the rear door of the van and set the bench out on the driveway. "Look at it. That chocolate stain will never come out of white velvet. We will have to replace this, and it will cost more than your deposit."

"I'll take you to small-claims court," Kaitlin threatened.

"We have before and after pictures of every piece you rented," Jorja told her, "so that might not be a good idea."

Taryn was glad Clinton was there, and she could have hugged Jorja. Her sweet little cousin had grown a backbone!

Kaitlin's eyes narrowed into slits. "I meant it when I told you I would never do business with you again."

"Even if you wanted to, our answer wouldn't be no but *hell no*," Jorja said. "We don't need this kind of stress from anyone—but I do have one question: What on earth made you think you were hiring us to be bossed around or to clean up your mess?"

Without even bothering to answer, Kaitlin got into her car and spun out with such force that she threw gravel all over the van and the trailer. Taryn whipped around and covered Zoe's face and body with her own. The small rocks stung when they hit her back, but that was better than them hitting the baby in the face.

Before the gray dust had even settled, Clinton was beside Taryn. "Are you all right? Did any of that hurt either of you?"

"We're fine. I just got a couple of little pings on my back, but it wasn't even as bad as a mosquito bite," Taryn assured him.

"Who would have thought that the flower business could be as bad as war?" he asked and then turned around to the other two women. "Are either of you hurt?"

"Nothing that a good cold beer won't fix," Anna Rose said. "Let's put this stuff in the storage room and go inside the trailer for a cold one. After this, I'm buying pizza for supper and having it delivered."

"Sounds good to me," Jorja said, "and I didn't even flinch when I told her hell no! Not only that, but I thought I heard applause in heaven."

"You probably did." Clinton opened the door to the shop. "Y'all go on in the trailer while I just set all of this stuff inside until tomorrow morning. We'll see what all we have to do to clean it up then."

"You won't get an argument out of me and Zoe," Taryn said. "It's hot out here, and this baby is sweating. I'm going to lay a quilt out on the floor for her so she can stretch out and get cool."

"Thanks," Clinton whispered.

"For what?" Taryn raised an eyebrow.

"For protecting her," he answered. "Like a mother."

"Instinct," Taryn said with a smile. "But let it be known I could do bodily harm to Kaitlin without regret for her not thinking about anyone—people or babies—being close by when she peeled out like that."

"I'm really, really glad we won't have to deal with her anymore," Clinton said and then picked up the bench and disappeared into the shop.

"Me too," Taryn agreed as she turned around and headed to the trailer behind her two cousins.

You sure made me feel special when you rushed over and checked on me and the baby, she thought.

Taryn was somewhere between asleep and awake when she heard a gentle knock on her bedroom door and then the old familiar squeak as it opened. The nightlight in the hallway reflected from the mirror above her dresser right into her eyes. She sat straight up in bed and threw off her covers.

"What's wrong? Is it Nana Irene?" she asked.

"No, nothing is wrong, except I can't sleep," Jorja said. "What happened with Kaitlin earlier this evening keeps playing through my mind like it's on a continuous loop."

Taryn patted the bed, and Jorja stretched out beside her.

"I've been living in fear and even denial for years. I thought if I didn't think about it that, pretty soon, it would all go away, like a forgotten dream, but now I'm angry," Jorja said.

"What's going on in here?" Anna Rose peeked into the room. "Are y'all having a slumber party without me?"

"Demons are keeping Jorja awake," Taryn said. "And she's finally getting angry. Isn't that a sign of healing?"

"Yes, it is. There are steps to grieving, and getting a good mad on is one of them, but I've got just the solution," Anna Rose said. "Meet me outside in five minutes."

"It's midnight," Jorja said.

"That just means you don't have to get dressed, because nobody is going to see us," Anna Rose told them.

"I'm not going to get drunk," Jorja declared.

"You might bring a bottle of water, but that's all you'll be drinking tonight," Anna Rose said. "Enough talk. Come on outside, and I guarantee you will be so tired after spending an hour in therapy with me that you won't have a bit of trouble sleeping."

Taryn pushed back the covers and got out of bed. "Do I need shoes?"

"Yes, but not flip-flops. Your work shoes will do fine," Anna Rose answered and then disappeared.

Taryn pulled on a pair of mismatched socks and her athletic shoes. "I wonder what she's got up her sleeve."

Jorja hopped up off the bed and headed out of the room. "I don't know, but I'll try about anything right now. I've figured out why wrath is a sin: it eats into a heart like a cancer. I need to get rid of these horrible feelings, but I don't know where to start."

"I think the last step is acceptance, so just know that you are working toward that," Taryn told her when she stepped outside.

"Have you made it past that step?" Jorja asked.

"Nope, not yet," Taryn answered honestly and glanced up at Clinton's apartment. She was glad that everything was dark up there;

the trailer's porch light would have shone right through her faded nightshirt, which barely came to her knees, and revealed the fact that she was not wearing a bra.

"Come on over here," Anna Rose said from the shadows.

Taryn crossed her arms over her breasts—just in case Clinton was looking out a window—and hurried out into the yard to find that Anna Rose had set up half a dozen flameless candles around the big oak tree at the end of the trailer.

"Where did those come from?" Jorja tugged at the bottom of her Minnie Mouse T-shirt. "We're not going to dance around that tree, are we? I may be trying to find myself and get past all this anger, but I'm not doing some weird dance."

"I keep them in my tote bag for occasions like this," Anna Rose said. "And trust me, this is something I learned in my therapy sessions, and we all need it. I've marked off a line here in the gravel. We have to stand behind it. I brought my tote bag full of things to throw. The lights are so we can get a better visual of the tree trunk."

"Why would we do that?" Jorja asked.

"When you are depressed or angry—but mostly when you're really mad, like you are tonight—your entire body tenses up," Anna Rose explained. "Those emotions affect your thinking, your muscles, and most of all, your heart and blood pressure. You can't sleep—which is what you and I've both proved tonight, Jorja. Lack of rest just makes everything even worse the next day. You need to work it out; throwing things helps. So we are going to stand behind this line and work out our tensions on that tree."

"Sounds insane to me," Jorja muttered.

Anna Rose dumped the contents of her tote bag onto the ground. "It did to me at first, too, but when I get all worked up, I get out the tote bag and I throw until the anger is gone. It might take ten minutes or an hour—but until I get all the tension out of my body, I keep at it."

Taryn frowned. "Those things look like dog toys."

"Yep." Anna Rose nodded. "These kinds work best because they don't bounce around. After we throw them all, we'll take turns gathering them up, and we'll do it again and again, until we are tired." She picked up a stuffed frog, wound up like a professional softball player, and sent it flying through the air. It hit the tree with a loud thump and fell to the ground.

Jorja chose a plastic bone and did the same thing, but it fell short of the tree.

"Come on, girl," Anna Rose said. "That was a baby throw if I ever saw one. Pretend that tree is Ford Chambers and you are throwing a stick of dynamite at him."

Taryn chose a stuffed octopus, held it by a long tenacle, and hit the tree with force. "Damn, that felt good," she said.

Jorja jogged over to the place where the bone had fallen and brought it back to the line. "Forget about his face and dynamite. This is me throwing his penis at the tree and smashing it so bad that he can't ever do what he did to me to another woman."

"I can't believe you said that word out loud," Anna Rose said with a giggle. "But now you're getting the idea. We're going to do this until our bodies say that we've worked out our anger toward the men who've caused us pain—and toward Kaitlin, for expecting us to be her servants."

"Enough talk," Taryn whispered, "more throwing."

Thirty minutes later, Taryn's arms were throbbing, but it was a good ache. Anna Rose had been right about the therapeutic value of giving the body a workout when a person was angry—whether it had been building for years and years or the moment had just happened in the past couple of days.

"Feel better?" Taryn asked.

"Not yet," Jorja answered as she gathered up the toys and came back to the starting line. "Y'all can go on in if you're done, but I've got some more frustrations to work out."

"Nope." Anna Rose sat down on the gravel and leaned her back against the van. "We're staying until we all three feel better."

Taryn sat down beside her and used the hem of her nightshirt to wipe sweat from her face. "Kind of like the rule in the military: no man left behind."

"That's it," Anna Rose said. "We might not agree on a blessed thing, but when it comes to our group therapy, we don't leave anyone out in the dark alone. So, Jorja, darlin', you keep pitching. That tree doesn't mind a bit."

Jorja didn't answer but picked up a toy in each hand. A good strong south wind kept the first one from hitting the tree, but the second one made a sound like the old oak had got the breath knocked plumb out of it. "I like this therapy. It's better than just talking and talking, and I feel my body letting go of the anger. How often should I do this?"

"As often as you need to. The toys are always in my closet. Come and get them anytime. They've taken lots of beatings," Anna Rose answered.

"I'm not so sure about that poor old tree, though," Taryn whispered. "It probably wishes that we were little kids again and fighting over the old tire swing that used to hang on the lower limb. What else did you learn in therapy?"

Anna Rose held up one finger. "Walking and breathing in fresh air clears your head and keeps you from having a stroke." A second finger shot up. "That talking can get anger out of the heart before it festers. There's no pills on the market that will cure what we've all been through—especially you, Jorja." The third finger came up slowly. "You gotta exercise—as in, batting practice or throwing toys at trees." And the fourth one even slower. "Teaching yourself to trust. I haven't come close to getting that one down yet."

"I'm not sure I could even begin to learn that last one," Taryn said. "How does a person teach themselves to trust?"

"I'm told that finding someone who is totally trustworthy and allowing yourself to trust your own judgment is the first baby step," Anna Rose answered. "I'm not so sure I'll ever get that far, but I still have hope."

Jorja gathered up the toys, put them back in the tote bag, and sat down beside Taryn. "Even after all these years, you still hold out hope? I gave that up a long time ago."

Taryn patted her on the knee. "Never give up hope. That's what keeps your heart strong."

Jorja leaned her head on Taryn's shoulder. "You and Anna Rose hope for me. I'm too tired to even think about trusting anyone right now."

"But the therapy worked, didn't it?" Taryn asked.

"Oh, yeah, it did. I just want a quick, cool shower and my bed," Jorja answered.

Anna Rose got to her feet and picked up the tote bag. "Just call me Dr. Duquette. My door is always open for patients if they're kin to me, but I'm getting the first cool shower. Don't fall asleep before you get in there, because you both stink. And please turn off the candles before you come inside."

"Will do," Taryn said and stood up.

Jorja followed her lead. "I'll help take care of them. Let's put them on the porch. That way if it rains, they won't be ruined."

"Good idea," Taryn said and glanced up at Clinton's apartment again. The curtain in the living room fluttered just a little, and she wondered if he *had* been watching them.

Chapter Twelve

*W*hat did that tree do to upset y'all last night?" Clinton asked the next morning when he arrived at the shop with Zoe in tow.

Anna Rose covered a yawn with her hand. "It's therapy—less expensive than a bottle of whiskey and a lot less strain on the body the next morning."

"Speak for yourself," Jorja muttered. "My arms and back are sore this morning."

"But you slept well, didn't you?" Anna Rose asked.

"Yes, but don't expect me to drink whiskey tonight," Jorja smarted off.

Anna Rose scowled at Jorja. "Oh, honey, I've got a bottle of Jameson in my room. I thought we'd play a game of shots with cards instead of a pool table. Then, tomorrow morning, we'll compare notes and see which one helps you sleep better."

"Oh, hush," Jorja hissed. "I'm not drinking with y'all. Tonight, I'll still be so tired that I won't even need to throw things at a tree, and I sure won't need to get drunk."

"You are welcome," Anna Rose said with a fake smile.

"For what?" Jorja shot back at her.

"For helping you sleep like a baby," Anna Rose told her.

"Speaking of a baby . . ." Taryn slid off her stool and reached for Zoe when Clinton had taken her out of the carrier. The fresh smell of baby lotion caused her biological clock to tick loud enough that she didn't even care that her cousins were arguing—again. "Good morning, precious darlin'. We need to tell your interim papa that the law doesn't say you have to carry a baby in a bucket all the time."

"Yes, he knows the law very well concerning babies, car seats, and all that," Clinton answered, "but this interim papa is afraid that he might stumble with her when he's coming down the steps. And if that happened, he could set her down on a step in the bucket and be less likely to hurt her when he fell."

A visual of Clinton stumbling and falling to the bottom of the steep stairs leading up to his apartment popped into Taryn's head and caused her to shiver. She hugged Zoe closer to her body and tried her best to get the image out of her mind. "Then carrier it is," she finally said. "We don't want you or this precious baby to get hurt."

"So, I'm not precious?" Clinton teased. "I can fall down the steps and it's okay?"

Or is he flirting? Taryn wondered.

"Of course you are precious," Jorja answered. "We'd be lost in this shop without you."

"Thank you for that," Clinton said as he took his place on his bar-stool and slid a roll of bright yellow ribbon over to his side of the table. "And speaking of being in the shop, I'm probably going to be out on Thursday because I've got back-to-back appointments with vets coming. If they all show up, I'll be gone most of the day."

"We better cross our fingers we don't have a funeral that day," Taryn moaned. "Because the wedding on Friday night is all fresh flowers, and we can't start making the arrangements until Thursday, or they won't hold up."

"I'll be here on Friday to help with the finishing touches," Clinton told them. "Thank goodness it's not a huge wedding like we did last week. Only one bridesmaid and groomsman, and it's an outside cere-mony. We'll need the bow hangers for folding chairs—not pews—and they have their own arch."

Taryn didn't want to talk about yellow pew bows, but she would have liked to visit with Clinton as one adult with another and see about these "vibes" she was sensing between them. She was sitting close enough to him that she could almost hear sparks sizzling, but he was acting so cool that she doubted if he even realized that there was chemistry between them.

Jorja rolled her eyes toward the ceiling. "Thank you, Jesus."

For a split second, Taryn thought that Jorja was giving thanks for the fact that Clinton didn't share all the chemistry that she felt. Then she realized that her cousin was grateful that this wedding wouldn't be like the Kaitlin Chambers fiasco.

"So, no prayer bench or candles?" Anna Rose asked.

"Just pew bows with three small daisies on each one, bouquets, and corsages and boutonnieres," Clinton answered. "Boston ferns will sit on pedestals on each side of the arch. If you want to look at it, the order is filed under 'Weddings.'"

Taryn slid off the barstool, riffled through the top drawer of the file cabinet over in the corner, and brought out the order. "Thirty pew bows; the bride's bouquet made from yellow daisies, roses, and white gladioli; and one bridesmaid is supposed to carry a nosegay of daisies and glads. Boutonnieres are to be one small yellow daisy with white ribbons. That really is a simple wedding, provided no evil wedding planner shows up."

"Compared to that awful issue at the church, it's going to be easy," Jorja said.

"Unless it rains," Anna Rose added. "What's their plan if it rains?"

"The backup plan is that it goes inside the three-car garage owned by the bride's folks," Clinton said. "Barring bad weather, the ceremony will be in her folks' backyard at the same address."

"Smart people." Taryn finished a bow and laid it to the side. "Keep it simple."

"The bride's name is Angela. She and her mother came in to make the arrangements," Clinton said. "Angela told Irene and Ruby that her mother gave her a choice: she could have a huge wedding or a down payment on a home. She took the latter."

"Even smarter bride," Anna Rose said with a nod. "I'd turn down a big wedding if my folks offered to buy me a washer and dryer—but a down payment would seal the deal for sure."

Taryn didn't want a big wedding, she admitted to herself—not really even on a cruise, like she had teased about. What she wanted was a marriage with a man she loved and a family. Her eyes shifted from the yellow ribbon she was wrapping into a bow over to Zoe. *Maybe just a sweet baby girl like that one would be a good start,* she thought.

Clinton nudged Taryn. "What would it take for you to turn down a big wedding?"

"A dollar bill," she said without hesitation.

"What?" Jorja asked.

"I'm saying that I'm not interested in an event. The long engagement, the planning, and all that isn't on my bucket list. I just want a marriage and a family." Out of the corner of her eye, she could see that Clinton was nodding.

That morning was so slow that they got all the pew bows made. Clinton suggested that they deliver the two orders they had gotten that morning on the way to Irene's for lunch.

"We can all go in my SUV," Taryn said as she locked up the shop.

Jorja shook her head. "I'm not sitting in that third seat. I'd feel like I was folding my legs up in a shoebox."

Clinton knew exactly how she felt. Someday, when he had a van for his business, he would offer to drive them in it so everyone would be comfortable. Later, when the nonprofit corporation was in full swing, he would buy a second one and then *borrow* it for times when the whole family needed to use it.

"You can go with me in my truck," Anna Rose offered. "Clinton and Zoe can ride with Taryn. You know they'll stay longer than we will, anyway. Nana Irene and Ruby both dote on the baby and will beg them to stick around for a while. I want to come home and get a nap before I go out tonight."

Jorja nodded and yawned at the same time. "I'm not going out this evening, but I could use a nap, so that sounds like a great idea."

At the mention of a nap, Clinton felt a yawn coming on, too, but he kept it at bay. Zoe slept fairly well at night these days, but she always woke up at least once. Being even a temporary father was a tough job, but he still loved every minute of it. He hoped Rebecca would feel a deeper sense of motherhood after she got some help at the center. She had said that she didn't think being there was going to work when he'd talked to her the last time. She hadn't mentioned missing Zoe, and that concerned Clinton.

"Will Anna Rose's truck be in good shape when y'all get there?" Taryn teased. "Do you both need to sign a contract not to get into a hair-pulling fight on the way?"

"I'll say a prayer before we leave," Jorja countered.

"And I'll have a shot of whiskey," Anna Rose added.

"Sounds about right," Clinton muttered as he loaded up the two deliveries in the back of Taryn's SUV.

Jorja waved from the trailer porch. "See you there."

The times that Clinton had had a chance to be alone with Taryn had been few, and now he couldn't think of a single thing to say to her. He'd only known her two weeks, but it seemed like a lot longer since they had been spending most of every waking hour together—most of the time with other folks around, though. Down deep in his heart, he knew that she was a good woman . . . but good Lord, a couple of weeks wasn't enough to really get to know anyone—was it? With that in mind, he could not possibly tell her that he had a huge attraction to her or ask her if she felt the same. What if he made the same mistake his grandfather and dad had when it came to women? Or what if she wasn't ready to put down roots? That would sure make things awkward between them.

He strapped Zoe's car seat and carrier into the back seat of the SUV, and then Taryn tossed him the keys. "You can drive, and I'll take the two deliveries up to the door," she said.

Clinton smiled as he got in behind the steering wheel. "I'm not going to argue."

"Have you heard from Rebecca in the last couple of days?" Taryn asked as she fastened her seat belt.

"She called last night," Clinton answered and started the engine, "and she's not doing well. I wouldn't be surprised if the doctors want her to stay more than six weeks. She never had anyone that loved her except for Larry, and she's so fragile right now. I'm not sure she'll be in any shape to take Zoe back for a while."

"That's sad," Taryn said with a long sigh. "Zoe won't even know her mother when she comes back for her if it takes months instead of weeks."

"She will; I'm not too worried about that. But I've got to admit that I'll sure miss our little girl when Rebecca is better. I'd like for Rebecca to stick around these parts, maybe even work part-time at the flower shop until she's completely well. You all will be gone by the end of summer, so there'll be an empty trailer that she could live in," Clinton said.

"Or she could live in the apartment, and you could take the trailer since you are outgrowing the place with all your veterans' business," Taryn suggested.

That sounded like a great idea, but he was thinking about a bigger building—maybe on Main Street—not a trailer behind a flower shop. The people who worked at the VA offices in the area were already sending him more and more vets who needed help.

"That's an even better idea." Clinton shook the thought off and started his drive toward the first delivery place. "Are any of you sticking around to help Irene when she gets her new knees this fall?" That could make a difference.

"I might," Taryn answered without much hesitation, "but I imagine that I'll stay with her in her house, not live in the trailer. I can't answer for my cousins. Even though they are getting better with each other, they've got a long way to go."

"Have you ever thought that maybe their bickering is the way they show affection to each other?" Clinton asked.

"If that's right, then I feel sorry for their husbands, if they ever do get married," Taryn said with a sigh. "I wouldn't want to spend every day for the rest of my life with someone who thought arguing was showing love."

"Me either, but I've known couples like that," he said. "One of my friends in the military and his wife were constantly bickering. He said it made the sex hotter." He pulled up into the driveway of a brick home and felt heat rising from his neck to his face. Was it too soon to use the *S* word so casually in front of her? Sure, she'd been in the service and heard worse, but it seemed disrespectful. He cleared his throat and said, "First stop. The vase with all the red roses goes in here."

Taryn got out of the vehicle, opened the back hatch, and picked up the arrangement. She carried it across the yard to the porch and rang the bell. When Diana Marlow opened the door, Taryn tried to say that she had a delivery for Polly Granberg, but words wouldn't form.

"Oh, how lovely." Diana clapped her hands. "Clinton has sent me roses. I'm so excited that I could just cry."

Taryn had forgotten that Polly was Diana's grandmother. "No, they're from—"

"It doesn't matter." Diana beamed. "I'm always glad to get flowers from anyone."

"They're for Polly," Taryn said. "I'm sorry. I should have told you that when you opened the door."

Diana's happiness turned into a mixed expression of anger and disappointment; then she laughed out loud. "It doesn't matter. Nettie Jones is watering her lawn across the street. She sees that you handed flowers to me, so she's going to think they're from Clinton. That puts me one over on Elaine and Mallory—so thank you, Taryn." She took the flowers with another chuckle and closed the door.

Taryn noticed that Nettie Jones *was* already talking on her phone when she left the porch. "You are not going to believe this," she said as she got back into the SUV. "Diana answered the door and is going to let people think that *you* gave *her* the flowers."

"But they were from a lady in Kentucky who said she was Polly's cousin, and the flowers were for her birthday." Clinton groaned. "I was hoping that this stupid contest had died out. None of those women have been around in a few days."

"Evidently, it's not over yet, and there doesn't seem to be an end in sight," Taryn said. "The next one goes to a teenager a couple of doors down from Nana Irene's house. They're from her boyfriend for her sixteenth birthday."

Clinton backed out of the driveway, rolled down the window, and pulled up to the curb across the street. "Good afternoon, Nettie. Your roses are beautiful. I believe your roses are even prettier than the ones we just delivered to Polly."

Nettie dropped her phone into the pocket of her apron. "Oh, I thought they were for Diana since she seemed to be so happy. She says that she's going to marry you by Christmas."

"Maybe Christmas in fifty years, if I have lost my mind," Clinton teased.

Nettie covered her giggles with the back of her hand. "In my day, girls didn't chase boys. It was the other way around."

"I wish it was still that way," Clinton told her. "You have a nice day, now."

Nettie laid the garden hose on the ground beside the rosebushes, sat down on a bench, and took her phone back out of her pocket. She was already talking by the time Clinton rolled up the window and drove away.

164

"Do you really not feel anything for any one of those women?" Taryn asked. "They've thrown their hats into the ring to seduce you, and brought you food, and tried to win your heart. What more do you want?"

"I want a woman who loves me for who I am, not for the money my family has or for the hero worship that isn't even real," he answered. "Those women don't want me; they want to win a contest so they can lord it over the others who lost. That's the foundation for a divorce. When I get married, I'm going into it with the conviction and determination that it is a forever thing."

"Amen!" Taryn agreed, glad to hear him voice exactly the way she felt about marriage and a permanent relationship.

Clinton grinned. "Was I preaching to the choir?"

"Little bit." Taryn smiled over at him.

Jorja laced her hands behind her head and tried to count the holes in just one ceiling tile, but she kept thinking about what Anna Rose had said about therapy. Throwing things helped, but maybe there were more tricks that would make her stop dreaming about what had happened ten years ago.

The last of Saturday's sun filtered through the lace curtains on the window in her bedroom and threw an array of patterns against the wall on the far side of the room. She lost interest in the ceiling and began to imagine what the shapes were—something she had done when she was a little girl.

She heard Taryn padding around in the kitchen and muted conversation between her and Anna Rose. They were probably talking about what bar Anna Rose was going to that evening and whether Taryn would go with her. Her cousin helped take care of the baby at the shop, but she was happy to help with her in the evenings, too. It seemed like Taryn was taking the role of Zoe's surrogate mother too seriously.

"Maybe the new me should offer to babysit Zoe and let all three of them go out this evening," she whispered, and then shook her head. She didn't want to change diapers and try to entertain a four-month-old baby, and she dang sure wasn't going to encourage her cousins or Clinton to go to honky-tonks.

A soft knock on the door made her forget about the patterns on the walls and even the holes in the ceiling tiles. "Yes?" she called out.

Anna Rose peeked into the room. "We're going to put Zoe in the stroller and take a walk. Want to go with us? My therapist says that a long walk is good for the soul."

Jorja sat up and slung her legs over the side of the bed. "Is Clinton going, too?"

"Nope," Anna Rose answered. "He got an emergency problem with a retired sergeant who needs help, so Taryn is keeping Zoe for him. She's putting her in the stroller now, so if you want to go with us, you better get your shoes on."

"Where are we going?" Jorja asked as she tied her shoes.

"Down to the Blarney Stone Plaza and then maybe to the Dairy Queen for some ice cream," Anna Rose answered. "Maybe we'll kiss the Stone again."

"What do you mean, kiss it *again*? I've never kissed that silly rock. There's no telling what kind of germs are on it." Jorja stood up. "I'm ready."

"Loosen up, girl," Anna Rose said with a frown. "We've got baby wipes to clean a little area. I intend to go all in and kiss it. Maybe if I renew my gift of gab, something lucky will happen to me this summer."

"You don't need any more of that gift," Jorja fussed. "You could talk a dead man into buying a second coffin as it is."

"Never hurts to have a little more power," Anna Rose told her as they walked down the hallway together. "You should wrap your arms around the stone and hug it like a brother, then kiss it a dozen times. Maybe you'll get a sense of humor."

"I do, too, have a sense of humor," Jorja argued. "My colleagues at the school where I teach think I'm funny."

Anna Rose rolled her eyes. "Jorja, you really need to tell Ford how you feel about him and let him know about the baby," she said. "That might bring you some final closure."

"I talked to him when we went to McDonald's," Jorja said through clenched teeth. "If you will remember, I even told him I wouldn't forgive him." She didn't want to ever see him again. Just thinking of his name stirred up a red-hot rage in her whole body. Him standing in front of her already made her want to blow the bottom right out of the Sixth Commandment.

Anna Rose opened the door and stood to the side to let Jorja go out first. "You talked *at* him. You barely threatened him, and that was only after Taryn and I both had our say-so. You need to really confront him—spit in his eye, slap the hell out of him, even double up your fist and give him a bloody nose. Then you just might be able to put everything from your past to rest and move on."

"What are we talking about now?" Taryn was waiting for them at the bottom of the steps. A small tote bag and her purse were in the basket under the stroller. Anyone who saw her would automatically think she was Zoe's mother, and Jorja felt a pang of jealousy shoot through her body.

Her baby would be nine years old if she had lived. She would be fussing about wanting to push the stroller. Ford had stolen not only Jorja's innocence but also her joy at having her first child.

"We're talking about Ford Chambers," Anna Rose answered. "Jorja needs to look him right in the eye and tell him to go sit on a barbed wire fence in the back forty acres of hell."

Taryn began pushing the stroller out of the parking area and toward the street. "That made a good visual in my head."

Jorja fell in step beside her cousin. "Did either of you ever tell the guys who hurt you what you thought of them?"

"I did," Taryn answered. "Before he walked out the door, I told my ex what a lyin' sack of crap he was."

"So did I"—Anna Rose took her place on the other side of the stroller—"but I used much more colorful language than that."

Jorja tried to imagine getting right up in Ford's face and telling him exactly what she thought of men like him, but the very idea made her chest tighten up so much that she could hardly breathe. The closest she'd ever come to telling anyone what she thought—other than her two cousins—was what she had already said to Kaitlin and Ford at McDonald's. Even then she'd been a little light-headed for a few minutes afterward.

You've got to face him and remind him what he did and what effect that has had on your whole life, the voice in her head said. *Until you do, you're always going to be looking over your shoulder to see if he's anywhere around.*

They reached the street and Taryn made a left-hand turn. At the end of the block, she pushed the stroller onto the sidewalk. They passed the Lucky Shamrock, and Jorja noticed that the baskets of petunias looked wilted.

"We need to take those flowers inside tomorrow and plant some lantana for the summer. It will take the heat and survive as long as we remember to water it. Do you think this might really be our lucky summer?" she asked. She wanted something lucky in her life so badly—but like everyone had said, including her inner voices, she had to take care of the Ford issue first.

"Of course it is," Taryn replied.

"That was a quick answer—but then, you're the one pushing that stroller," Anna Rose said.

"What's that supposed to mean?" Jorja asked.

Anna Rose nudged Taryn on the shoulder. "That she's getting her baby fix, which she needed badly, and she's found a friend in Clinton that could turn into a relationship. Maybe it's her lucky summer, but not ours. We haven't found a new friend."

Jorja frowned. "Don't say that. We might not all agree on everything—"

"Or anything," Anna Rose cut in quickly.

"Let me finish," Jorja snapped. "What I was going to say is that we're taking a walk and trying to help each other get over the past and not arguing about every little thing."

Taryn waved at someone who honked at them. "You are right about me getting my baby fix, but it's gone beyond that. I'm worried about the depression I'll fall into when Rebecca comes back from the center and takes Zoe. It took me weeks to get over Alicia leaving my world. I still look at little-girl clothes every time I . . ." She stopped in front of a boutique and pointed to a cute little lacy bonnet in the window. "Like right now. Isn't that adorable?"

"It is," Jorja said, and wondered if she would ever look at little-girl things without thinking of the baby she hadn't wanted at the time. She laid a hand on Taryn's shoulder. "We'll be here to help you. We can throw things at the tree or go for long walks in the evening like we're doing now."

"Y'all both need to get a cat," Anna Rose said. "Goldie has helped me as much as any therapy I've ever had. I've told her secrets that I can't even tell either of you, and she doesn't judge or fuss at me. Petting her is soothing."

"You could share her with us," Jorja suggested.

"Nope, she's mine, and I told her to run from y'all," Anna Rose teased.

"I don't need a cat," Taryn declared.

"That's right," Anna Rose agreed. "You've got a baby and Clinton. But, honey, you will leave them behind, and I'm taking Goldie with me. When I do, she's going to be an inside cat."

Jorja clucked like an old hen and then wondered if that's what she would wind up like—just an old hen living a lonely life without kids or a husband to share everything with. "Do you really expect that cat to adapt to being confined in a hotel room or a temporary apartment?

She has a home here, where she can roam all over town and come back to the trailer when she wants to eat or be petted. She'll wither up and die if you make her move every time you get a whim to chase off to another place to take pictures."

"Do you think that's what we're doing?" Taryn asked. "Is the fact that Anna Rose and I have moved around so much going to cause us to wither up and die, never having put down roots or trusted people?"

"But look at you." Anna Rose leaned forward enough to see Jorja. "You don't travel like we do, but you bury yourself in the safety of a school routine to keep from facing your demons. You haven't really put down roots, either. You still live in a small apartment. That makes it easier to pack up and leave at a moment's notice."

Jorja nodded with a twinge. Anna Rose had nailed it. "We're a bunch of misfits, aren't we?"

"But we do have the choice to change if we want to," Taryn said as she turned at the next corner and passed under the arched sign that read "Blarney Stone Plaza." The whole plaza was just a small strip of concrete and gravel, with some shrubs, a couple of trees, a plaque, and the stone—which was about waist high on Jorja and had been painted green. According to what was on the bronze plaque, it had been brought over from Ireland in 1959. A different sign that showed a picture of the Blarney Castle said that there was so much disagreement about a piece of the castle being taken away from its home in Ireland that it had to be delivered with armed guards.

"Did you ever read this other stuff when we lived here?" Anna Rose pointed to the smaller print at the bottom of the sign. She read aloud the part that said the stone was also rumored to be either part of the rock that Moses had struck in anger or that it could be part of the very thing that Jacob had rested his head on when he had the dream about the ladder. "It's biblical, so being as religious as you are, you definitely need to kiss it for good luck, Jorja."

Taryn locked the stroller wheels and stepped off the sidewalk. "I don't care who's put their mouth on it, I'm kissing it. I need even more luck than what we're getting by working in the Lucky Shamrock." She walked over to the stone, hugged the round thing like a brother—or a sister, or cousin, on the days she liked Anna Rose and Jorja—and kissed it twice.

"Are you going to kiss that baby with those lips?" Jorja asked with a shiver that went from her ears to her toes.

"Not until I have a shot of Jameson to wash all the germs off," Taryn teased.

Anna Rose was next, but instead of hugging the stone, she laid across it and wiggled. "I need more than just a kiss's worth of luck; I need a whole body's worth. If I'm going to feel the need to settle down here in Shamrock, it'll take more than putting my lips on this thing."

"Are you even considering it?" Jorja gasped.

"Maybe," Anna Rose answered. "Nana Irene will need someone to help her out either with the shop or to be there for her personally when she has her knees replaced. Have you noticed how she limps and hangs on to things to get around? I don't know how she and Ruby are making it."

"Ruby might be able to take care of her—but then, who's going to run the shop?" Taryn asked. "I've been considering staying on awhile longer, even after my vacation time is up. I can work from anywhere. Are you going to kiss the stone or not, Jorja?"

Jorja took a deep breath and held it while she hurried over to the stone and planted a kiss on the edge of its round top. She hoped that most folks kissed the center and not the side.

"There. I did it," she said, but she couldn't keep another shiver from chasing down her spine. "I have a job, so I can't stay. I could come back on holidays and relieve y'all if you wanted to go somewhere."

"Have you signed next year's contract?" Taryn asked as she turned the stroller around and started walking north.

"Not yet. It should be ready by July first," Jorja answered.

"Then you've still got time to test the waters and see whether you want to stay here or go back to teaching," Taryn told her.

"I might be able to land a teaching job here." Jorja hadn't really thought about moving, and even if her cousins did decide to stay awhile longer, their jobs didn't require them to sit in one place for nine months. "But only if—and that's a big *if*—y'all are sticking around."

"Do you realize that it's a mile to the Dairy Queen?" Anna Rose asked. "That didn't seem like so far when we were kids, but I'm tired, so I'm stopping off at the trailer."

"Me too," Jorja agreed. "We've got ice cream in the freezer, and a mile in this muggy weather is too far for me. And besides, Ora Mae called and begged me to come to church tomorrow morning and then go to lunch with her. I don't want to do it, but . . ."

"Tell her no, then," Taryn said. "Is it tough for you to tell people no?"

"A little bit," Jorja answered. "I hate to disappoint people."

"If you don't want to go, then tell her thank you but you have to take a rain check," Anna Rose suggested. "I'm taking my camera out away from town and taking some night photos. My agent says that we need a few more for the Texas book that will be published next year. I haven't taken any of the Blarney Stone or of anything with Route 66 on it. Y'all want to drive around with me?"

"Not me," Jorja declared. "I've got a good book that's calling my name."

"I don't know when Clinton will be done, so I'll stick close to home," Taryn answered. "Zoe is already getting fussy. She likes her bath, and her bedtime is about now."

All three women stopped in their tracks when a car came to a screeching halt at the curb near them. Taryn yanked the stroller back close to the building they were standing beside; Anna Rose and Jorja both plastered themselves against the door.

"I thought someone lost control and that car would jump the curb," Anna Rose gasped. Jorja grabbed her arm to steady herself.

Nana Irene's voice popped into Jorja's head: *Here's your chance. No wife. No kids. Unload on him. Get it off your chest.*

Ford Chambers flung open the door and jumped out of the car. He had an angry expression on his face and determination in his walk when he rounded the vehicle and stood at the passenger's side. "I don't appreciate the way you treated my wife at the church or the way you acted in McDonald's, and it better not happen again."

A black curtain flickered at the edges of Jorja's vision. Anna Rose gave her a gentle shove, knocking her out of it. "Here's your chance," she whispered—the same words that Nana Irene had said just seconds before. "Your adrenaline has to be rushing, and there's no kids or wife to embarrass. But truthfully, I wouldn't care if Kaitlin *did* get a bit of comeuppance."

Jorja took a step forward, and her heart pounded like a drum in her chest. She wished she had that whole tote bag of dog toys to throw at Ford—no, that wasn't right. She wanted a tote bag full of bricks. Finally, she took one step forward and then another, and she kept walking until she was nose to nose with him.

"How dare you even speak to me after drugging me and then raping me on the night we graduated from high school? You got me pregnant, and I suffered through a miscarriage. I kept my mouth shut and didn't tell anyone about any of what happened, but it scarred me for life. So"—she poked him in the chest with her forefinger—"you got off easy with us just embarrassing you in front of your wife and sons. If you drugged other innocent girls during that time, you might think about the fact that you could have other children out there somewhere, maybe being raised by a single mother or in foster homes. So don't come at me in anger; it's me that should be mad—and believe me, I still am even after all these years."

"You are lying," he said, his voice barely above a whisper. "If you spread that around, I will sue you for defamation of character."

"Want me to send you the hospital bill and notes about my miscarriage?" she asked. "Or maybe the skirt I wore that night with your DNA probably still all over it? I didn't report the rape, but I did take pictures of the bruises on my body and the blood in the back seat of my car. Want to see those?"

He edged out around her and rounded the back of the car. "You've always been weird, and no one would believe a thing you say."

"Maybe so, but I didn't ruin someone's life like you did mine," Jorja yelled at him.

He got in his car and drove away, leaving long black streaks on the road behind him.

Anna Rose threw an arm around Jorja's shoulders. "Feel better?"

"A little—no, a whole lot," Jorja answered. It wasn't in court, but she had faced her attacker and told him what she thought of him, and that brought a tiny bit of closure.

Chapter Thirteen

A hard south wind causing the limbs of a scrub oak tree to brush against Taryn's bedroom window awoke her on Sunday morning. From the way the sun kept peeking out from behind dark clouds, she realized a storm was coming. Then the siren sounded, telling them that a tornado was most likely headed their way. Her phone rang, and she grabbed it off the nightstand.

"Nana Irene, are you both okay?" she asked.

"Ruby and I are headed for the cellar. Didn't the tornado siren wake y'all up?" Irene's voice was high and squeaky. "You girls and Clinton get over to the shop and go down into the basement. Don't argue with me through the phone. Just do it."

"Yes, ma'am," Taryn answered. "See you on the other side."

"Hopefully without any damage," Irene said.

Anna Rose met Taryn in the hallway with Goldie in her arms. When they made it to the living room, Jorja was already there with the shop keys in her hands. She flung the door open, and a strong wind blew through the screen door.

"Y'all look like one of those cartoons of people with their hair all blown back from the wind," Taryn said.

"Well, darlin', you don't look a bit better," Anna Rose told her. "I don't imagine the tornado cares about our appearance. It just wants to grab us up, twirl us around like rag dolls, and throw us back down up in Kansas."

Taryn didn't even think about her looks when she slammed the trailer door shut and looked up to see Clinton carrying Zoe down the steps.

"The sirens woke me up," he yelled over what sounded like a freight train moving toward them.

Taryn met him halfway up the steps and took the baby from him. "I can see it traveling this way, so we need to hurry."

Together, they ran through the back door of the shop. Clinton took a moment to close and lock it and then followed her down into the basement. Not even slamming that door shut canceled out the noise of the storm.

"Everyone all right?" he asked.

"I hate basements," Jorja answered, "but we're fine. I saw a huge piece of wood twirling in the air about the time I opened the back door."

A twin-size bed was against the wall on one side of the room, and two rocking chairs were over on the far end. In the corner, at the end of the bed, was an old safe that Irene and Ruby had used years ago. Nowadays, they tallied up the money in the cash register daily and took it to the bank on their way home each evening. Taryn had spent time in this little room, as had her cousins, when she was a child because Nana Irene and Ruby were both terrified of storms.

Her hands trembled, but she hugged the baby up close to her chest and sat down in a rocking chair. Just thinking about what could have happened if something had fallen from the sky before they could get inside made her chest tighten. If anything had hit the baby, they wouldn't have even been able to get her to the hospital or a doctor until the storm passed.

"There's nothing like getting woken up by a tornado siren not a block away from the house," Anna Rose said and covered a yawn with the back of her hand.

"Welcome to Texas—but then, we're all Texans by birth and raising, I guess," Clinton said and took the rocking chair next to Taryn. "At least it'll pass through in a little while. It's not like those hurricanes that hit the coastal towns. They take up squatter's rights and stick around a long time."

Jorja sat down on the twin bed. "Or the earthquakes in California that rattle your teeth. I've said it before, but I'm declaring it again: I hate storms. I prayed the whole way across the parking lot that it would go around us, but that's not right, either. If it doesn't tear Shamrock up, then it'll get someone else. So praying that we are saved to the death or injury of others isn't what we should be asking for."

Clinton set the rocking chair in motion. "I saw a sign in a store window that said 'Don't Tell God How Big Your Storm Is. Tell the Storm How Big Your God Is.'"

"Amen," Jorja agreed. "But I didn't take you for a religious man."

"I'm not *church* religious, but I do believe in a higher power. If I didn't, I wouldn't be alive today," Clinton said. "Some of the guys I served with would turn from being nonbelievers when bad things happened to good people."

"Are you thinking of Rebecca?" Taryn asked.

"Yes," he answered. "I hope that she finally gets to a place where she can see the good that could come of all the things she has had to endure."

Anna Rose plopped down on the other end of the bed, but she still hugged Goldie close to her chest. She scanned the walls and the ceiling before she leaned back. "I'm as afraid of scorpions as Jorja is storms, and I've seen a couple down here through the years."

"Seems to be safe right now." Taryn set the rocker in motion with her foot. "Do y'all realize that we've been coming down here during storm season since we were Zoe's age?"

"That's right. Nana Irene put the bed down here so we could sleep through the storms," Anna Rose said. "I remember all three of us curled up right here while we waited for the storm to pass."

Jorja pointed toward the old safe. "She always kept a scented candle on the top of that thing to keep the place smelling nice."

"Well, I'm just glad we've got a shelter like this to protect us. If the storm comes right through this area, the upstairs apartment and the trailer might be hit hard," Clinton said. "So, when we get out of this place, we could have a mess to clean up. Irene and Ruby will be devastated if they lose the shop to a tornado."

"But we'll all still be alive. Buildings can be rebuilt and trailers replaced." Taryn had been through more than one storm in her life—both natural and mental—and survived all of them, but this one felt more ominous than the ones before now. Could it be a sign that there were too many storms to weather in Shamrock for her to survive them?

It's because there's a baby in the mix, her grandmother's voice whispered in her head. *When you have responsibilities beyond yourself, life changes.*

But Zoe isn't mine, Taryn argued with the voice.

Tell your heart that, Irene shot back at her.

"You look like you're fighting a battle in your mind," Clinton said. "Your expression keeps changing."

"I am. With my grandmother," Taryn answered without hesitation. "I hope she and Ruby made it to the cellar out behind Nana Irene's house without any problems."

Anna Rose finally let Goldie loose, and the cat turned around three times on the pillow, lay down, and put her paw over her eyes. "If the trailer is flattened and the shop is torn all to pieces, Goldie and I are going over to Nana Irene's house for breakfast. I'm starving."

"What if her place is gone?" Jorja asked. "Or worse yet, what if all our vehicles have been blown into the next county?"

"Then we will meet her at the Dairy Queen," Anna Rose answered. "It's all just stuff that can be replaced, if we have to."

Taryn shot a sideways glance over at Clinton and shrugged. If the trailer and the shop were demolished, then she was going to take it as a sure sign that she shouldn't stay in Shamrock. A tornado blowing away her place of business would be sad, but it would also definitely be an omen.

Taryn thought of the possibility of an era passing in the twenty to thirty minutes it took a tornado to sweep through the panhandle of Texas. She'd practically been raised in the flower shop. The basement room had looked bigger back when she'd rocked her baby dolls in the old wooden rocking chairs and played school with her cousins. Since she was the oldest, she always got to be the teacher, and they were the students. She wondered if they remembered those days as clearly as she did.

The noise above them finally died down, but another ten minutes passed before they heard the all-clear siren.

"We should have a moment before we go out there," Jorja whispered and bowed her head.

"Not me," Anna Rose declared as she started up the stairs. "I'm going to see if we've got a place to live and, more importantly, to make waffles. That's what I want for breakfast this morning."

Jorja raised her head after saying what appeared to have been a quick prayer, then followed her cousin. When she reached the top of the stairs, she shouted, "The shop is still standing! Not even any broken glass. Going out now to check on our vehicles and the trailer."

Taryn wasn't aware she'd been holding her breath until it all came out in a whoosh. "Thank God!" she whispered as she stood up with Zoe still in her arms. "You've been such a good baby, darlin' girl."

Clinton got to his feet, reached up, and pulled the wooden thread spool hanging from a length of cord and sent the basement into semi-darkness. A shaft of light from the open door lit up the stairway enough that they could make their way to the top. "We should have realized that we were okay when the electricity down here didn't go out. I try to be patient, but I'm not so good at waiting. All kinds of things ran through my mind in this last half hour. Could Rebecca find us if everything got destroyed? What if all my files were blown away? I have them backed up in the cloud, but I like hard copies."

Taryn stopped at the bottom of the stairs. "Me too. The storm brought back some good memories for me, of all weird things—the times when all three of us cousins played or took naps in this basement. I want Zoe to have good memories like that. But I also half hoped that her mama couldn't find us so we wouldn't have to give Zoe back to her. It's not fair, I know."

Clinton wrapped his arms around her with the baby between them. "No, I know that, too, and I sure don't want her put into foster care, but my fear is that Rebecca is too fragile to raise her."

Taryn looked up into his brown eyes. "I'm here to help with her as long as you need me."

She barely had time to moisten her lips before his found hers in a kiss that stopped the world from turning. There were no more tornadoes, no past or future—just the here and now, and that kiss.

"Hey, what are y'all waiting on?" Anna Rose yelled.

Clinton took a step backward and whispered, "I've wanted to do that for days, and it was even better than I dreamed about."

"We're on our way," Taryn said, raising her voice for Anna Rose before she turned back to Clinton. "Me too, but we'd better go see what's going on right now."

"Talk later?" he asked.

"Yes, definitely," she answered with a smile.

Anna Rose was already out in the yard, standing in the bed of her truck in pouring-down rain, checking out the trailer's roof. "Looks like we're good from out here."

Jorja opened the trailer door and shouted across the parking lot. "No leaks inside. We got lucky. Our throwing tree lost some limbs, and the scrub oak out back has been uprooted. Nana Irene called and said they're both good, and everything looks good, too. They're back in the house now."

"I need to go check my apartment, but I don't want to climb those slippery steps with the baby in my arms," Clinton said.

"Go!" Taryn motioned with her free hand. "We'll be fine right here in the shop until the rain slows down; then I'll take her to the trailer. You go on and make sure everything in your apartment is safe."

"Thank you," Clinton said. "Not only for this but for everything you've done since Zoe . . ." He paused. "Well, you know."

She smiled up at him. "It's totally been my pleasure. I've fallen in love with this child."

"Me too," Clinton said and then darted out into the rain.

Taryn put the baby in her playpen and started the mobile. Zoe's chubby little cheeks broke out in a smile, and she kicked her legs.

"You're going to be a dancer, aren't you?" Taryn pulled a barstool over close. "Are you going to like jazz, tap, or ballet better? Or maybe you'll be like Anna Rose and enjoy line dancing or two-stepping best of all."

Tears filled Taryn's eyes when the baby cooed up at her and kicked even harder. "Oh, baby girl, I can't even think about you going away, but I want you to have a good life with your mama."

She wiped her eyes with the sleeve of the T-shirt she'd slept in the night before and walked over to the door to see if the rain had let up enough to run across the lot to the trailer. Her mind hopped from the kiss she'd shared with Clinton to the idea of all three cousins staying in Shamrock past the end of summer.

She jumped when her phone rang, and thinking it was Clinton, she answered it without even looking at the caller ID. "Hello, is everything all right up there? Is the roof leaking?"

"Up where?" Irene asked.

"I'm sorry, Nana," Taryn apologized. "I thought you were Clinton. He braved the rain to see if his apartment was dry, and I'm in the shop with Zoe until the rain slacks up a bit."

"Everything is fine in the apartment," Irene said. "I just talked to him, and Jorja says the trailer is still standing but there's some tree limbs on the ground. I guess we're lucky, aren't we? Though I'll miss that scrub oak. Anyway, I wanted to know if you checked the front room. The last hard rain we got from the south blew water under the door, and we had to mop it up."

Taryn spun around and crossed the work room, went through the doorway into the front, and checked everything. "All looks good here. No water on the floor. Glass is still intact, but the petunia baskets out front are gone, and it looks like some of the shops across the street got some of their shingles blown away. There's a lot of debris everywhere."

"Damn tornadoes!" Irene swore. "They're as unpredictable as a horse race."

Taryn wasn't sure if her giggles came from nerves or relief. "Nana Irene, just how is a horse race unpredictable?"

"Didn't you watch the Kentucky Derby last year?" she asked. "Ruby and I always wear a big hat and watch it on television. Last year, the winner had an eighty-to-one chance to win that race. That's like a tornado. It will suck up a cow and put it in a tree thirty miles down the road but leave a three-ounce box of Jell-O sitting on the shelf in a grocery store that has had all the windows blown out and the roof taken off."

"Yep, I've seen that happen, too, but we dodged a bullet this time. Nana Irene . . ." She paused.

"Your voice changed. Are you about to tattle?" Irene asked.

"No, ma'am," Taryn answered. "But can I come over and talk to you later this evening?"

"Nope," Irene replied. "If I let you come over here, then I'll have to let the other two, and y'all need to work out your problems amongst the three of you. I won't be around forever."

"This hasn't got anything to do with Anna Rose and Jorja," Taryn said. "We've kind of formed a therapy group to talk about our problems—and believe it or not, we are getting along a little better. This has to do with me and Clinton. I'm afraid I'm projecting my feelings for Zoe over to him. He kissed me today, but the baby was between us. Literally between us—as in, I was holding her and he had to lean around her to kiss me."

"And?" Irene asked.

"And it felt right, but . . ." Taryn sighed. "But all three of us cousins have trust issues. I'm not going to tell Anna Rose's and Jorja's stories, and this isn't the time to get into my own story." She paused. "I made so many stupid mistakes as a teenager here in Shamrock that it hurts my heart to think of how much pain it had to have caused you."

"You were an ornery kid, for sure." Irene's tone was serious. "But keeping things bottled up for years isn't good for a person. I've prayed every day for you girls, and now I find out that you've all kept secrets from me. You are all going to come clean before you leave if I have to lock you back down in the cellar until you tell me what has happened."

"We'll tell you when the time is right for them," Taryn said. "But it's so hard to trust again—"

"You can trust Clinton," Irene butted in. "He's a good, honest man. If he wasn't, he wouldn't be working for me or with you girls. You have to figure out for yourself if you are really loving him as a man or if you are just wanting a family. That's your job, Taryn. I wouldn't begin to steer you in any direction on that issue."

"Hey," Jorja yelled from the back door. "It's just drizzling now, so I brought an umbrella to help you get the baby to the trailer. Where is her diaper bag?"

"You go on and take care of things," Irene said. "We'll talk more later."

"Thanks, Nana Irene, for listening," Taryn said.

"Anytime—but mark my words, the truth will come out," Irene said and ended the call.

"The diaper bag is probably still in the basement," Taryn called back, raising her voice. "I didn't see Clinton pick it up."

"I'll get it, and you get Zoe." Jorja's voice faded as she headed down the steps.

By the time Taryn had picked up the baby, Jorja was back, with the bag thrown over her shoulder. "We can all huddle up under the umbrella. Anna Rose and I were both soaking wet when we got back to the trailer. We got into dry clothes, though, and she's making breakfast for us. I already called Clinton, and he was on his way down when I came to get you and Zoe. Who were you talking to?" She opened the door and popped the umbrella up.

Taryn avoided the question. "Thank you so much for helping us out."

"No problem," Jorja said as she took them across the wet parking lot and into the trailer.

Taryn inhaled the mixture of freshly brewed coffee and frying bacon when she was in the house. "I didn't realize I was hungry until now," she said as she made a pallet on the floor for the baby. "Everything smells wonderful."

"Bacon and scrambled eggs, and waffles with whipped cream and strawberries, or else butter and syrup," Anna Rose said.

Clinton stopped right inside the door and inhaled deeply. "I don't know if it's relief from our places still standing or if I'm really this hungry, but I feel like I could eat an elephant."

Taryn looked up from the floor and caught Clinton's sly wink and imagined that he was thinking the same thing she was.

If just a kiss can make us this hungry, what would a night in bed cause?

Chapter Fourteen

"I'm worried whether you are ready for this step," Clinton told Rebecca.

"I'm fine. The therapy helped, and it's time for me to move on," Rebecca assured him. "Where's that trash bag I brought the rest of her things in?"

She pushed a strand of red hair back behind her ear. Her blue eyes darted around the room, looking for the used trash bag. Clinton wanted to help her, but it was evident that she just wanted to take Zoe and run.

"I threw it away when I unpacked her things." Clinton picked Zoe up from the playpen and hugged her close to his chest. "There's a whole roll under the kitchen sink. Rebecca, you can't run from your problems. You've got to face them and get better before you can be a mother to this baby."

Her hands shook as she peeled off a single bag from the roll and threw the baby's neatly folded things into it helter-skelter. "We don't have room in the car to take her playpen or anything else, and Kyla's waiting for me, so I need to hurry." She reached out her hands for Zoe. "Thank you for all your help, but a new place with down-to-earth, healthy people is what I need, not listening to a bunch of people depressing me with their war stories."

Clinton couldn't let go of the baby. "Please, Rebecca, leave her with me until you get settled, and then I'll bring her over to Arkansas myself, along with whatever she needs. She's outgrowing the playpen. Why don't I just buy her a crib and bring it at that point?"

Rebecca took the baby from him and shook her head. "Thanks again for everything and for the offer, but she's my daughter." She slung the bulging diaper bag over her shoulder, held on to Zoe with one arm, and opened the door. Within seconds, her new friend from the center had gotten out of an older-model car and come to the bottom of the stairs. The woman looked as frazzled as Rebecca; she couldn't stand still, and her whole body seemed to hum with anxiety. Clinton had seen soldiers in that shape when they had severe PTSD. Knowing that Zoe was leaving with Rebecca and that woman caused his chest to tighten.

Rebecca hitched up sweatpants that seemed to be at least two sizes too big for her, picked up the garbage bag, and tossed it out the door to the landing. When she stepped outside, she kicked it to the bottom of the steps and yelled, "Throw that in the trunk, and we're ready to go once I get her car seat out of Clinton's truck."

"I'll do that for you," Clinton offered as they walked down the steps.

"I can do it," Rebecca said, shifting the baby to her other hip. "I don't want to listen to you try to talk me out of what I'm doing. The little commune in the hills of Arkansas will be a good place for me and Kyla both to heal from our problems. My baby will grow up with a mama who is there for her."

Dread and hope warred in Clinton's gut as he picked up his truck keys and opened the doors. "If you ever need anything or change your mind, you've got my phone number."

She nodded. "Yes, I do."

He was a grown man, and he'd known from the beginning that having Zoe was temporary, but he couldn't stop the tears from flowing down his unshaven cheeks or the ache in his heart.

"Please call me when you get to the end of your trip," he called out.

"I don't have a phone, but I can use Kyla's," Rebecca agreed as she settled Zoe into the car seat. "Goodbye, Clinton."

"Bye." He waved but was worried about her lack of a phone. He made a mental note to buy half a dozen prepaid ones next time he was at a store that sold them, just to have on hand for times like this.

Taryn heard the bell above the shop door jingle and slid off her barstool and headed toward the front. She fought down a rush of anger when she saw Diana standing in front of the counter with a Bundt cake in her hands. Would the three women ever give up on dragging Clinton kicking and screaming down the aisle? Diana set the plate on the counter and rolled her eyes toward the ceiling. "I was hoping to see Clinton today. Maybe I should take this up to his apartment."

"I wouldn't bother him if I was you," Taryn told her. "He's got business going on up there, and I doubt that he would appreciate being disturbed, but hey . . ." She held up both palms. "It's your call, not mine."

"I'll leave it here," Diana said through clenched teeth. "But it's for him, not for all y'all."

"I'll tell him what you said. What else can I do for you today?" Taryn asked.

"It's an applesauce cake. There's a surprise filling of brown sugar and cinnamon in the center, and it stays moist for days." She took a step toward the door. "I mean it about it being just for him."

"I heard you the first time—but what if he says he doesn't like cinnamon and wants to share with us?" Taryn asked.

Diana flipped her hair over her shoulder in what Taryn thought was supposed to be a classy—or maybe sexy—gesture. "He loves cinnamon. I'm planning to use this same recipe for our wedding cake."

Taryn sniffed the air. "It certainly smells delicious. Would you share the recipe so we can make one of our own if he's not in a sharing mood?"

"I don't share my recipes *or* my men," Diana snapped.

"We haven't seen any of you contest women coming by in the evenings. Have Elaine and Mallory given up on the whole idea of roping him into a wedding?" Taryn's tone sounded downright chilly in her own ears.

"I've been busy helping some friends with a couple of weddings. I thought I could get some ideas for my own, which I hope will be happening at Christmas. I love velvet, and my grandmother and I are designing a velvet wedding gown with a cape that has the train attached to it." Diana practically swooned.

Elaine pushed her way into the shop with a wrapped package in her hands. She set it on the counter beside the cake. "Stand back, Diana. You haven't won this contest yet," she said and looked over at Taryn. "This is a little present for Clinton that I found on my trip to New Mexico. Nothing fancy, but I thought he might like it. Either call him out of that back room or I'm going in there."

"He hasn't come in yet. Maybe the baby had a bad night," Taryn said, before muttering under her breath, "So, I guess now there's two down, another ugly one to go."

"What did you say?" Elaine demanded.

"You heard me. Two down—both of you standing here in the shop, vying for Clinton's attention. One to go—where is Mallory?" Taryn answered. "This is downright ridiculous. Clinton should put a restraining order out on all three of you for harassment. Has he given any one of you the first sign that he's interested in a relationship?"

"Are you accusing us of being stalkers?" Diana asked in a demanding tone.

"That's *exactly* what I'm doing," Taryn replied. "Everyone in town is probably laughing at you for acting like lovestruck teenagers, but hey"—she frowned—"I'm not complaining one bit. When they're gossiping about you, they're leaving me and my cousins alone."

"You are wrong," Diana said. "Clinton is just trying to decide which one of us he likes best, and we're all showing him how much we care about him."

"What you are doing is shameful for grown women. Come to think of it, girls in grade school would have better sense than you are all showing. You are a hairdresser"—Taryn pointed at Diana and then swung her finger around to Elaine—"and you have a prosperous real estate business. Use what brain cells you have in your head and think about how the whole town is gossiping about you and probably laughing behind your backs. What eligible bachelor—or even divorced guy or widower—is going to ever think about dating you when he hears about all this mess? 'Course, as long as you're bringing food to us—and I'm telling you right now that he's been sharing ever since we got here—I really don't care if you are making fools of yourselves. I'm hoping there's a T-shirt in your present, Elaine, because my nightshirt is getting holes in it, and I'm thinking Clinton might share his new one with me."

Diana flipped her hair over her shoulder and glared at Taryn, then stormed out of the shop. Elaine set her mouth in a firm line, picked her package back up, and followed Diana outside.

Anna Rose came through the back room and patted Taryn on the shoulder. "You are my hero. I couldn't have done better, but I'm real glad Diana didn't take her cake. I'm going to have some with a second cup of coffee for my breakfast."

"So, y'all heard all that?" Taryn asked.

"Sure, we did." Jorja raised her voice so that her cousins could hear her. "But maybe you better ask Clinton since Diana said it wasn't for us."

Anna Rose picked up an ivy and carried it to the back room. "I'll call him and ask if it's all right if we cut it, but we all know he's going to say yes."

"Say yes about what?" Clinton asked as he came through the back door. "Do I smell cinnamon? Is there a bake sale going on somewhere?"

"Yep, in Diana's house or maybe in her grandmother's place—or one of her customers down at the Cut and Curl might have brought this cake to her. But you do smell cinnamon," Jorja answered.

"If you're willing to share, we can have a cake-tasting to see if you want this kind when you and Diana get married," Taryn teased.

Jorja laughed. "Diana explicitly said that it was for you alone, just be aware."

Something didn't look right. Clinton didn't have a diaper bag thrown over his shoulder, and she didn't hear Zoe cooing or fussing.

"Anytime those women bring anything at all here or to my apartment, we'll share it. You don't even have to ask anymore," Clinton said with a long sigh. His tone and expression looked like he carried the weight of the world on his shoulders.

Jorja picked up the cake and carried it to the back room. "Thank you for that. I thought maybe they had given up on this stupid contest, but I guess they've been busy with other things."

"I wish they would all give up. I'd rather buy my own food or cook than have to deal with all this crazy stuff," he said. "Especially today."

Taryn followed Jorja and went straight to the playpen, but there was no baby in it. When she realized the carrier wasn't on the worktable, fear filled her heart. Was Zoe sick? Who was watching her? "Where's the baby?" She looked over at Clinton, and it hit her like a Class 5 tornado. "Rebecca came back, didn't she?"

"She showed up around an hour ago with a friend she met at the center. She's going to Arkansas with Kyla, this new friend, to live in the mountains and make jams and jellies to sell at farmers' markets," Clinton answered. "I tried to talk her out of taking Zoe with her, but she insisted that she was better and could take care of the baby, and she thinks this move is just what she needs. There was nothing I could do."

Taryn felt as empty as the playpen, but her inner voice reminded her that Zoe belonged with her mother. Even knowing that didn't help with the tears damming up behind her eyelashes. She blinked them away and sat down on her barstool, her legs almost giving way before she could.

"I'll pray that Rebecca is healed enough to take on the responsibility of a baby," Jorja said.

Anna Rose brought the cake to the table, then poured four cups of coffee and set one at each place. "Clinton, you have seen lots of these cases. In your opinion, is she ready to leave rehab after such a short time?"

He shook his head and then took a sip of his coffee. "Not by a long shot. I'm worried about Zoe, but the papers I have say that the guardianship is temporary, and Rebecca can take her with her at any time."

"Are you okay, Taryn?" Jorja asked.

"No," Taryn answered, "but I'm going to hope that the baby is taken care of right and loved and . . ." She blinked back tears. "Would someone please cut that cake and let's talk about something else before I start ugly crying?"

Anna Rose quickly removed the plastic wrap from the cake and cut several slices. "Food has always been our comfort," she explained to Clinton as she served up a piece to each of them. "Nana Irene said that everyone needs fuel to help them through tough times."

"I need a lot of it to get me through this day," Taryn whispered.

Clinton took a bite and nodded. "Irene and Ruby told me the same thing when I would come in upset because I couldn't get some help for a homeless vet. I'm not sure if it was the food or the talking about things that really helped, though."

"Is Rebecca going to call when she gets to Arkansas so we'll know that she and the baby are safe?" Anna Rose asked.

"She doesn't have a phone, but her friend does, so Rebecca promised me that they would let us know when they arrive," Clinton answered with a sigh. "It's over four hundred miles from here to where they're going, and they're not planning to stop to sleep. Just the trip to Pampa and back exhausted Zoe, so the poor little girl is going to be beyond tired by the time they get there tonight."

Jorja finished off the last bite of her cake and cut herself another piece. "With Rebecca and her new friend both having PTSD, I need to pray that a whining baby doesn't trigger their anger." She bowed her head and closed her eyes.

Taryn hoped that her cousin's prayers went higher than the ceiling and shot right on upward all the way to God's ears. Life was going to be lonely without Zoe, but she wanted the baby to be happy and to be in a loving environment.

No, I don't, she argued with herself. *I want Zoe to live right here. I want to watch her grow, help her pick out dresses for her proms, and listen to her give the valedictorian speech at her high school graduation. I want to hold her when she cries over her breakup with her first boyfriend and listen to her fuss when her best friend is mean to her.*

She wiped away a tear with the back of her hand and picked up an order ticket from the basket. Glad that it was a plant that just needed pretty paper and a bow, she headed to the front of the shop to get a hydrangea. She had just picked one off a display case when the doorbell jingled, and Kaitlin's mother, Linda, came through the door with Diana right behind her.

"My uncle, Amos Landry, died last night, and I need a wreath fixed up and taken to the funeral home as soon as you can get it there. The old codger made arrangements to be buried as soon as he could," Linda said curtly. "Daisies will do just fine. Roses are too expensive. Maybe with some orange ribbons or yellow ribbons."

Diana patted Linda on the shoulder. "Daisies do seem to be more manly than roses, but just think of it this way: you won't have to put up with him dropping in to embarrass you when you have guests, like he did last week. His watermelons are good, but holy crap—coming to your house uninvited is downright disrespectful."

"I know," Linda said with a long sigh. "That's what Kaitlin said, too. Amos embarrassed her more than once when he came by the house while she had friends over."

"I remember," Diana said in a sympathetic tone.

"Thank you for coming with me today instead of Kaitlin," Linda said, "Her head cold is disgusting. I will say that, as his only surviving relative . . ." She paused and clamped her mouth shut like she had forgotten that Taryn was standing behind the counter.

"It's my pleasure. I'd stopped by to check on Kaitlin when you arrived to tell her that Amos had passed away," Diana said. She turned to face Taryn. "Is Clinton here now? I could sure use his big, broad shoulders to cry on."

"For God's sake!" Linda's tone went from grief to ice in an instant. "Don't pretend that any of us are going to cry. I've been waiting and wishing he would kick the bucket for years. I'm going to sell that farm to the highest bidder and buy a beach house in Florida."

"I'll do my best, but I always cry at funerals and weddings. Kaitlin and I are both passionate women." Diana sniffled. "I really could use a strong man's comfort. And some of that cake that better not have been eaten." She sniffed again, this time almost pointedly.

Taryn pulled out the order pad and deliberately wrote down Linda's order wrong just to see if it mattered enough for her to raise a fuss. "*White* daisies with orange ribbons. Check, credit card, or cash?"

Linda glanced down at the bill. "Don't you have something a little less expensive?"

"I can do a plant for about half that," Taryn answered and motioned toward the few pots with green plants that were left in the shop. "We don't get an order in until Wednesday, so there's not a lot to choose from. The cheapest one we have right now is a sunset bromeliad."

"We could go halves on it." Diana turned to Linda. "I've always felt like you and Kaitlin were my second family, and her precious little boys are like nephews to me."

"That sounds great." Linda fished around in her purse and brought out a credit card. "Put my part on this."

"I'll pay cash," Diana said.

Taryn tore up the first two orders and made change for each of them. "Still want an orange bow?"

"Yes," Linda answered, then almost growled, "and get it there before closing today."

"Yes, ma'am," Taryn said with a nod. "Anything else?"

Linda pointed her forefinger with a perfectly manicured nail—done in orange—at Taryn. "You were mean and hateful to Kaitlin—but then, I wouldn't expect anything else from you. At least her children are legitimate. That baby you've had at the shop is a . . ."

Taryn rounded the end of the counter and stuck her own forefinger right under the woman's nose. "Don't say that word. Don't even think it."

Linda pushed her hand away and stormed out of the shop.

"That was harsh," Diana snapped.

"Yes, *she* was and totally uncalled for," Taryn said through clenched teeth.

"I wouldn't like it if someone called my child a bad name. But then, I don't plan on having children," Diana said with a shrug. "You should have some consideration for Linda. She just lost her uncle." She spun around like one of those little ballerina figures in a cheap jewelry box and marched out of the shop.

"I probably liked old Amos better than she did," Taryn muttered as she took the bromeliad to the back. "And she's not calling Zoe names without there being consequences."

Nana Irene's tuna casserole was one of Taryn's favorite dishes, and Anna Rose made it for supper that evening. Maybe it was because she thought Taryn was heartbroken over Zoe—but most likely it was because she liked it just as well as Taryn did. Still, that evening, the food had absolutely no taste. Taryn might as well have been eating sawdust or wet dirt. Even the sweet tea had no flavor.

"Are you sick?" Jorja asked as she took a second helping. "I remember when you used to scrape the bowl clean when Nana Irene made this."

"Leave her alone," Anna Rose fussed. "She's missing her baby girl. She'll be fine in a few days."

"Imagine how Nana Irene misses us when we leave and don't come back for several months at a time." Taryn picked at the food still on her plate. "Or how much she misses our parents since they've all moved away."

"I've been so busy living my own life that I never thought of how lonely she must be when we just pop in for a couple of days and then don't come back for months," Jorja said. "She had us around all the time right up until we graduated from high school, and we only had Zoe in our lives for a couple of weeks. I'm so worried about her that my heart hurts. I can't imagine how Nana must feel when we are gone."

Clinton nodded in agreement. "She talks about y'all all the time. Maybe the real reason that she doesn't want you to come over every day is because of what Taryn and Jorja just said. Six whole weeks of seeing you all the time and then, poof"—he snapped his fingers—"you're gone."

Anna Rose brought a box of Dilly Bars from the Dairy Queen to the table for dessert. "But our lives aren't here in Shamrock anymore. I've got books to make, pictures to take, and places to see."

"Life is where you make it," Clinton whispered.

"What did you say?" Taryn asked, not quite believing what she'd heard.

He repeated the words. "I would never have thought about living here in Shamrock permanently. I wasn't even sure I'd stay very long when I moved into the apartment. My original plan was to live in one place and help as many vets as I could, then move on."

"What changed?" Taryn asked.

"I found that vets are more than willing to come to me. Word of mouth gets around quickly, and I've built up quite a list of those who need help from Kansas, Oklahoma, and Texas. The icing on the cake is that when I'm not busy with that job, I get to work in the flower shop with Irene and Ruby," he answered.

Get *to work*, Taryn thought, *not* have *to work. That's the attitude I should have.*

Anna Rose could almost feel the roots growing from her own heart and into the ground right there in Shamrock. When she left the town, she'd vowed she would only come back for short visits. Her folks had moved right after she left, and her grandmother was the only real tie she had to Shamrock. Someday, Nana Irene would be gone, and then nothing would draw her back to the small town.

The silence that filled the room as they worked on orders that afternoon was so thick that Anna Rose didn't think it could be cut with a machete. She tried to picture what a photograph would look like if she could capture even one of the emotions that she and her cousins were experiencing.

Jorja's would be a sapling tree in the winter, with snow clinging to the fragile limbs, because she was confused—not only about life but that day. She had prayed, but her expression told Anna Rose that her cousin was still struggling with whether Jesus would even hear her prayer after she had drunk a beer. Hopefully, when Jorja found herself, the picture would change into a lovely full-grown evergreen with daisies growing at its base.

Clinton would be a rock—strong, dependable, confident that he was doing good. But that day, a chip had been knocked out of the middle of it. Rebecca had taken a little piece of his heart with her when she went away with Zoe. In Anna Rose's mind, she held the camera up to her eye and saw a before and after picture—one from that day and one from sometime in the future, when the rock was complete and solid again.

Does that mean Rebecca will bring the baby back? Anna Rose wondered as she looked over at the empty playpen.

Tears pricked her eyes when she glanced across the table at Taryn. She blinked the moisture away and pretended she was looking through her camera lens again. She saw a big heart, like the ones they had made for their valentine boxes as children. The heart was cracked down the middle. Not broken—just flawed, with a long, jagged crack. Then she heard the tinkling of the bell above the door and the vision disappeared.

"I'll get it this time," Jorja said as she slid off her barstool.

Anna Rose left the worktable and peeked around the doorjamb so she could see who the customer was. Then she straightened up and whispered, "It's Ora Mae, probably trying to get Jorja to help her with something at the church."

"Sounds like she's crying," Taryn whispered back.

"She is," Anna Rose reported.

"Oh, Jorja, my dear friend Amos is dead!" Ora Mae broke into hard sobs.

Jorja opened her arms and Ora Mae walked right into them. "He was my neighbor and such a good friend," she sobbed.

Jorja patted her on the back and let her cry it out. "Linda was in here just a little while ago to order a plant for him."

"Linda Sullivan and her daughter, Kaitlin, treated him so shabby. He told me . . ." She paused and wiped her eyes on a lace-trimmed handkerchief that she'd pulled from the cuff of her long-sleeved blouse. "That . . . that"—she hiccuped, making it hard for the cousins to hear— "when he took them watermelons, he felt like a homeless beggar. They made fun of him every chance they got and were embarrassed when he wore his overalls to church."

"I'm so sorry," Jorja said. "I didn't know him very well, but he was always kind when I saw him."

Ora Mae took a step back, sucked in a long breath, and nodded. "He believed in showing people his religion by living it every day—he never missed a single church service. I knew something had to be wrong yesterday morning when he didn't meet me right on the front pew. His bibbed overalls and his shirt were always spotless and ironed, and he was clean shaven. I don't know why his last living relative had to treat him like dirt, but she's about to learn the cost of her actions. Like the good book says, you reap what you sow."

"Why did he sit on the front pew?" Jorja asked.

"He was a little hard of hearing." Ora Mae's voice had gotten a little stronger. "To tell the truth, I am, too, especially these days, but me and Frank—that was my husband, God rest his soul—we been best friends with Amos all of our lives."

"I'm so sorry for your loss," Jorja said.

"Poor Forrest," Ora Mae went on. "He's going to be lost. All he had in this world was Amos and me. We've all lived close together for years now. Amos and I each have a house that are close together—just a picket fence separates our yards. And Forrest has his own little trailer house out in Amos's backyard."

"If there's anything I can do, other than fix flowers, just let me know," Jorja offered.

"Thank you." Ora Mae managed a weak smile and laid a credit card on the counter. "I want to buy a big, nice casket piece for him. You girls and Clinton can fix it up with red roses, and if you run out of those, then use whatever you've got in the shop to make it beautiful. We have such lovely wild roses growing on the fence between my house and his. We took turns keeping them watered in the hot weather. When Frank died, Amos bought all my land, but I kept the house and one acre. Amos mowed it for me in the spring and summer, and I often took his supper over to him and Forrest, and we'd sit on his front porch and visit while they ate. Some folks thought he was odd, seeing as he never married, but he was just what folks call an *introvert*. I always thought that's why he took Forrest in and treated him like a son. They were so much alike."

Anna Rose remembered going out to Amos's old barn on the back side of his property. That's where the kids gathered on weekends, and either he never did find out about them being out there, or he didn't care. She used to have good memories of all the fun they had listening to music and dancing by the headlights of all their vehicles. But after what had happened to Jorja, every time she thought about that area, she got mad all over again.

"Do you remember Amos?" Taryn whispered.

Anna Rose nodded and put a finger over her lips to shush her cousin. After what Ora Mae had said about Linda and Kaitlin reaping what they sowed, she didn't want to miss a single word.

"I never thought Amos would go before me," Ora Mae said with a long sigh. "I'm glad that he had a will in place. I helped him fix it up a couple of years ago, and when you girls came back to Shamrock, it seemed like an omen that we'd done the right thing."

Jorja came around the end of the counter and picked up an order pad. "I didn't know Amos as well as you, but he'll be missed."

"I'm glad that you were the one to wait on me, darlin'," Ora Mae said. "And I'm glad you girls are here to help Irene. It would be good if you would stay—and maybe you will, once you read these letters. We talked to our lawyers at the same time and made sure that the wills are ironclad so that Linda can't contest anything in his."

"What letters?" Taryn asked in the back room.

"Shhh . . ." Anna Rose put a finger over her lips.

"Letters? Why would you have letters for us? And what is going on with your wills?" Jorja asked.

Ora Mae twisted the hankie into a ropy looking mess. She pulled three manila envelopes from her oversize black purse, laid them on the counter, and straightened her back. "After I leave, you and the girls can open these. But right now let's talk about the casket piece. I want it to show that someone loved and cared for Amos."

"What's your budget?" Jorja asked.

Anna Rose wished she hadn't been so quick to change the subject.

"There is no budget," Ora Mae answered. "Amos was my best friend. He and Forrest and I made up a quarter of the population of Twitty, Texas. Our little community has dwindled down to just twelve people. Used to be a nice-sized place, but these days our mail even comes out of Shamrock. I want the biggest, most expensive, nicest piece that you've ever made," Ora Mae said. "You be sure you make it a work of art, and I do *not* want anyone to know that I paid for it. They've gossiped enough about me and Amos being neighbors. After my Frank died, he and Forrest became my family, and I've always loved Amos like a brother."

She lowered her voice to a whisper, and Anna Rose had to strain to hear the words.

"I wish you would have had a best friend like Amos to help you through tough times," Ora Mae said. "The funeral is tomorrow. Amos didn't believe in putting things off, and I'm abiding by his wishes. God stamps all of us with an expiration date, and we never know who is next in line. We figured that when Amos's time came, you'd find out about what he has done, but it sure makes it better that you are right here in Shamrock."

Anna Rose leaned back to see Jorja tear the credit card receipt from the machine and hand it and a pen to Ora Mae. She wished that Ora Mae would stop beating around the bush about whatever was in those envelopes and tell Jorja what was going on.

"Just sign the bottom, and we'll take care of the rest—and again, I'm so sorry," Jorja said.

Ora Mae signed and then laid the pen down. "The funeral is tomorrow, and I hope to see y'all there. Our preacher gave out a phone number and link to those who can't attend . . ."

"We will be there," Jorja assured her.

"Me and Amos weren't blind, but there just didn't seem to be anything we could do at the time," Ora Mae said. "But now we can sure show the whole town how we feel." She rounded the end of the counter and hugged Jorja again. "I'll see y'all at the funeral. It's going to be just like Amos wanted . . ." Ora Mae wiped her eyes. "And I want you all three to know that we're both real sorry."

"I will do that," Jorja said. "Sorry for what?"

"The letters will explain." The bell above the door let them know that Ora Mae had left.

Anna Rose stepped out around the corner and raised her eyebrows. "What in the world is going on?"

Jorja picked up the flower order and the envelopes. "I guess the answer is in these. She ordered a big casket piece. She didn't even flinch when I showed her the bill. We'll have to use every red rose in the place to fill it, but we'll make it beautiful." She took everything to the back room, put the order in the basket, and gave each of her cousins their envelope.

"We heard the conversation," Taryn told her.

Anna Rose stared at the one with her name on it. "I never knew that she and Amos were such good friends, but back when we were living here, we didn't pay much attention to the folks that were older than us."

"And they didn't have kids," Taryn added.

"Now I feel guilty for not going to church with her," Jorja said with a sigh. "She's such a great cook and always bringing food to folks who were sick or who had babies or to those who were grieving. I'm hoping this has one of her special recipes."

The bell above the door let them know there was another customer, so Jorja got up and headed out front. "Don't open those until I get back."

Anna Rose figured that Jorja had been right. They had probably each inherited a copy of Ora Mae's famous recipes. Maybe the key was that they were Amos's favorite recipes, too. But even with only the anticipation of some silly recipes, Anna Rose knew she wanted to be there for moments like this with her cousins and hoped they did, too. After the way she'd felt when she first arrived in Shamrock, that was just barely short of a miracle.

"Recipes for what?" Clinton came through the back door and took his place on the barstool where he always sat. "What did I miss this morning?"

"Hello, Jorja." Forrest's eyes were red, probably from crying, and he held his hat in his hands. "I need to buy one of them flower things that go at the end of a casket for Amos Landry."

"I'm so sorry for your loss, Forrest," Jorja told him. "Linda and Ora Mae have both been in this morning."

He took a red bandanna from his pocket and wiped a fresh batch of tears from his cheeks. "Thank you. Amos was like a father to me. But Linda wasn't nice to him, and Kaitlin was even worse."

Jorja laid a hand on his shoulder. "I can't imagine losing my father." She needed to be strong for Forrest, so she blinked back tears, but she really wanted to wrap him up in her arms and weep with him. She had felt pain—maybe not the kind he was experiencing—but hurt came in all forms.

"It's tough," Forrest said and tucked the bandanna into the hip pocket of his jeans.

Jorja took her place back behind the counter. "Do you want to look at a book to decide what you want?"

"Yes, thank you," Forrest answered.

She flipped one of their sample books around so he could leaf through it, but after turning only two pages, he pointed at one. "Like that, only scatter some red roses in it. Ora Mae said she would have her casket piece done up with roses and that Amos liked the ones that grew on the fence out at the farm." He removed his wallet and laid several bills on the counter.

She made change and handed it back to him. "Thank you, Forrest. And again, I'm real sorry about Amos."

"I appreciate that. We kind of knew his time was short, but I wasn't ready to give him up." Forrest ducked his head and headed for the door.

"No one ever is," Jorja assured him.

She took the order to the back room. "Can you believe that his niece, Linda, haggled over the price of a plant? Ora Mae spends a fortune on a casket piece, and Forrest buys the biggest, nicest wreath we sell?"

"Yes, I can," Anna Rose replied. "Where do you think Kaitlin learned her ways?"

"The apple never falls too far from the tree," Taryn reminded them, and then tore into the envelope with her name on it.

Anna Rose did the same; she took one look at the stack of papers and passed them over to Clinton. "You're the one who knows about legal stuff. What is this all about? I thought we'd be opening up copies of her cookbooks, not what appears to be a will."

Clinton glanced down at it. "It is the last will and testament from Amos Landry." He flipped through a couple of pages. "He's leaving his house and all his belongings jointly to Taryn O'Reilly, Anna Rose Duquette, and Jorja Butler. He is leaving his niece, Linda Sullivan, one dollar, and he's already set up a trust fund for Forrest Flannigan but asks that you three please keep him on as the foreman of the ranch."

"He did what?" Taryn gasped.

"Holy crap!" Anna Rose whispered.

"Why would he do such a thing?" Jorja asked and gripped the edge of the table to steady herself. "Mine has two legal documents in it. Would you take a look at this one?" She shoved it across the table toward him.

"I guess you need to read those letters to know the why, but this looks pretty solid to me," Clinton answered. "There's a lawyer's card attached to it with a sticky note that says he will be at the church after the funeral to answer any questions. It says for all three of you to read the letters. Looks like y'all have come into a windfall that will help you put down roots if you have a mind to do so."

All three women opened their letters at the same time. Tears flowed down Jorja's cheeks as she scanned through hers and then went back to read it more carefully.

I'm writing this for me and Amos both because he says his handwriting looks like chicken scratching. He's right. It does, and we're sitting here on my porch as I write this laughing like teenagers. We plan to give copies of our new wills to you in the next couple of weeks, unless one of us kick the bucket before you leave town. Amos has pancreatic cancer and only has a few weeks left, but we can both see he's getting weaker with each passing day.

We knew that you and Taryn were just normal, ornery teenagers that got a bad reputation mainly because of other folks. One of us might have poor eyesight and the other one can't hear so good, but we aren't wearing blinders when it comes to seeing what's really going on, both in the past and right now. There's not much two senile—that's what folks call us—old people can do with nothing but hearsay, but we know. And it's for that cause that we changed our wills and have not changed our minds one bit since then. Irene and Ruby were always so good to me and Amos. Irene taught Bible School with me and talked about you girls all the time. She and Ruby both knew that y'all weren't treated right, so we're kind of making up for all that now. Their money is tied up in the shop, and all you have to live in is that tiny trailer out back, so we're hoping that this will help you three girls have a place and land of your own so that Ruby and Irene can have you close by in their golden years. We know Ruby and Irene will be delighted.

My will is included in the envelope, and it states that my land and house belong to you girls as well, but that it's mine as long as I am alive. I will live in it until that time and will be grateful to have you as my neighbors.

Get in touch with our lawyer if anyone gives you an ounce of trouble about our wills and what we want done.

Sincerely,

Amos Landry and Ora Mae Stephens

P.S. Amos's handwriting really does look like chicken scratch.

Anna Rose looked up from her letter, but Jorja barely noticed. Taryn had dissolved into tears. Clinton slid off his stool, grabbed a roll of paper towels, and handed it to Taryn. She peeled off two and passed them over to the other side of the worktable.

"That must've been some letter," Clinton said.

Anna Rose shoved hers over to him. "Read it and weep with us. We didn't even know those two folks so well, and yet they *know* us."

Jorja tried to dry the tears, but they just kept coming. "Now I really feel guilty about not visiting Nana Irene more often."

Clinton scanned through the letter and handed it back to Anna Rose. "I don't envy you ladies the moment when Linda and Kaitlin find out."

Jorja folded her letter and started to put it back in the envelope when she realized it held another piece of paper. She pulled it out and unfolded it. "This seems to be a letter just from Amos. His handwriting really isn't good, but I can read it." She gasped when she scanned down through it and then looked up with tears in her eyes. "It seems that Ford and his friends were still in the barn at dawn after our graduation, and Amos overheard them bragging about how many girls they had drugged the night before. Ford bragged that he got the best prize because he got a virgin, and . . ." She looked up at her cousins and blushed. "And . . . ," she stammered, "and Ford named me." She went on to read out loud:

> "Times was different back then, and Ford's family was pretty big in town. It was well known that they could buy him out of any trouble he got in, and besides we didn't have an ounce of proof other than what I heard, and the folks around here wouldn't take my word for anything. I kept it a secret, other than telling Ora Mae, and we kind of nudged each other to leave

our land and houses to you girls. It seemed the right thing to do to make up for the way you've all been treated, and besides, Ruby and Irene have been among the handful of folks who treated us and Forrest right."

Clinton slapped the table so hard that two vases fell to the floor and broke into a million pieces. "Does Irene know?" he growled.

All three women shook their heads.

"We didn't even know until Jorja told us since we've been back this time," Taryn answered.

Jorja couldn't take her eyes off the letter. "Amos says that he tore down that barn and put up 'No Trespassing' signs all over his property after that happened."

"And to think that Ford Chambers helps with the youth at the church and does volunteer work with the sheriff's department," Clinton snapped. "A fine upstanding citizen he is. Are you all right, Jorja? I know this happened years ago, but that kind of thing can cause problems for years."

"It has caused her too much grief," Anna Rose said. "And even after ten years, the memories hang on like a bulldog, right, Jorja?"

Jorja finally had the courage to raise her eyes. "Yes, they do, and the guilt that goes with some of them feels like it will suffocate me at times. I got pregnant that night and lost the baby before the second trimester."

"Holy crap!" Clinton gasped.

"But I'm getting better now," Jorja declared. "Us cousins have formed a therapy group. Sometimes we throw things at trees and sometimes do crazy things like kissing the Blarney Stone. Working together these weeks has helped me more than y'all will ever know." She paused. "And I pray every night that the Lucky Shamrock really does bring all of us good luck."

"If y'all need me, I'm more than glad to sit in on your therapy sessions," Clinton offered. "It's kind of what I do with the men and women I work with."

"You are welcome anytime, and I might need a meeting of some kind tonight since Zoe has been ripped away from my heart," Taryn admitted.

"Sweet Jesus!" Anna Rose finally exploded. "What are we going to do with acres and acres of watermelons and two houses?"

"Harvest them and maybe live in the houses?" Clinton suggested. "Maybe build a third one if you are tired of living together? You've got some decisions to make this week—but right now, we've got a huge casket piece to make."

"And a couple of really nice arrangements to put together to set at each end," Taryn said. "One from us and one from Forrest. We should close the shop so every one of us can attend the funeral tomorrow morning."

"I'm not leaving Shamrock," Jorja whispered. "Nana Irene and Ruby need us, and this gives us a place to live and a farm to run."

"Me either," Anna Rose said. "I'm going to be a watermelon farmer, and I hope Forrest will teach me what I need to know. Taking pictures and being semi-famous for my art has been fun, but it is time to move on." She stopped and nodded toward Taryn. "You need to do the same."

"I'm in," Taryn said.

Jorja shifted her gaze over toward Clinton.

He raised his palms and grinned. "I made the decision to stay right here in Shamrock a long time ago."

"Great," Jorja said, and went back to work. When she had first learned that Nana Irene had brought in Taryn and Anna Rose to live in the trailer with her, she had started a countdown calendar and marked off each day with a red pen. Now she didn't know how she could ever survive without her little support group.

Chapter Fifteen

The trailer was so quiet that Taryn could hear her own heartbeat, but she couldn't sleep. She tried imagining a black hole that got bigger and bigger, but that didn't work. She finally went outside, sat down in the rocking chair, and drew her knees up to her chin. The evening breeze cooled her face, and the full Strawberry Moon lit up the area rather nicely. She remembered asking her grandmother what that kind of moon was and why it was named such a thing. The answer had been that it was the first full moon in June and was called that because it was a time when harvesting began.

The aroma of Clinton's cologne—a masculine scent that blended the woods, vanilla, and maybe just a hint of coffee beans—wafted across the porch even before he came out of the shadows from behind the van.

"Having trouble sleeping?" he asked as he sat down on the top porch step.

"Little bit," she answered. "This has been a heck of an emotional day for all of us. I'm sure Linda will throw a real hissy fit about all this. It's kind of amusing that the only flowers that were ordered were the ones we sent, Forrest's wreath, Ora Mae's gorgeous casket piece, and that plant from Linda and Diana."

"That little bromeliad will kind of pale in comparison to the others, won't it?" Clinton said with a chuckle.

Taryn nodded. "But it does show just who loved Amos. Have you heard from Rebecca? She should have been there a couple of hours ago."

"I was hoping you were still awake," he answered. "Rebecca called about ten minutes ago. I could hear Zoe crying in the background, but Rebecca assured me that the baby was just tired from the long drive. She had put her to bed and propped her bottle on a pillow rather than holding her."

"How many times have you propped a bottle for that sweet child? Ever?" Taryn's eyes filled with tears for the umpteenth time that day. "Either I rocked her to sleep or you did. I'm worried, Clinton, that she won't get the love and care she needs in that situation."

"Me too"—Clinton nodded again—"but there's nothing we can do. She is Rebecca's daughter, and unless Zoe is in danger or is living in unfit surroundings, we are helpless. I want Rebecca to be well and get better—but at the same time, I wish I could adopt Zoe. Does that sound crazy?"

"Not to me," Taryn answered. "I'm rowing in the same canoe you are when it comes to Zoe."

"Want to take a walk with me? I'm too antsy to sleep. Maybe we can go up to the convenience store for an ice-cream sandwich?" Clinton asked.

Taryn stood up. "I would love that. A nice walk and ice cream might settle me down enough to sleep."

Clinton held out his hand and she put hers in it. They walked out to the road, made a left and then a right, and headed up the street. Taryn remembered holding hands with her first boyfriend back when she was about fifteen; that boy's sweaty hand in hers hadn't created nearly as many flutters in her stomach—and Clinton's hand wasn't the least bit sweaty.

"We'll be okay," he whispered.

"Are you trying to convince me or yourself?" Taryn asked.

"Both," Clinton answered.

They walked along in comfortable silence for another block, and then Clinton asked, "Have you all talked about what you're going to do about your inheritance?"

"We've talked around it, but we all have to have a little while to think about what all it entails. Will you go with us?" Taryn asked.

"Be glad to," Clinton answered. "I didn't know either Amos or Ora Mae personally, but I'll be there for you all."

Taryn gave his hand a gentle squeeze. "That should set the gossip vines on fire."

"Why?" Clinton asked.

"When word gets out about those wills," Taryn answered, "the fact that we closed up shop for the funeral will cause all kinds of rumors. Plus, if you are there with us . . . ." She hesitated.

"It would be nice if me being there made the women stalking me quit. But I really think that it would bring Jorja some peace to broadcast what happened to her—even maybe put a letter to the editor in the newspaper," Clinton suggested. "That kind of gossip would override the inheritance story. Who knows? It might even bring some comeuppance to Ford and those boys who were doing the same thing to the girls."

Taryn slowed down so that they could talk longer. "The headlines would be humiliating for Jorja, but I wonder if Ford has continued to do such ugly things or if he's repented for all his sins."

"I can't even imagine what Jorja has lived with all these years," Clinton said. "My mind goes to all kinds of scary places when I think about what I could do to a man who does that kind of thing to a woman."

Taryn stopped in front of the convenience store. "Here we are, and I'm ready for ice cream. This whole day has been an emotional roller coaster that never ends." She didn't tell him that just walking down the street of her hometown with his hand in hers didn't do a lot to slow the ride down.

"Have a seat right there." Clinton pointed to the park bench in front of the store. "I'll go get ice cream and root beers, and we'll talk about something else."

Taryn let go of Clinton's hand and sat down. He had barely gotten inside when Elaine pulled up in her car and parked in front of the store. She got out, popped her hands on her hips, and glared at Taryn.

"I heard that you were . . ." She seemed to be so angry that she couldn't get her words out.

Clinton stopped at the door and gritted his teeth. Couldn't he go anywhere without one of those women showing up? He went on outside in time to hear Elaine stammering. "You heard what?" he asked. "That Taryn and I have taken a walk, and I bought us ice cream and soft drinks? Do I need your permission to do that?"

"No, but you might have not led me on for the past weeks and months," Elaine fumed.

"I have not done any such thing," Clinton told her. "I told you right up front that I wasn't interested in dating any of you."

"You took our food and were sweet to us," Elaine said, her voice turning into a whine.

Taryn stuck her root beer into the pocket of her baggy sweats and unwrapped her ice-cream sandwich. Elaine wasn't worth letting good ice cream melt in her hands. She took a bite. Then she did her best to ignore the woman and her hateful, glaring eyes, but when that didn't work, she envisioned her glittery wand from her sixth-birthday party in her hands. She waved it toward Elaine, and poof! Just like that, she disappeared.

Clinton eased down on the bench beside her. "That's called good manners. When someone brings you something, I was taught to tell that person thank you with a smile on my face—even if I don't like sauerkraut and hot links."

"Why haven't you brought that down to the trailer for supper?" Taryn asked. "That's Jorja's favorite dish."

"Sorry, but I tossed it in the trash," Clinton answered.

Elaine threw up her hands. "I'm done, and I hope you're happy with the talk of the town sitting beside you."

Clinton peeled the paper from his ice cream. "So far, so good. You have a nice day, Miz Ferguson."

"Do you even know about Taryn's reputation?" Elaine asked. "She's bad news, and I hear she got kicked out of whatever military branch was crazy enough to take her. You'll lose every bit of the respect you have built up when you're seen walking down the street, holding hands with her like a couple of teenagers."

"So what? I also know who ruined a few acres of Amos Landry's watermelon fields. And who set the tires on fire on Main Street when y'all were teenagers." He pointed at Elaine. "Or better yet, who wrote graffiti in the girls' bathroom at school, and rather than be a rat, Taryn cleaned it all up herself and had to do in-school suspension for more than a week?" Clinton took a bite of his ice cream. "You have no right to look down your nose at her or to act like you've got wings and a halo. You should be glad that she wasn't a snitch, or you'd be the one who had a bad reputation in town."

Elaine opened her mouth, but nothing would come out. Finally, she snapped it shut, spun around in a blur, and popped the spike heel right off one of her fancy shoes. She looked somewhat like a drunk person with one foot on the curb and the other on the street as she hobbled to her car. She peeled out and had to have left at least five hundred miles of rubber off her tires as she squealed away.

"Where's a cop when you need one?" Taryn asked. "And how did you know all that?"

"Ruby told me," Clinton said with a shrug. "One down, two to go."

"Are you sure that she was the one who brought the sauerkraut? Maybe if she wasn't and she runs to the other two, one of them will get mad and pull out of the contest, too. Then it'll be two down and only one to go," Taryn told him.

"One can only hope and pray."

"Good ice cream. Good company. Thanks for both and for taking up for me." Taryn smiled up at him. There was no sense in beating the dead contest horse when, hopefully, Elaine was being truthful about giving up her place in the contest and not getting the wedding of her dreams.

Clinton shot a sly wink toward her. "Anytime, darlin'!"

Taryn put a note on the door of the shop the next day, locked the doors, and then raced out to the trailer to get ready for Amos's funeral. "What are y'all wearing?" she called out as she hurried down the hallway. "I don't own a black dress."

"I've got an extra one I'll loan you," Anna Rose answered. "I'm dressed, so I'll bring it to your room. Have you got shoes?"

"Yes, I've got a pair of black flats." Taryn peeled off her T-shirt and jeans and jerked the clip out of her red hair. She seldom bought anything black because it seemed to make every single freckle on her face pop out.

Anna Rose came into her room wearing a simple black wrap dress, a necklace with a single pearl in a gold shamrock, and shiny black high-heeled shoes. "I keep two dresses for book signings and switch them off." She laid her extra dress on the bed and then sat down in a ladder-back chair at the end of the dresser.

Jorja knocked on the doorjamb, came into the room, and touched the necklace around her neck—the one that matched Anna Rose's. "I hate funerals. I hate wearing black, even though according to my color chart, it's one of my best colors. Do you think it's because when I came to by myself that night, everything around me was dark?"

"Possibly," Taryn answered as she slipped into the dress Anna Rose had brought. "I don't know if it means anything, but the night I learned that my boyfriend wasn't only married but had another girlfriend in addition to me, I was wearing black. Maybe that's the reason I don't like it, either."

"Hey, you didn't tell us the part about him having another girl-friend," Anna Rose fussed at her.

Taryn slipped her feet into a pair of flat shoes and opened a small jewelry box on her dresser. "That seemed kind of minor compared to the existence of his wife." She slipped a necklace that matched the one her cousins were wearing around her neck. "We might as well give everyone the subtle message that we stand together."

"A pearl in the middle of a gold shamrock." Jorja fidgeted with her pendant.

Anna Rose touched hers. "Remember what Nana Irene said when she gave us each one for our sixteenth birthdays?"

"That our grandfather had bought Nana Irene a necklace with three pearls on it when she had her third child. She had the pearls reset in the middle of the shamrocks—one for each of us," Jorja answered. "The pearl to remember our heritage, the shamrock to bring us good luck in whatever we chose to do with our lives."

"And now we're all back in Shamrock together, at least until we decide what we're going to do with a big chunk of land and two houses." Taryn fastened her necklace. "Kind of symbolic, isn't it?"

"What *are* we going to do?" Jorja asked as she led the way down the hall.

"I'm staying and learning all I can about running a watermelon farm," Anna Rose answered as she left the room. "This seems like an omen to me. I can still take pictures, but I'll do it around this area. If a book sells, that's fine. If not, then I'll make a living selling watermelons."

"We could make watermelon wine," Jorja suggested as she followed her.

"And maybe watermelon-rind pickles." Anna Rose opened the door just as Clinton was starting to knock.

"I hadn't thought of that," Taryn said. "I might see what else we can make to sell in our roadside market."

"Thought of what?" Clinton asked. "And by the way, you all look very nice."

"Thank you," they chorused.

Taryn tried not to stare at him, but it wasn't easy. He wore creased jeans, a white pearl-snap shirt, and freshly shined black cowboy boots. "You clean up pretty good yourself. What vehicle are we going in?"

"We can take my truck, and I'll chauffeur," Clinton said and stood to the side. "I'll be the envy of everyone in town."

"Except for Diana, Mallory, and Elaine," Anna Rose said as she got into the back seat of the truck. "They'll want to put us in the casket with Amos."

"If they start something, they just might find that they're the ones in the casket," Jorja stated with conviction.

"You can leave Elaine out of that picture." Taryn told them what had happened the night before. "And I wouldn't do that to Amos. It would be downright disrespectful. That sweet old man wouldn't rest in peace for one minute with all three of them bickering throughout eternity."

Clinton fastened his seat belt and then started the engine and drove toward the church. "Amen to that. I hope this contest crap dies in its sleep. I wouldn't even mind making a wreath for its funeral and saying a few words over it."

"I'll help," Taryn offered.

"And I'll speak at it, for sure," Jorja added. "They might not be nice words, but I'll speak from the heart."

Anna Rose giggled. "You are moving on right well, Jorja."

Taryn was surprised that there were only a few vehicles at the church. She had expected the lot to be full and maybe a few cars parked out along the curb. Amos Landry had been born and raised in Shamrock. Even if people weren't religious, they should have come to pay their respects for all the watermelons he had given to folks for different events through the summer.

"Doesn't look like we'll have trouble finding a seat," Jorja said when Clinton had parked.

"Do you think that folks have already found out about the will?" Anna Rose asked.

"Who knows?" Taryn said with a shrug. "If they did and disagree with the way things are going, then that's their problem, not ours."

Jorja unfastened her seat belt, opened the door, and got out of the truck. "You sounded just like Nana Irene."

Anna Rose pointed at the car parking right beside them. "Looks like she and Ruby have decided to attend the funeral."

Taryn flung open the truck door and started fussing at Irene the moment she was out of her small vehicle. "Nana Irene, why didn't you call me? I would have come over and driven for you and Ruby."

"Don't gripe at me, girl," Irene said. "Just get Ruby's walker out of the back seat and help her out. She's doin' real good today, and this was our test drive to see if she's able to get in and out of the car before we go to the doctor tomorrow for her checkup."

"And I'm doing just fine," Ruby declared as she stood up and took her walker from Taryn. "In another week, I'm throwing this thing out in the yard and using a cane."

"There's no talking to her," Irene fussed. "When she sets her mind, a block of C-4 couldn't blow the idea out of her head."

"Ain't that the truth," Ruby said. "But we are here to pay our last respects to Amos, so we need to be nice."

"Yes, we do," Taryn agreed and held the door open for Irene, Ruby, and her cousins. She had thought about telling her grandmother about the letters but decided to wait until after the funeral.

Then Clinton took a step to one side and motioned for Taryn to go ahead of him. "My grandpa would disown me if I wasn't a gentleman."

"Thank you," Taryn whispered.

They all sat on the second pew, leaving the first one for family, but when Linda and Diana arrived two minutes before the service began, they chose to sit across the aisle and a couple of rows back.

"Why isn't Kaitlin here?" Taryn asked her grandmother.

"After what happened at the wedding and when she found out we would be here, Kaitlin refused to come to the funeral," Ruby reminded them.

"So she talked her best friend Diana into being here to support Linda," Ruby added.

"Guess Linda's not going to sit on the front pew and claim her relative even in death," Irene whispered. "Would it kill her to sit on that front pew? Ora Mae called me last night and told me about the will, but she said Jorja had to tell me her story about why they left everything to y'all and not to Forrest. That boy was like a son to both of them. I tried to drag it out of her but couldn't get the job done. She just said that it would do Jorja good to get it out and talk about it. Do *you* know why she and Amos left everything to y'all?"

"Whatever the story is, we're glad that you girls have the means to stay right here in Shamrock," Ruby said with a smile.

"So are we," Taryn said. "And the story is Jorja's, so you need to make her tell you what happened."

Ora Mae came in and sat on the front pew. She turned around, smiled at all of them, and whispered, "Thank you for being here. It means the world to me, and I can feel Amos in this moment, too."

Brother James took his place behind the pulpit and cleared his throat. "I was expecting a much bigger crowd today, but knowing Amos the way I did, I'm sure he doesn't really care about numbers. It was a blessing we got the news early enough on Sunday that we could send out an email newsletter to everyone in the church telling them they could listen to the service on their phones; so many friends of his find it difficult to get out. Now, to get on with his wishes. He gave me a letter when he learned that he didn't have long to live. He told me that it was to be opened when he died." He picked up a letter opener and slid it across the top of the envelope.

Taryn felt the hairs on the back of her neck stand up. If the letter he'd left behind to be read at his funeral contained anything like what the ones he left for the cousins had—Lord have mercy!—the crap that would hit the fan in Shamrock would be catastrophic.

She shivered slightly and glanced over at Jorja. Her cousin's eyes were as big as saucers. When Taryn leaned up slightly to see past Jorja, Anna Rose just winked at her and nodded.

The preacher cleared his throat and said, "Amos asked that this letter be read first and that I would then read the parable about the seeds and the soils. After the reading, he wanted me to end the service with 'Lead Me Home' by Jamey Johnson, and then those who want to can gather around the casket to tell him goodbye one final time. Before I start, let me say that I'm glad that Amos didn't write this in longhand but had someone type it up. If we went by his handwriting, then we would think he should've been a doctor." The small crowd chuckled. "'To everyone who's at my funeral: I'm writing this because I couldn't do a thing about it back then, but the time comes for everyone to pay the fiddler. Ten years ago . . .'"

Taryn raised an eyebrow at Anna Rose, who covered up a giggle with a cough.

Jorja bowed her head and closed her eyes. Taryn had no doubt she was praying that Amos wouldn't tell the whole community her secret.

The preacher had stopped, and Taryn noticed that his hands trembled so badly that he dropped the letter on the floor. "I'm sorry, Ora Mae," he said in a hollow voice. "I cannot read this out loud. This service is being sent out all over the county."

"I can," she said and marched up to the pulpit. "*You* can go sit over there on the deacon's bench." She picked up the letter. "First of all, I see Amos's and my lawyer on the back pew. Linda, you are invited to stay and hear about his will when the song is over. That said, here's what the preacher can't seem to read, but I won't have a bit of trouble doing—and for all y'all's information, I typed this letter word for word for Amos."

She cleared her throat and began: "'Ten years ago, I overheard three boys in my barn talking about a hideous thing they had done the night before.'"

Taryn heard Jorja suck in air and turned to see her cousin's face turning bright red.

"'They were bragging about having drugged some sweet girls and taken advantage of them the night before. I only heard one name, and

I won't name her because it's up to her to decide whether she wants her story told. But I will name those boys. They are Ford Chambers, Donald Jones, and Billy Johnson. Even though they won't be punished by law, since it's been so long, they deserve to have their sins brought to light, even if it is just by making people aware that they are not what everyone in Shamrock thinks they are. They all thought it was a grand thing they had done and was even slapping each other on the backs to celebrate hurting those girls. It's for that reason I have left my entire farm, house, and all my earthly possessions—including my two cats—to Jorja Butler, Taryn O'Reilly, and Anna Rose Duquette. This property will help them stay here near family they loved and cared for—unlike my family, who never bothered with me. If you are here, Linda, don't try to contest the will. It's ironclad. And now the preacher can read the parable.'" Ora Mae folded the letter and tucked it into her pocket. "But first, I've got one more thing to say. Linda, I want you to know that you are like that hard seed the preacher is going to read about. You have no roots in kindness or the love of family."

With a straight back, Ora Mae marched right back to her place on the pew. The preacher stumbled through the parable and then the song began. Taryn had bitten her tongue to keep from laughing, but now, listening to the lyrics, she began to weep. That poor old man had carried what he'd heard with him, but in death he had spoken his mind. Taryn hoped that in doing so, he could truly rest in peace.

When the song ended, Linda popped up. "This is ridiculous, and I would sue him for defamation of character if he was still alive. Ford is a good man, a good father to my grandchildren, and a good husband."

Jorja got to her feet and turned to face Linda. "This isn't the time or place."

The preacher held up a hand. "Jorja is right. That concludes the service. Amos didn't want any kind of service at the grave, so when you all have told him goodbye, the casket will be moved to the cemetery. The fellowship hall is open if any of you want to gather there."

The funeral home director moved the flowers to the end of the casket and opened it for anyone who wanted to go forward, then stood at the other end beside the preacher.

"I don't need to tell that old codger goodbye," Linda said. "I will want a copy of that will." She paled and laid a hand on her forehead. "Good God almighty! Everyone in town that was listening in on their phones will have heard all that! Ford will be disgraced. My poor Kaitlin will have to bear the burden of all these lies."

"I bet Nettie didn't miss listening to a word and is already heating up the phone lines," Clinton whispered for Taryn's ears only.

"Will y'all go with me to tell him goodbye?" Ora Mae asked Irene and Ruby.

"Of course," they answered, and Irene took Ora Mae's hand. Together, the old ladies made their way to the front to pay their last respects to Amos, and the others followed and gathered around the coffin.

"I wonder if he's chuckling at what just happened," Ruby mused.

"You know it," Ora Mae said with a nod. "He just turned this town inside out and upside down." She patted his hand. "You look right natural in your overalls, Amos, and your letter was real nice. I hope you heard me read every word that the preacher couldn't. And . . ." She leaned down and whispered, "And you'll be pleased to know that folks all over town who couldn't get out to the service just heard every word that was said."

Irene giggled under her breath. "So much for what was in that letter staying in this sanctuary, huh?"

"That was kind of the purpose," Ora Mae said. "Amos Landry just spoke from the grave."

"Vengeance might belong to the lord, but Amos is an angel," Jorja said under her breath. "I wonder how many other girls got drugged that night—or for that matter, any night before or since then."

"Who knows," Anna Rose said. "But this might give them the confidence to come forward."

"Which one of you are the one those boys . . . ," Irene asked. Concern was written all over her face, and Taryn could swear she saw smoke coming out of her ears. If her grandmother had a heart attack over this, Taryn vowed that Ford Chambers would do more than lose his reputation in town.

Jorja raised her hand. "That would be me, and I got pregnant. I lost the baby that first semester of school."

"It's about time he was brought to justice, even if it's too late for a real court of law," Ruby growled.

"He needs more justice than just this much." Irene's fingers clutched her handbag till her bony knuckles turned white.

Who would have ever thought that a small country funeral would turn out this way? Taryn thought.

Chapter Sixteen

"This is Mr. Terrance James," Ora Mae said, introducing the lawyer when they were all in the fellowship hall.

Mr. James—a short, baldheaded man, with gold-rimmed spectacles that he wore halfway down on his nose—beamed at them. Taryn wondered whether this was the wildest case he'd had to date. His briefcase was open on the table in front of him, and several copies of legal papers were lined up beside it. "Thank you, Ora Mae. There seems to be enough chairs around the table for us all to sit down."

Ora Mae took a seat beside the lawyer, and Jorja sat down beside her. Irene and Ruby chose to sit on the other side of him at the long table. Taryn joined her cousins, and Clinton sat across from them. Linda's expression suggested she'd rather be sitting beside a rattlesnake, but she and Diana finally took their places at the end of the line—Diana sitting beside Clinton, and Linda at the very end. Diana kept shifting her eyes toward the door, like she couldn't make up her mind whether to continue to fill in for her best friend or make a mad dash away from what was about to go down.

"This won't take long. Amos was very adamant in his wishes." Mr. James slid a thick copy of the will across the table. "This is for you, Mrs. Sullivan. Ora Mae delivered these young ladies' copies to them yesterday. You don't need the one from Ora Mae."

"Why, oh why"—Linda swiped a tear from her cheek—"would he tell lies on my son-in-law and leave what is rightfully mine to these . . ." She shot dirty looks around the table.

Taryn leaned around Clinton and looked the woman right in her shifty eyes. "These what, Linda?"

"You know exactly what I'm talking about," Linda hissed.

"Be careful," Irene said. "You might find yourself wading into waters too deep for you to swim out of."

Linda's hoity-toity gaze landed on Irene. "What's that supposed to mean?"

"It means that you should have been nicer to Amos, and it also means that Ford needs to be held accountable for what he did. The fallout from today will be your comeuppance for thinking you are better than your own kin and better than my granddaughters," Irene answered.

Linda crossed her arms over her chest and shook her head. "Those are all lies from an old man who didn't know what he was talking about."

The lawyer cleared his throat and went on, "I'm not here to determine what is truth or not. I'm just here to deliver Amos's will to you and the money he is leaving you. You will find one dollar attached to your copy. All of Amos Landry's property goes to these three cousins. Ora Mae is giving her house and one acre, which makes up her estate, to them after her death. Are there any questions?"

Linda picked up the copy lying in front of her and stood with such force that the metal chair she had been sitting on flipped over and hit the floor, sending an echo bouncing around the whole room. "I'm not taking your word for this being ironclad—I'm going to have my own lawyer take a look at it."

"Please do, but you will be wasting your money," Mr. James told her. "You each have one of my cards attached to your copy of the will. If you have questions or need me for anything else, just call."

Taryn raised her hand. "I have a question: When can we take possession?"

"Right now," he said as he snapped his briefcase.

Ora Mae clapped her hands and then did a fist pump. "Does that mean you are all going to live on the farm?"

"Yes, ma'am," Taryn, Anna Rose, and Jorja said at the same time.

Linda started toward the door, then turned around and motioned toward Diana. "I'm glad Kaitlin decided not to come so she didn't have to deal with you people. Come on, Diana, we are leaving!"

Diana took a deep breath and shook her head. *Is this the moment?* Taryn wondered. Maybe Diana was about to crack.

"I'm not going with you. I don't want my name tied up with the crap storm that's about to come down on your family."

"Traitor," Linda spat. "You have always been Kaitlin's best friend. How can you not stand beside her in her time of trouble? She would never forsake you if the tables were turned."

Diana gently pushed her chair back and stood. "Sorry, but I can't take that chance. I've got a beauty shop to run. You can bet that the news of what Ford did is already all over town, and I could lose customers if I'm associated with you. My next appointment is in thirty minutes, so I'm leaving."

"Just wait till Kaitlin hears about this! You are never welcome in my home again!" Linda shouted.

"That's probably for the best," Diana said.

Taryn wondered if Linda would start tearing out her hair, but she simply stormed out of the fellowship hall through the back door—and left the chair on the floor.

"Y'all have a good day," Mr. James said, and whistled the whole way out of the building.

Ruby got to her feet. "I got to admit, this has been the most interesting funeral I've ever been to."

Irene stood up and situated Ruby's walker in front of her. "And it ain't over yet. The fallout from this will last for years."

"Yep," Ora Mae agreed with a nod. "Here's the keys to Amos's house." She passed them out to all three girls. "I'd love to show you around later this afternoon and let you get acquainted with Forrest." She gave each girl a hug. "Like I said before, we all have an expiration date, darlin'. I'm going to miss Amos something fierce—but when it's my time to go, I'll know that we did something right and good." She took a step back. "I've been working my whole life for that day when I face my maker and hopefully hear him say, 'Come on in, Ora Mae. Frank and Amos have been waiting for you.'"

"Save me a seat," Irene said with a smile.

"You know I will, and I don't know if any of you noticed, but Forrest was sitting on the back pew today and left before we all went up to tell Amos goodbye," Ora Mae replied. "I wanted him to sit with us, but he said that he had always sat on the back pew and that's where Amos would expect him to be."

"We would have made him welcome to sit with us," Anna Rose said. "I got in big trouble for punching a guy once when he was being mean to Forrest. I had to spend a week in the in-school suspension room for it."

"He told me about that, and he said that Jorja and Taryn were kind to him, too," Ora Mae said, wiping away a small tear. "I'll see you in a little while out at the farm."

Jorja stepped up for one more hug. "Thank you . . . and Amos . . ." Her voice cracked. "For everything."

"You are welcome. We just wish we could have done something at the time, when all those bad things were happening," Ora Mae said and headed toward the door.

Taryn swallowed several times, but the lump in her throat refused to budge. The week had been—hands down—the most emotional one she'd ever experienced. At that moment, it seemed as if time stood still—like everyone around her had stopped breathing and their hearts weren't beating. The quietness was deafening.

Clinton finally broke the silence. "What a day!"

"What a *week*," Taryn added as she stood up. "Is anyone hungry? I'll be glad to treat us all to a burger at the Dairy Queen on our way out there."

Clinton shook his head. "My treat today. My grandfather wouldn't like it if I let ladies pay for lunch. Let's all meet there and talk this through before we continue to the farm."

Ruby started across the room. "I'm not arguing about who is paying for dinner, and I agree with Clinton: we need to take a breath and talk about this thing that's happened—especially with you, Jorja."

"If I'm telling my story, then Anna Rose and Taryn have to fess up, too," Jorja declared.

"What have y'all been keeping from me?" Irene asked.

"We'll talk while we eat," Taryn answered. "It's too long of a story to start now."

What if, the voice in her head whispered, *Anna Rose decides she hates sweating in the watermelon fields and Jorja goes back to teaching?*

Clinton nudged her on the shoulder as they stepped out into the bright sunshine. "You are in that deep-thinking mode again. What's on your mind?"

"Just that we never know what might happen in the blink of an eye. None of us had planned on telling Nana Irene about our past, but Amos kind of outed us. But to tell the truth, I was thinking right then about watermelon farming and wondering if we are all up to it."

Clinton took her hand in his. "Miracles still happen; I'm living proof of that. The doctors said I would never walk again, so I made up my mind to never fuss about my limp."

"What fixes damaged hearts? I mean, in a virtual sense," Taryn asked.

"Love and lots of it," Clinton answered.

Taryn hoped that someday love wouldn't be in a virtual sense but in a very real one . . . because she was falling in love with Clinton McEntire.

"Jorja, you can start talking while we wait on our food," Irene said as she helped Ruby before sitting down beside her at the table for six. "I can't believe you've kept this from me for all these years, but it sure explains why you don't date. Have you talked to your parents about what happened?"

"No," Jorja said in a low voice. "I was afraid that they would be disappointed in me for even going out to Amos's old barn for that graduation party. I was too embarrassed to even tell you, for fear you would all hate me."

Nettie Jones breezed into the Dairy Queen and waved a hand in front of her face. "I swear, if it's this hot in June, I hate to see what July will be like." She made a beeline toward the table, and Jorja had to battle to keep from rolling her eyes. "I take it that you-all were at the funeral. That was some letter that Amos wrote, wasn't it? I'm glad he left his farm to you girls, though, but I got to admit, I figured he would let Forrest have it. But then, maybe Forrest ain't too good with the management business. Now, I don't know that for a fact. No sir." She stopped for a quick breath and went on. "But Linda needs to taste a little humble pie after going around telling everyone what she intended to do with the money when 'the old geezer'—her words, not mine—kicked the bucket. Anyway, I called our preacher right away and told him that Ford Chambers should be investigated, and if this is true, he shouldn't be working with the youth. I think it's the gospel truth, though, because Amos was as honest a man as ever walked." She patted Jorja on the shoulder. "Well, y'all enjoy your dinner when it gets here. I came in for an ice-cream sundae. When you're eighty-five years old, you can eat sweet stuff for dinner if you want." She hurried to get to the counter before the large group coming in from outside could put in their order.

"If there was a committee for gossip, Nettie would be the president," Ruby whispered.

"What in the . . . ?" Jorja gasped.

"That didn't take long," Taryn said.

"It's good enough for the sorry sumbitch," Anna Rose declared.

"No, it's not." Irene's tone dripped icicles. "Nothing, short of being run out of town, is good enough for any of those three men."

"I don't know if I'm bewildered or if I'm happy," Jorja whispered.

"You'll figure it out in time," Ruby told her. "But go on with your story."

Jorja kept her voice low and the story short. "I still have nightmares about that night, but Anna Rose and Taryn are helping me. I don't think we should be talking about this in public. Remember what you used to tell us, Nana Irene?"

"Which time?" Irene asked.

"Little corn has big ears," Anna Rose and Taryn said at the same time.

Ruby giggled. "So do big corns."

The same lady who had taken their order at the counter brought their food to the table and then leaned down and whispered, "Did y'all hear about Ford and those other two boys? Do you know who old Amos was talking about? That one name he heard?"

Jorja's chest tightened. "Who do *you* think it might be?"

"I was at that party, and it could have been me. That jerk Billy Johnson would not leave me alone," the woman said. "By the way, I'm Paula, and I was a couple of years behind you in school, Jorja. Ford and I ran into each other at a party a few years later. I never spoke up because I was too embarrassed—but nine months and one big spiked drink later, I had a baby. He's blond and blue eyed, just like Ford. I confronted Ford about the baby when he was born, but he refused to do a paternity test. His dad offered me a settlement to keep my mouth shut, but I didn't take it."

Ruby laid a hand on Paula's arm. "I'm so sorry."

"It was tough at first, but I finished high school," Paula said with a smile. "My son is the light in my world, but I'm glad Amos left that letter. If there's other girls, I hope they are as happy as I am that someone stepped up and exposed that man for what he is. Y'all enjoy your food, now."

Jorja sucked in a lungful of air and let it out very slowly. "So, I wasn't the only one."

Irene gave her a sideways hug. "How does that make you feel?"

"I hate that . . ." Jorja hesitated and looked around the room before she whispered, "That young girls suffered, and I feel sorry for them."

"I hope they all come forward now that Amos broke the news," Taryn said. "The time has come for them—especially Ford—to have to face the music."

"Are you preaching to yourself or to the world in general?" Irene asked.

"Both. But for the most part, I faced my fiddler long ago," Taryn answered.

Jorja stiffened her spine and pushed her chair back. This had gone on too long, and Anna Rose had been right when she said that talking to others helped. Maybe it would do even more to visit with the girls who had been drugged that night. "I'll be back in a minute."

She walked over to the counter, where Paula had just finished taking an order. "Do you know of any other girls that . . . were . . . ," Jorja stammered, her sudden resolve failing her.

"That have been raped?" Paula finished the sentence for her. "Yes, I do, but there was no way to prove that what happened wasn't consensual. Of course, now the whole town knows."

Jorja nodded. "And who would have believed it back then, anyway?"

"Right," Paula said. "I'm sorry for what happened, especially if Amos was talking about you in that letter. You were one of the few who were always"—she paused when a young couple came into the restaurant with two little children—"nice to me, even if I was rebellious."

"Thank you," Jorja said. "And I'm sorry for what happened to you, too. None of us deserved to be treated like that." She already felt like a few bricks of the load she'd been carrying for ten years had been tossed away, and her heart was lighter when she went back to the table.

"What was that all about?" Irene asked.

"Just talking to her a little more about Ford and how he would claim that it was consensual."

Ruby dipped a french fry in ketchup and popped it into her mouth. "How is it that I've never heard of any of this?"

"Probably because the victims were too embarrassed to come forward," Anna Rose answered. "I wonder if they will now."

"There's a lot of good people in Shamrock who will support them if they do," Irene said. "Ruby and I are two of them. I always knew that Ford Chambers was shifty, but I thought he was just a big flirt."

"I wonder if Kaitlin will stay with him," Clinton said.

"Maybe she will play the martyr and stand by her man," Taryn said and then hummed a few notes of the old song by Tammy Wynette.

"I recognize that song," Clinton said. "Grandpa listens to classic country music all the time. Kaitlin might be playing it right now."

Irene polished off the last of her fries. "I betcha that Kaitlin kicks him out. She's not brave enough to face the gossip. She might even move out of town."

Anna Rose's eyes twinkled. "Speaking of old songs, the lyrics of 'Diggin' Up Bones' are running through my head. One of the lines is about exhuming some stuff that's better left alone."

"You think I should leave it alone?" Jorja asked.

"Nope, but I bet Ford sure wished those old bones would have stayed buried," Anna Rose answered.

"You can't bury those kinds of bones deep enough for them to stay in the ground," Clinton said. "'Specially when you've now got a little kid with those bones himself."

"Amen," Jorja whispered.

Chapter Seventeen

As Clinton followed Irene's car out of town to the west, Taryn wondered what the two houses that she and her cousins now owned looked like and how many acres the farm covered. Big green melons lay in the fields on both sides of the road. Crews were busy loading them into old stripped-down school buses that looked like they'd been filled with straw. Had Amos owned all this? Were she and her cousins now proud owners of a couple of acres or thousands?

"They've sure got getting those things from field to bus down to an art," Clinton said. "Reminds me of that kids' game."

"I remember that game. It was called Hot Potato," Taryn said. "And we've all got to learn this whole watermelon process if we're going to settle down in Shamrock."

"I'm ready—hopefully, Forrest will teach us," Anna Rose declared as Clinton made a slight turn and then parked behind Irene's vehicle. A picket fence with red roses blooming on both sides separated two well-kept yards. The two white frame houses looked almost identical—wide front porches with a couple of rocking chairs set back in the shade and yellow shutters.

"Is that Forrest, sitting on the porch?" Taryn asked. "I could hear him when he came into the shop to buy flowers, but I didn't see him. I remember him being tall and kind of lanky in school, but he's filled out some."

Forrest waved at them and raised his voice when they started getting out of the car. "Y'all come on in. Ora Mae has brought some cobbler over here—she's inside already."

He wasn't a heavy man by any means, but his sleeveless shirt left no doubt that whatever he was doing on the farm had built up some nice muscles. His jet-black hair was pulled back in a ponytail, and his straw hat hung on the back of the rocking chair where he sat. Two cats—one black and white, and one that looked predominantly like a Siamese— sunned themselves on the porch steps.

"Hello, Forrest," Irene called out.

He met them at the bottom of the steps. "Afternoon, Miz Irene. I'm sorry I left the church before y'all went up to view Amos. I want to remember him helpin' me supervise the watermelon crews and the cotton harvesters, not layin' there in a casket. Miz Ora Mae has made us a blackberry cobbler, and there's ice cream in the freezer."

"You girls help Ruby get into the house," Irene said as she crossed the yard and wrapped Forrest up in a fierce hug.

He wept like a baby on her shoulder, and Taryn had to swallow several times to get the lump out of her own throat. He finally took a step back, pulled out a hankie, and wiped his eyes; then he nodded toward the rest of the group. "Amos took me in and taught me this business when everyone else thought I was worthless."

"We sure hope you'll agree to stay on," Anna Rose said, "and help us learn. We don't know anything about farming."

"I'd love to do that," Forrest said. "Y'all come on in the house and have some cobbler while we talk a spell, and then I need to get out to the watermelon shed and help load the boxes. It's been a while, but I remember all of you except . . ." He glanced over at Clinton.

"But me, right?" Clinton stuck out his hand. "I'm Clinton McEntire."

Forrest shook hands with him. "Pleased to meet you. Amos said kind things about how you help veterans and don't charge them. I tried to join the service, but I don't do too good when it comes to written tests."

"But evidently, you know how to grow watermelons," Jorja told him as she headed into the house.

"That, I can do," Forrest said, holding the door open to allow the rest of them to go inside.

Taryn helped Ruby up the steps and then stepped into the living room, an open area with the dining room and kitchen all visible.

"That would make Amos happy," Forrest told her.

Taryn had promised herself when she graduated and left for basic training that she would never live in Shamrock again, and now she didn't have to. "The population of Twitty might increase since Anna Rose says she's ready to learn the watermelon business, and I expect Jorja and I better be ready to do what we can, too."

"And I've got a cat, Goldie, that I'll be bringing with me," Anna Rose announced. "When can you start teaching me?"

"We're in full harvest now, and it will last through the first week of July," Forrest told her as he led the way to the kitchen area, where Ora Mae was getting bowls down out of the cabinet. "Then we'll start to plow the fields to get them ready for spring planting. We also grow a few acres of cotton, so we have a fall crop to tend to. Listen to me, talking like Amos is still here." His voice quivered slightly when he said Amos's name.

"He will always be here in our hearts," Jorja told him. "What he's done for all of us, and especially for me, can't be measured in dollars and cents."

Forrest opened the freezer and brought out a gallon of vanilla ice cream.

"Were you . . ." Forrest's face turned scarlet. "I mean . . . don't answer that. It's too personal."

Jorja set the ice cream on the counter and laid a hand on Forrest's shoulder. "I was, but let's enjoy this moment. This cobbler looks amazing and smells wonderful, Ora Mae. Can I help by dipping it up into those bowls?"

"Yes, you can," Ora Mae answered. "Blackberry cobbler was Amos's favorite dessert, so it seemed fittin' to make one for today," she said.

"I'm so sorry." Forrest tucked his chin down to his chest.

"That Amos liked blackberry cobbler?" Jorja asked.

"No, for not being there on that night. I went to that party that night, but I stayed back at the side a few minutes, then went home. If I'd stuck around, I might have kept what happened from . . ." He raised his head and locked eyes with Jorja.

"We can't undo the past, but I sure appreciate your feelings," Jorja told him with a smile. "Who all wants ice cream? Help me out, Forrest."

Everyone's hand went up, and Forrest began topping every bowl with a big scoop of ice cream. Taryn admired Jorja's calmness; the funeral and this party would be mentioned a lot over the next few weeks—at least until some new gossip took its place.

Forrest brought a tray with coffee mugs and a full pot of coffee, and Jorja helped Ora Mae carry the bowls to the table.

"This just seems right: you girls and Clinton and Forrest all being here. Amos would love it. When something was perfect, he used to say that it was the icing on the cake," Ora Mae said, but she dropped her spoon on the floor in the middle of her sweeping gesture. She got up to put the dirty utensil in the sink and get another one but paused for a long moment, staring at the whole bunch of them gathered around the table.

"I've been thinking since the funeral this morning, and now . . ." She stopped and smiled. "My older sister down in Amarillo has been begging me to move over there and live in an assisted-living place with her. She called right after I got home from the funeral to check in and says there's an apartment right next to hers that's come open. The folks there told her they would hold it for me a couple of days. Seems like an omen to me. I'm going to call her back and tell her that I want to move in soon. Y'all can form your own new friendships with Forrest and the folks who live in this little community. It's time for me to go—I know that every time I look at this house without my friend in it, it will make me sad. Y'all are all going to be a new breath of air here."

"But, Ora Mae, what if you don't like it?" Jorja argued.

"I get up every morning and make the decision to be happy. This is the right move because I feel it in my bones," Ora Mae said. "Don't argue with me. If you have two houses, it will give you room to spread out a little." She came back to the table and sat down. "Now, let's eat this cobbler."

"Reckon you could give me the recipe?" Jorja asked. "I'll make it every year on this day to remember Amos, and you can come over here from Amarillo to spend a couple of days with us."

"Of course I will share the recipe with you." Ora Mae smiled. "Maybe when y'all come to Amarillo to shop, you can drop by and see me."

"You can count on it," Taryn said.

"And we'll take you and your sister out to dinner when we do," Anna Rose told her.

The cobbler was delicious, but Taryn was having trouble swallowing. Like she had said before, things were happening so fast that thinking about it made her dizzy. A big farm and two houses had been dropped in their laps, not to mention whatever money Amos had in the bank. But if Zoe could come back, she would gladly give it all up.

She finished her last bite and picked up her coffee. "Would it be rude for me and Clinton to take our coffee to the porch?"

"Not one bit," Irene said, "but that doesn't mean you won't have to tell us your story later this afternoon. If it's worse than what Jorja's is, me and Ruby might be loading up our automatic shotguns."

"Yes, ma'am," Taryn agreed and then spun back around to face her grandmother. "What are you doing with automatic guns?"

"Rattlesnakes," Ruby answered. "Our eyes ain't good enough to pop a snake's head off at ten yards, but if one comes around—slithering on the ground or standing upright on two legs—we can shoot until we run out of shells. I bet Forrest has inherited Amos's arsenal, so y'all don't have to worry about such things out here."

"Lord have mercy," Taryn said under her breath as she headed outside.

She and Clinton settled into the rocking chairs on the porch. "Can you believe that my grandmother has a shotgun?"

"Nothing surprises me about those two gals," Clinton said with a chuckle.

"What do you think will happen to the shop if Jorja and Anna Rose move out here?" Taryn asked.

"Irene and Ruby won't be satisfied sitting at home and doing nothing," Clinton answered. "They need something to keep them busy. Irene told me she's been bored out of her mind these past few weeks and that she's not having her knees replaced. They want to be back in the shop as soon as the doctor releases Ruby. Are you going to live out here with Anna Rose or with Jorja?"

"Everything has happened so fast that I haven't had time to even think about that, but my first thought had been to continue living in the trailer," Taryn replied. "I might build a house somewhere on the property later on, if all of us will learn how to be watermelon and cotton farmers."

"Sounds like a plan to me," Clinton said and took a sip of his coffee.

Taryn drank in the sight of watermelon fields as far as the eye could see. "I wonder just how big this place is."

Forrest came outside and nodded at Clinton and Taryn. "It was nice to see all y'all again and to meet you, Clinton. I need to get back out to the fields. A thousand acres of watermelons don't harvest themselves."

"There's your answer," Clinton said with a smile.

"I was just wondering out loud about the size of this place," Taryn explained.

"A thousand acres of melons and not quite three hundred in cotton," Forrest told her. "Are all three of you planning to move out here?"

"Well . . . ," Taryn answered and then made up her mind in that moment. "Anna Rose will be, but I'm not sure about Jorja. Since Ora Mae is moving, though, I expect she'll want to come on out here, too. This is all so sudden that I'm having trouble wrapping my mind around it."

"Amos was like a father to me, and he did right by me," Forrest answered. "Wrapping my head around what he's left me is mind-boggling, too. I could live off the interest from the trust fund that Amos left for me. I wouldn't have to work another day in my life, but I love working outside and then sitting on the porch with a glass of sweet tea in the evenings and realizing that I've helped bring in a good crop. It'll be good to keep doing just that." He picked up a wide brimmed hat from the porch swing. "Y'all going to move in here soon?"

"We don't want to rush Ora Mae, so we may all live in this house until she's got her moving plans in place," Taryn said.

"Good," Forrest said as he crammed the hat down on his head and started out across the yard. "It'd be lonely out here without Ora Mae or Amos."

"I thought you were staying in the trailer," Clinton said.

"Me too, but I know I need family around me. Sounds crazy since I didn't want to live with Anna Rose and Jorja—but now I can't imagine not having them close by," Taryn told him.

Clinton reached over and laid his hand on hers. "I'm glad you'll be close. But I will miss just walking across the back lot to the trailer to see you."

"I vowed to never live in Shamrock again," Taryn told him.

Clinton gave her hand a gentle squeeze. "This isn't Shamrock, darlin'. It's Twitty."

"Yes, it is, and it's only seven miles out here. You are more than welcome anytime. This would have been a great place to raise Zoe."

"I was just thinking the same thing," Clinton said.

Anna Rose came out the door. "Y'all want to come inside and tour the rest of this place with me and Jorja? I'm a little spooked. Seems sad that a man had to die for Jorja to . . . Well, you know," she stammered. "And for us to . . ."

"I know." Taryn stood up. "It's like fate, or God, or the universe stepped in to avenge Jorja, and to make sure that all three of us will stay in this area. Speaking of that, am I going to live with you or Jorja?"

"Whichever one you want to live with will be fine. The houses are just alike, from what Ora Mae says. Three bedrooms and a bath and a half in each, and the layout is the same," Anna Rose answered. "It sounds like neither place has had a makeover in years."

"I'll take the coffee cups into the house if you want to be with your cousins," Clinton offered.

"Thanks," Taryn said and then turned to Anna Rose. "Are we going to give Amos's place a big face-lift before we move in?"

"Maybe not," Anna Rose answered. "When we walked into this house, I felt peaceful."

"Kind of like coming home to Nana Irene's, isn't it?" Taryn commented.

"Right, and I like that feeling," Anna Rose said as she went up the steps to the second house, opened the door, and went inside ahead of Taryn. "I think that Jorja might be friends with Forrest—and maybe on down the road, it could be more."

"Don't be pushing her too fast," Taryn scolded. "She's making progress, but it's in baby steps."

"I'll give you the tour," Ora Mae said. "The furniture is seventies style, but it's in good shape—all except for that recliner in the corner with a stack of books on the end table beside it. I always expected Amos would die because the chair collapsed on him. Of course, he wouldn't hear to getting a new one."

Taryn checked out the titles on the well-worn books for a moment while Ora Mae told the other two cousins more about when the two houses were built. "We had the bathroom remodeled twenty years ago, and I had the walls all painted white about five years ago. Got to where

I couldn't see as well as when I was a kid, and brightening up the walls seemed to help."

Most of the books were old Westerns and had been read time and time again, from the look of them. Taryn sat down carefully in the recliner and caught a whiff of Old Spice, the same shaving lotion that her maternal grandfather used. Was Amos's spirit still in the house, making sure that the girls were going to be happy? She took a deep breath, but the scent had disappeared.

"We'll take care of things for you, Amos," she whispered.

She could have sworn that she heard a faint chuckle.

"You girls are not going to like these beds," Ora Mae said when they reached a bedroom. "They don't even have box springs, and not a one of them is a queen or king size—he was such an old bachelor. You really should buy new ones, for sure."

"We can shop for those sometime this week," Taryn answered, "but let's keep this old recliner. It looks like crap, but it's very comfortable."

The past meets the future, the voice in Taryn's head whispered.

Chapter Eighteen

*C*linton closed the door behind Rebecca with a rush of light-head-edness. He had just taken on the biggest responsibility of his life. Even though he knew in his heart and soul it was the right thing to do, he felt so sorry for the baby in his arms, sucking her thumb.

Rebecca had called the night before, miserable about her time in Arkansas. She'd said that she couldn't handle it and wanted to move to California. She was bringing the baby back to him and needed, in her words, "a permanent reset." He hadn't believed it, especially not with all the drama she'd revealed, until she had knocked on his door an hour before. She only intended to stop by and drop Zoe off on her way to her new spot with her former foster sister.

Clinton had gotten in touch with his grandfather the minute Rebecca hung up. Legal papers had been faxed over to him—just in case she really went through with the idea of giving her child to him. Then he'd used his Veterans Affairs contacts to talk to a different lawyer, just in case there would be a fuss stirred up later about her signing away her rights under duress.

"Are you sure about this?" he had asked. "I want you to think about it long and hard before you sign the papers, and you need to read every single word, Rebecca."

"Absolutely." She'd flashed a dirty look his way and hadn't even hesitated when she picked up the pen and signed all the documents.

Her hair had hung in limp strands, and her eyes had looked tired, but there'd been no signs that she was on anything.

"I want you to promise me that you aren't high or drunk," he had said.

"Neither one." Rebecca had shoved the papers across the table. "I've made up my mind. I've tried to be a mother, but that's not who I am now."

He had wondered how the cousins would adapt to a brand-new lifestyle of having a lot more money than they'd been accustomed to. Now he knew how shocked they had to have been when it had all happened so fast. He was holding a baby in his arms who needed a bath soon—and food sooner—and all that Rebecca had brought back with her was the diaper bag. His shock still hadn't worn off several minutes after she'd walked out the door without telling her baby goodbye or even looking back.

"Okay, little girl, let's get you cleaned up and go to work," he whispered and kissed Zoe on the forehead. "I'll do my best to be a good daddy to you, darlin'."

A whirlwind of emotions and thoughts had been tumbling in Taryn's mind for two solid days. She and her cousins had talked about when they might move to the country. Anna Rose was all gung ho to move into Amos's house and begin learning about watermelons. Jorja was ready for her own space and said that she would make the ten-minute drive back and forth to Shamrock to the shop. Taryn could usually make up her mind on the spur of the moment, but not lately. Thoughts of that one kiss from Clinton, and a little hand holding, seemed to circle back around to her mind every few hours—and then, to top it all off, she dreamed about him almost every night.

Clinton had business to attend to that morning, so just the three cousins were at the Lucky Shamrock, making pew bows for still yet another wedding coming up soon.

"I'm so sick of bows that I want y'all to promise to never let me have them on every pew when I get married," Jorja declared.

"I, being as sick of them as you are, hereby vow to refuse to be your maid of honor if you want bows on the pews—but only if you'll do the same for me," Taryn agreed.

Anna Rose brought the coffeepot to the table and refilled all their mugs. "And me. I want in on this deal. Now that that's settled—Taryn, have you made up your mind which one of us you are going to live with?"

"Not yet," Taryn answered. "Maybe I'll just buy an old trailer and move it out there so neither of you will have to put up with me."

"That's crazy," Anna Rose fussed. "We've got three bedrooms in each house. You can live with me if you don't want to listen to Jorja reciting Bible verses."

"Or you can live with me if you don't want to find one of Anna Rose's strange cowboys in the kitchen every morning," Jorja shot right back.

"I'll make up my mind about which house to live in later," Taryn said. "Don't y'all think we should wait until Nana Irene and Ruby come back to the shop? Someone needs to be close by if—"

"Clinton lives upstairs," Anna Rose argued. "He can keep an eye on things after work hours. That's what he always used to do."

Taryn glanced over at Jorja. She was wearing tighter-fitting jeans that day and had put on a bit of makeup. "Are you really going to send in your resignation and live here, even after the news that Amos let out of the bag?"

Jorja finished a bow and started another one. "I sent it in yesterday, and it's been accepted. I called Mama and Daddy last night and explained the whole story to them. Mama cried, and Daddy said that everyone pays for their sins at one time or another and that he was glad that Ford got outed at the funeral. I feel like a little bird that's been let out of its cage—so the answer is yes, I'm really going to live on the farm. I figure that Forrest can teach me and Anna Rose about farming at the same time. You should start learning about the bookkeeping. Forrest says that it's all on the computer, and you are a whiz at that. I don't want to have to sit behind a desk and input data into a machine."

"Okay, okay!" Taryn said. "I'll move whenever y'all are ready, but . . ."

Anna Rose raised both eyebrows. "Does that *but* have anything to do with Clinton?"

"That *but* has to do with not moving until we know that Nana Irene and Ruby are doing okay in the shop without us." Taryn gave her a dirty look. "We need to think about this for more than a day. What if we don't like growing watermelons? What if we hate living in Twitty? Not a one of us has ever lived more than a few blocks from a grocery store. All this has fallen in our laps too fast. We need to take a step back and—"

Jorja threw up a palm. "Like Ora Mae said, I intend to get up every morning with a positive attitude. I won't have to worry about what to wear to work, if I'm going to have problems with the kids—or worse yet, the administration or parents. If you think I'm going too fast, then you are wrong."

"Again," Anna Rose said with a grin, "what Jorja said. Only my new career won't involve having to deal with publishers and hoping my books sell enough to get me royalties."

"Good mornin'," Clinton said, coming through the back door with Zoe in his arms. "Look who has come home."

At first, Taryn couldn't believe her eyes. Surely, she had to be dreaming, but then Clinton turned the baby around, and Zoe smiled at her. Taryn slid off the stool, and Clinton met her halfway across the room. She took Zoe from him, and the baby snuggled down against her shoulder.

"Oh, you sweet little darlin'," Taryn whispered. "You can't know how much I have missed you." She looked up at Clinton. "How long can she stay?"

"Forever, I guess," Clinton answered.

Taryn took a really deep breath and let it out slowly. "Don't joke with me."

Clinton slung an arm around her shoulders and gave them a gentle squeeze. "I'm not teasing. Rebecca is on her way to California, and she made it clear that she doesn't ever want to be tied down with a baby—not Zoe or any others. Grandpa told me once that there are some people you can't help. I didn't believe that was possible, but I do now. She signed all the legal papers to allow me to adopt and raise this baby. I'm still in a bit of shock over it all."

Anna Rose motioned toward his barstool. "You'd better sit down and explain what has happened. Don't worry about Zoe. Taryn isn't going to let her go for at least an hour."

"Maybe longer." Taryn couldn't believe that Zoe could possibly be there forever.

"Rebecca called late last night and told me that things weren't working in Arkansas, and she hated it there. She'd been in touch with a friend she had when she was in foster care who wanted her to come to California and work with her in a café." He sat down on the barstool and motioned for Taryn to do the same. "I asked her if she wanted me to keep Zoe until she got settled, but she said that she didn't need temporary help."

Taryn shook her head. "I don't want to sit just yet. I'm afraid if I do, this will be a dream and I'll wake up."

"She was"—Clinton paused—"was going to . . . ," he stammered. "I can't hardly say the words."

"Spit it out," Anna Rose snapped. "Was she going to leave the baby at that commune?"

"No, she was going to drop her off at the nearest fire station or hospital, and she had found one five miles from where she was when she called."

"No!" Taryn's voice was high and squeaky in her own ears. The room took a couple of spins, and for a moment, she thought she would faint. After several deep breaths, everything came back to normal, and she sat down on her barstool.

"Are you all right?" Jorja asked. "Your face lost all color for a second there."

Taryn hugged the baby closer. "I'm fine now. I couldn't bear not knowing if this precious child was all right. Why would Rebecca do that?"

"Her story is that she wasn't ready to be a mother when she got pregnant. Her own mother took her to a fire station when Rebecca was a couple of days old, and she's always had abandonment issues," Clinton explained.

"Knowing that, how could she . . ." Jorja's voice cracked.

Clinton shrugged. "She needs therapy, but that takes time and work. It's part of why she was in the trauma-recovery center. But she wants to be healed instantly. I told her that the Safe Haven law wouldn't work for Zoe because she's not a newborn. I convinced her to bring Zoe to me, and then I called my grandfather and a person I know who takes care of legal stuff for veterans. Rebecca has relinquished all rights to the child, and after a few months, I will legally adopt her," Clinton said. "That's the short version."

"And the long one is what?" Taryn kissed the baby on the forehead and inhaled deeply to get a whiff of sweet-smelling lotion.

Clinton rubbed his chin and frowned. "You won't like it. She said that every time she looked at the child, she saw Larry and couldn't forgive him for abandoning her just like her mother had done."

"There's more, isn't there?" Anna Rose asked.

"Well"—Clinton shook his head—"Zoe hadn't had a diaper change in the hours it took Rebecca to get here with her, and she was crying when she first arrived. Her last bottle was before they left Arkansas."

Hot tears ran down Taryn's cheeks, but she didn't even attempt to wipe them away. Poor Rebecca had no idea what she was giving up or how much she might regret her decision in the future. The baby wouldn't even remember her, but knowing that her mother hadn't wanted her would affect her whole life.

"We need to weave a story"—Taryn sniffled—"to tell this precious child. She should never feel unwanted, so we will tell her that her mother loved her so much that she wanted her to have a better life than she could give her. We don't ever want her to have abandonment issues like Rebecca has."

"You are so right," Jorja said. "I want to hold her, please."

"I thought you didn't like babies," Taryn said.

"I'm moving forward, remember?" Jorja stood up and rounded the end of the table. "And besides, I thought I would be leaving, and I didn't want to get attached to her. Look what it did to you."

Taryn kissed Zoe on the forehead and then handed her over to Jorja.

"I get her after Jorja has her five minutes." Anna Rose handed Taryn a box of tissues. "This baby is never going to want for love or anything else. She should be raised out on the farm, not in a tiny apartment. I'll live with Jorja, and you and Clinton can have Amos's house. You can each have a bedroom, and the third one can be fixed for a proper nursery. I'll buy her a swing set when she's old enough for one, and we'll all be her family."

"That's planning ahead," Clinton said with a chuckle.

Taryn crossed her arms over her chest. "I wish she would have never left."

"So do I," Clinton agreed. "But why?"

"Because neither of these two"—she pointed at her cousins—"wanted much to do with her before now, and she was all mine and yours, Clinton. Now they've got baby fever just like I do."

Anna Rose took Zoe from Jorja. "Evidently, it's contagious."

Jorja went back to her barstool. "That's the gospel truth—we will be a family for this child."

Clinton reached over and took Taryn's hand in his. Never before, not in her previous relationships, had she felt so complete with nothing more than a touch. Words were not necessary. He felt the same way she did—not only about Zoe but about her.

"Yes, we will," Taryn whispered, and she saw a bright future ahead.

Are you sure? the niggling voice in her head asked.

She nodded just slightly. *I'll go slow,* she promised herself, *and give everything time.*

Chapter Nineteen

*T*aryn awoke the next morning with a lighter heart than she'd had in days. She hummed as she made herself a bowl of cereal and carried it to the front porch. She had just sat down in the rocking chair when the crunch of tires caused her chest to tighten. Had Rebecca changed her mind and come back to get Zoe?

She didn't realize she was holding her breath until she recognized her grandmother's car, and it all came out in a loud whoosh. She set her cereal on the porch and walked out across the warm gravel in her bare feet.

"What are y'all doing here this early?" she asked as she opened the passenger door and helped Ruby get out.

"Early?" Ruby scolded. "Girl, we been up since the dawn, got the Monday-morning laundry done, and fixed a big breakfast."

Taryn got Ruby's walker from the back seat and popped it open. "Good for you, but we just grab and go in the morning, unless there's something sweet in the shop."

"We are bored out of our minds. The doctor said if Ruby doesn't overdo it, she can come back to work part-time," Irene said. "We figure we can be here until noon. Clinton called a little while ago with the news about Zoe, and we can't wait to see her. Plus, he's got vet stuff this morning, so y'all can use our help."

Ruby pushed her walker toward the back door. "We'll see y'all when you get up and around. Don't worry about me. The boss lady that can't wait to get into her shop has a plan."

"And that is?" Taryn asked.

"She's going to set up a card table for me. I can turn this walker around and sit on it, and . . ." She lowered her voice. "We can *spill the tea*, as you girls call a good old gossip session these days."

"Promise you won't try to sit on a barstool?" Taryn asked.

"I already signed an affidavit in blood for Irene that I wouldn't try to use my new hip to pop up on a barstool and that I will behave myself and let y'all bring me materials to work with," Ruby declared.

Taryn opened the door for her and stood to the side. "Okay, then, can I see the paperwork?"

Ruby let go of one handle of the walker and air-slapped Taryn on the arm. "Don't you get sassy with me. If I have to stay in that house another day, I'm going to start drinking—a lot!"

Irene already had set up the small table and motioned for Ruby to bring her walker over to it. "You turn that Cadillac around and sit down right here."

"She's so bossy that even the angels couldn't live with her," Ruby grumbled. "I thought I could get some payback when she had her knees done, but now she's decided that she's not going to do that."

"After seeing what you went through with one hip, there's no way I'm getting my knees done. When I get to heaven, I won't need them anyway, and I can get around in the shop on them just the way they are," Irene told her. "Taryn, go get dressed, and wake up your cousins. If y'all get out here in the next few minutes, we can gossip for a good hour before we have to unlock the front door."

"We know Jorja's story, but you and Anna Rose never got around to telling us yours," Ruby said. "Irene, put on a pot of coffee so it will be ready for the girls, and get that box of doughnuts out of the car."

"Now who's being bossy?" Irene asked.

Taryn whipped around, went out the door, and jogged to the trailer.

When Taryn returned with Anna Rose and Jorja, Irene and Ruby were sitting across from each other at the card table. Three plants were on the end of the big worktable and one in front of each of them.

"Neither of us feel like getting up and down off those stools, so this is where we'll work," Irene explained.

"Until our new lower worktable arrives," Ruby said.

"Where's the doughnuts?" Taryn asked. Ruby probably thought the sly wink she gave Irene was quick enough that no one saw it, but Taryn did, and she wondered what inside joke they had about something as simple as worktables.

"If Irene didn't eat the whole dozen, they're over there by the coffee-pot," Ruby answered. "We got a dozen and a half, so hopefully, there's one left for each of you. Clinton is bringing the baby down, isn't he?"

Jorja went straight to the doughnut box, put two on a paper plate, and poured herself a cup of coffee. "He's supposed to call Taryn as soon as she wakes up. I'm surprised that my dear cousin didn't move in with Clinton last night just so she could be near Zoe."

"I thought about it, but it would have been moving in with Zoe, not Clinton." Taryn helped herself to a couple of doughnuts with chocolate icing.

"At what point would that change?" Anna Rose asked. "Don't give me the old stink eye, girl. I see the way you two look at each other. The time is coming, but my second question is: Are you ready to trust him?"

Irene laid aside the arrangement she was working on. "Why wouldn't she trust Clinton? He's one of the finest young men I've ever known. How many guys would help vets like he does, and how many would adopt a baby to keep her out of foster care?"

"Tell them," Anna Rose said.

Taryn bit a chunk of doughnut to give herself time to think about how to begin. She chewed slowly, then took a sip of coffee. "I kind of fell in love with a married man. I thought he was serious about me, but . . ."

Jorja came to her defense. "And she didn't know he was married until he was getting out of the service and going home."

"How on earth did you not know?" Irene asked.

"We worked on different bases and only saw each other a couple of times a week. He had told me he had a surprise for me, and I just knew he was going to propose," Taryn answered. "When he arrived, he informed me that he was getting out and going home, and I thought he was about to ask me to join him when I finished my enlistment. That's when he told me the relationship that we'd had had been fun, and he would never forget me—but he had a wife and a couple of kids."

"What did you do?" Ruby asked.

"I threw a fit and used words that would blister the paint on the walls," Taryn said. "And then he told me that his other girlfriend at the base where he was stationed didn't act like a banshee, and he left."

"Good God!" Irene said.

"Yep, He is," Ruby agreed, "and hopefully, that man has had an up-close-and-personal talk with the heavenly Father by now."

"Does your daddy know about this?" Irene practically growled.

"He does," Taryn answered, "but he was on a deployment when it happened. Mama and I talked him out of going AWOL and taking care of things in his own way. It all happened years ago, so don't let it raise your blood pressure." She was glad to finally get the whole story off her chest.

"Don't matter when it happened. Men like him and Ford should be hanged, but I won't say by what," Irene muttered through clenched teeth.

"I agree," Ruby said. "I'm going to pray hard every night that his wife has found out what kind of man she was married to. I hope she took him out into the woods and nailed his tally-whacker to a tree stump. I will be nice, though, and pray that she would give him a butcher knife and tell him when he got ready to cut that thing off, he could come home and sign the divorce papers. I'm real sweet about giving a person a fighting chance. You should have told me when it happened so I could have been talking to God all this time."

"Yes, ma'am, but it won't ever happen again," Taryn promised.

"That's a sorry excuse for a husband," Irene muttered. "His poor wife was sitting at home, raising kids and waiting for him like I did when your grandpa was off fighting in the war of that day. That man deceiving you and her both like that should have gotten him shot."

"And that's why we don't trust men for long-term relationships," Anna Rose said.

"What's your story?" Ruby asked.

"Manipulation and abuse. I got involved with a guy who slowly took me away from my friends and then all of you, and when I disagreed with him about going out to dinner one evening, he started hitting me," Anna Rose answered, and went on to tell them what had happened to her. "And yes, my folks know—but like Jorja and Taryn, I was too embarrassed to tell you, Nana Irene. I didn't deserve your support after cutting you and my family out of my life for all those months just to make him happy."

"You did right by not telling us," Ruby said. "We would have both been spending our last days in prison if we'd known at the time. This walker's real heavy, girls. I might still get to see what the inside of a cell looks like because I *can* get to Ford Chambers."

Irene pointed at her. "Not if I see him first."

"Okay, now we've told you our deepest secrets"—Anna Rose took her place across from Irene—"I hear there's some tea to be spilled."

Irene got out of her chair and refilled her coffee cup. "Kaitlin had the locks changed on her house and threw everything that belonged to Ford out in the yard. His underwear was all tangled up in his golf clubs. Nettie called to tell us that if we wanted to see it all before he got home from work and weaseled his way back into the house, we'd better hurry."

"So, we did," Ruby went on. "We sat on Nettie's porch and watched the circus when he got home: Kaitlin screaming like a fishwife—"

Irene butted in. "I always wondered what a screaming fishwife sounded like, and now I know."

Ruby nodded and said, "It was a sight to behold, but he finally threw all the stuff into his car and drove away. I hear that Linda is hiding out in the cabin they bought up in Kansas and refuses to come home until the dust settles."

"Where did Ford go?" Jorja asked.

"He moved in with Donald and Billy, his old buddies. They're living over near Erick, Oklahoma, in Billy's grandpa's house out in the country," Ruby replied. "A far cry from the fancy house he had here in Shamrock."

"How the mighty have fallen," Irene quipped.

"He's also been relieved of any duties he had at the church with the young people, and he was laid off from his job at the bank," Ruby went on, spilling a few more drops of tea. "They said it was because of the way things are today in the financial world, but we all know the real reason."

"Oh, really?" Jorja asked. "He actually lost his home, his job, *and* his family over this?"

"Yep, and it's good enough for him," Irene declared.

"I just wish those sorry suckers that did you other two wrong would meet the same end," Ruby said.

"Miz Ruby, we should pray for our enemies," Jorja scolded.

Ruby laid the bright green bow she was making to the side, closed her eyes, and bowed her head. "You are right, Jorja. Our most gracious Holy Father, please hear my prayer. If You could infect Billy's house with roaches and rats, that would be good. And please, relocate a nest of rattlesnakes under the trailer, and if You have a mind to do some vengeance like You did in the Bible to those folks who had Your people enslaved, maybe a few boils on those parts of their body that was responsible for ruining young women's lives—well, that would be an answer to an old woman's prayers. And what I have asked for these men,

I would pray that You would visit the same on the men who caused Anna Rose and Taryn such emotional pain. Amen." She raised her head and went back to work.

"Good grief!" Jorja gasped.

"You told me to pray," Ruby said with a shrug, "and I prayed."

"But . . . ," Jorja stammered.

"Not all prayers are as sweet as rainbows and unicorn farts," Irene said. "David asked for his enemies to be abolished. Ruby used her sweeter side and didn't ask God to strike them graveyard dead."

"Not funny," Jorja got out before she let it go and laughed even harder than Taryn.

"Yes . . . it . . . is!" Anna Rose disagreed in between bouts of giggles.

Irene held up a hand and high-fived Ruby. "I'm right proud of you."

"Did someone die?" Concern was written on Clinton's face when he came into the shop with Zoe in his arms.

Taryn grabbed a fistful of tissues and wiped her face. "No," she answered. "We were laughing, not crying."

"Well, that's good news." Clinton crossed the room and handed Irene the baby. "I hate to leave the baby, but I've got a full day of work with a million government agencies," he said.

"We'll probably fight over who gets to play with her the longest." Taryn smiled at him.

Clinton smiled back at Taryn. "My luck changes for the better every single day. Diana showed up at my apartment to collect a couple of dishes this morning and said the contest was done and over. I wouldn't be getting any more food."

"That's some good news right there," Ruby said.

"We might have lost those hot links and sauerkraut that Jorja loves—but why don't we pick up some fried chicken and take it out to the farm when we close up?" Anna Rose asked. Taryn heard Jorja muffle a laugh. "We'd like to show Zoe where she'll be spending a lot of time pretty soon."

Taryn took the baby from Irene and settled her into the playpen. Zoe giggled and cooed at the mobile when Taryn hit the button to turn it on. "Nana Irene, are you sure you can handle all three of us living nearby?"

"It'll be tough," Irene teased, "but I'll do my best, especially if Anna Rose and Jorja will put a lid on all the bickering."

"Then I guess we'd best sell the farm or give it to Forrest," Taryn said with a long, fake sigh. "Because that won't happen until the devil sets up a snow cone stand in the middle of hell."

"And gives them away for free," Jorja added.

"You got it!" Anna Rose chimed in.

"We can argue amongst us, but if an outsider comes in to say anything to us or about us, we can and will stand together," Taryn told her grandmother.

"That's exactly what I wanted to hear when I brought you all home this summer," Irene said. "You are on your way to becoming a family."

"At last," Ruby agreed and raised a hand toward the ceiling. "Thank you, kind and loving Father, for answering our prayers. Now, if You would consider the one I just prayed a few minutes ago, I would appreciate it greatly. Amen." She lowered her hands and started wrapping a plant in colorful foil paper.

How could so much happen in such a short time? Taryn wondered as her eyes shifted from one cousin to the other and then to Ruby and her grandmother.

Irene finished her own job and smiled. "We'll be here in the mornings for the rest of this week, and then next Monday morning, we'll be back full-time."

"Did the doctor say so?" Anna Rose asked.

The whole big picture hit Taryn like a ton of bricks. "Wait for it! Wait for it!" she said.

Anna Rose drew her eyebrows down into a frown for several seconds, and then they popped straight up. "Oh, my!"

"Yep," Taryn said with a nod.

"What?" Jorja asked.

"Nana Irene and Ruby could have come back to work a week ago or maybe earlier. *Light duty* is probably what the doctor said, right?" Taryn asked.

"Busted!" Ruby's grin and twinkling eyes told the whole story.

Irene's giggle made Zoe smile. "But we got away with it as long as we needed to."

"Are you kidding me?" Jorja's eyes settled on Irene. "Did y'all know what Amos and Ora Mae were doing, too?"

"Nope," Irene and Ruby said at the same time.

"But," Irene went on, "it's a sign that it's time for y'all to put down roots and come home, where you belong. Shamrock is a sweet little town, and despite the few bad apples—"

"Which every town has," Ruby said.

Irene agreed with a nod. "It's still a good place to raise kids."

"And watermelons and cotton," Anna Rose added.

"What's most important is that we get to be a part of your lives," Irene told them.

"You always have been and always will be," Taryn assured her.

Chapter Twenty

The quietness in the trailer was overwhelming that Sunday evening. Anna Rose and Jorja had packed up and moved after work the day before. Since the new beds had not arrived for Amos's house, they'd made the decision to move in together to Ora Mae's place. She'd found a set of young men who were super-fast at packing her moving truck. Taryn wondered if they'd all still be single by the time they hit Amarillo. Ora Mae was a force of nature.

"Evidently, the new house does not have magical powers, but I do think that the shamrock on the front of the shop has done a good job," she whispered as she watched the sunset and kept the rocking chair in motion on the front porch.

"Hey," Clinton called out from the top of the stairs.

She raised her voice. "Hey, yourself. Come on down and keep me company. This place is as quiet as a tomb."

"Can you come up here?" Clinton asked. "Zoe just went to sleep."

Taryn stood up, crossed the lot, and climbed the stairs. "Have you heard anything from Rebecca? It's been more than a week now, and I keep waiting for the other shoe to fall."

Clinton opened the door for her and then followed her inside. "Nope, and I really don't think we ever will." He motioned for her to sit on the sofa and took two beers from the refrigerator in the small galley kitchen.

Zoe was curled up in a portable crib across the room. She had a thumb in her mouth and her forefinger crooked around her nose. Taryn wanted so badly to pick her up, reassure her again that she would be loved and that she had a family.

Clinton handed Taryn a beer and then sat down close to her on the sofa. "We need to talk now that things have settled down this past week."

Taryn's concern meter jacked up several notches. The last time a man had said that they needed to talk was the night she found out her boyfriend was a married man. Her heart seemed to lie in her chest like a heavy stone that couldn't beat. She took a long gulp of her beer and waited—that other shoe she'd been worried about was hanging in the air, ready to hit the floor with a thud at any minute.

"I'll go first," Clinton said. "For a while now, I've wondered if these feelings I have for you are because you are so good with Zoe."

Taryn had wondered the same thing, and Nana Irene had weighed in heavily about it, too. But living alone and spending more time with Clinton this past week, she had decided that what she felt for him was very different from the maternal love she had for the baby.

"But"—Clinton paused to take a drink of his beer—"I've got my emotions sorted out. Looking back, I realized that the chemistry between us was still there when Zoe was gone those several days. I'm not real good with romantic words, but I know that I want you in my life as more than a babysitter or a surrogate mother for Zoe. Now, your turn. How do you feel about *us*?"

"How do you feel right now?" she asked.

"Like my future is in your hands," he answered.

"That's how I felt when you said we needed to talk," she told him, and then went on to tell him about the betrayal she'd experienced with her ex. "I didn't think I'd ever trust a man again, but I was wrong. I trust you, Clinton, and I feel the same way you do, but I really don't want to rush this amazing thing between us. I like the idea of us moving into one of the houses out on the farm together, but I'm in no hurry . . ."

He set his beer down, cupped her cheeks in his hands, and before she even had time to moisten her lips, he kissed her with so much passion that the world stopped spinning. She wrapped her arms round his neck and tangled her fingers in his thick hair.

They were both panting when he leaned back slightly and stared into her eyes. "Just how slow do you want to go?"

She brought his lips to hers for another scorching-hot kiss. He scooped her up in his arms and took a couple of steps toward the open door into his bedroom. "You can say that this is too fast, and we'll go back to the sofa."

"I could, but I'm not going to," she whispered.

Sunrays slipped through the window and warmed Taryn's face the next morning. Her eyes popped wide open, and her mind went into overdrive. Something wasn't right. The window was in the wrong place, and the alarm clock was putting out cooing sounds. Strong arms held her in an embrace. Then she realized that she'd spent the entire night in Clinton's apartment, and slowly, her heart stopped pounding.

"Sounds like our baby girl is awake," Clinton muttered. "Want to go fix breakfast and get her ready for the day?"

"Yes, I do," Taryn answered. "We've got about an hour until Nana Irene and Ruby get to the shop."

Clinton drew her closer to him and kissed the soft, tender spot on her neck. Little spurts of desire chased down her spine. One more minute of that, and they'd not only have to go to work with no breakfast, but she'd be answering a million questions from Ruby and her grandmother. *Slow* might not mean taking baby steps in the bedroom, but she would like to savor each moment with Clinton before everyone in the family found out they were in a very serious relationship.

Good Lord! the voice in her head seemed to shout. *You've known him less than a month, and you've already slept with him.*

Yep, I did. She couldn't have stopped smiling if she'd tried sucking on a lemon.

"Zoe isn't fussing." Clinton's warm breath sent another series of vibes down her body. "Want to . . ."

The baby monitor that Taryn had mistaken for the alarm clock suddenly let them know that Zoe wasn't happy anymore. "Guess the answer to that would be 'not right now,'" Taryn said as she threw back the sheet and got out of bed. "Our baby is hungry and needs changing."

Clinton propped up on one elbow. "You are even beautiful in the morning with your red hair all mussed up."

She covered a yawn with her hand. "That could be the most romantic thing anyone ever said to me. If you can think that when I look like this, then it's possible we've got a real thing going here between us." He slung his long legs out over the side of the bed, and she saw all the scars. "Clinton McEntire, did you lie to me?"

He jerked the sheet over his leg. "About what?"

"What really happened to you?" she asked.

He hurriedly put on a pair of pajama pants and jerked a T-shirt over his head. "I'll tell you the truth while I make breakfast."

Taryn dressed in the same denim shorts and shirt that she'd worn up to his apartment the night before. "I'll take care of Zoe while you talk and cook."

"Okay," he agreed. "I owe you the truth since we're taking the next step in our relationship. I don't like people to feel sorry for me or treat me like I did something amazing. I didn't. I just happened to be in the wrong place at the wrong time." He opened the door, crossed the room, and stopped at the portable crib long enough to kiss the baby on the forehead. "Good morning, Princess Zoe. Are you hungry? I'll heat up a bottle while I cook, and Taryn is going to get you ready for the day."

Romance and family all mixed together seemed to Taryn like a good combination. She picked up the baby and hugged her tightly, then changed her diaper and got her dressed for the day while Clinton prepared her morning bottle.

"Your story?" she reminded him.

"Sometimes I was sent on a special mission," Clinton said as he whipped up batter to make waffles. "Not very often, but I had some special skills, and so did Quincy. Neither of us batted an eye when we were included with a new team."

"What kind of special skills?" Taryn asked.

"Defusing bombs," he said, as calmly as if he were telling her a fairy tale. "I was going too fast, and the thing detonated. That's the real story, but I like the story I tell people much better. It says I'm just a common old boy, not some kind of hero—because I'm not. It's not a big lie because I did get an injury when I was out running."

Taryn sat down at the end of the small table and fed Zoe her bottle. "Thank you for telling me, but, honey, I thought I was your only friend," she teased.

"Quincy is my *best* friend, darlin'." He stopped working long enough to cross the room and give her a lingering kiss. "You are my soulmate, and I think I knew that the first time I laid eyes on you. And now that we know each other's past, are we good?"

"We are," she answered. "What you said a while ago about the past being gone but we have a million futures in front of us comes to my mind. I only want one future, Clinton, and that's with you and this precious child."

Clinton turned around and cocked his head to one side. "Why, Miz Taryn O'Reilly, are you proposing to me?"

"No, darlin', that's your job, but let's don't get in a hurry," she said.

Chapter Twenty-One

*J*orja climbed the ladder and carefully hung a filmy length of illu-
sion from the top of the window and down the sides to the floor.
Then she attached one silk calla lily to each of the two corners.

"One side is longer than the other," Anna Rose said from across
the room, where she placed a hurricane lamp set in the middle of white
lilies and roses in each window. "You'll have to redo it."

Jorja picked up a pair of scissors from her work basket and lopped
off the side that was too long. "There, does that satisfy Miss Perfection?"

"Yep, it does," Anna Rose answered.

"Stop your bickering," Irene said. "We're making good money on
this wedding."

"I'm glad you girls are here to help. Us two old women couldn't
have crawled up and down on that ladder twenty times like you have
done," Ruby said.

"Speak for yourself," Irene snapped. "We've done bigger events that
this before."

"Yes, when we were forty years younger," Ruby threw back at her
and adjusted Zoe to a better position on her lap. "I told you back in the
spring when you contracted this huge event and agreed to do all this
decorating that we'd have to hire extra help."

"And I told you the girls would be here to lend a hand," Irene
argued.

"How did you know that?" Jorja asked.

"I figured I'd be the one laid up with knee surgery this summer," Irene replied with a shrug. "But Ruby stepped ahead of me and broke her hip. I didn't have a single doubt that if I needed y'all to run the shop, you would take on the job. I wasn't wrong, was I? And just look at what the last month has produced in all three of your lives."

"Some days I want to strangle Anna Rose," Jorja grumbled.

"I understand. Sometimes I want to kick your grandmother in the hind end," Ruby said with a grin. "I'm so glad to be back in my own house and not be smothered to death"—she pointed at Irene—"by this old woman. The way she's made me eat these past weeks has probably put ten pounds on me. My britches are getting too tight, and I refuse to buy new clothes at my age."

"Food makes fuel to heal a body," Irene told her. "Now that you can get around with a cane and can fix your meals for yourself, you'll lose what little weight you gained."

"Yes, I will," Ruby declared. "Come on over here and get this baby. She's getting bored with me. The doctor says I can live by myself and do light duty at the shop. He didn't say I could carry Zoe around the sanctuary."

"If you'd eaten more, you could," Irene grumbled as she took Zoe from Ruby. "Come on to your Nana Irene, baby girl. We'll go look at all the pretty decorations for this wedding."

Jorja folded the ladder and picked it up. "I'm taking this back to the fellowship hall."

"We should be done in here in five minutes," Anna Rose called out from the other side of the sanctuary.

"If Taryn is done, we'll meet you back here in the sanctuary," Jorja told her.

Sure enough, Taryn was tweaking the last of the centerpieces for the tables.

"Time has sure gone fast since we first got here, and so much has happened," Jorja said as she carefully wove through the tables to the utility room.

"A lot has happened, for sure," Taryn agreed. "Do you really think Nana Irene and Ruby are ready to take over on Monday without any of us being there?"

Jorja put the ladder back in the exact spot she'd found it and then pulled out a chair and sat down at one of the tables. "They think they are, and we don't have a choice but to let them try."

Taryn eased down in a chair right beside her cousin. "I suppose if they get into trouble, we're only minutes away."

"That's right," Jorja said, "and if Anna Rose is driving, you can cut that time in half."

"How are y'all getting along, now that you've been in the same house for more than a week?" Taryn asked.

"I love her, but sometimes I don't like her, and I'm sure she shares the same feeling," Jorja answered. "How about you and Clinton?"

"We're doing fine," Taryn was glad to say. "We've only had one disagreement since we moved in, and we settled it pretty quickly."

Jorja wiggled her eyebrows. "In whose bedroom?"

Taryn could feel her eyes getting wider and wider. "I can't believe you said that. You really have changed a lot in this past month. You wouldn't have asked that question before without blushing, and you aren't even pink. Have you taken someone into *your* bedroom yet?"

"Nope, but the possibility might be there—someday," Jorja said with a grin. "Right now, I'm ready to go home, have some supper, and sit on the porch with Forrest. He might be an introvert, but I do enjoy visiting with him."

"That's a good thing," Taryn told her. "I'm proud of you for letting your hair down a little and trusting a man to be a friend."

Jorja stood up and pushed the chair back in under the table. "They should be done with the sanctuary, and the shop is closed. Nana Irene says that Clinton has a vet—a woman—who needs a job, so Nana is going to let her go to work on Monday. I guess we've gone from weddings and funerals now to cotton and watermelons."

"Which one do you like better?"

"The jury is still out, and this next week will be the first time we don't work at the shop every day, but I think I'm going to like farming better. Is that strange?" Jorja asked.

"Kind of," Taryn answered. "Three months ago, if someone had told you that you would be living in a house with Anna Rose on a watermelon and cotton farm, what would you have told them?"

"That one of the Ten Commandments says, 'Thou shalt not lie,'" Jorja said. "How about you?"

"I would have told whoever came up with such a harebrained idea that they were talking sheer nonsense," Taryn replied.

"I like your answer better." Jorja giggled.

The sun had set an hour before Anna Rose left the farm that evening. She waved at Jorja and Forrest from the window of her truck as she drove away, and then she plugged her phone into the system and started her favorite playlist. "Are You Gonna Kiss Me or Not" by Thompson Square popped up as the first song, and it immediately reminded her of Jorja and Forrest. There was no doubt in her mind that this new friendship would blossom into something beautiful, but it wouldn't happen overnight. She thought about the conversation the cousins had had about weddings. Jorja had declared she wanted the whole church thing, just not overdone like the one they'd set up for that afternoon.

Anna Rose would bet that when the time came in another year or maybe two, since neither of them would rush this thing, that they would either make a trip to the courthouse or else get married in the middle of a watermelon field. Of all three of them, it seemed to her like Jorja was taking to this business of farming better than either of her cousins.

"Good for her," Anna Rose said. "If the Lucky Shamrock was going to work out romantically for any of us, I'm glad it's Jorja. We've all had our problems, but hers was worse than mine and Taryn's."

Anna Rose had left Shamrock in her rearview mirror by the time the song ended and the music from Blake Shelton's "God Gave Me You" started. She smiled and tapped her thumbs on the steering wheel. That was Taryn and Clinton's song, and they would not wait a whole year to make a quick trip to the courthouse. She stopped tapping her thumbs on the steering wheel and wondered if Zoe's first word would be *mama* or *da-da*.

"The next song is for me," she muttered, and then laughed when Brooks & Dunn's old song "Boot Scootin' Boogie" began to play.

If that song was as strong an omen for her future as the first two had been for her cousins, then she didn't have to pick out a wedding dress for a long time. There was a lot of dancing in honky-tonk bars left in the boots she was wearing that night. A vision of the shamrock painted on the flower-shop window popped into her head. The plant had three leaves, so that should be a sign that each of the cousins would have good luck.

But it doesn't mean all at the same time, her grandmother's voice whispered, so clearly that Anna Rose looked up in the rearview to see if Nana Irene was sitting in the back seat.

She opened her mouth to say something but clamped it shut when "Broken Halos" started playing. After Amos's funeral, the song pricked her heart. She thought of her grandmother and Ruby, and tears began to roll down her cheeks. "Please, God," she prayed, "give them the third leaf on the shamrock. I'll forfeit my lucky day if you'll let them live for a few more years."

She'd barely gotten the words out when she heard a loud pop, and her truck began to swerve to the right. She hadn't passed a single car coming or going since she'd left home, so it looked like she wouldn't be getting any help from a knight in shining armor who knew how to change a tire. She quickly pulled over to the side of the road, got out, and saw that the tire wasn't just flat but had blown out, leaving strips of rubber back along the highway. She wondered if this was an omen telling her that, when she had changed the tire, she should turn around and go home.

"It's not a sign," she said, arguing with what she knew Jorja would tell her.

She had the spare tire in her hands when a truck slowed down and then parked right in front of her vehicle. The driver was nothing but a silhouette in the lights of her truck when he got out and waved, but she could tell that he was a tall, hunky cowboy by his broad shoulders, hat, and boots.

"Need some help?" he asked.

Anna Rose squinted and shook her head.

"I'm Quincy Jameson. Don't think we've met. I'm moving to Shamrock to help my friend. You can call him if you're worried. His name is Clinton McEntire."

"I'm Anna Rose." She smiled. "And I would love some help—I know Clinton well. It's nice to meet you. Clinton told us you were coming to help him, but we didn't know when."

Quincy covered the distance in a few long strides, slid the jack into the right place, and then removed the lug nuts. His biceps filled out the sleeves of his pearl-snap Western shirt, and his boots were a testament to the fact that they'd been worn for more than just two-steppin' around a dance floor. "Looks like you ran over something back along the road. Know what it was? I could drive back that way and get it off the road before it causes a wreck." He pulled the ruined tire off and tossed it into the back of the truck.

She handed him the spare and said, "I have no idea what I hit. I didn't feel a bump, but I did hear a pop, and then the truck began to swerve, so I pulled over."

"Have you been crying?" he asked bluntly as he put the spare on and began to tighten the lug nuts.

"Yes, I have," she answered. "I was listening to a sad song by Chris Stapleton. Why do you ask?"

"Was it 'Broken Halos'?" Quincy asked. "That one always makes me get a lump in my throat. I only asked because you have black streaks running down your cheeks."

"Yep," Anna Rose admitted, with a swipe at her rogue mascara. "It made me think of a couple of people I know. Amos and Ora Mae, and then of Nana Irene and Ruby. Do you believe in omens or signs?"

"I do," Quincy answered. "Do you?"

"I didn't—but here lately, I've been changing my mind," she answered.

He finished the job, stood up, and put the jack away. "What caused you to change your mind and believe in omens and fate?"

"The Lucky Shamrock," she answered. "Looking back, it seems as if . . ." She paused. "Well, that fate had a hand in it."

He leaned against the fender of the truck and nodded. "I can believe that. Clinton moved to Shamrock because he liked the place when he visited as a child. Talking to him these last months and hearing happiness in his voice, especially since all y'all came to town, made me want to have whatever is in that small town that made him glad to be there. Besides, I miss him. So yes, I believe that fate steps into our lives sometimes."

"Thanks for that. I should be getting on back to the farm. I don't want to take a chance on driving home without a spare in the early-morning hours," Anna Rose said.

He flashed a bright smile her way. "I'll follow you. Can't let someone as beautiful as you are get stranded on the road again."

"Thank you, but I can call Clinton or—"

Quincy butted in before she could finish. "Oh, honey, Clinton would be very upset with me if he had to leave Taryn and the baby behind on this fine evening when I can feed my ego by rescuing you."

"Where were you headed?" she asked.

"To have a cold beer and maybe a shot of Jameson over at a bar in Erick, but"—he took a step forward—"do you have cold beers at the farm?"

"I do," she answered. "Would you like to sit on my porch, have a beer or two, and swap funny stories about Clinton with me? Seems like that isn't nearly enough to repay you for missing an evening of dancing and—"

"I'd rather go home for a peaceful visit, but if you've got a mind to dance, we could always put on some music and do some two-steppin' by the light of the moon out in the yard."

She hadn't expected Quincy to be so good looking, to make her heart flutter, or to flirt with her upon first meeting—but she loved it all.

"Will it be all right if I take off my boots and prop my feet up on the railing?" Quincy asked as he headed back to his truck.

"Absolutely," she answered and wondered how much more he would be willing to take off before the evening ended.

Oh, no! the voice in her head screamed. *You do not need a one-night stand, and if this little flirtation goes wrong, it could cause all kinds of problems. You are going to take whatever this evening produces even slower than Jorja and Forrest.*

"Lead the way out to your farm," Quincy said.

She waved at him, got into her truck, and headed back toward home. When she started her playlist again, Mary Chapin Carpenter was belting out "I Feel Lucky."

Taryn heard the vehicles coming down the lane before the headlights actually appeared. "Sounds like we've got company," she said, and leaned forward in one of the rocking chairs on Amos's front porch. Someday she might stop thinking of the place where she and Clinton lived with Zoe as Amos's and think of it as theirs, but that would be later.

Clinton reached across the few inches from his rocker to hers and covered her hand with his. "Yep," he agreed. "But I'm being selfish and hoping they aren't coming here."

"Why?" Taryn asked.

"Because I only get a few hours in the evening with you, and I don't like to share," he said. "I miss the flower shop, where we got to sit beside each other all day."

"But we weren't the only ones in the shop," she told him.

"In my mind we were, darlin'." He grinned.

"That is pretty romantic for someone who declares that they aren't," she reminded him.

"You bring out the best in me," Clinton said. "Looks like we don't get company after all—that's Anna Rose. Wasn't she going out dancing tonight?"

"Yep—and who is that behind her?" Taryn asked.

"Looks like . . . Quincy?" Clinton stood right up.

"Your friend that is going to help with the vet business?" Taryn was surprised, not only to see him but also to see her cousin back from the bar that early.

Anna Rose parked and got out of her truck, waved at Taryn and Clinton—who sat back down—and yelled across the rose-covered picket fence, "I had a flat tire."

Quincy was parked behind her and already out of his vehicle. "And I was the knight in shining armor that saved her."

"Y'all want to come over and visit with us?" Taryn asked.

"No, we're going to stay over here on this porch and have a couple of cold beers," Anna Rose answered. "See y'all tomorrow."

"Thank you, Jesus," Clinton muttered under his breath.

"Amen," Taryn agreed and grinned. She and Clinton were enjoying a quiet moment after Zoe was asleep on the porch where Amos used to live. Jorja was back behind the two houses, sitting on the swing on the porch of Forrest's trailer house. Anna Rose and Quincy were about to have beers on Ora Mae's porch. The future sure looked bright—and it was all because of the Lucky Shamrock.

Epilogue

*T*aryn watched Zoe chasing first one cat and then the other while they all waited on Irene and Ruby to arrive that Sunday afternoon. Zoe had learned to walk by holding on to Goldie's tail a few months before. She had finally made friends with both cats the cousins had inherited with the farm—Blanche, the black-and-white cat, and Rosy, the blue-eyed one who had Siamese in her—but Goldie was her favorite. Clinton came out of the house and slipped his arms around Taryn's waist. She leaned back against his chest and loved the sheer chemistry that was still there when he touched her. Bright sunlight lit up their gold wedding bands, and thinking of the fact that all three cousins had opted for simple rings put a smile on her face.

Forrest and Jorja had taken advantage of a slow time in December to wed in a simple Christmas wedding at the farm. Jorja's folks had come from Africa and spent the holidays in the trailer behind the shop. In March, Quincy and Anna Rose had gone on a weekend trip to Las Vegas and come back to Texas wearing wedding rings. Taryn and Clinton had been married a couple of months before at the courthouse.

"We're the luckiest cousins to ever come out of Shamrock," she whispered. "And of the three of us, I get to top the list."

"I'm glad you feel like that," Clinton whispered, and his warm breath on her neck sent desire shooting through her whole body. "But, honey, I think Quincy, Forrest, and I might disagree with you on that issue. We all feel like we're the lucky ones. I hear Forrest's old truck rattling down the lane. I bet Irene is floating on cloud nine today."

"No doubt about that." Taryn turned around and kissed him on the cheek. "All of her chickens are home for the summer. Jorja's folks don't leave until August for their new mission. My parents might even move back permanently now that they have a grandbaby; Zoe has stolen their hearts. And Anna Rose's mama and daddy have declared that they want to be here to share their grandkids' lives. Here comes a whole string of vehicles."

In that moment, she remembered slapping the steering wheel and yelling, "No, no, no!" when she had reached the flower shop the year before. Today, she wanted to holler, "Yes, yes, yes!"

"Our first family reunion—and here comes Forrest, carrying the first watermelon of the season," Clinton said. "I truly believe that the flower shop has some lucky powers."

Taryn nodded. "They don't call it the Lucky Shamrock for nothing."

Dear Readers,

Sometimes I'm asked if I'm a plotter—do I plot out every single scene in a book before I start writing?—or if I'm a pantser. (That means that I more or less start writing and then just see where the story goes.) Here's my answer: I start out with a plot in mind and maybe an outline for the first five chapters. Then I imagine myself as the pilot of a big jet airplane, and all my characters are the passengers. We take off and get through maybe two or three chapters, but then the characters hijack the plane. That's when we go on an amazing adventure to experience emotions that I never dreamed I would write about. The characters are so real by then that they tell me what to write, and if I don't give one of them enough room, they wake me up at night and fuss at me. It's always with a little sadness that I finish their story—by the end, it hardly belongs to me—and have to tell them goodbye. I sincerely hope that you have the same emotion when you finish reading *The Lucky Shamrock*.

As always, there are people I want to thank for helping me take this story from an idea to the book you are holding in your hands today: my agent, Erin Niumata, and my agency, Folio Management Agency, for believing in me for the past many years; my team and editor, Alison Dasho, at Amazon/Montlake for everything they do; Krista Stroever, my developmental editor, whom I adore; and of course, my family, for understanding what deadlines mean. I always owe a big debt of gratitude to my husband and soulmate for the past fifty-six years. It takes a special person to live with an author, and he has always been there to support me. And last but never least, to all my readers who continue to support me by buying my books, reviewing them, dropping me a note to cheer me up, and recommending my stories to other folks: you are all truly the wind beneath my wings.

Until next time,
Carolyn Brown

About the Author

arolyn Brown is a *New York Times, USA Today, Washington Post, Wall Street Journal,* and *Publishers Weekly* bestselling author and RITA finalist with more than 125 published books. She has written women's fiction, historical and contemporary romance, and cowboys-and-country-music novels. She and her husband live in the small town of Davis, Oklahoma, where everyone knows everyone else, knows what they are doing and when, and reads the local newspaper on Wednesday to see who got caught. They have three grown children and enough grandchildren and great-grandchildren to keep them young. For more information, visit www.carolynbrownbooks.com.